Twin Crossing

By
Jerry Leake

We've reached a crossroads, my younger twin
This battle may be yours, but the war I will win
On this plane, parallel lines don't meet
Yet I overlap same, and my life is complete

Excerpt from a prisoner's journal – November 6, 1999

"Places, please. Initiate satellite link. Check sound and 3-D graphics. Date log-in: February 2021. Okay, Elizabeth... In 3, 2, 1."

"Good evening, and welcome to 'Topics Above The Line,' a show featuring interviews with new authors. Tonight's guest is Brad Genova, who is here to talk about his suspense thriller, Twin Crossing. Brad, welcome to our show."

"Thank you, Elizabeth. It's nice to be here."

"Brad, please tell us how your characters, Chance and Cassandra, initially met."

"They actually met on the Internet. In today's world, such meetings are all too common. However, twenty-five years ago, in the year 1995, the Internet was relatively new. One night, Chance booted up his home computer to catch up on some work."

Chapter 1

Chance Macklin turned the key, the familiar click echoing through the foyer as he stepped inside his humble abode. The darkness enveloped him, a reminder of the shifting priorities that governed his life. Discarding his jacket onto the chair, he retrieved the mail and traversed the first floor of his cozy two-family house nestled in the heart of Framingham, Massachusetts. Weariness tugged at his senses, but the demands of his architectural business held him captive. Requests from clients for sketch revisions clamored for his attention, and he knew his timely email responses were anticipated. During nights like this, working from the solace of home offered him a semblance of peace. As a bachelor, his career became his steadfast companion.

Ascending the stairs, he heard the footsteps of his second-floor tenants, Lisa Genova and her bright-eyed eight-year-old son, Brad. The energetic boy sprinted up the steps, their creaking echoing through the main hallway. Brad, an only child with an insatiable appetite for reading, spent his evenings engrossed in the world of books that adorned their apartment above Chance's. Chance knew precisely where the young boy would find comfort—a reclining chair nestled near the living room radiator.

Chance longed to sink into his favorite chair and peruse the paper or architectural journals, yet the weight of his responsibilities as a business owner denied him such luxuries. By focusing on community services, schools, and hospitals, he managed to sidestep direct competition with larger firms, ensuring his livelihood through competitive compensation. But on this particular night, the pangs of loneliness bore down upon him, amplified by the mounting clutter that had taken root over days of neglect. The ever-growing heap of papers on his dining room table stared back at him, a testament to his inability to keep up with his domestic obligations.

With a resigned gaze, he observed the computer nestled beside his stereo—a silent machine beckoning him to a realm beyond mere monetary pursuits. There were treasures far more valuable: his passion for music, his cherished collection of literature, antique model cars fashioned during the exuberance of his youth, and his prized possession—a meticulously crafted wooden model of the USS

Constitution that had ignited his fascination with design. Determination filled his steps as he approached the computer, his finger pressing the startup button, heralding the illumination of the living room with a soft, ethereal glow. As the monitor flickered to life, an electronic voice pierced the room's silence, signaling the arrival of a new message.

Chance composed his response to the first of many letters, printing a copy for his records before proceeding to the next. By the stroke of eleven, the burden had lifted, relief washing over him as he realized that answering fifteen detailed letters had only claimed two hours of his evening. The resonant sounds of the Brandenberg Concertos, which had long since ceased playing, were replaced by the tranquil hush of the suburban night.

Realizing it was too late to invite Brad downstairs for a round of "Road Rash," Chance contemplated whether to power down the system or delve into the mysterious chatrooms he had heard whispered about. Colleagues at work incessantly gossiped about secret online friendships, while local and national newspapers stoked the hype with their coverage of digital romances. "Can't be that big a deal," he mused, casting a fleeting glance at the menu options before making his selection.

Within seconds, he found himself in the virtual lobby, perusing the array of menus. Popping into a room, he discovered a multitude of ongoing conversations, the chaos of typed voices vying for attention. The sign-on names—TreKre, PandaBear, Lust-o-fun, SaxyLady, and countless others—elicited a chuckle as he glimpsed their personalities through their chosen aliases.

He typed, "Hello from Boston," leaning back and awaiting a response.

"Welcome, Beantown," RussX replied.

"Hey, Russ. What's the topic?"

As he anticipated a reply from Russ, his attention was drawn to a conversation unfolding between two women—JstJL and AngelEyes— as they bemoaned the "rude hunters" in the vast expanse of the Internet.

JstJL: The guy said what?

AngelEyes: That he wanted me to be his foot slave. Can you believe that line of bull?

JstJL: Sounds kinky, honey.
AngelEyes: You interested, JL? Go for it!

Amidst the flurry of so many conversations, Chance focused on their ongoing dialogue.

JstJL: One guy asked for my measurements, and I told him I was a size seven.
AngelEyes: I'm sure he has no clue what that means. All they want to know is my weight and cup size.
JstJL: I feel like I'm back in high school inside this thing.
AngelEyes: Some of these guys are probably brainstorming clever lines for their next encounter.
RussX: Hey gals, wanna join me in a private chat room for some fun?
JstJL: You're quite the charmer, RussX. Let's see if you can keep up with my wit.
AngelEyes: Haha, I'm a speed demon on the keyboard too. Let's see if you can handle it!

Then a message appeared, this time directed at Chance. Man-o-Action typed: "I didn't see your profile. Are you a woman?"
Chance typed, "I don't have a profile. Man."
He explored the menus and managed to access the profiles of JstJL and AngelEyes. Reading JstJL's profile, he discovered she was twenty-eight years old, though their conversation made them sound much younger. He recalled her remark, "I feel like I'm back in high school inside this thing."
Curiosity piqued, he delved into AngelEyes's profile. It revealed that she had recently graduated with a master's degree in psychology and worked as a full-time intern. But where? In what city? Chance raised an eyebrow as he read her hobbies. One entry caught him off guard: "My favorite activity is canoe dumping." *Canoe dumping?* Only a few would understand the significance.
Fifteen years ago, during summer camp, Chance and his twin brother Seth had reveled in the joy of overturning aluminum canoes, allowing them to fill with water while remaining afloat just beneath the surface. It created a makeshift bathtub of sorts, allowing them to paddle with their hands. Canoe dumping had been their favorite camp

activity. Following the menu prompts, Chance created his own profile. He was about to log it into the system when an instant message appeared.

"Male or female?"

"Male."

"Sorry, looking for single women interested in some cyber fun."

Chance wasn't surprised by the antics of men seeking online seduction. He had recently read an article in the Boston Globe about the need for government regulation to discourage such behavior of "rude hunters." Continuing to read their conversation, Chance found himself increasingly intrigued by AngelEyes, pondering how best to introduce himself. *Something poetic or amusing?* Finally, he summoned the courage to send her a personalized instant message.

"The eyes of an Angel can see the entire world."

Pausing, he sent the message and watched it disappear. Seconds stretched into minutes as he wondered if she had received it. Mixing orange juice and soda water into a glass, he stole glances at the scrolling conversations on the computer screen—twenty members engaged in digital banter. *How could anyone take this place seriously?* Suddenly, the familiar chime of an incoming instant message interrupted his musings.

Chance replied to SandalMan, "I'm not your type!"

As AngelEyes continued her simultaneous conversations, Chance remembered their shared hobby and typed, "Hey, AngelEyes, ever been canoe dumping in the Upper Peninsula?" Shaking his head at his audacity, he thought, What the hell, just send it. So he did.

Without slowing down her dialogue, AngelEyes carried on, and Chance leaned back, closing his eyes and rubbing them until sparks danced in his vision. He was eager to tear himself away from the monitor, but the computer chimed, signaling another instant message. "Leave me alone, guys," he muttered, but when he opened his eyes, he saw the name—AngelEyes!

She had responded: "I read your profile, Chance2. You sound like a nice guy."

Now what? Chance struggled to find the right words, typing and deleting sentences as cleverness eluded him. Another instant message from AngelEyes appeared: "So, stranger, tell me more about you."

Chance2: I'm single and own my own architectural business and home near Boston.

AngelEyes: It looks like we're neighbors, sort of. I live in Jersey. Also single.

For the next hour, they delved into a discussion about the peculiar realm of internet encounters. To her, it was a world of playfulness, where one could embrace daring and mystery from the comfort of their own home. She was surprised to discover that this was Chance's maiden voyage into the scrolling chaos, admiring his approach to catching her attention.

"What's your real name?" he typed, his words carrying a hint of playful skepticism. "You could always lie. I'll never know."

A momentary pause lingered in the digital air before she responded, "Beth."

"Hi, Beth," he greeted.

"No, really, it's Delia."

Chuckling, he leaned back in his chair. "Hi, Delia."

"Actually, Dorothea!"

Amidst the silence of his room, Chance's laughter resounded. "Hi, BethDelia-Dorothea. Although I prefer to call you AngelEyes."

A message popped up that would become a familiar refrain: "LOL. So, what's your real name, stranger?"

He deliberated for a moment, considering his options. "Harold."

"Is that true?"

"No, it really is Chance."

An eternity seemed to pass before the reply appeared. "Chance, it's nice to meet you. My real name is Cassandra."

As Chance delved deeper into Cassandra's world of psychology, a distant voice whispered within his mind, tempting him with the possibility of unraveling the complex nature of his twin brother, Seth. However, that voice remained imprisoned, unable to rise to the surface where he could utter—or type—the words. For years, Chance had suppressed all memories of his incarcerated twin, secretly hoping that the judicial system would provide Seth with the healing he desperately needed. His inquiries about Cassandra's career remained within the realms of general curiosity, allowing her the space to expound upon her philosophies for understanding the intricacies of the human mind. At one point, she inquired if Chance had studied psychology in college.

"Not formally, but the subject always fascinated me," he replied. "I guess it's a way for me to better understand myself."

"Good answer," she typed. "I'm naturally analytical, but I strive to maintain an open mind."

"Especially when it comes to canoe dumping," Chance responded, a playful smile dancing on his lips.

Cassandra decided to pose a more challenging question. "Okay, Chance, if you could use one word to describe who you are, what would it be?"

Chance laughed, eyeing her message. "My lucky number is seven, so my word has seven letters—sincere." As he hit the send button, a part of him feared Cassandra would find his response corny or predictable.

"My God!" she eventually replied. "A friend of mine mentioned today that 'sincere' in Greek means 'without wax.' Apparently, sculptors like Michelangelo used hot wax to mend broken pieces of marble that accidentally chipped off during the creation process. Today, I ended a letter to a colleague by saying 'without wax, Cassandra Grey.' That's so funny, Chance."

With a twinkle of audacity, Chance typed, "I wonder which part of Michelangelo's 'David' wasn't 'sincerely' done."

Cassandra laughed at his jest, realizing she had never before found such genuine amusement while engaging with others online. His wit left an indelible impression on her, and she found herself reluctant to let the evening come to an end. Yet, as the hours crept past midnight, they agreed that it was time to bid farewell and log off for the night. Chance dared to ask if they could meet again.

"How about tomorrow at nine?" he proposed.

"Perfect!" AngelEyes typed, "Goodnight," and disconnected.

Chance stared at her parting words before powering down the computer. As his head settled on the pillow, he contemplated the past year, with its series of casual encounters that led nowhere. *Am I too consumed by work? Too comfortable in my bachelorhood?* Deep within, he knew he yearned for a companion—a kindred spirit who shared his passions and values. *You don't even know what she looks like.* Yet, for reasons he couldn't fathom, he felt a magnetic pull towards AngelEyes. He closed his eyes, envisioning the two of them canoe dumping in the warm embrace of a lake. Within moments, he succumbed to the meandering realms of his dreams, pondering the enigmatic question, *Who is this woman?*

* * *

Cassandra Grey curled up in her bed, her heart torn between the gripping pages of Sidney Sheldon's Nothing Lasts Forever and the enigmatic man, Chance, who had entered her life through the digital realm. As the suspenseful story of three nurses unfolded before her, she found her thoughts continually drifting back to their online encounter. He had written words that stirred her soul and elicited genuine laughter. "Read your novel. He's just another cyberguy!" she muttered to herself, attempting to regain focus on the book. Yet, her mind remained captivated by the tantalizing prospect of Chance's presence in her life. She closed the book, placing it on her night table, and settled into her pillow, her feet playfully kicking beneath the covers. Glancing at the alarm clock's radiant red numbers, glaring "1:30," she couldn't help but think about the thrill of canoe dumping.

Morning greeted Cassandra with the gentle melody of her alarm, serenading her with light classical music. Throughout the day, she valiantly tried to maintain focus on her work as an intern, yet as the hours passed and evening approached, she grew increasingly aware of the passage of time. Lost in her thoughts, she barely registered the words of a patient, needing to constantly redirect her attention.

"Miss Grey, what do you think?" the patient inquired.

"Hmm? Sorry. Please continue," Cassandra replied, swiftly reengaging in the conversation. *Wake up, girl!*

As the late evening descended, Cassandra left work and slipped into her car, only to find herself ensnared in the clutches of tangled traffic caused by a road construction crew. Hunger gnawed at her, frustration building within. She tightened her grip around the steering wheel in a futile attempt to alleviate her growing impatience. "Come on!" In her moments of clarity, she acknowledged the implausibility of an online relationship and the slim odds of Chance being there to meet her. She understood that nothing substantial could blossom from this chance encounter.

Crossing the threshold of her home, Cassandra became acutely aware that Chance had inadvertently infiltrated her life, though she couldn't fathom why. She resided in a realm of tranquility, free from unnecessary distractions. She passed by her office, her gaze briefly lingering on the computer. In the kitchen, she popped a pizza pocket into the microwave, poured herself a glass of wine, and pressed the button on the answering machine. Her mother's voice resounded through the speakers, reminding her of her brother Morgan's upcoming party. Morgan's voice followed, echoing the same reminder. It seemed typical of both her mother and Morgan to ensure she dutifully fulfilled her expected obligations since her father's tragic demise seven years ago.

Thoughts of that fateful night, when her mother received the late-night phone call about her father's accident on the expressway, flooded Cassandra's mind. The weather service had warned of treacherous icy conditions, but her father, Jonathan Grey, remained bound by the responsibilities of his insurance salesman role. Unseen by his eyes, a tractor-trailer veered into his lane, and in a heartbreaking instant, he was gone. Since that tragic event, Cassandra's life had undergone a radical transformation. To the dismay of her mother and Morgan, she often found herself disconnected from family events, occasionally sinking into periods of melancholy.

The microwave's beep pierced through Cassandra's ruminations, reminding her of her hunger. She pondered if Chance would have waited for her arrival. As she logged into the internet, an instant message materialized before her, even though she had barely signed on. He had reached out to her almost instantly.

Chance2: Good evening, AngelEyes.
AngelEyes: Hi, yourself. I thought you would have logged off by now.
Chance2: I almost did but decided to give it one more try. How was your day?
AngelEyes: Horrendous. I couldn't wait to get home.
Chance2: Cassandra, are you apprehensive about engaging in online conversations like this?
AngelEyes: A little. I mean, we know so little about each other.
Chance2: Ask me anything you want. It's your dime, too.
AngelEyes: LOL! Okay, here goes.

For a while, they delved into various facets of life, discussing family, careers, vacations, and music. Determined to maintain a lighthearted atmosphere, they exchanged silly jokes received from friends via the internet. At one point, Chance posed a question, inquiring about the word Cassandra strived to embody in her life. Her response surprised him, igniting a spark within his soul.

"My lucky number is also seven, and my word of choice is—genuine." Thirty seconds elapsed, and Cassandra wondered if he had received her message. "Chance, are you still there?"

"Still here," he responded promptly. "I looked up 'sincere' in my book of synonyms and found 'genuine' listed there as well. It's a small world, my genuinely sincere stranger."

Cassandra smiled, her fingers dancing across the keyboard. "Two lucky sevens. I wonder how well we would fare at the craps tables in Vegas?"

"If I were a betting man, which I am not, I believe good fortune would smile upon us," he replied, his words carrying a glimmer of hope and possibility.

Their connection grew stronger with every typed word, defying the limitations of distance and skepticism. Fate had woven their paths together, and neither Cassandra nor Chance could deny the allure of what lay before them.

Cassandra reveled in the knowledge that Chance was not a gambling man, a fact that brought her immense relief. Constantly surrounded by patients battling addictive tendencies, she often found herself pleading with her mother to curb her excessive lottery ticket purchases. The internet became her sanctuary, a place where she could explore the realm of innocent flirtation without enduring the weighty obligations and commitments demanded by a live relationship. Within this digital realm, she could freely bare her soul, knowing she held the power to control the situation with the simple act of turning the computer on or off. For the most part, her online encounters had been safe, and whenever someone attempted to delve too deeply into her personal life, she adeptly stepped back, safeguarding her heart.

However, in the span of just twenty-four hours, something new and exhilarating had unfolded in her life. Curiosity gnawed at her, wondering what Chance truly looked like. Her emotions swayed as she reflected on her unfortunate history with men she had met through the internet. People she had grown to respect eventually revealed their true colors: "Sorry, Fred, I don't share your affinity for whips and chains," or "Gee, Stan, I'm not interested in threesomes. You and your wife can have a great time without me." She had even discovered a devastating secret about a man she had grown fond of online—he was only thirteen years old! The audacity of his deception stung her to the core. "Why did he fool me like that?" she had asked, to which he simply replied, "Because I knew I could." It was the knowledge that some people reveled in the thrill of keeping their true identities a secret, savoring the moment when the truth was finally unveiled, that disturbed her the most.

Her psychologist's mind constantly reminded her to exercise caution and let prudence outweigh desire. The prospect of finding her soulmate through the online realm seemed infinitesimally small. Yet, despite these reservations, she couldn't help but notice the growing anticipation that welled within her as she awaited their next online rendezvous.

As the weeks melded together, their cyber meetings became an integral part of both their lives. They exchanged emails whenever possible, both keenly aware that the possibility of romance lay tantalizingly in the background. On one particular day, Cassandra logged on, disappointed to find that Chance hadn't arrived yet. Undeterred, she mustered the courage to send him an email: "The treasures we find in this beautiful world..." Her heart raced with a blend of excitement and trepidation.

Venturing into the chatrooms, she hoped for Chance's appearance, but instead encountered TomTom, Spanker, Casinofool, and a host of others, leaving rude and explicit instant messages. "Are you M or F? Age, measurements, height, where do you live?" Their words reeked of transparent sexual innuendo. After receiving a graphic instant message from SizzlDik, she decided it was time to log off for the night, unrealistically missing Chance.

* * *

Far away from New Jersey, Chance found himself pulled from one meeting to another, putting the final touches on his sketches for two hospital wings and a children's park, projects he had undertaken pro bono for the community. As the minutes ticked by, he glanced at his wristwatch. It was well past nine, and he had given up hope of making his online date.

"I hope she's not still there," he moaned, booting up his home computer. Nervously tapping his fingers on the table, he waited with bated breath as the system loaded at a painstakingly slow pace. His watch reminded him of the ticking seconds—ten fifty!

The internet chimed, indicating the arrival of new mail, but Chance brushed it aside in his search for Cassandra. Alas, she was no longer signed on. He opened his mailbox, skipping past previous emails until he found hers. His eyes locked onto the words she had written: "The treasures we find in this beautiful world..." Reflecting on the melodic flow of her words, he began to type his response: "...are for us to share, forever and a day..." With anticipation and affection, he pressed the send button, his words vanishing into the digital abyss.

In the rush of getting ready for work the next morning, Cassandra hurriedly logged on to her computer, hoping to find a response from Chance. A burst of adrenaline coursed through her veins as she read his words: "...are for us to share, forever and a day..." She found herself lost in a daydream, completely oblivious to the incessantly ringing phone as she typed her reply, "...for the heart is a sacred place to reside," and hit send, her mind already spinning with possibilities. While engaged in a conversation with her mother, she couldn't help but wish that she could turn back time and craft a more creative response.

That night, as she logged on again, disappointment washed over her when she discovered that Chance hadn't yet replied. The realization that her emotions were being controlled by a mere connection of a computer left her irritated.

Later in the evening, as Chance contemplated his next letter to Cassandra, he felt excitement and nervousness. He knew their literary duet had become something special, a bridge that connected their souls in an inexplicable way. With a smile on his face, he sent: "...when two hearts beat as one with the rhythm of life."

Suddenly, a realization struck him—he had forgotten to mention his upcoming meeting in New York City. The idea of finally meeting Cassandra had been percolating in their conversations, but the prospect both thrilled and scared him. *What if there was no chemistry between us?*

Dearest AngelEyes,

Our poetic exchange continues to captivate my heart, revealing deeper facets of our being with each passing letter. I wanted to tell you that I will be in New York City on business next week. I find myself curious if you would be interested in finally meeting in person. I would catch a cab to any location you desire in New Jersey. Perhaps a restaurant or cafe?

Without Wax, Chance

That evening, Cassandra found two letters from Chance in her inbox. Eagerly, she opened the first, savoring the continuation of their poetic journey. As she read his second letter, a flurry of thoughts raced through her mind.

Dearest Chance,

Our connection has transcended the boundaries of this digital realm, and I find myself yearning to meet you in person. However, I believe it would be wise for us to meet in the city for dinner. I feel more comfortable bringing along a friend as a chaperone, not because I don't trust you, but rather due to the cautionary tales I've heard about online dating. Besides, my friend would never allow me to embark on this adventure alone.

You will find a second letter from me, the next installment of our shared poem.

Genuinely, Cassandra

A smile graced her lips as she pressed send, yet the prospect of actually meeting him left her feeling both excited and apprehensive. What if he didn't live up to her expectations? The thought slithered through her mind like a snake in the underbrush, whispering doubts and fears. *But what if he did?* They lived hundreds of miles apart, and suddenly the situation seemed overwhelmingly complex. Suddenly, an instant message appeared on her screen.

Chance2: I'm looking forward to our meeting.
AngelEyes: Me too, although I must admit, I'm a bit nervous.
Chance2: Is there anything I can say to help?
AngelEyes: Could you describe yourself in more detail? I know we agreed not to exchange pictures, but my curiosity is piqued.
Chance2: Ah, good old-fashioned chemistry. Well, I'm 300 lbs with a full beard and a really cute beer belly!
AngelEyes: What?
Chance2: Is that okay?

AngelEyes: Of course! I'm amazed because, minus the beard, that's exactly what I look like.

Chance2: LOL. Well, you already know that I'm 27 years old.

AngelEyes: And you know I'm 25.

Chance2: I'm 6 feet and weigh 175 lbs. I have black curly hair and blue eyes.

AngelEyes: That sounds nice. I'm 5 feet 6 inches, fit, with brunette hair and blue eyes.

During their conversation, they exchanged similar views and shared subtle hints of attraction, without delving too deeply into the subject of sexuality. Cassandra felt a wave of relief wash over her as she realized that she was genuinely drawn to Chance.

* * *

As Chance sat in his dimly lit study, bathed in the glow of his computer screen, he found himself lost in the labyrinth of his own thoughts. The gentle hum of the computer fan provided a steady backdrop to the whirlwind of emotions churning within him. His fingers hovered over the keyboard, hesitating before typing out his next message to Cassandra, the enigmatic woman who had captured his attention like no other.

"Hi, Cassandra. Hope your day went well. Mine was... eventful."

As he hit the send button, he couldn't shake the gnawing feeling of unease that had settled in the pit of his stomach. The events of the past few years had taken a toll on him, stirring up memories and emotions he had long buried deep within. Among them, the shadow of his identical twin brother, Seth, loomed large. Seth's incarceration was a constant weight on Chance's conscience, a reminder of the rift that had torn their lives apart.

The screen flickered to life as Cassandra's response appeared, her words illuminated against the dark backdrop of the chat window.

"Hey, Chance. Sorry to hear your day was rough. Anything you want to talk about?"

Chance hesitated, his fingers tracing the edges of his keyboard as he struggled to articulate the turbulent storm raging inside him. Finally, he typed out a response, the words flowing from his fingertips with an urgency he couldn't explain.

"It's just... things have been strange lately. Memories I thought I had left behind are resurfacing, and I can't shake the feeling that something isn't right."

Cassandra's reply was swift, her words a beacon of comfort in the sea of uncertainty that threatened to engulf him.

"I'm here for you, Chance. Whatever you're going through, you don't have to face it alone."

As he read her words, a sense of warmth washed over him, momentarily dispelling the shadows that loomed on the horizon. But even as he basked in the reassurance of her presence, a nagging doubt lingered at the back of his mind, whispering tales of danger and deception.

With a heavy heart, Chance pushed aside his misgivings and focused on the connection he shared with Cassandra, determined to unravel the mysteries that bound them together. Little did he know that their journey would lead them down a path fraught with peril and betrayal, where the line between truth and illusion blurred with each passing moment.

As the clock struck midnight and the world outside faded into darkness, Chance found himself drawn deeper into the web of intrigue that surrounded him, his fate intertwined with that of the woman who had stolen his heart and the secrets that threatened to tear them apart. But amidst the uncertainty, one thing remained clear: the specter of Seth's incarceration would haunt him every step of the way, a constant reminder of the brother he had failed to save.

* * *

Twenty-four hours before their meeting, Cassandra's heart raced with anxiety, robbing her of much-needed sleep. Like an eager child on Christmas Eve, the anticipation kept her wide-eyed and restless. Overwhelmed by curiosity and the desire to learn more about Chance, she reached for her phone and dialed Helen's number, despite the late hour.

"Helen, are you awake?" Cassandra whispered.

Startled from her slumber, Helen responded in a groggy tone, "Who is this?"

"It's Cassandra. I apologize for calling so late, but I can't sleep. Tomorrow is the day I meet Chance!"

"I know, and you're picking me up around three-thirty, right?" Helen replied.

"What if he's just another guy who picks up girls on the internet?" Cassandra's voice trembled with worry.

"Cassandra, take a deep breath and calm down. Just try to relax and get some sleep," Helen advised, yawning.

"I can't," Cassandra confessed, her anxiety refusing to subside.

After a pause, Helen said, "Trust your instincts and try to have fun. Goodnight, little Angel."

Cassandra spent an hour tossing and turning in bed, unable to find peace. Finally, she gave in to exhaustion, only to be roused by the blaring of her alarm clock a few hours later.

With the day of their meeting finally upon her, Cassandra left work at three o'clock to pick up Helen, who was eager to witness the outcome of an online connection turned real-life encounter. Helen had contemplated the idea of meeting someone online herself, hoping for a positive outcome for both Cassandra.

"Nervousness suits you," Helen remarked, studying Cassandra's radiant appearance as they climbed into the car.

Cassandra glanced at her watch repeatedly, praying for smooth traffic and punctuality. She prided herself on being on time, and today was no exception. Helen attempted to ease the tension by regaling her with tales of her recent Florida vacation, but Cassandra's mind remained fixated on the approaching hour of six.

Parking the car in a nearby garage, Cassandra and Helen made their way to the restaurant, their steps infused with anticipation. Every passing man caught Cassandra's eye, sending a shiver of both fear and excitement through her. Could this be Chance? Please, don't let it be him. *Please, let it be him!* The suspense gnawed at her, but she was grateful that the long-awaited day had finally arrived—sparks would either ignite or fade away.

"Table for two?" the maitre d' inquired.

Distracted by the bustling activity of the restaurant, Cassandra's nerves were on edge and barely heard the question.

"Actually, we're meeting someone here," Helen replied. "His name is Chance Macklin."

Recognition lit up the maitre d's face. "Ah, yes. The gentleman arrived ten minutes ago. Waiter, please seat these two ladies at table twelve."

"Right this way," the waiter gestured.

Cassandra felt her legs weaken under the weight of anticipation she had been carrying for months. She stood frozen in place as Helen motioned toward table twelve. Her heart skipped a beat. *Oh my, he's absolutely stunning!*

"Chance," Helen began, her voice filled with warmth, "I'd like you to meet Cassandra Grey."

Chance's eyes widened as he rose to meet the mysterious AngelEyes. "Nice to meet you, Cassandra. I'm Chance Macklin." A genuine smile danced on his lips, revealing his delight in her appearance, her sensitive eyes and hair cascading over her shoulders. He briefly glanced at her figure, his eyes conveying a subtle excitement. *More beautiful than I ever imagined!*

Cassandra regained her composure, her confidence renewed. "Chance, at last we meet," she greeted, struggling to contain her awe. He was everything he had described and more—an athletic build, deep blue eyes that twinkled when they met hers. The touch of his hand sent a surge of warmth through her veins, and she couldn't help but smile.

"Please, have a seat," Chance offered, standing and extending his arm.

Over appetizers, laughter filled the air as they reminisced about the letters they had exchanged, each anecdote recalled with almost telepathic synchronicity. Helen observed their interaction and seductive glances, silently amazed and captivated. It felt necessary for her to act as Cassandra's escort, and she knew she would gladly do it again.

"Cassandra, it's getting late," Helen interjected gently. "I'm sorry, Chance, but we have quite a drive ahead of us, and both have work tomorrow."

"I understand," Chance replied, refusing to accept money as he settled the dinner bill.

Cassandra, her voice tinged with concern, asked Chance, "How are you getting to the airport?"

"By cab. Thankfully, my flight isn't for another two hours, and I know the time will pass quickly," Chance reassured her with a warm smile.

His gaze met Cassandra's, a magnetic link establishing between them, unaffected by the cacophony of New York traffic engulfing them. An air of awkwardness settled upon them, disrupted only by the impatient cab driver's honking horn. Cassandra longed for Chance to bridge the gap between them, but circumstances denied them their first kiss. The magic of the moment was momentarily stripped away.

Chance extended his right hand, gently raising Cassandra's hand to his lips. With a soft kiss on the back of her hand, he whispered, "Thank you for being everything you said you were."

"You too. I had a wonderful time," Cassandra replied, her voice filled with sincerity.

Chance waved goodbye and entered the waiting cab. As the vehicle drove away, Helen couldn't help but feel a twinge of envy. "Don't let this guy slip away," she urged.

"Helen, I can't thank you enough for coming with me. I just hope he doesn't turn out to be someone entirely different," Cassandra confided.

"He seems like a nice guy, and handsome! By the way, does he happen to have a brother?" Helen joked.

Cassandra paused for a moment, contemplating Helen's question. "That's a good question. I'll have to ask him more about his family. Our conversations online, and now that I've met him in person, it all feels surreal," she confessed, her voice tinged with awe and disbelief. Cassandra gazed out the car window, lost in her thoughts.

That night, images of Chance filled Cassandra's mind as she lay in bed, consumed by excitement. Reading a book became impossible, as her thoughts wandered elsewhere, her fingers absentmindedly turning the pages. Unable to resist, she sat up and walked to her home office, determined to conduct a search of her dashing prince.

Sitting in front of her computer, she whispered to herself, "Okay, Macklin. Show me what you've got." Her search led her to an article about a certain Seth Macklin's arrest, but she quickly dismissed it, discovering that the name Macklin was more common than she had thought.

"Brad, it seems that true love has finally found its way into Cassandra's life. Or has it?" Elizabeth inquired, her voice laced with intrigue.

"In every new relationship, doubts, concerns, and hesitations inevitably arise. Despite the distance that separated them, their online courtship was not immune to these challenges," Brad Genova, author of Twin Crossing, responded.

"Indeed. For those just tuning in, I'm here with Brad Genova, discussing the complexities of their virtual romance. Please, enlighten us further," the host prodded.

"Their struggles, both logistically and emotionally, weighed heavily on their hearts. The physical distance between them only amplified their yearning for each other."

Chapter 2

Cassandra lingered in Chance's thoughts long after their dinner together, her image etched into his mind like a beautiful dream. The subtle glances she had offered, the mesmerizing beauty of her blue eyes—it all felt surreal to him. The idea that he had met such an extraordinary woman in the vastness of the Internet left him questioning its reality. But deep within, he knew without a doubt that she was real, and he couldn't help but smile at the thought. The possibilities that lay before them both excited and frightened him. He chuckled as he reminisced about the missed opportunity to kiss her. *Why didn't I seize the moment?* In his mind's eye, he traced her every movement, bridging the physical distance that separated them.

Back at home, Chance composed an email to Cassandra, expressing how much he had enjoyed their time together. His words were brief, yet they carried a sincerity that resonated with her. Cassandra responded in kind, her cautious nature mirrored in her reply. As the days turned into weeks, their online courtship continued to blossom, becoming a cherished highlight of their hectic days. Sometimes their conversations were brief, lasting mere minutes, while at times, they lost themselves in the passage of time.

One Monday night, as Chance read journals in bed, the sound of footsteps from his upstairs tenants reminded him of how little time he had spent with Brad lately. A pang of guilt and longing washed over him, and he resolved to devote quality time to the young boy during the upcoming weekend. There was an unfinished project awaiting them—a tree fort in the backyard that Chance had promised to build.

Chance recalled the day Brad had shared his personal journal, revealing the emotional toll of losing his father. Although Brad seldom discussed it, their friendship meant a great deal to him. He wanted Chance to understand the reason behind his occasional bouts of sadness. The memory of the nightmarish days surrounding his father's illness haunted the young boy.

The concept of cancer eluded his comprehension as he visited his father, William, in the hospital. He wondered why his mother always left in tears, even though his dad assured him he would soon be coming home. But as months went by, the harsh reality settled in—a reality that crushed the hopes of the six-year-old boy, as his father's hospital bed became his final resting place.

Chance envisioned the details of the tree fort, planning the amount of wood they would need, the perfect spot on the tree, and how to involve Brad in the construction process. Suddenly, Cassandra's presence invaded his thoughts. Before retiring for the night, he logged onto his computer and discovered her letter.

Chance,
The magic we share, forged through the mystery of my
computer screen, is a treasure I hold dear. Coming home and finding
a letter from you brings me immense joy. It's all so strange, yet I
revel in this feeling.
AngelEyes

* * *

Chance stood amidst the bustling activity of the construction site, his watchful gaze tracing the progress of the hospital wing taking shape before him The Contract Manager, whose wife was enduring a difficult delivery, had asked him to lend a hand. While it wasn't his usual role, he understood the urgency of the situation. Chance noticed the foreman of the construction crew standing idly by—a man known for his occasional belligerence.

"Where are the beams we ordered?" Chance inquired, his tone betraying his frustration.

"They were supposed to arrive from the Steelworks in Pittsburgh this afternoon," Dan Jacobs of Gaffney Construction replied.

"What's causing the delay?" Chance pressed, his impatience mounting.

"They haven't arrived yet," Dan replied curtly.

"I can see that, Dan!"

"Look, Chance," Dan retorted, his hand gesturing angrily, "I'm not the trucking company. I have no idea where that rig is. My crew is waiting, as you can see. What do you want me to do?"

"Call me when the truck arrives," Chance said tersely.

With a heavy sigh, Chance walked toward the construction trailer, reviewing all phases of the project. He meticulously double-checked requisition forms against his design, finding solace in the fact that everything aligned perfectly. It was only when the truck from Pittsburgh finally arrived that he grabbed his hard hat and micrometer. As he approached the truck, his eyes fixed on the beams, but anger welled up within him as he checked the measurements.

"Tell me where this registers," Chance demanded.

"Seven-sixteenths. What difference does one-sixteenth of an inch make?" Dan retorted, his condescending attitude clear.

Chance's patience wore thin. "It means that every patient in this wing is at risk. Not from their own medical conditions, but from the instability of a building that I'm responsible for. Do you understand?" The intensity in his eyes left no room for doubt.

"So, boss, what's your plan?" Dan asked confrontationally.

Chance placed his hand on Dan's shoulders, attempting to diffuse the tension. "Dan, I value your company. I have plenty of work that I could send your way. But when it comes to *my* work, I don't compromise. If you don't share this same commitment, then we can never do business again."

"These beams won't pose a problem," Dan argued, refusing to back down. "You design, I build."

Chance halted in his tracks, his gaze unwavering. "You can leave. I'll send this driver back to steel country." He began walking toward the driver.

"Wait!" Dan called out, approaching Chance. "I'll pause construction and get the required supports."

"Now we understand each other! But next time you try to cut corners, make sure you have another project lined up," Chance warned sternly.

"Where will you be?" Dan inquired cautiously.

"In the trailer, double-checking all shipments. Unless you want to come clean now and save me the trouble," Chance added, a hint of skepticism in his voice.

"Everything will meet the specifications," Dan assured.

* * *

That evening, as Cassandra settled before her computer, the familiar chime of an awaiting message brought a gentle curve to her lips.

Dear AngelEyes,

Even though you seem so far away, a mere moment is all it takes for me to close my eyes and envision you walking into the restaurant. You have captured a part of me that I didn't even know existed. I hope your day was filled with sweetness and ease.

Yours, Chance

In the comfort of her bed, Cassandra's thoughts turned to the sexual energy that Chance had ignited within her. She allowed herself to envision their passionate encounters, a longing stirring deep within her. Sleep evaded her as her mind wandered into uncharted territory.

Doubts began to creep in—meeting Mr. Right through the internet seemed too good to be true. She sought distraction and turned on the television, aimlessly flipping through cable channels. However, nothing captured her interest.

Just as she was about to give up, CNN caught her attention. The news story from California recounted the horrific ordeal of a young woman who had been attacked after meeting a man online. Her heart sank as she listened to the details of the investigation. The anchorwoman's warning echoed in her ears, cautioning against the potential dangers of online meetings. The three words, "exercise extreme caution," haunted her thoughts.

Days later, Cassandra found herself at the hospital, reviewing case files with fellow interns in the break room. As they chatted, a conversation about the recent news caught her attention. Kendra, one of the interns, had taken time off due to a personal emergency involving her sister.

"It's all over the news," Stacey remarked, her voice filled with concern.

"I hope Kendra's sister will be okay," Angie chimed in. "Such a terrible situation."

Cassandra couldn't help but ask, her hands trembling around her coffee cup, "What happened to Kendra's sister?"

"She got attacked last night," Stacey answered somberly. "It's awful."

Martha, another intern, expressed her frustration. "These guys think that just because we go out with them, we owe them something. It's infuriating!"

As Cassandra listened to the interns' conversation about Kendra's sister, her mind raced with memories of her own past. The night in college when she narrowly escaped a date rape flashed before her eyes, the scarf that was used to hold her down serving as a constant reminder of the importance of trusting her instincts. The intercom's blaring interrupted her thoughts, and she snapped back to the present.

As the interns began to leave the break room, Cassandra said, "Martha and this guy. How did they meet?"

Stacey tossed her empty coffee cup into the wastebasket. "In one of those cheesy Internet chatrooms."

Cassandra felt her body freeze in her chair, the weight of those words crashing down on her. She closed her eyes, the warning to exercise caution echoing in her mind.

* * *

On a sunny Saturday morning, Brad stood outside Chance's door, his ear pressed against it as he softly knocked. "Chance, are you there?"

Chance's eyes snapped open, jolted from sleep by the familiar sound of Brad's voice cutting through the silence of the room. "I'm coming, Brad," he called out, quickly throwing on a pair of shorts and a t-shirt. Days had passed since Cassandra's last letter, and he anxiously awaited her response. He opened the door, mustering a smile. "Sorry, I worked late last night."

"No problemo." Brad walked in and made his way to the computer. "What's our plan for today?"

Chance attempted to shake off his sleepiness. *Where is she? Four days without a letter.* "First, I'll make some coffee and take a shower. And you, my co-foreman, could gather the tools from the shed. We'll need a saw, hammer, nails, level, two sturdy horses, and anything else you can think of."

"I'm on it." Brad left the room, eager to assist.

With his hair still damp from the shower, Chance emerged from his house in his work clothes. In one hand, he held a cup of coffee, and in the other, his cell phone. "We need to call Home Depot and confirm that everything is in stock."

Brad watched as Chance inspected the array of tools. "How did I do?"

"Excellent job, Bradley," Chance praised, playfully ruffling the boy's hair.

"I hate that name," he laughed.

As Chance dialed the phone, he couldn't help but notice the mischievous look on Brad's face. After ending the call, he questioned the young boy, "What's going on?"

Brad burst into laughter. "I just realized you're left-handed."

"Call me southpaw," Chance winked. "Now, let's get to work."

An hour later, they unpacked the supplies in the backyard, ready to embark on their project. "It's ten a.m., and we're right on schedule," Chance declared, pointing to a large oak tree. "A tree fort will soon be born right over there."

Brad handed Chance every tool he requested, their teamwork seamless as they carried planks to the sawhorses. Engrossed in their work, they hardly noticed Brad's mother, Lisa, arriving with a tray of lemonade.

"Cold drinks for the crew," Lisa announced cheerfully.

"Break time!" Chance declared, the two of them gulping down their glasses. After a brief pause, he said, "Break's over."

Lisa smiled. "Any requests for lunch?"

Brad, dragging a heavy load of 2x10s, gasped, "Bologna!"

"Light on the mayo," Chance added. "I'm running out of belt loops." Lisa laughed, appreciating their banter.

The project progressed throughout the afternoon, their conversations flowing as nails were hammered, wood was measured, and cuts were made. Chance was pleasantly surprised by Brad's occasional blunt remarks, reminiscent of Arnold Schwarzenegger's character in The Terminator.

"Hey, Chance. How come you don't have a girlfriend?" Brad asked out of the blue.

Caught off guard, Chance realized the innocence behind the question. His thoughts wandered momentarily, his mind filled with concerns over Cassandra's silence. "I suppose I'm waiting for the right woman to come along."

"My mom is hoping to meet someone too. She's been lonely since Dad died," Brad revealed, a wide grin on his face. "Hey, you know what?"

Chance sensed where the conversation was heading. "Brad, your mom and I are great friends. That will never change, you understand?"

Brad nodded. "Yup. Still, I wish..."

Placing a hand on Brad's shoulder, Chance reassured him, "Someday, she will." A few moments later, he added, "I actually did meet someone."

"Really?" Brad's eyes widened with curiosity.

"Do you remember when I showed you how the internet works? How I can talk to people all over the world?" Chance began, a hint of sadness in his voice. "Well, I met a woman on online who lives in New Jersey, and we've been in touch for the past few of months."

Brad's response was filled with melancholy. "I wish Mom could meet someone like that." He continued hammering a nail into a 2x4. "Hey, Chance, what's this?" He rhythmically tapped his hammer, a familiar sound echoing in the air.

Chance joined in, hammering twice in response. "Do you know what that is called?"

"It has a name?"

"It's called 'Shave and a Haircut, Two Bits.' Have you ever seen the movie 'Who Framed Roger Rabbit'?"

"No way! A movie about a shave and a haircut?"

Chance chuckled. "No, they use that rhythm throughout the movie. We'll watch it together sometime, okay?" Brad nodded eagerly.

They continued their work, measuring and sawing with each passing moment. As the sun began to set, Lisa appeared in the backyard.

"Dinner will be ready in an hour. Should I delay it?" she asked, a knowing smile on her face.

"That sounds about right," Chance winked at Brad.

Soon, the tree fort stood tall and majestic, its structure a testament to the hard work and bond between Chance and Brad. They stepped back, their eyes filled with pride as they admired their creation. Several lower branches supported the different rooms and levels of the fort, and Brad walked around to examine the windows. One faced their house, another looked out onto a neighbor's home, and his favorite was a skylight that allowed him to gaze at the stars from the top floor.

Behind the toolshed, Chance retrieved a sign he had made earlier. "And now for the most important feature."

Brad gasped as he read the sign: "'Brad's Tree Fort. Everyone Welcome.' Chance, you're awesome!"

Chance nailed the sign to the front entrance, and Brad climbed through each level, testing their strength and feeling the smooth wood beneath his hands. Later, they sat down for a celebratory dinner in the fort. Chance raised his glass.

"A toast to our new backyard fort."

Brad clinked his soda against Chance's glass. "Here's mud in your eye."

The following morning, the sounds of laughter and play emanated from the fort, waking Chance from his sleep. He groggily left his bed, his gaze shifting to the computer. Drawn by an irresistible force, he approached it and logged on. But there was nothing. *Are you still there, Cassandra?* Fearing the worst, he composed a heartfelt message.

Cassandra,

I'm starting to get worried. It has been nearly a week since I last heard from you, and I hope everything is alright. Please, if you can, send me a response so I can ease my mind. If you wish to end our correspondence completely, I suppose I'll understand. Regardless of what happens, know that I consider you a dear and valued friend.

Chance

* * *

Cassandra hesitated before opening her email. What did she expect? For him to vanish without a trace? Guided by her logical mind, she read his letter, struggling with the ambivalence of her decision. Memories of the CNN story and Martha's recent attack played in her thoughts, reminding her of the dangers of trusting someone she had met online. Her own experiences with meeting people in cyberspace reinforced her belief that severing all contact was the best course of action. However, her heart felt a pang of guilt for abruptly ending their relationship. And now, faced with his fifth unanswered letter, her rationality clashed with her intuition. *He's a good guy. Don't trust him. It's just email. Women have been raped and attacked. Remember what happened in college!* With a heavy heart, she signed off.

Sitting in a cafe, Cassandra shared her decision with Helen over a cup of coffee. "Martha is still in the hospital. That guy tried to kill her."

Helen nodded understandingly, aware of Cassandra's close call with a rapist in college. Taking a sip of her coffee, she said, "Even with men you date in person, you never truly know what they're capable of. It's unfortunate, but even women who have been married for years can experience such things. Sometimes, it feels like the only option is to remain celibate and embrace life as an old maid."

Cassandra shook her head. "No, thank you! Mr. Right is out there somewhere. Probably not in Boston, though."

Helen sighed. "Honey, you'd be a fool to let Chance slip away. That's all I have to say!"

Lost in her thoughts, Cassandra recalled Chance's most recent letter. "He's worried that something might have happened to me. I haven't responded to his email."

"Really?" Helen asked, raising an eyebrow.

"Do you think I'm being unreasonable?"

Helen grinned, recalling Cassandra's favorite psychology cliché. "What do you think?"

Cassandra chuckled. "Very funny." After a moment of reflection, she added, "I suppose there's no harm in writing back. He doesn't know where I live or have my phone number."

* * *

"You've got to be kidding," Chance muttered as he logged on that night.

Chance,
I apologize for not writing sooner. I should have realized that you would be worried. Still, I believe it's best for us to stop writing. It's a long and painful story, and I hope you can understand. It's nothing personal.
Cassandra

Chance couldn't help but feel a mixture of frustration and longing. The thoughts "And to think I found myself falling for you" echoed in his mind. Was it true? Did he truly have those feelings for her? After much contemplation, he made the decision to include those words in his final reply. With a deep breath, he hit the button, launching his message into the abyss.

* * *

Helen's voice crackled through the phone the following evening. "He said what? Read it again."

"He said, 'And to think I found myself falling for you.' What do you think, Helen?"

"It sounds like he's serious," Helen replied.

"Or he's trying to deceive me," Cassandra muttered, her voice laced with uncertainty.

"Or..." Helen paused.

"Or he genuinely had feelings for me," Cassandra said, causing Helen to laugh. "What's so funny?"

"Cassandra, he's a real guy! You've met him, and I have too," Helen said. "Maybe I should make my move. I've been hoping you'd end it anyway. He's cute, and I think he likes me."

Now it was Cassandra's turn to laugh. "Are you using reverse psychology on me?" A pause hung between them, with each waiting for the other to speak. "Helen?"

"Hmm? Oh, sorry. Just lost in thought. I have to go, Cassandra."

"Hold on… What a mess…" Cassandra anxiously awaited a response. "Stop with the long pauses, Helen. I can't stand them!"

"Now you know how Chance feels. Are you going to let him slip away? After what you said to me in New York about the possibility of finding Mr. Right?"

"You know, there's always room for you in my profession if you ever want to change careers."

Helen chuckled. "Send me the bill. Just be careful, but not too careful. Remember, it's only email."

After they hung up, Cassandra sat at her desk, drumming her fingers on the wood surface. *He must think I'm crazy. Perhaps I am.* She powered up her computer, her eyes fixed on her empty inbox. She opened Chance's last letter: "And to think I found myself falling for you." *And to think, Chance, I found myself afraid to feel the same way.*

Dear Chance,

I would like to continue our friendship and I hope you don't find me foolish for being so ambivalent. There are many things going on in my life, and I guess I feared getting too close and complicating things even further. I would understand if you choose not to reply.

A sincere friend. Truly!

In a separate email, Cassandra bravely shared the details of her college assault, when she had met a man who had said all the right things, only to take her to an expensive restaurant and fulfill his own selfish desires. Chance appreciated her honesty and assured her that he would always be there to lend a thoughtful ear whenever she needed.

Their friendship gradually blossomed, and for months they chatted online. After some hesitation, Cassandra gave Chance her home phone number. Sometimes days would pass before he would call or reply to her emails, not because he wanted to tease her, but to protect his own heart. They discussed their experiences with others they had dated, laughing on the surface while silently wondering about the true depth of their own connection. Chance purposely avoided any mention of meeting in person again, hoping that Cassandra would take the initiative.

* * *

Cassandra dedicated herself to her work at the medical center in Denville, making strides in helping patients trapped in abusive relationships. Wives sought her guidance, their bodies bearing the signs and scars of physical abuse. "Pam," she gently suggested to one patient, "perhaps it's time for some intervention. Your husband is causing you harm. Don't you think it's time to make a change for yourself?"

"But I know he loves me," Pam replied as she held back the tears.

"I'm sure he does in his own way," Cassandra responded thoughtfully. "But if the situation is physically or mentally dangerous for you, then intervention becomes crucial. It's time to prioritize your well-being."

Cassandra's thoughts wandered back to the day she had decided to pursue a career in psychology, the day the campus police had apprehended the man who had attacked her. One of the most distressing aspects of her profession was dealing with abusive relationships involving innocent children. The stories were endless and varied, with parents attempting to blame their child's injuries on mere accidents.

"He's just a clumsy kid," Cooper said dismissively about his six-year-old son.

Cassandra knelt down to meet the tear-stained face of the boy. "Mark, did you fall down and hurt yourself?"

"I told you—" Cooper began to interject, but Cassandra's icy stare silenced him.

She smiled at the boy. "Okay, Mark, I want you to come with me and sit in a special room I have. It's filled with all kinds of fun toys. Have you ever heard of the Teenage Mutant Turtle Ninjas?"

"Ninja Turtles," Mark replied between sobs.

"That's right," Cassandra corrected herself. "Well, I have all of them in that room over there." She pointed towards the end of the hallway. "There's a nice lady waiting there, eager for you to show her how they play. Would you like that?"

Mark nodded cautiously, stealing a glance at his father.

"Go on," his father said, motioning with his hands. Sarcastically, he added, "I'll talk to this nice shrink for a while."

Once David left, Cassandra locked eyes with the father, sensing the brewing anger within him. "Cooper, we have reached a critical point. I have no choice but to report my suspicions of child abuse to the authorities. This isn't just a single bump or bruise; it's an accumulation of injuries. During our previous sessions, I provided suggestions on how to release your anger in healthier ways. However, now you have directed it towards Mark, and I cannot allow that to continue."

"You're bluffing. You can't take my child away from me!"

"I don't play games, and I never bluff," Cassandra stated firmly.

"Damn it, lady, this is none of your business. I'll leave the boy alone."

"I'm sorry," she calmly replied. "Mark will need to stay with the authorities, and he will not be returning home with you tonight."

Cooper yelled with rage, and Cassandra braced herself, half-expecting him to strike her. Instead, she pressed the alarm button, and within moments, two security guards entered the office.

"Please escort this gentleman out the door," she instructed them.

Many exhausting hours later, Cassandra successfully had Mark placed in a safe foster home, while his father faced charges of abuse. The family would require months of counseling to rebuild their lives, but Cassandra knew she had made the right choice for Mark. As she drove home, the event replayed in her mind, filling her with dread about the upcoming night's sleep.

Slumped in her chair at home, Cassandra wondered what to do next. She had lost her appetite. Her thoughts turned to a friend she had been missing. *Chance, how did you spend your day?*

* * *

Chance jolted awake, his heart racing like a stallion galloping through the darkness of his room. The tendrils of his nightmare still clung to him, tightening their grip with every beat of his pulse. Sweat trickled down his brow, cold and clammy against his skin as he struggled to shake off the remnants of the dream.

"Get up, convict!"

The harsh voice echoed in his mind, a cruel reminder of the past that refused to release its hold. In the murky depths of slumber, Chance found himself ensnared within a labyrinth of shadows, where the ghosts of his past danced in haunting silence. Each whisper, each cry for help, reverberated through the corridors of his consciousness like a relentless echo, driving him further into the depths of despair.

"Chance, help me!"

The anguished plea tore through the darkness, a desperate cry for salvation from a soul in torment. He jolted awake, his chest heaving with the weight of his nightmares. But even as he emerged from the suffocating embrace of sleep, the specter of his past lingered like a shadow, refusing to be banished by the light of day.

As dawn's tentative fingers began to paint the horizon with hues of amber and gold, Chance found himself drawn to the soft glow of his computer screen, a beacon of light in the sea of darkness that threatened to engulf him. With trembling hands, he reached out, fingers hovering over the keyboard like a hesitant lover seeking solace in the embrace of an old flame.

And there, amidst the silence of the early morning hours, he found her—the promise of sanctuary in a world fraught with turmoil. With each word she penned, Cassandra wove a tapestry of hope and redemption, a lifeline cast across the tumultuous seas of his troubled mind.

The transition from the haunting depths of his nightmare to the comforting embrace of Cassandra's letter was like emerging from the depths of a storm-tossed sea into the warm embrace of a sunlit shore. In her words, he found solace, a beacon of light guiding him through the darkest corridors of his soul.

Dear Chance,
In the midst of my busiest days, the thought of our friendship brings me peace and joy.
Love, Cassandra

After reading Cassandra's letter, Chance sat in silence, the soft glow of the computer screen illuminating the dimly lit room. He felt a stirring within him, a mixture of emotions swirling like a tempest in his chest. The two words she had written—*Love, Cassandra*—had pierced through the veil of his darkness, offering a glimmer of hope amidst the shadows that threatened to engulf him.

But along with the sense of relief came a flood of other emotions: longing, desire, and a twinge of guilt. Guilt for allowing himself to be consumed by the ghosts of his past, for wallowing in self-pity instead of seizing the opportunities that lay before him. Guilt for the pain he had caused those he loved, especially Seth, whose memory haunted him like a ghost in the night. Yet, amidst the turmoil of his emotions, there was also a glimmer of something else, a flicker of determination, a spark of hope.

Closing his eyes, Chance allowed himself to envision a world where the darkness no longer held sway, where he could walk in the light without fear of stumbling back into the shadows. And in that moment, he made a silent vow to himself—to seize the opportunities that lay before him, to confront his demons head-on, and to embrace the love and friendship that Cassandra had offered so freely.

With a newfound sense of resolve, Chance set aside the letter and rose from his chair, the weight of his burdens feeling lighter than they had in years. The journey ahead would not be easy, he knew, but for the first time in a long while, he felt ready to face whatever challenges lay in store.

As he extinguished the soft glow of the computer screen and made his way towards the window, the first rays of dawn painted the horizon. And in that fleeting moment between darkness and light, Chance felt a sense of peace wash over him—a peace that he knew had been a long time coming.

Holding a picture of Cassandra dancing at a friend's wedding, an erotic fantasy took hold of his imagination. He vividly envisioned every detail of her graceful movements.

Dear Angel Eyes,
I feel compelled to share with you a story of my growing desire. I seek your permission to send my thoughts in the form of a mild fantasy. Please don't hesitate to say no.
With thoughts of you filling my heart,
Love, Chance

The next morning, Cassandra found his story and immediately printed it. She curled up on her couch, bathed in the soft glow of her Victorian lamp.

I Love to Watch You Dance
Throughout the day, I called you at work to express how much I yearned for you. Each time you answered the phone, you wondered if it would be me, softly whispering my desires into your ear. By the time five p.m. arrived, you walked in a daze, consumed by my longing.

I left work early to prepare for the evening, purchasing your favorite bottle of wine and luscious strawberries. As the hour drew near, I turned off the lights and waited in silence. A single candle flickered on the dining room table, casting enchanting shadows on the walls.

I heard the sound of your key turning in the lock, anticipating your arrival. As you entered, I sensed your curiosity and excitement. You felt my presence as you cautiously made your way through the kitchen, peeking in before stepping into the dining room.

The room was bathed in a gentle yellow glow. I saw the smile that graced your face, and in an instant, the room seemed to grow warmer. You noticed that I wore only a bathrobe, the soft contours of my body revealed in the flickering candlelight. With a seductive glance, I motioned for you to approach. Our closeness allowed me to savor your intoxicating scent as I lifted a glass to your lips.

Without physical contact, the electricity between us surged. Setting the glass down, I gently placed my hand against your cheek, causing you to melt against me, your body seeking comfort. Holding you in my arms, I felt an overwhelming warmth flow through me as our lips met. You pressed a finger to your lips before lightly touching it to mine. Your eyes conveyed a message of anticipation, and I released you. As you left the room, I sat down, wondering and waiting.

Soon, the sound of music filled the air. The rhythm transported you to a world of your own, setting my heart ablaze. Draped in a long, sheer white gown that swayed with every movement, you entered the dining room. Floating on a cloud of mounting passion, my eyes fixated solely on you.

You knew your dancing drove me to madness as you moved in perfect harmony with the music. Your hair glistened as it cascaded over your eyes, and with a look of desire and wildness, you glanced at me. Enraptured by your spell, my hope had been to ensnare you in mine. You danced before me, your alluring body tantalizingly close, but every time I reached for you, you eluded my grasp. I could only watch as your dress concealed the essence of my adoration, the soft light revealing a mere hint of your exquisite silhouette.

I was at your mercy. Your exotic dance continued unabated, your attention barely grazing my longing gaze. Desperate for your notice, you teased me with your self-control. As you circled, the gentle fabric of your dress brushed against my legs. I reached out for you, capturing you in my arms as you swayed.

The music slowed, your body responding to each subtle beat. I surrendered entirely to the enchantment of your seduction. As the final drumbeat echoed, one dance ended, and another began. We remained entwined in heart and body, aware that the music had ceased, yet feeling as though we had just begun.

"Oh my god," she muttered and read it again.

"I don't want to spoil the surprise for our viewers or your readers, but the tension in this next chapter was completely unexpected," Elizabeth, the interviewer, remarked.

Brad Genova, the author of Twin Crossing, said, "After all, this is not just the beginning of a romance, but also a journey involving identical twin brothers."

Elizabeth leaned closer, intrigued. "Which explains the title you've chosen for your novel. Brad, let's hear your final thoughts before we dive in."

Brad took a moment to gather his words. "I think it's important to reflect on the power of communication in our modern world. It's incredible how the smartphone, the computer, and other forms of connectivity have shaped our lives. However, as we'll soon discover, this power can also be terrifying."

Chapter 3

Part I

The shrill ring of the phone shattered Chance's peaceful slumber, his mind still filled with thoughts of Cassandra's enchanting dance. He glanced at the clock, mumbling, "Three-thirty." As the phone continued its persistent melody, he grabbed the receiver, his voice groggy from sleep. "Who is this?" he grumbled, annoyance seeping into his words. But the only response he received was a chilling silence. "Who the hell is this?" he repeated, his anger intensifying.

A man's voice dripped with sarcasm as he replied, "Take a guess."

"Seth?" Chance's breath caught in his throat.

"Bingo! Miss me?" Seth's voice oozed with coldness, sending a shiver down Chance's spine. "Don't you just love these awkward moments, Chance?"

"I... I wasn't expecting to hear from you. How did you find me?" Chance's mind raced, wondering if Seth was in town.

"I have my connections, little brother," Seth replied, his voice lowering. "I've spent a great deal of time thinking about you. We're so close I can feel you. Surely you must have sensed my presence?"

"You're in Boston?" The implications of the question filled Chance with dread.

"I'm here to arrange a little family reunion with my long-lost twin. What better opportunity for us to share a beer and catch up on old times? How about tonight?"

In Seth's mindset, bitterness simmered beneath the surface, fueled by years of feeling abandoned and misunderstood. As twin brothers, they shared a psychic bond that allowed one to finish the thought of the other. The trauma Seth endured at home and at their New Hampshire property on the lake was more than he could bear. The shame, guilt, and feelings of being lost and alone weighed heavily on him. Seth wondered if Chance ever truly understood or cared about his pain. His years in prison did little to temper these feelings of anger and resentment toward his brother.

"No," Chance firmly replied. "I have some business to attend to. Perhaps—"

"Business? What the fuck do you think I'm doing here?" Seth snapped. "We're going to catch up on unfinished, festering business!"

"Look, you have no right to insist we meet just because it's convenient for you!" Chance retorted, his voice tinged with frustration and defiance, expecting Seth to explode.

"I understand your career comes before family," Seth said, his tone dripping with contempt. "For me, however, blood is thicker than water, and I'm just oozing with feelings of togetherness. We'll be in touch." With that, he abruptly hung up.

Moments passed, but the echo of the dial tone still reverberated in Chance's ear. He stared at the wall, replaying every word of their conversation, dissecting the subtle nuances in Seth's voice. For five years, Chance had managed to push Seth out of his mind during his brother's incarceration. But how could he expect Seth to simply disappear?

Chance's thoughts swirled in a tumultuous storm of guilt and regret. Every word exchanged with Seth echoed in his mind like a relentless drumbeat of condemnation. Guilt gnawed at his insides, a weighty burden that threatened to suffocate him. He questioned his choices, his actions—*or lack thereof*—over the years. Had he abandoned Seth when he needed him most? Could he have done more to steer his brother away from the destructive path he now walked?

Regret, like a bitter poison, seeped into Chance's soul. He replayed memories of their tumultuous childhood, each one a painful reminder of his failure to save Seth from himself. The image of their father, belt in hand, and Seth's defiant smirk haunted him, a constant reminder of his inability to protect his brother.

The breaking and entering incident from years ago, which he had almost forgotten, resurfaced with terrifying clarity. Running from his past seemed futile.

In their youth, Chance had fruitlessly attempted to help Seth as he fell into a pattern of selling marijuana to their classmates. Seth was despised by teachers and parents, yet he wielded influence and fear among his peers. It always bewildered their family how Seth could stay out of trouble for brief periods, only to stumble back into it. Their parents, Kevin and Maggie Macklin, struggled to comprehend the paradox of their twin sons: one a model student who respected authority, the other a constant rebel who flouted rules and failed academically.

Painful memories flooded Chance's mind. He vividly recalled the evening their father had erupted in anger when the police caught thirteen-year-old Seth drinking alcohol and smoking pot at Jewette Park.

* * *

"Get in here this minute!" Kevin had demanded, his voice seething with fury.

The officer escorted Seth inside, standing guard by the doorway. Unsteady on his feet, Seth stumbled and giggled. Kevin slapped him in a fit of anger. "You think this is funny?"

Seth's body went limp, his head snapping back. He looked at Chance and grinned. "Hey, look," he slurred drunkenly, "that's me over there. Aren't I a good little boy?"

Chance watched in disbelief, his schoolbook slipping from his grasp. He knew Seth was in serious trouble and fear gripped him. Sensing his brother's intoxication, he pleaded, "Do as Dad says."

"Fuck off!" Seth retorted.

Overwhelmed with rage, Kevin slapped Seth, causing him to stumble and fall at the base of the staircase. "You ungrateful slob! Get upstairs!" he bellowed.

"Thanks for leading the way," Seth jeered, his words laced with defiance.

Seth struggled up the stairs, his hands and knees scraping against the cold surface. The sound of his barking, resembling that of a desperate dog, pierced the air. The police officer stood by, holding up a beer bottle and two joints as evidence of Seth's misdeeds.

Shame washed over Kevin's face as he turned to the officer. "This will never happen again," he vowed.

"See that it doesn't," the officer sternly replied before leaving. Kevin's gaze turned intense as he spoke to Maggie, requesting a few moments alone with Seth. As he ascended the stairs, he unbuckled his belt, the metallic sound echoing ominously. Chance watched his father's actions, a sense of dread settling in.

"We've tried everything, but Seth won't listen," Kevin confessed, his voice heavy with frustration.

The noise from upstairs consumed Chance's thoughts. The silence that followed frightened him the most. He sprinted up the stairs, bursting into the room where his father loomed over Seth, the belt raised high. Seth, perched over his knee with saliva dripping from his mouth, became the target of his father's wrath. Chance pleaded for mercy.

"Please, it hurts me too," he implored.

Kevin tightened his grip on Seth's hair. "It's going to hurt him a lot more. Now get out, or feel this belt!"

Feeling powerless, Chance retreated from the room, the impact of the belt reverberating through his own body. He sought solace in the basement, burying his head in the couch. He tried to cover his ears, but the sound and the pain seeped into his being.

"Stop it, Dad! Stop it!" he cried out in desperation.

* * *

Chance's thoughts shifted to another painful memory—the aftermath of Seth's beatings. He remembered entering Seth's room, struck by how little pain his brother seemed to show, while he himself suffered with every lash. These memories, like an unwanted torrent, flooded his mind. In that moment, he yearned to hold on to the happier times they had shared as carefree boys, like when they were eight years old at summer camp in Michigan, fishing together and landing a record-breaking walleye.

But as the years went by, Seth's troubles only grew, becoming entangled with the belt and the beatings that failed to curb his antisocial behavior. After graduating with honors from the Architectural Institute of Boston, Chance had landed a prestigious job in the Windy City. He chose not to share his successes with Seth, knowing how much his brother resented him. He had offered financial assistance, but was met with hostility and intrusion into Seth's personal affairs.

"I don't need your handouts!" Seth had spat during one heated call.

Chance was aware of Seth's meager income as a janitor and how he wasted it on vices like drinking and gambling. "It's not charity, Seth. We're family, and I want to help."

"Screw yourself and your corporate world!" Seth angrily retorted.

At that time, Chance listened to his brother's bitter words, shouldering the blame for Seth's troubled path. Since then, he had no contact with Seth until one fateful evening when his desperate brother appeared on his doorstep.

The pounding on the door startled Chance, jolting him from his thoughts. Through the peephole, he saw Seth.

"Open up!" Seth demanded.

"What's going on?" Chance asked, cracking the door open with the chain still in place.

"Open this goddamn door!"

Chance complied, unlocking the door as Seth barged in, his face etched with desperation. He turned off the lights, peering through the drapes as police spotlights illuminated the street. Chance filled a kettle with water, contemplating the irony of Seth's sudden appearance after years of absence.

Seth closed the drapes, shutting out the intrusive lights. "What the hell are you doing?"

"Making tea," Chance muttered, his voice calm amidst the chaos.

"Tea?" Seth laughed derisively. "How about a helicopter? Got one of those?"

Chance opened the cupboard, his gaze shifting from left to right. "Nope, fresh out of choppers."

"When did you become so damn funny? Oh yeah, dear old Dad. Wasn't he hilarious swinging that belt of his?" Seth walked over to the refrigerator, yanking it open, causing the door to crash against the wall. "Why don't you drink beer like everyone else in this world?" He slammed the refrigerator shut, the contents rattling within.

Still waiting for an explanation, Chance asked, "What's new?"

"Check this shit out." Seth reached into his coat and pulled out a handful of jewelry and watches.

As time passed, an interminable silence lingered, punctuated only by bursts of anger. Chance knew he was harboring a wanted criminal, and doing nothing meant watching his brother sink deeper into a destructive spiral.

"You can sleep on the couch," Chance finally offered.

Chance lay awake, contemplating his limited options as Seth slept on the couch. Allowing Seth to stay the night and leave quietly in the morning felt like enabling an addict while avoiding the difficult conversation about rehabilitation. He longed to extract the goodness from Seth's soul and discard the rest, hoping that his brother would recognize the untapped potential within him. Yet, deep down, Chance knew that nothing had changed so far. If Seth continued down the path of crime and deceit, there would be no turning back. The second option terrified Chance the most. But doing nothing was even worse.

Hours later, he reached for the phone and made the most difficult call of his life. Within minutes, squad cars arrived, their flashing lights casting an eerie glow on the stillness of the night. Chance opened the door before they could even knock.

"He's on the couch. Please, don't hurt him. He's my brother," Chance pleaded with the officers.

An armed officer swiftly disarmed Seth, removing the gun he had tucked under his shirt. Another officer barked at Seth, "Get your ass out of bed!"

Seth's eyes burst open to find himself confronted by half a dozen revolvers, their barrels aimed directly at his head. Instinctively, he reached for his gun, only to realize it had been confiscated. Silence engulfed the room as he locked eyes with Chance and grinned.

Chance knew that no words could bridge the gap between them. Helplessly, he watched as the officers handcuffed Seth and escorted him out the door. Later, he provided testimony during the trial. When the proceedings came to an end, the jury handed down a five-year sentence for Seth, his prior record playing a role in the strict penalty.

Over the years, memories faded as Chance distanced himself from Seth through the silence of their past. He advanced in his architectural career, eventually leaving behind the corporate world to start his own business in Boston.

* * *

That evening, as Chance turned the key to his front door, he marveled at how suddenly his life had been plunged into turmoil. No matter how hard he had tried, the Seth situation refused to fade away. He walked over to his computer, unsure of what to say to Cassandra. After much contemplation, he logged on and stared at the blank screen. Emotions surged through him as he fell into a trance-like state, his mind drifting into reflection, interrupted only by the sound of a voice.

"Welcome home, dear brother," a voice echoed in the room.

Chance's neck hairs stood on end as he turned, startled. "How did you get in?"

Seth's physical presence slowly materialized. He stood before Chance, a beer in one hand and a casually tucked gun in his waistband. "You have no time for me, so I decided to make time for you," Seth taunted.

Using the gun to coerce him, Seth motioned for Chance to sit on the couch. Concern for his personal safety paled in comparison to the worry that Brad and Lisa, his neighbors, might hear the commotion. From his seat on the couch, Chance listened to Seth's tales from jail, his thoughts straying uncontrollably to the computer that remained connected to the internet. Desperate for any opportunity to shut the system down, he stood up.

Seth waved the gun. "Where do you think you're going?"

"The bathroom!" Chance avoided any glances towards the monitor, fearing what awaited him. He almost stopped breathing when he heard the friendly but unwelcome prompt, "You've got mail."

Seth peered at the computer, confusion furrowing his brow. "What the hell does *that* mean?"

"Remember? I told you I had some business to take care of tonight, and there it is," Chance quickly improvised, his forehead glistening with sweat.

Seth approached the monitor, his curiosity piqued. He manipulated the mouse, scrolling through menus until something caught his attention. "You don't mind if I read your business correspondence, do you?"

"It's just work," Chance offered, hoping to divert Seth's attention.

This only heightened Seth's curiosity. In a mocking tone, he read the words aloud, relishing in the discomfort he caused Chance.

Dear Chance,
The overwhelming passion that exudes from you thrills me beyond measure. In this moment, all I desire is to continue feeling this way.
Love, Cassandra
P.S. Your fantasy was exhilarating.
I can only imagine the real you.

"Fancy a little fantasy, huh? How naughty, Chance," Seth taunted.

"No matter what I say, you won't understand," Chance said, his frustration mounting. Seth had unearthed a fresh vulnerability, and no amount of convincing would change that. Chance's mind drifted back to the incident in high school that had shattered their bond.

* * *

Soccer practice had run late that day, with the coach insisting on an extra hour of defensive training. Chance, playing offensive left wing, saw no need to stay. It was his first date with Barbara, and he wanted to make a lasting impression. Hurriedly, he ran home to his room.

"Mom, have you seen my leather jacket?" he asked, finding his mother folding clothes from the dryer.

Maggie looked up, a hint of concern in her eyes. "I saw Seth trying it on earlier. He was heading toward town."

Frustrated, Chance grabbed a worn-out jean jacket and stormed out of the house. Arriving at the Always Arcade, he scanned the crowd, surprised not to find Barbara. Spotting the owner, he approached Tony with anger and desperation carved into his face.

"Tony, have you seen Barbara Connors?"

"Yeah, she was here. I thought she was with you. You're Chance, right?" Tony replied, noting the anger etched on Chance's face.

Rage welled up within Chance as he searched every hangout spot in town, contemplating how he might confront Seth, what anger would surface. Eventually, he returned home, waiting anxiously as each second ticked away. Finally, Seth entered with a taunting smile.

"Hope you don't mind the jacket, but—"

"Shut up, asshole!" Chance grabbed Seth, forcing him up the stairs to his room. "She was my friend," he seethed, knowing that if Barbara ever found out what had transpired, she would want nothing to do with him.

"If you're too busy, I'll fill in for ya. Check out my hickey," Seth goaded, his laughter mocking Chance's pain. Chance's fists connected with Seth's body, but his hits were poorly aimed, easily blocked by his brother. They crashed into the night table, the alarm clattering to the floor. Seth wrestled Chance into submission, holding his arms in place.

"How could you?" Chance cried, utterly exhausted.

* * *

"Are you still there?" Seth interrupted, snapping Chance out of his flashback. The terror in his brother's eyes was intoxicating. "We have a fun day planned for tomorrow. Since you're the boss, you get the day off. Time for bed. Oh, and I removed the phone from your bedroom."

Concerned, Chance asked, "What will you do?"

"Watch TV. I just love Nickelodeon," Seth sneered.

Chance reluctantly stepped into the bedroom, wishing he could snap his fingers and either heal his brother's troubled soul or make him vanish altogether. Meanwhile, Seth, fascinated by his brother's email affair, put his mechanical skills to work and within minutes was browsing the internet. He read every intimate letter exchanged between Chance and Cassandra. "Busy lovebirds," he scoffed, patting the monitor before entering Chance's room.

"Wake up," Seth repeated until Chance stirred, opening his eyes to the barrel of Seth's gun.

"You're drunk," Chance stammered, his voice trembling.

"Hell, no, I'm as wired as that computer of yours. Get up!" Seth commanded.

In the living room, Seth instructed Chance to sit while he picked up the phone and dialed. "Hi, sweetie. It's Chance. I hope I'm not calling too late?" Seth winked mischievously, his voice carrying an air of sincerity. "Everything is great. I got home late and just read your wonderful letter."

Chance started to rise from the couch, on the verge of yelling, "Cassandra, hang up!" But before he could utter a word, Seth covered the mouthpiece and pulled back the trigger.

"Chance, if you move, I will blow your head off. And then, my dear brother, I will have a field day with this woman," Seth warned, a twisted smile playing on his lips. Chance sat frozen as Seth continued his conversation. "I'm sorry, sweetie. I was just distracted. I'm calling because I'm desperate to see you. We've been immersed in passionate thoughts for far too long, and I would love for you to visit me here in Boston this weekend." Chance gasped, realizing the complete extent of Seth's revenge. "Saturday would be perfect."

Seth proceeded to give Cassandra directions to Chance's home. Covering the mouthpiece, he chuckled, "She really likes me." Hanging up, he grinned at Chance. "I have a date this Saturday. That's the day after tomorrow, tiger!" He crushed his fifth beer can, tossing it to the floor.

"I'll give you anything you want. Money. My computer. Just take it. I promise I won't call the police," Chance pleaded desperately.

"Can you imagine? I might actually find true love. But for now, I have no option but to request your presence for the duration," Seth said, the twisted smile still on his lips.

Seth led Chance, still sore from his hours of confinement, into the living room. The slow passage of time weighed heavily on Chance, his exhaustion preventing sleep as he remained vigilant. His mind worked tirelessly, strategizing his next move against his brother. The following morning, Seth untied Chance and allowed him to use the bathroom. Stiff-legged and aching, he emerged to find Seth lounging on the couch, his feet propped up on the coffee table.

"Now you have a taste of prison life," Seth remarked, a hint of amusement in his voice.

"What I did five years ago, I would do again today!" Chance retorted, his anger boiling over. "If you can't handle the time, don't commit the crime."

Seth ignored the cliché retort, making himself at home in the living room. Furniture had been rearranged, and Chance noticed the absence of the television and camcorder. "Do you honestly believe those things hold any value? Go ahead, sell them for drugs," Chance scoffed, shaking his head in disbelief. He sensed no admission into his brother's mind or soul, their connection severed long ago.

Seth distracted himself by exploring the Internet on Chance's computer, stumbling upon a chat room filled with random typed conversations. "So, you met this woman, *Cassandra*, in here?" he asked with contempt as he emphasized her name. Chance paced the room, biding his time. "Chance, how could you let your life sink so low that you need a computer to find a woman?" he taunted, idly toying with the mouse.

Seeing an opening, Chance lunged at Seth, and they both tumbled to the floor. The computer crashed down with them, sparks flying as the internal components sputtered. Seth laughed, glancing at the broken machine.

"You've killed Cassandra," he declared, relishing in the chaos.

With a fierce punch to Seth's stomach, Chance tried to reach for the pistol. Seth tossed it into the kitchen, where it slid across the tile floor, coming to a stop under the table. As Chance struggled to stand, Seth tripped him, causing him to fall face-first onto the floor. He quickly rose and delivered a forceful kick to Chance's side, sending him rolling onto his back. Blood trickled from his mouth.

"You need a few years in jail to learn some lessons. Now, sit back down on that damn couch and don't move, or I swear on your future grave that she will die!" Seth threatened.

Struggling to make his way back to the couch, Chance fought against the pain. Seth walked into the kitchen and retrieved the gun, while Chance pressed his hands against his stomach, feeling for any cracked ribs.

"Feeling better?" Seth asked in a mocking tone.

"Just leave me alone, Seth! I'm not trying to ruin your life," Chance said as he caught his breath.

Seth grinned as he leaned forward in his chair. "You never once visited me in jail, not that I missed you all that much. I only needed to look in the mirror to see you laughing at me, while I was left to rot with a cell block full of lunatics. Did you ever think about what you did to me? Squealing to the authorities like a pathetic coward?" Seth wanted to say more, but the pain from the darkest recesses of the past was too much to bear at the moment, causing his headache to intensify.

"Tell me you won't hurt her," Chance implored, his voice trembling.

"Who? Cassandra?" Seth laughed bitterly. "It's you who will be hurting her, not me. You have a debt to repay, so take it like a man!"

* * *

The afternoon dragged on, the two brothers engaged in a bitter argument that seemed to have no resolution. Chance couldn't fathom how a mere ten minutes in their birth could have created such contrasting souls. It was as if their astrological paths had diverged, sending Seth down a dark, twisted universe separate from his own. They were locked in a perpetual struggle, teetering on opposite ends of a seesaw, unable to find balance or compromise.

Chance knew he had exhausted every effort to help Seth throughout their years together, but now it felt futile. Seth withdrew into a solemn silence, consumed by his own thoughts and plans, hardly acknowledging his brother's attempts to provoke pointless arguments. Chance's eyes grew heavy, and he drifted into sleep. In his dream, he relived the moment of their conception, battling against Seth to overpower him, erasing the possibility of a twin birth entirely. He awoke later, surprised by the length of his slumber. The swelling had subsided, and he could move with less pain. He chose not to engage with Seth for the remainder of the afternoon and into the early evening. Eventually, Seth led him into the bedroom, securing his bonds for the night.

"Sweet dreams," Seth taunted.

Slowly, the coolness of Friday evening gave way to the warm embrace of Saturday morning. Chance dreaded the thought of Cassandra embarking on a four-hour drive to Boston, silently praying for any kind of miracle: a flat tire, a detour, anything to keep her away from the danger he was trapped in.

Silenced by Seth, Chance was led out of his apartment into the hallway, guided toward the basement door beneath the stairs. Upstairs, the sounds of Lisa and Brad's routine chores filled the air: music, vacuuming—the usual Saturday morning rituals that would keep them occupied for a while.

Seth forcefully pushed Chance down the stairs, his arms still bound, as he descended into the dimly lit, musty basement. Cobwebs clung to his face, and the scent of mildew filled his nostrils. He could hear the scurrying of a mouse in the shadows. In the far corner, a wooden chair sat near the gas burner of the heating system, facing the television that belonged to him.

Forced to sit, Chance couldn't help but make a painful joke, attempting to alleviate the tension. "Time for Nickelodeon?"

Seth tightened the ropes, securing Chance's hands to the main heating pipe. "I would've brought the remote so you could surf the channels. Unfortunately, though, your hands will be tied."

Chance struggled to think clearly or move his hands, but the situation felt surreal and incomprehensible. Seth admired his handiwork, ensuring the bonds were secure. Just as Chance spoke, Seth stuffed a washcloth into his mouth, sealing it with duct tape. He turned on the television, adjusting the picture.

"I'm sure this little film will be quite the hit," Seth taunted.

Chance gasped at the image that flickered on the screen—it was his own bedroom!

Part II

As the miles stretched between Cassandra and her home, she couldn't help but question her own sanity. Was she crazy to embark on this journey to Boston, driven by her feelings for Chance? Doubts lingered in her mind, partly because Chance had never been so forward before. He had always been reserved and gentlemanly. But alongside the doubts, excitement coursed through her veins; the prospect of finally being alone with him ignited a flame within her

Her logical mind, honed by her profession, clashed with her decision to visit Chance. The hesitations crept in like a storm, intensifying with every passing mile. What was it about him that drew her in, despite her resistance? She reflected on her past relationships, learning from them what she didn't want. Memories of heartbreak and disappointment surfaced, reminding her of the risks and vulnerabilities that came with opening her heart.

But despite the doubts and fears, there was a glimmer of hope, a voice within her that whispered of the possibility of love and happiness. She had spent so long guarding her heart, shielding herself from potential pain, but now, faced with the chance for something real, she couldn't ignore the longing stirring within her.

With each mile marker that passed, Cassandra found herself torn between reason and desire, between the safety of her walls and the allure of Chance's presence. She knew the journey ahead would test her in ways she hadn't imagined. Deep down, she couldn't shake the feeling that it was a risk worth taking.

"Get a grip," she murmured, clasping the steering wheel tighter. "You know this man. Mr. Without Wax."

Her heart raced with anticipation as she continued down the road, the uncertainty of what awaited her in Boston mingling with the undeniable pull she felt toward Chance. It was a journey into the unknown, but one she was willing to take, if only to discover what lay on the other side.

* * *

Seth glanced at his watch, his excitement mounting. "Just another hour, and my romance will begin. Aren't you thrilled for me, Chance?" Laughter echoed through the staircase as Seth left the basement, making his way into Chance's bedroom. His eyes fell upon the camcorder hidden behind a bookshelf, ready to capture every moment for Chance's torment. Inflicting pain upon Cassandra would be more than mere revenge—it would shatter Chance's soul.

That final hour felt like an eternity to Chance as he strained his ears for any sound. And then he heard it—the doorbell rang.

Seth nonchalantly opened the door, a smile gracing his face. Cassandra looked at him, noticing his strikingly bright blue eyes. In the warm embrace of the Saturday morning, Seth appeared in a new light. Stepping inside, she glanced around the room.

"I love your home, Chance," she remarked.

"Home is where the heart is," Seth replied, his smile enchanting, saying all the words she longed to hear. She reached over and hugged him, unable to resist his charm. With a wink, he said, "Time for the grand tour."

Cassandra draped her windbreaker over a chair near the entrance. "I want to see it all," she said, her heart skipping a beat at the thought of exploring Chance's world.

They moved through the living room, with Seth apologizing for the slight mess. His broken computer was laying on the floor, a result of a recent mishap. "One of the legs of my desk snapped last night, causing this little accident. But not to worry, I'll be back online soon."

Cassandra's gaze lingered on the shattered computer. "Really?" she asked, puzzled by how such an accident could occur.

Thinking quickly, Seth diverted her attention. "You must be hungry from your journey."

Her gaze remained fixed on the computer. "Hmm?" She turned to look into his eyes. "Yes, I am. Thank you for asking."

Seth reached for her hand, marveling at its softness. "You look absolutely beautiful, Cassandra."

He led her into the dining room, where he had prepared a spread of sandwiches and coffee. From the depths of the basement, Chance strained to catch fragments of their conversation. The sound of Cassandra's laughter pierced his heart, causing him to cringe and struggle harder against his restraints.

Half an hour passed, and then they moved from the dining room into the kitchen. As Seth guided her on a tour of his home, Cassandra admired the many features.

"The ceramic tile is stunning," she remarked, her eyes taking in the beauty.

Finally, they stood outside the bedroom door. Seth's voice carried a glint of mischief. "I think we should save this for later," he said, a smile playing on his lips.

Suggesting they go for a walk around the neighborhood, Seth delighted in tormenting Chance with the unknown. For Cassandra, it was an opportunity to relax and slow down, tempering the growing passion she felt for him.

As they strolled hand in hand, Seth gradually placed his arm around her shoulder, drawing her closer to him. She reveled in the warmth of his body against hers, a sense of comfort and security enveloping her.

Twenty minutes later, they returned. Silently, Seth led her to the bedroom, his touch gentle as he held her hand. She squeezed it, conveying trust and reassurance. With the grace of a gentleman, he escorted her into the room. From the prison basement, Chance's eyes widened in disbelief as he watched Seth seat her on the bed. Cassandra closed her eyes, aching for their first kiss. Adjusting her position, her desire for him grew evident.

"Don't be afraid," she whispered, sensing his nervousness. How endearing, she thought. He's really shy. "It's okay."

Seth tenderly caressed Cassandra's hair, his gaze fixated on the camcorder lens capturing every moment in the basement. Are you watching, dear brother? With a slow, deliberate motion, he tilted her head back, his lips puckering as they drew closer to hers.

She sighed, closing her eyes and whispering his name. For the sake of his brother, Seth turned her sideways, their profiles now fully visible. Their lips met in a gentle, tantalizing kiss, and Seth relished the taste of her soft, supple flesh. She moaned in response, her mouth opening slightly. Seth, having long forgotten the taste of a woman's kiss, allowed his tongue to mingle with hers. The power he held over her fed his growing passion.

They embraced passionately, their bodies entwined on the bed, their lips locked in a fervent dance. Seth wished he could witness the sheer torment on Chance's face in that moment. Meanwhile, Chance's eyes burned with fury and hatred. He kicked and thrashed against his restraints, desperate to free himself.

Cassandra! Run!

After several moments, Cassandra gently brushed her fingers across Seth's face and excused herself to the bathroom on the opposite side of the room. Seth winked at the camcorder, his eyes glinting with malevolence. He opened the night table drawer and retrieved a large kitchen knife, lovingly caressing its wooden handle and admiring the gleaming steel blade. With care, he returned the knife to its place.

Cassandra returned, taking her seat on the bed next to him, her hand resting on his lap. Their intimate embrace resumed,

In a sudden jolt, Chance realized he was positioned near the same corner where Brad liked to read. He adjusted his college ring against the heating pipe and tapped loudly, hoping Brad would recognize their secret code: Shave and a Haircut, Two Bits.

Brad was at home, engrossed in a book after finishing his cleaning chores. As he stretched his arms, he heard a familiar rhythm resonating through the pipes. "Why is the heating on in the middle of August?" A grin spread across his face as he recognized the familiar beat—it was Chance, signaling him to come down. He descended the stairs and knocked on his friend's door. Seth ceased his passionate kiss with Cassandra and looked up.

"What's wrong?" she asked, her voice laced with confusion.

"I thought I heard something. Wait here, my sweet," Seth replied, concern evident in his eyes.

Exiting the bedroom, Seth's fake smile transformed into a mask of rage. Cassandra, still clothed, lay her head on the pillow, perplexed but content to be in his home. He's so irresistible, she thought, struggling to control her desire. As she rolled on his bed, the warmth of her arousal consumed her. Ignoring the nagging words of caution in her mind, she reassured herself that she had taken reasonable precautions. He had passed the test and won her heart. It was a fantasy come true!

Chance was astonished by his brother's smooth manipulation, pretending to be shy only to ignite Cassandra's desire for him. Trapped in a state of terror, Chance could only wait to see the outcome of his signal to Brad: a diversion, a chance to gather his thoughts, and a silent prayer that Brad would be okay. Seth's heavy footsteps reverberated through the house. He grabbed a beer, guzzling it down in three large gulps. Storming through the living room, he flung the front door open, glaring at the unwelcome visitor.

"Shave and a Haircut?" Brad grinned.

Seth crushed the empty beer can in his hand. "I'm not interested in any cookies!"

Brad's smile vanished. "I thought you wanted me to—"

"Scram, kid!" Seth barked, slamming the door shut.

* * *

Brad rushed upstairs, terror coursing through his veins as if he had seen a ghost. He flung himself onto his bed, tears streaming down his face, questioning what he had done to anger his friend. His gaze fixed upon the ceiling, his eyes blurred with tears. Then, his gaze shifted to the antique cone top beer can he had recently found at a flea market, and a realization struck him—Chance didn't drink beer.

Brad returned to the living room, his ear pressed against the heating pipe. As he turned his head, his gaze fell upon the phone, triggering an uneasy feeling. Memories of the day they built their tree fort flooded his mind. Chance had held the phone in his left hand. This guy, however, held a beer can in his right hand. Something strange was definitely happening.

Back in the basement, Chance watched helplessly as Cassandra lay on the bed beside Seth. He strained to hear any signs of struggle or violence, assuming Seth had shut the door on Brad. Tapping their code against the heating pipe once more, he prayed for a response. But as he saw Seth reach in front of the headboard and retrieve nylon rope, he tapped harder, knowing Seth couldn't hear the noise from within the bedroom.

Cassandra fought against Seth's suddenly aggressive advances, now attempting to resist his touch and the firm grip of his hands. Fear washed over her, realizing that this man was no longer the Chance she had come to know. "Chance, please stop," she pleaded, her voice filled with desperation.

Seth secured her firmly to the bed, restraining her arms and feet. "We're just getting started," he whispered.

Just as she was about to scream, he silenced her with a gag, stealing her voice. Panic consumed her as he reached for a knife on the night table. *This can't be happening!* He positioned the knife over her breasts, sliding it between the buttons of her blouse, each button popping free with a sharp sting. With slow, deliberate movements, he leaned back, savoring the sight of her lace bra. Placing the knife against her flesh and the strap of her bra, he twisted the blade, causing it to split, revealing her bosom.

* * *

Meanwhile, Brad made his way down the stairs. Standing near Chance's door, he surveyed the hallway and noticed that the basement door was padlocked shut. "This is never locked," he muttered. Curiosity piqued, he pressed his ear against the door, straining to hear any sounds. Silence. He hesitated for a moment before heading toward the foyer. Exiting the house, he made his way to a basement window on the side. As his eyes adjusted, he noticed a faint bluish light emanating from the corner.

Brad squinted and observed some movement, as if someone were struggling against the light. Determined, he found a broken limb behind a nearby tree and used it to shatter the window, shards of glass falling to the basement floor. "Who's down here?" he demanded.

The musty scent of old wood and dust filled his nostrils, triggering a wave of nostalgia mixed with dread. With a trembling hand, he reached inside for the window latch, carefully avoiding the shards of glass that hung like knives. As he turned it slowly, the hinges creaked in protest, adding an eerie soundtrack to the tense atmosphere.

As the window swung open with a low groan, Brad's heart pounded in his chest, his palms clammy with sweat as he carefully maneuvered into the basement. The air grew thick and stifling, the faint scent of mildew and decay assaulted his senses, making him wrinkle his nose in disgust.

More movement in the corner caught Brad's eye, accompanied by faint moans. His heart raced as he cautiously approached the source of the blue light. A television? Down here? His gaze fell upon Chance, who was tied up, and Brad hurried to his friend's side. He removed the gag, his voice filled with concern. "Chance, are you alright?"

Gasping for air, Chance spoke urgently. "Untie me." His gaze darted to the monitor displaying Cassandra's struggles. "Don't look at that!"

As Brad freed Chance from his restraints, he glanced at the monitor. "What show are you watching?"

Chance swiftly shut it off. "Brad, I need your help, but it could be dangerous." Brad nodded, ready to assist. Once they were outside, Chance outlined his plan. "If you sense any danger, just run."

"I'll be okay," Brad reassured him.

Following Chance's instructions, Brad knocked loudly on Chance's apartment door. Startled by the interruption, Seth placed the knife on Cassandra's stomach and left her momentarily. He swung open the door, feigning concern as Brad rolled himself into a ball, pretending to be in pain. "Chance, you have to help me. My stomach! It hurts!"

"Take a deep breath, kid, you're going to be alright," Seth replied, concealing his anger beneath a facade of neighborly concern. "Where's your mom?"

He's going to kill me! You must escape! Cassandra's panic surged as she stared at the knife poised on her stomach. She began thrusting her body up and down on the bed, trying to dislodge the knife and direct it toward her bound hands. The knife slipped off her stomach, grazing her ribs before coming to rest by her side. Those words of caution became obsolete in her mind. She knew this man would not only violate her but likely end her life. Her bonds tightened, causing painful lacerations on her feet and hands. *Please, God! Give me a second chance!*

* * *

Chance made his way around the side of the house, reaching the window of his first-floor bedroom. Peering inside, he watched Cassandra's valiant attempt to escape. He positioned his elbow against the top of the window and struck it with his fist, shattering the glass. Cassandra watched in disbelief as he climbed his way into the room. When he spoke, his voice carried a sense of urgency and determination.

"It's me, Chance! This other guy is my brother. Trust me." He swiftly removed her gag.

"Let me go, or I'll scream!" Cassandra pleaded, her voice trembling with fear.

"His name is Seth, and he's dangerous. He just got out of prison and found your number from my emails," Chance explained, his words filled with urgency and concern.

As Seth began moving back toward the bedroom, Chance pleaded for Cassandra to play along. Meeting her terrified gaze, he replaced the gag, urging her to remain calm. He retrieved the knife and concealed himself behind the bedroom door. Cassandra's eyes widened in disbelief as Seth entered the room. The resemblance was uncanny—one brother gripped the knife tightly, while the other grinned with the unsettling lust of a deranged lunatic. Seth positioned himself near the door, seemingly unaware of the broken glass at the window.

Suddenly, Chance emerged from behind the door, knife at the ready, confronting Seth with determination. "Don't move!"

Seth glanced at Cassandra, smiling briefly before lunging for the knife. Catching Chance off guard, he managed to restrain his arm. "How rude, dear brother. And in front of my new girlfriend," he sneered.

With a swift smack across Chance's face, Seth sent him sprawling to the ground. Now in possession of the knife, Seth continued to engage in a fierce struggle with his twin. Cassandra gasped, her heart pounding, as she watched the intense confrontation unfold before her eyes. Seizing the opportunity, she kicked and fought until she freed her legs from their bindings. Moments later, she successfully released her other leg. Curled into a protective ball, she used her feet to push against the wall of the headboard, causing the bed to inch forward. However, her leverage was short-lived as the bed reached its limit, leaving her powerless to escape.

Brad, who had been observing the fight from the doorway, knew he had to act swiftly. He dashed upstairs, placing his desk chair under the bookshelf, and reached for his prized possession—the last gift his father had given him.

As the struggle between the brothers intensified, Chance landed a blow to Seth's face. In retaliation, Seth thrust the knife toward Chance's stomach, but he managed to dodge the attack, striking Seth's arm in the process. Determined to disarm his brother, Chance fought to free the blade from his grip, slamming Seth's arm against the bed frame. However, Seth used his legs to trip Chance, sending him crashing to the floor.

"Go ahead, Chance. Beg for your life. Cassandra won't mind," Seth taunted.

Just as the situation seemed dire, Brad burst into the bedroom, wielding his weapon. He issued a stern warning, "Don't move or I'll shoot!"

Seth erupted into laughter upon seeing the BB gun in Brad's hand. "Spare me, kid," he scoffed, raising his hands in mock surrender as he approached. "Thought you had a stomachache. Now you think you're John Wayne? Give me that toy!"

Brad focused his resolve before taking aim and firing. The pellet struck Seth's eyeball, causing him to crumple to the ground, cursing in pain. "You fucking brat!"

Taking advantage of the respite, Chance grabbed the lamp from the end table and delivered a forceful blow to Seth's face, rendering him unconscious. He urged Brad to retrieve some rope from under the kitchen sink. Within moments, Brad returned, only to witness Seth stirring.

"Chance, look out!" Brad shouted, alarmed.

Chance turned just in time to see Seth crawling toward the knife. He seized the BB gun and cocked it, taking aim. Seth coughed up blood, his hand reaching for the knife. In the next moment, the pellet struck his fist, causing him to recoil in pain.

As Brad provided cover using the gun, he struggled to comprehend the surreal scene unfolding before him. All he had wanted was to finish reading the first book of the Lord of the Rings trilogy, but the events he had become entangled in would leave an indelible mark on his life. Once Seth was securely bound, Chance freed Cassandra from her restraints.

"Cassandra, I am so sorry," Chance apologized, remorse lacing his words.

"Don't you dare use my name!" Cassandra snapped.

"I should have told you about my twin. It's over," Chance confessed, the weight of regret heavy in his voice.

"Yes, it is definitely over!" Cassandra retorted, her eyes filled with anger and pain. She glared at him, struggling to comprehend how everything had gone so horribly wrong. He made the call to the police, his heart heavy with sorrow. Tears streamed down his face as he tried to console Cassandra.

"I am not like him. He was in prison, so I saw no need to mention him to you, at least for now," Chance explained, his voice choked with emotion. Cassandra stared at the man she once believed she knew so well. Thoughts of their letters and shared emotions seemed insignificant now. He raised his head, his eyes pleading. "Can you forgive me?" he asked, his voice trembling.

Cassandra began to cry, her heart shattered into a thousand pieces. She knew she could never forgive him, and he understood. She had ignored her instincts and paid the price. Chance tried to offer comfort, but she recoiled, creating a painful distance between them. Taunting echoes from the bedroom served as a painful reminder of the torment Seth had inflicted upon him. Seth had exacted his revenge, forever altering Chance's life. The wailing sirens of the approaching police snapped Chance out of his daze. He opened the front door and spoke with hollow detachment.

"In the bedroom."

As the police took Seth away, he muttered a chilling promise. "We'll be in touch."

"Get moving," the officer commanded, pushing Seth through the door.

Chance knew better than to respond to the veiled threat. He turned to Cassandra, but she backed away, shaking her head. "Don't come near me," she warned, her voice laced with pain and disillusionment.

A moment passed before Brad rose from the couch. "It's okay, Chance. None of this was your fault," he reassured him.

Chance knelt down, embracing the young boy who had shown such bravery. "Brad, I can't thank you enough for what you've done."

Cassandra sought solace in the backyard, the weight of the ordeal heavy on her heart. She sat in a patio chair, tears streaming down her face, unable to comprehend how she could have been so blind. When Chance approached, she could only see the face of a monster, no longer recognizing the man she had once came to love. His apologies meant nothing to her, as her trust had been shattered beyond repair.

"Your brother tried to kill me. We will never talk again!"

Part III

Chance sought a distraction, a long-term project to occupy his mind. He decided it was time to renovate a portion of his Victorian house, beginning with the dining room. Loathing the lime green paint left by the previous owner, he painstakingly removed the molding and trim, inadvertently tearing away sections of the old drywall. Realizing the extent of the work involved, he sealed off the dining room to prevent drywall dust from spreading throughout the house. Amidst the arduous task of restoring the walls, he spent evenings meticulously sanding the surfaces.

Brad occasionally stopped by to check on Chance's progress, wearing a face mask to shield himself from the dust. "It's like a cloud in here," the boy observed.

Chance laughed, switching sandpaper. "The more I work, the thicker it seems to get. In a few weeks, this room will shine."

"Are you planning to tackle the living room next?" Brad inquired.

Chance shook his head, a weary expression on his face. "No, I'm taking a break after this. It's just too much work." He walked over and patted Brad on the head, releasing a cloud of spackle dust from his hair. "I wouldn't wish this on my worst enemy."

Brad nervously chuckled, trying to lighten the mood. "Yeah, let's get Seth to help," he joked.

Each mention of Seth's name pierced Chance's soul, filling him with a profound hatred he had never experienced before. Brad struggled to come to terms with the traumatic events that unfolded, eventually finding solace in writing a short story as a form of catharsis. The dining room project served as a coping mechanism for Chance, providing an outlet for his complex emotions. However, despite his progress, he couldn't escape the loneliness that clung to him like a blanket of spackle dust.

"I have to go," Brad announced. "Mom's making lasagna. Want some?"

Chance weighed the proposition, glancing at the pile of unfinished work. "Duty calls." He started his sander, waving as Brad departed.

Days turned into weeks, and Chance began to witness the fruits of his labor. The walls regained their former glory, their smooth finish a testament to his dedication. Having stripped the old trim and molding, he savored the part he enjoyed most— applying two coats of cherry stain, followed by three coats of polyurethane. With the completion of the dining room project, he commenced the process of resetting the molding and trim. The French cabinet with glass doors gleamed, unrecognizable from its previous state. Stepping back, he admired his handiwork. Was it all worth it? he questioned, feeling the stiffness in his back. Running his hand along the smooth, stained wood, he couldn't help but feel a sense of pride. "Absolutely worth it!"

Determined to celebrate his accomplishment and express gratitude to those who had supported him throughout the project, Chance decided to host a lavish dinner. He invited Brad and Lisa, who had offered moral support, along with two employees who had provided assistance. Seated at the head of the table, he raised his glass, ready to commemorate the transformation of both his dining room and his journey.

* * *

Chance's life moved forward in the months following the incident with Seth. His architectural business began to thrive, and he expanded his team by hiring three additional employees to meet the growing demand. However, amidst the success, he couldn't escape the lingering ache of singlehood and the fading dream of a life with Cassandra.

Karen, his office assistant, sensed his melancholy and encouraged him to go on a blind date. "Come on, Chance. It's just one date, and she's very attractive."

Reluctantly, Chance agreed despite feeling out of touch with the dating scene. Karen's attempt to play matchmaker didn't bear fruit, and the date with Sheila ended in disappointment. He didn't need to ask Karen for Sheila's feedback; he could tell by her interactions with him at work that it hadn't gone well. It seemed that Cupid's arrows had missed their mark.

Work became Chance's refuge from the lingering emptiness. The more time he spent at the office, the more comfortable he felt. Paradoxically, his computer, once a vital tool for his business, had become his nemesis. Each night, he logged in, hoping to receive a message from Cassandra, but his inbox remained empty. She despises you, he thought. *And who could blame her?*

As more weeks turned into months, Chance reluctantly went on more blind dates, but none of the women he met captivated his interest. He joked about being a terminal bachelor, convinced that he wasn't cut out for a committed relationship.

* * *

Nine months after the "Seth incident," Chance arrived home early from work, feeling restless and lonely. Brad was out, and he had no desire to play video games by himself. Scanning his bookshelf for a distraction, he realized that he needed to take a chance once again.

Turning on his computer, Chance felt a surge of hope as the monitor came to life. He checked his emails but found nothing awaiting him—no work matters to attend to, and no personal messages. Intrigued, he entered a singles chatroom, reminiscing about how he had met Cassandra online.

However, his attempts to engage in conversations proved futile. Few people showed interest, and he quickly left the first room. Despite his desire to connect and say something clever, the words eluded him in his subsequent attempts. After an hour, he contemplated signing off, but it was still early—nine thirty. "Get a life, Chance," he muttered, browsing aimlessly through various rooms without finding any real purpose.

In the kitchen, sipping on juice, he watched the silent dialogues scroll across the monitor. The assortment of usernames caught his eye, and then he saw it—AngelEyes. He knew Cassandra still maintained her internet subscription because his letters to her hadn't returned with an "Address Unknown." Now, through sheer luck, he had stumbled upon her, chatting away with strangers from the comfort and safety of her home. *If I say something, she'll know I'm here.*

Strangely, Chance felt a twinge of jealousy as virtual men vied for Cassandra's attention, offering virtual bouquets of roses. He tried to access her profile, only to discover that she hadn't registered one. Remembering her desire for a place to play without getting too close, he understood her intention of avoiding personal connections.

Engaged in casual dialogue with strangers like SvenGollie, PorkPie, and PassnFruit, Cassandra seemed disinterested. A sense of sadness washed over Chance. Hello from Beantown, he typed, but hesitated then deleted it. It's the same old routine, he thought, attempting to make a second connection but erasing his words in frustration. After ten minutes of observing her growing boredom, his inner voice screamed at him: Do it!

Chance2: Anyone know how to undump a canoe?

He leaned back, waiting anxiously for a response, but a wave of disappointment washed over him when he saw the reply.

PorkPie: Are you crazy? Get back on track with the conversation!

Chance's attempts to catch Cassandra's attention had backfired. Instead of sparking a connection with her, he became the target of mockery and dismissive remarks. It seemed that everyone noticed him except her. Each response brought a pang of disappointment and a growing sense of frustration.

PorkPie: Hey Chance, how much do you hicks get for a canoe, anyway?

PassnFruit: The fish are biting in the next room. Move it on.

Chance2: I said, anyone know how to undump a canoe? Without wax?

Minutes passed, and Chance received a barrage of rude instant messages calling him idiotic and suggesting he remove the wax from his ears to clear his brain. Feeling defeated, he finally signed off and shut down his computer. In bed, he stared blankly at the surrounding walls, ceiling, and pillow. *Get out of my head!* The more he obsessed, the less sleep he got. The next day, he threw himself into work, grateful for the full load of new projects that provided a much-needed distraction.

* * *

Cassandra and Helen sat in their favorite cafe, surrounded by the gentle hum of patrons engrossed in their own conversations and activities. Helen sensed Cassandra's preoccupation and decided to break the silence.

"What's going on?" Helen poured milk into her coffee.

Cassandra sipped her drink, appreciating its rich flavor while her mind remained occupied. "This place is like a chatroom," she remarked, observing the myriad of voices around them. "So many people talking, but so little meaningful conversation."

"Hmm?" Helen responded, sensing Cassandra's distraction. "How's the new internship going?"

Helen had refrained from discussing relationships with Cassandra since her breakup with Chance. However, now she recognized that familiar look in her friend's eyes. Leaning forward, she prodded, "Okay, out with it! Something's on your mind, and I don't mean caffeine!"

Cassandra chuckled. "Do you remember Chance Macklin?"

"Duh, of course I do. Prince Nearly Charming," Helen replied playfully.

"I heard from him yesterday. He didn't say anything to me. I mean, I... I saw him in a chatroom last night."

Helen leaned in, intrigued. "So?" she urged. "I hope the plot thickens here."

Cassandra nervously laughed. "He said, 'Anyone know how to undump a canoe?'" Helen's eyebrows furrowed, perplexed. "He said it twice."

"And?" Helen pressed, sensing there was more to the story.

"And what?" Cassandra replied, evading the topic.

Helen shook her head. "I have to leave in two minutes."

"I didn't say anything. He was just being silly, trying to get my attention."

"That doesn't sound silly to me. Why didn't you say anything?"

"A few minutes later, he signed off, and I did too," Cassandra explained.

Helen leaned back in her chair, a smile playing on her lips. "So here we are, discussing this incredible coincidence. You could have called and told me this!" She understood that Cassandra couldn't forgive Chance for what had happened with his brother. However, her inner voice urged her to explore further: 1) mind your own business, 2) don't mind your own business, and 3) all of the above. Cassandra's smirk indicated that Helen's laughter had hit a nerve.

"What's so funny?" Cassandra asked.

"You are. You want me to be that little voice inside your head, guiding you. Well, I charge double for impersonations. So, either pay up or get back to work," Helen teased.

"This is ridiculous! *You* met him, and you, of all people, should understand what I'm going through," Cassandra replied, frustrated.

Helen's expression turned serious. "Do you like him or not?"

Cassandra paused, her mind drifting to the complexities of Chance's life with a look-alike twin determined to ruin her existence. She fought against the sympathetic feelings, reminding herself of the near-tragic ordeal she had endured. A long silence hung in the air as they watched people come and go. Among the patrons were college students celebrating the completion of an exam. In the midst of the celebration, one student accidentally spilled her coffee, nearly causing another customer to trip. Helen extended a helping hand, receiving gratitude in return. A few moments later, she glanced at her watch.

"I have to run. We can talk later. How about we meet in a chatroom tonight?"

"No!" Cassandra objected. "The last thing I need is for him to send me an instant message. That would ruin my day."

* * *

Some weeks later, Helen guided Cassandra blindfolded into her apartment, filling the space with anticipation. Finally, she instructed her to open her eyes. Cassandra stood in awe, surrounded by a breathtaking display of affection. Three dozen red and white roses adorned the room, complemented by two heart-shaped boxes of English candy she was known to be addicted to. Colorful balloons, each with a unique expression, filled the air, and a small golden teddy bear stood proudly among the gifts.

Cassandra, bewildered, asked, "What's all this?"

Helen grinned mischievously. "Read the card."

Cassandra's hands trembled slightly as she reached for the card, her eyes scanning the heartfelt words. "Cassandra, for months I've been wanting to say I'm deeply sorry, and I miss you. Your friend, Chance." Panic surged through her body, mingling with confusion and visible distress. "Explain! Now!"

Helen took a deep breath, preparing herself to reveal what she had done. "Cassandra, please listen to me. I know you're still hurting and scared, but I saw how much you cared about Chance. He's been trying to reach out to you, to make amends. I couldn't bear to see you both suffer anymore."

Cassandra's emotions swirled, torn between anger and the lingering feelings she had tried to bury. "Helen, how could you?" she mumbled, her voice trembling.

"I couldn't stand by and watch the two of you lose what could be something truly special. I had to try," Helen explained earnestly.

Cassandra's eyes brimmed with tears, mirroring her inner turmoil. "I don't know what to do. I'm still scared, Helen. Scared of getting hurt again."

Helen moved closer, wrapping her arms around her friend in a comforting embrace. "I understand. Just remember that sometimes, taking the plunge is the only way to find happiness. You deserve to be happy, Cassandra."

Cassandra clung to Helen, finding calm in her friend's words. "Thank you for looking out for me, even when I didn't want you to."

Helen smiled softly. "That's what friends are for. And remember, love can heal wounds, even the deepest ones."

As Cassandra stared at the array of gifts before her, the turmoil within her began to settle. She realized that, despite her fear and uncertainty, there was a part of her that still longed for Chance's presence in her life. Perhaps, with time and forgiveness, they could build something beautiful together. Emotional turmoil consumed her and she started to cry. "Why did you do this?" she gasped, overwhelmed with confusion.

"I... I gave Chance my address, and he sent you these gifts," Helen confessed, her voice filled with remorse, sensing Cassandra's rush of conflicting emotions.

"When?" Cassandra questioned, her voice laced with disbelief.

"After you and I talked. I thought it was the only way to get you two back together again," Helen explained, her words tinged with regret.

"Goddamnit, Helen!" Cassandra's voice rose in frustration, her anger spiraling out of control.

Helen took a step back, taken aback by the intensity of Cassandra's reaction. "I'm sorry. I just... It's just that... You two belong—"

"Mind your own damn business!" Cassandra snapped, her words filled with anger.

Cassandra stormed out of the apartment, slamming the door behind her. Helen stood alone in the quietness, feeling the weight of her actions. She turned off the living room light and sat in silence, reflecting on her interference. Ten minutes later, the phone rang, but Helen let it go unanswered. She listened as her own voice echoed from the machine, followed by Cassandra's anxious voice.

"Helen, it's Cassandra. Are you there? I feel terrible. I didn't mean what I said. You're my best friend, and, well, I screwed up. Sorry. Please, if you're there, pick up the phone. I need to—"

The machine abruptly cut her off. Helen couldn't help but smile at her friend's persistence. The phone rang again, breaking the silence of the room.

"Your machine killed me. I guess I deserved it. I'm coming back. If you don't answer, no problem. But if you do, can I please have a hug?"

Minutes later, there was a knock at the door. Helen opened it, her expression void of emotion. "Yes?"

"I could really use a piece of chocolate," Cassandra said, her voice laced with vulnerability.

"Sorry. Fresh out," Helen retorted, trying to maintain a stern facade.

Cassandra studied Helen's expression, searching for a hint of forgiveness. "Friends?" she offered tentatively.

Helen laughed, her voice holding a touch of warmth. "Only if you get all of this stuff outta here. I have no room for gifts from almost-boyfriends."

Cassandra stepped inside, her gaze shifting to the array of gifts. "He's just too much," she muttered. Turning her attention back to Helen, she added, "And so are you."

Helen took Cassandra's hand, leading her toward a small bureau by the phone. Confused, Cassandra glanced around the room. Helen motioned toward a tiny handmade replica resting on a small table.

"What is it?" Cassandra asked, her curiosity piqued.

Helen rolled her eyes playfully. "Look around, Cassandra."

Cassandra followed Helen's gaze and picked up the intricately crafted memento. "It's a miniature birch bark canoe," Cassandra whispered, her voice filled with awe.

Helen smiled as she said, "Read the poem on the side."

Squinting her eyes, Cassandra deciphered the delicate words etched on the canoe. "Our paddle's keen and bright, flashing like silver. Swift as the wild goose flies, dip, dip and swing." She marveled at the sincerity of the words and the intricate craftsmanship. "It's beautiful."

* * *

Two weeks had passed since Helen's revelation and Cassandra's emotional rollercoaster. Now, seated in the car with Helen behind the wheel, Cassandra couldn't help but feel a surge of nervousness. "I'm more nervous now than before. What if he hates me? I mean, I've been acting like such a jerk," she confessed, her voice filled with uncertainty.

Helen glanced at Cassandra in the rearview mirror, a mischievous glint in her eyes. "You're right. Maybe he'll fall in love with me. How's *that* for a plot twist?"

Cassandra laughed, adding, "Then I'd get to play the nosy friend."

Helen had suggested they pretend to meet for the first time, an idea Cassandra initially dismissed but later found merit in. As she thought back to their earlier conversations, a smile graced her lips. "Helen, sometimes I feel like you're my therapist."

Helen chuckled softly. "My bill is in the mail."

A half-hour later, they pulled into the parking lot of the same restaurant where they had first met Chance. Cassandra's nerves fluttered within her, but she mustered the resolve to remain calm. "Just stay calm and be nice," she coached herself.

As she stepped out of the car, Cassandra caught her reflection in the side mirror and adjusted her appearance one last time. Together, they walked into the restaurant, the familiarity of the surroundings stirring memories. Cassandra had chosen a new dress for the occasion, while Helen dressed conservatively, not wanting to intrude with her presence.

Helen led the way, guiding Cassandra toward the designated table. There, standing before them, was Chance Macklin, casually dressed, a warm smile adorning his face. He extended his hand as they approached. "Nice to meet you, Cassandra. Please, have a seat," he invited graciously.

As they settled into their seats, the conversation initially felt halting, burdened by the weight of the past. But gradually, the words flowed more freely, bridges being rebuilt and hearts rekindling their connection.

Later, outside the restaurant, Cassandra's gaze shifted to the bustling city traffic. "Chance, how are you getting home?" she inquired, using the same words from before.

A smile danced upon Chance's lips. "I'll take a cab to the airport. My flight is in a couple of hours, but I know the time will fly by."

Cassandra's eyes sparkled with recognition as she quoted a line from the poem Chance had written on her miniature canoe. "As swift as the wild goose flies."

"Dip, dip, and swing," Chance responded seductively, moving closer to her.

Helen turned her gaze away, waving at three anxious cabbies as they passed. She had played her part, now leaving them to find their own path.

"Chance, can you ever—" Cassandra began, her voice tinged with vulnerability.

"Shh," Chance whispered gently, cutting off her words. "Cassandra, I love you."

As their eyes met, the world around them seemed to disappear. In that moment, they knew that their hearts had prevailed, erasing the pain of the past and opening the door to a future filled with hope and possibility.

He approached Cassandra, his arms open and inviting, but for a moment, she hesitated, the fear of Seth's presence still lingering in her mind. She knew she had to confront these fears, to let go of the past and embrace the future. As he wrapped his arms around her waist, she felt a sense of warmth and safety envelop her. Looking into his eyes, she saw a different man—not the face of a killer, but the face of the loving and generous man she had once fallen for. Their lips met in a tender kiss, and in that moment, all doubt and fear melted away.

"I love you, too," Cassandra whispered, her heart overflowing with emotions. Oblivious to the honking horns and bustling city around them, they kissed again, sealing their commitment in that stolen moment.

* * *

As weeks turned into months, Cassandra and Chance planned their future together. Trust was rebuilt, and they often found themselves joking about how they almost let each slip away. They would chat about their earlier attempts at dating, realizing that their paths had always been leading them back to one another.

As the weeks turned into months, Chance made every effort to visit Cassandra in New Jersey. He became acquainted with her parents and her younger brother, Morgan, instantly becoming a part of her family. One evening, during a family gathering, Morgan covertly asked Cassandra a playful question that caught her off guard.

"So, are you going to marry this guy?" he quipped, raising an eyebrow.

Cassandra whispered back with a smile, "One step at a time. And what about you?"

Morgan chuckled, his eyes filled with mischief. "Sisters first."

Later that night, as they sat alone on Cassandra's veranda, Chance summoned his courage and asked the question that had been weighing on his heart. "Cassandra, would you be interested in moving to Boston and living with me?" His words hung in the air, surprising both of them. Embarrassed by the sudden confession, Chance quickly tried to backtrack. "Forget it. I shouldn't have—"

But Cassandra interrupted him. "No, it's okay. Actually, a position opened up at our branch hospital in Boston. I... I submitted a proposal to see if I'm qualified."

Chance's eyes lit up. "Really? What did they say?"

A joyful laugh escaped Cassandra's lips. "I found out yesterday. They're interested."

Chance couldn't help but ask, "So, the answer is...?"

Cassandra smiled, her eyes shining with warmth. "Yes."

However, as their dreams began to align, Cassandra couldn't help but feel the grip of apprehension. The idea of moving to Boston meant leaving behind her work, her family, and enduring more painful memories of Seth's attack. Chance assured her that selling his house wasn't an option, not quite yet, and together they would face any obstacles that came their way. Looking into his eyes, she saw the adoration and devotion, and she knew that they would create a home filled with happiness.

"It's what I've dreamed of ever since you asked for advice on how to undump a canoe," Cassandra confessed, her voice filled with excitement.

Chance's expression turned to one of shock. "Why didn't you say hello? Did you notice how many people were insulting me and my 'without wax' joke?"

Cassandra giggled, feeling a sense of completeness and belonging. All the pieces had fallen into place, and their dream was taking shape. Chance could hardly wait to welcome her into his home, to create a life together. But deep down, both of them knew that a missing piece still remained—Seth, serving his sentence in jail, a ticking clock reminding them of an uncertain future.

And then what?

"Brad, it seems Cassandra has found true happiness, despite the challenges she faced with Chance's twin brother, Seth," Elizabeth announced to her audience.

"Indeed, Cassandra's journey has been a rollercoaster ride of emotions, but love triumphed over adversity. As she aptly said, 'It's either sink or swim,' and they chose to swim," Brad replied.

"You delved into the complications they faced during Cassandra's move to Boston, but our viewers are undoubtedly curious about their life together," Elizabeth continued, pressing for more details.

"After overcoming the many obstacles involved with relocating her job while staying connected to her family and friends, Cassandra and Chance embarked on a new adventure together. They decided to christen their new life with a well-deserved vacation," Brad revealed.

Chapter 4

Part I

Cassandra stood on the serene beach, marveling at the grand wall of flagstones that encircled the charming bed and breakfast in Michigan's upper peninsula. It was Chance's idea to bring her to this secluded corner of the country, a place he held dear from his summers spent at a nearby boys' camp. Here, he had learned the art of canoe dumping and immersed himself in the wonders of nature.

As she gazed across the tranquil expanse of Lake Michigamme, she couldn't help but notice the streaks in the water caused by iron sediments. Chance had shared during their flight that Michigamme meant "Streaked Water" in the language of the Anishinaabe/Ojibwe peoples. Sitting on the beach, she relished the coolness of the water enveloping her body and marveled at the untouched beauty of this pristine land. A few scattered boats dotted the lake—a water-skier here, a fishing enthusiast there—each person finding peace in the serene stillness.

Moments later, Chance emerged from their private cabin, a towel draped over his shoulders, donning a blue and white boxer-style bathing suit. A smile adorned his face, reminiscent of a mischievous young boy. Cassandra, dressed in a vibrant purple one-piece swimsuit, waved excitedly as a small water plane prepared to land on the lake. Chance, his eyes darting between the ground and the sky, almost stumbled on a hidden root along the path. Cassandra couldn't help but laugh.

"It's as if a bird is swooping down," she remarked, pointing to the plane's graceful descent as it skimmed the calm waters before coming to a rest.

"Amazing!" Chance mentioned his dream of building his own plane someday, to which Cassandra playfully slapped his shoulder.

"I wouldn't be caught dead in a homemade plane, no matter how calm the runway might be," she teased, their laughter blending in the air.

Soon, they found themselves immersed in the refreshing waters, the sand tickling their toes and the warm sun casting a golden glow on their skin. Despite the approaching mid-August, the relatively dry spring had spared them from the torment of mosquitoes. Without mentioning Seth's name or the many summers they had spent together as campers, Chance reminisced about the record-breaking walleye he caught, and the countless practical jokes they played on their fellow campers. As he shared these memories with Cassandra, a sense of joy and newfound experiences enveloped them.

After their swim, Chance showcased his canoe-jumping skills with aluminum canoes. Cassandra observed from a lounge chair on the shore as he paddled a few hundred feet away. Turning the canoe toward her, he positioned his paddle inside and then skillfully balanced himself on the back gunnel. With rhythmic hopping, the bow of the canoe rose and fell in the water, propelling it forward. His motions became livelier, and the canoe accelerated, generating a chorus of splashes upon touching the water's surface. As Chance neared the shore, he attempted to flex his muscles, aiming to impress Cassandra. But fate had different plans, and he lost his balance, tumbling into the water and capsizing the canoe.

Without a second thought, Cassandra sprang from her lounge chair and dashed into the water, swimming toward Chance. Anticipating her arrival, he paddled to the partially submerged canoe and admired her graceful form as she swam toward him. Together, they sat in the water-filled "dumped" canoe, facing each other, using their hands as makeshift paddles and delighting in playful splashes. With their combined efforts, they maneuvered the canoe back toward the shore, the water gently carrying them to the sandy beach. Laughing, they remained seated in their floating vessel, their kisses blending with the soothing sounds of the lake. In that moment, Cassandra cherished Chance's playful and carefree spirit, hoping that he would never lose touch with his inner child.

As the day wore on and the beach remained deserted, Cassandra reclined on the soft sand, a sigh escaping her lips as Chance gently massaged warm coconut-scented oil onto her body. The sun cast shimmering reflections on the calm waters, and a solitary gull soared gracefully across the sky.

"Chance, reach into my bag," Cassandra whispered, her heart pounding with anticipation.

Chance retrieved the envelope and read its title, his laughter filling the air. "You little sneak," he chuckled, appreciating her playful surprise.

Faithfully Falling
The Treasures we discover in this beautiful world...
...are for us to share forever and a day...
...for the heart is a sacred place to reside...
...when two hearts beat as one with the rhythm of life...
...and two souls unite in the ecstasy of passion...
...a passion that is fueled by the depth of their eternal love.

Cassandra turned towards him, her fingertips tracing a path across his chest, down his body, expressing her desire. Later, in the cozy seclusion of their cabin, they ventured into that sacred place where their bodies, souls, and minds melded together in a glorious union.

* * *

Back in Boston, Chance uttered, "Cassandra, this is your home now. Feel free to make yourself completely at ease." She felt a rush of affection for the spacious Victorian house, floating through each room with excitement, savoring the joy of being with him. As they entered the dining room, she finally noticed a subtle change.

"Has something changed here?" she inquired.

He recalled the laborious weeks spent on a project, a coy smile playing on his lips. "Just a few weekend projects," he replied.

Captivated by his craftsmanship, Cassandra eagerly anticipated discovering the rest of the house. In the living room, she gazed at him seductively, conveying a message that stirred his desires. He marveled at her allure, recognizing her insatiable appetite. With a sly grin, she led him to the bedroom, overcoming her fears as she entered the space where she had previously encountered Seth.

"There's only one thing I need from you now," she whispered softly.

Chance unbuttoned her blouse, bestowing gentle kisses upon every exposed inch of her skin as her clothing gracefully dropped to the floor. Her body responded to the sensations, each touch igniting her senses. His fingers traced a path along her shoulders and down her back. In turn, she unbuttoned his shirt and pants, shedding his garments with excitement.

After they shared their first intimate moment in his home, she battled against the haunting memories of Seth wielding a knife. Rolling onto her side, she summoned the courage to speak.

"Chance, could we talk?" she hesitantly requested.

"About anything," he reassured her.

* * *

The alarm pierced the stillness, jolting Cassandra from her sleep. Momentarily disoriented, she struggled to shake off the remnants of a confusing dream. The first image that greeted her eyes was that of Seth, sending chills down her spine. She sat upright, frozen for a few breathless seconds. Sensing her distress, Chance opened his eyes and reached out, placing his hand on hers. She scanned the room, her heart rate gradually slowing as she realized it looked different than in her nightmare.

"Care to talk some more?" Chance inquired, recalling their previous conversation about Seth.

"I'm alright," she replied, her voice tinged with uncertainty and determination. "You need to get going, and I have a mountain of unpacking to tackle. My boxes are definitely in the way." She caught his concerned gaze. "Truly, I'll be fine. It'll take some time."

Chance leaned over, planting a tender kiss on her cheek, before rising from the bed. He made his way to the bathroom but couldn't resist glancing back at her. She sat there, head bowed, hands trembling, silently weeping. His instinct urged him to say something, but he sensed that she needed space to adjust at her own pace. Don't rush it, he reminded himself.

Ignoring his earlier resolve, he retraced his steps, sitting on the bed and placing a comforting hand on her shoulders. "Let it all out. It's alright," he whispered gently.

Through a torrent of tears, Cassandra managed a weak smile. "Thanks for being my pillar of strength."

After dressing, Chance joined her in the kitchen, where she had prepared a light breakfast. The contentment of having her in his home filled him with a profound sense of happiness, understanding that it would take time for her to find that same peace within herself. Following breakfast, he bid her goodbye with a kiss.

"Make yourself at home," he encouraged.

"Really?" she responded, a playful glint dancing in her eyes.

He paused momentarily, considering her mischievous expression. "Sure, go for it," he replied with intrigue.

Chance reluctantly left, knowing a busy work week awaited him—new client meetings, preliminary sketch reviews for an elementary school. Cassandra, eager to settle into their new life, had chosen to take the week off before starting her new internship at Beth Israel Hospital. As she kissed him goodbye, her seductive glance revealed exactly what was on the evening's menu. Throughout the day, Chance called her multiple times, informing her of changing plans, offering apologies, and finally settling on a return home time.

In a playful exchange, she reminded him, "Take care of business, but remember, when you're home, you're all mine."

Now at home, he turned the key in the front door, remembering the teasing lilt in her voice. She stood in the doorway, adorned in a delicate lace nightgown. Her slender fingers reached for his briefcase, revealing the allure of her sultry figure. His gaze swept over the scene, taking in the softly glowing candles adorning the dining room table. The rich mahogany surface gleamed with a fresh coat of wax. It had once been cluttered with sketches and paperwork, but now it was transformed into a setting befitting a romantic evening. A beautiful lace cloth draped over it, accompanied by a floral centerpiece of exquisite Victorian crystal, surrounded by silver and glassware.

He stood there, awestruck, as she guided him to his seat. The mouthwatering aroma of scallops, shrimp, and artichokes filled the air, evoking a new sensation. Never before had such delectable scents wafted through his house. His usual fare consisted of quick microwaved or stove-heated meals. He took a deep breath, savoring the tantalizing fragrance.

"In less than ten hours, you've created all this?" he marveled.

"That, and more," she replied with a glimmer in her eyes.

During dinner, soft jazz music played in the background, casting a romantic ambiance throughout the room. "I love to watch you dance," Chance declared, his words harkening back to a fantasy he had once shared with her.

Inspired, she rose from her chair and gracefully moved into the living room, turning up the volume as she swayed to the swing in her lavender nightgown. "What did you say?" she playfully winked, momentarily revealing a glimpse of her bosom.

Blowing out the candles, she gestured for him to stand—it was time for dessert. Leading him through the house, she guided him to the bedroom. The bed was adorned with lace sheets and matching pillowcases. The comforter she had purchased earlier that day blended seamlessly with the beige-colored walls. His eyes caught sight of a jewelry box positioned at the end of her dresser, showcasing her earrings and bracelets.

Observing his silent admiration, she asked, "Are you sure you don't mind?"

"It's wonderful," he said, grateful she had transformed the room that held so many dark memories for them both.

* * *

As the days went by, Chance noticed the subtle touches that Cassandra added to their home. She kept herself occupied, setting up her office, purchasing new drapes, and infusing feminine touches that he had longed for. He admired how she filled the empty shelves of the French cabinet he had painstakingly refinished, previously disappointed by its bareness. Now, it displayed beautiful glassware and dishes that they used to celebrate their evening meals together. Throughout the week, Cassandra grew fond of Lisa and Brad, and on Friday, she discussed the dinner menu with Chance before extending a formal invitation for them to join them in their new home.

"What time did you ask them to arrive?" Chance inquired, hastily getting dressed.

Assuming he didn't know the details, Cassandra playfully replied, "You have five minutes." As a knock echoed through the front door, she chuckled. "Oops, I guess they're early." She made her way through the house and opened the door with a wide smile. "Come on in."

"Thank you," Lisa said, presenting her with a bottle of wine.

Cassandra took a moment to admire Lisa's appearance—shoulder-length brunette hair, brown eyes, and a flawless complexion. Noticing her figure, Cassandra wondered why Chance hadn't been drawn to her. Closing the door, she heard Brad exclaim, "Hey, wait!"

"Sorry. Come on in, Brad. I was have lost in my thoughts," she apologized.

Brad, wearing a suit and pretending to look cool, asked, "How do I look?"

"Very dapper," Cassandra complimented, playfully tweaking his chin.

Lisa laughed when Chance entered the living room. "Well, well. Love seems to be doing wonders for you, Chance."

"This old thing?" he responded, casually brushing off his jacket. "I completely forgot I owned it."

Cassandra held a tray with two glasses of Merlot and two glasses of Seven-Up for Chance and Brad. As Brad reached for the wine, she swiftly handed him a glass of soda. She served her favorite dishes of pasta and chicken. Over dinner, they exchanged stories about the remarkable transformation of the house.

"Cassandra, I absolutely adore the new curtains. Where did you find them?" Lisa inquired.

Brad exchanged a knowing glance with Chance, who reciprocated the look. Sensing their silent communication, Cassandra replied, "Chance helped me pick them out."

Chance sheepishly nodded at Brad. "I took her to Roper's in town. They have the most incredible selection."

Brad burst into laughter, only to be silenced by a pointed look from his mother. "Yeah, those curtains are really something, Cassandra. You should have seen Chance covered in dust when he fixed up the dining room."

Chance ruffled Brad's hair as he reminisced about the clouds of dust that had formed above his head.

On Monday, Cassandra would embark on her internship at Beth Israel Hospital, but for now, work was the farthest thing from her mind as she basked in the joy of seeing her guests and her beloved enjoying the delightful dinner and atmosphere.

"That was a fantastic dinner," Lisa complimented, gesturing towards Brad, who eagerly nodded in agreement.

Later, they found themselves on the front porch, relishing chocolate cake, sipping coffee and drinks, and savoring the soothing sounds of the evening. Their conversations flowed, touching on Brad's schoolwork, Chance's business endeavors, and Lisa's recent job at the local supermarket's deli counter. The relaxed ambiance suddenly transformed when a lively dog bounded towards Brad, showering him with affectionate slobbers. Brad struggled to free himself, his laughter reverberating through the calmness of the evening. He eventually gave in, collapsing onto the ground as the exuberant dog continued its playful antics, its tail wagging in exhilaration.

"It tickles," Brad exclaimed, surrendering to the delightful assault.

"Bodger, come here," a middle-aged man called from the walkway. Waving a leash, he approached, apologizing for the dog's antics. He couldn't help but watch Brad enjoying the playful encounter.

"As you can see, they've already become good friends," Chance remarked.

Cassandra, ever the gracious hostess, offered John a cup of coffee. "I'm Cassandra."

John had recently retired from teaching mathematics at the local high school. Chance recognized the school, mentioning that his company had designed the new auditorium that had opened the previous year. As their conversation continued, Brad and Bodger continued their lively play.

"Well, I should probably head back. Thanks for the coffee," he said appreciatively.

"Feel free to bring Bodger by anytime," Brad chimed in.

Chance couldn't help but revel in the excitement twinkling in Brad's eyes. It occurred to him that having a dog of his own would be a wonderful addition to their lives. However, he decided to discuss it with Lisa privately first. A few minutes later, after bidding Lisa and Brad farewell, Chance and Cassandra found themselves undressing for bed. From across the room, Chance admired Cassandra's form as she hung her dress in the closet. He approached her from behind, softly kissing her shoulder. She leaned back, turning to him, her voice filled with sleepy contentment. Despite her desire for him, exhaustion weighed heavily on her.

"I'm a little tired," she murmured.

They crawled into bed together, finding comfort in each other's embrace. Cassandra drifted off to sleep, and soon, Chance followed suit, his gentle snores creating a soothing harmony in the room.

Later in the night, Cassandra awoke in a haze, feeling disconnected from her new home and longing for her family back in New Jersey. Her sleep was fitful, disturbed by restlessness. She awoke for the third time, her gaze fixating on the clock glaring 2:30 in the morning. Chance remained peacefully asleep beside her, his gentle snoring providing a reassuring soundtrack. However, tonight, she couldn't shake off the strange sensations plaguing her. As she dozed off once more, her mind was flooded with vivid images of her traumatic encounter with Seth. The same nightmares that haunted her in New Jersey had returned in full force since she moved in with Chance.

A grimace escaped her lips as she visualized Seth brandishing the knife over her. The tension grew until suddenly, her eyes flew open, and she saw Seth lying next to her. Realizing it was Chance, her heart rate slowed, the perspiration cooling on her skin. She slipped out of bed, perching at the edge and cradling her head in her hands. She dragged herself into the bathroom, seeking respite in the cold water splashing against her face. Yet, her body still trembled with unease.

Leaning over the sink, she tried to rationalize her psychological turmoil. "You look awful," she muttered to her reflection. She retraced the events of the evening in her mind, and it struck her that the kitchen knife she had used to cut the cake bore an uncanny resemblance to the one Seth had used to threaten her. *It couldn't possibly be the same one!*

Stepping out of the bathroom, she moved through the dining room to the living room, where the rhythmic ticking of a clock in the foyer echoed. The distant sound of a passing siren gnawed at her senses, and she sighed, attempting to regain her composure. Her gaze swept over every detail of the house, her fingers gliding over the texture of the furniture as she approached the bay window adorned with new drapes. Everything seemed safe and comforting.

She walked into her office, sinking into her chair and reclining, her head rolling from side to side as she stared out the window at the darkened backyard. The faint silhouette of the tree fort that Chance and Brad had constructed took on an eerie appearance in the dim light. She turned her attention to the bookshelf, her gaze falling on the birch bark canoe that Chance had lovingly crafted for her. Lifting it gently, her fingers traced its delicate lines, tears welling in her eyes. A solitary tear cascaded onto the canoe's surface, and she chuckled to herself, remembering the shared experience of canoe dumping.

Walking into the kitchen, a sense of trepidation filled Cassandra as she approached the cutlery drawer. She retrieved a bottle of water from the refrigerator, admiring the lively wallpaper trim adorned with colorful fruits and flowing vines. This house had become her haven, her dream come true. Letting out a nervous sigh, she braced herself and opened the drawer. And there it was, staring at her with its black handle and a six-inch blade. Her hand froze, hesitant to touch it.

With trembling fingers, Cassandra picked up the knife, turning it over, its silver blade gleaming under the light. She settled at the kitchen table, holding the knife in the way that evoked her deepest fears. *Chance should have thrown it away!*

Later, as she entered the bedroom, Cassandra slipped into bed, sensing movement as Chance rolled onto his side. She lay on her back, closing her eyes, battling against the memories that threatened to engulf her. Chance drew closer, wrapping his left arm around her waist. She intertwined her fingers with his and silently wept, finding calm in his presence. Eventually, exhaustion claimed her, granting her a few precious hours of sleep.

When morning arrived, Chance was taken aback by Cassandra's weary appearance. "Are you alright?"

She responded solemnly, "I didn't sleep well. I guess I'm just anxious about starting my new job." She rose from the bed and made her way into the bathroom, barely sparing him a glance.

Raising his voice, hoping his words would reach her, he declared, "I love you!"

She peeked her head around the bathroom door. "I'm okay."

As Chance brewed coffee, he couldn't help but wonder if Cassandra had experienced a nightmare about Seth. He heard the sound of the shower ceasing and set the coffee and eggs at her place. As she passed by, he reached out, gently caressing her cheek. He wanted to ask, "What's wrong?" as she walked over to the kitchen drawer and paused. Opening it, she retrieved the knife, her voice laced with nervousness.

"Does this look familiar?"

"What do you mean?" Suddenly, Chance knew. He comprehended the conflict that tore at her heart. Her body began to tremble, and he quickly stood, stepping closer to her. "No, Cassandra. That's not the same knife. I swear, I disposed of the other one immediately."

She broke into tears, lowering the blade onto the counter. "I was up all night, wondering if it was... if it was..."

Placing a finger on her lips, he brushed away her tears. "Promise me that if you ever feel uneasy, you'll wake me up."

Crying into his shoulder, she whispered, "I'm sorry I doubted you."

After their embrace, he suggested, "Let's go for a walk. We should talk about this outside."

As she left, Chance's gaze fell upon the knife resting on the counter, bearing an uncanny resemblance to the one Seth had used on her. He wrapped it in several bags and deposited it in the trash. Cassandra appeared at the door, her smile laced with sorrow.

Chance hugged her and said, "After our walk, we'll go shopping for new cutlery."

* * *

"Brad!" Chance called out from Cassandra's office window. The boy jumped down from his tree fort, rushing to the front of the house. "Come around to the front."

Confused, Brad hurried around, his eyes widening in astonishment. "Wow! What's all this?"

Lisa exclaimed, "Surprise!"

Brad approached the cocker spaniel puppy, joyfully petting it as its tail. "Is he mine? No way!"

"Yes. And remember, taking care of him is your responsibility," Lisa said, suggesting that he take the pup to the backyard, to their fort.

"Come on, boy."

The puppy yapped happily, following its new master. Chance knew that Brad didn't have many friends at school, often feeling left out of activities in the neighborhood. Now, he had found a loyal companion who would adore him unconditionally. Laughter filled the air as the pup stayed a few steps ahead of Brad, successfully retrieving a branch but failing in returning it. Exhausted from the chase, Brad collapsed to the ground, catching his breath. The playful pup bounded over him, dancing merrily.

Chance shouted, "Look out!"

The pup dashed over Brad, catching him off guard. Tripping in his steps, the branch slipped from the dog's mouth. Brad swiftly scooped it up, displaying his prize. Suddenly, the pup lunged forward, snatching the branch from his hand. They played a spirited game of hide-and-seek within the fort, yet the dog found Brad each time. Later, Brad named him Peanuts due to the brown spots that adorned his fur.

As the days passed, Brad proved himself responsible in caring for Peanuts—feeding, walking, and even washing the pup on a regular basis. Together, he and Chance worked on building an extension to the fence, ensuring that the backyard remained secure.

"Now, remember," Chance reminded him, "you have to close this gate and make sure it locks shut, alright?"

"No problemo," Brad assured him with a confident grin.

* * *

Cassandra pulled into the driveway around eleven in the morning, surprised to find Brad sulking on the front steps. "Is there a guy nearby who can lend me a little hand?"

Groaning, Brad slowly approached her car. As they unloaded groceries from the trunk, she asked him what was bothering him. A long pause ensued before he grunted. Sensing his solemn mood, she said, "Give me a hand, and I'll whip up some sandwiches." Brad began taking the first load of groceries into the house. Later, in the kitchen, she informed him, "We have turkey."

He sat at the table, his response subdued. "No bologna?"

Cassandra shook her head, offering an alternative. "We have extra chunky peanut butter and jelly." Soon, she handed him a paper plate with a neatly cut sandwich. "Where's your mom?"

"Upstairs, sleeping. Peanuts is too."

Taking a seat at the table, Cassandra inquired, "Do you wanna play catch?" She was aware of his grumpy mood and wondered if it had anything to do with the neighborhood street hockey game she had noticed on her way home. "I was hoping to show you my fast ball and famous curve. Come on, slugger. I bet you can't catch my slider."

His interest piqued, Brad asked, "Can you really throw all those pitches?"

"I may be a bit rusty, but I'm sure it'll all come back to me."

Once outside and properly equipped, Cassandra wound up and threw a fast ball toward Brad. Gasping in amazement, he caught the perfect strike. He returned the throw with a fast ball of his own, slightly off target but with impressive speed. As they played catch, Brad occasionally turned to observe the progress of the street hockey game nearby. A puck whizzed down the street, retrieved by a boy who ignored their game.

"How are you doing?" Cassandra asked the boy.

He glanced their way but didn't respond. "Found it!" he yelled to his friends up the street.

"They don't want me to play with them," Brad muttered, tossing the ball halfheartedly.

"Did you ask?" Cassandra caught the lazy lob and tossed it back in the same manner. He shook his head, frowning. "We don't need them," she said with a mischievous grin.

Shortly after, Chance arrived. "Do you have an extra glove?" he asked.

Brad shook his head.

"I think there's one in the basement," Cassandra mentioned.

Remembering his old glove from youth, Chance dashed into the house to search for it.

"I have an idea," Cassandra exclaimed. "Let me grab my bat, and we'll play Five Hundred."

"Five what?"

Chance returned, slamming his fist into the worn leather glove. "You've never played Five Hundred?"

Brad shrugged his shoulders. In a matter of minutes, Cassandra was sending pop flies soaring through the air, while Chance and Brad competed to catch the ball, with each successful catch earning one hundred points. The first to reach five hundred would get the chance to bat. The neighborhood kids eventually noticed their game, but they were engrossed in friendly competition. Chance chased after a ball that had rolled into the field hockey area.

"You guys wanna play?" he asked.

"We're playing hockey," the goalie responded.

Chance threw the ball back to Brad, who passed it to Cassandra. Moments later, Brad caught the game-winning ball. Chance saluted the victory, and Brad eagerly took his place as the next batter. Soon, the field hockey game ended, and as several kids walked by on their way home, Brad greeted them with a friendly nod before launching another soaring fly ball into the air.

After forty minutes of exhilarating play, Chance declared, "That's it. I'm exhausted."

Brad agreed. "You were really good, Cassandra."

"Of course I was," she laughed. "Lemonade?"

"Sure!"

As they quenched their thirst, Brad blurted out, "Cassandra, can we do this again?"

"Anytime you want." She ruffled his hair, noticing that he had forgotten his earlier sadness, if only for a couple of hours.

* * *

In late October, Cassandra and Chance were jolted awake by loud knocking on their door at eleven in the evening. She nudged him, whispering, "It sounds like Brad."

"Alright, I'm up." Chance donned his robe, opening the front door to find Lisa and Brad standing there. "What's going on?"

"Sorry to wake you," Lisa said apologetically.

"Chance! It's Peanuts!" Brad blurted out.

His heart raced with worry as Chance looked at Lisa. "Is he alright?"

"He escaped through the fence," she explained.

"Alright. Let's see," Chance paused to think. "There's only one thing to do: get dressed and start searching the neighborhood. Brad, do you know how to think like Peanuts?"

Brad nodded. "I guess."

"Then you're in charge."

Chance returned to the bedroom. "Peanuts got out," he whispered to a drowsy Cassandra. "You've only been at the hospital for two months, and you're already swamped. Go back to sleep. I promise I won't be too long." He quickly dressed in jeans and a shirt.

Cassandra nestled her head back onto the pillow. "Good luck."

As the search for Peanuts continued outside, Brad called out, "Peanuts! Where are you?"

Chance and Lisa followed closely behind, encouraging Brad to keep calling. As they scoured the area, some of the older neighborhood teenagers playing Ghost in the Graveyard became curious about the commotion. "What's going on?" one of the boys asked.

"My dog got out of our fence," Brad explained with a touch of sadness.

Several more kids approached, their curiosity piqued. Lisa noticed their gathering and motioned to Chance.

"Hi, guys. I'm Chance," he introduced himself. "This is Brad and his mom, Lisa. We're neighbors up the street. Have any of you seen a stray puppy?" The boys looked at each other, shaking their heads in response.

Brad's shyness began to dissipate. "His name is Peanuts."

"Can you guys help finding him?" Chance asked the group.

The oldest boy glanced at Chance and nodded. He turned to his friends and said, "Sure, why not." Soon, they split into different directions, calling out Peanuts' name.

"That was really kind of them," Lisa commented, impressed by the teenagers' willingness to help.

"That boy is the son of one of my employees," Chance revealed. "Good thing he noticed my stare."

Lisa laughed, "You sneaky one."

After half an hour of searching, someone finally yelled the words everyone was waiting for, "I found him! I found him!" Peanuts emerged from behind a row of bushes and rushed into the street.

"Peanuts!" Brad scolded, "Bad dog!"

Peanuts lowered his head and tucked his tail between his legs. Chance and Lisa stood on the sidewalk, not wanting to interrupt the interaction between Brad and his beloved pet. "Peanuts, roll over and break dance!" Brad commanded. Peanuts obediently squirmed onto his back, impressing the onlookers. "I trained him myself. You should see how we play hide-and-seek in my fort."

Listening to the commotion, an idea suddenly struck Chance. "Hey, kids, how about we have a barbecue at my house tomorrow to celebrate finding Peanuts?" Excited squeals filled the air. "Make sure to get permission from your parents and bring them along. My address is four-seventeen Haywood Knolls Drive, just up the street. How about eleven a.m.?"

Everyone eagerly agreed to the plan. As they made their way back to the house, with Peanuts leading the way, Brad prepared himself for the punishment he anticipated.

"Do you know what I am going to say?" Lisa asked sternly.

"To be more careful with Peanuts," Brad replied, knowing he had learned his lesson.

"What else?" she pressed.

"Oh, yeah. Chance, thanks for helping."

"No problemo," Chance grinned.

Brad laughed as he bounded up the stairs to the second floor. Peanuts scampered ahead, reaching the top of the stairs and wagging his tail in anticipation.

* * *

The next morning and inspired by an idea, Chance called Greg from his home phone. "Good morning, Greg. It's Chance. I hope I didn't wake you."

"Not at all. Is everything alright?" Greg, a young employee at Chance's firm, wondered why his employer was calling him on a Saturday morning.

"I wanted to invite you to a barbecue at my house," Chance added, keeping his motivations close to his chest. "We haven't had much opportunity to chat over the past few weeks, and I know you're new to the area."

"Ahh... well... sure... Sounds like fun." Greg jotted down the directions, agreeing to arrive shortly before noon.

Later, Chance knocked on Lisa's door. Brad answered, with Peanuts wagging his tail in anticipation of something exciting. "Let's go, Brad." Peanuts bounded down the stairs, leading the way. "Man, that dog can run."

"Tell me about it," Brad laughed, excited for the day ahead.

Chance opened the shed, pointing to the old Weber grill. "There it is." He removed the top and gasped. "I haven't used it in years."

As they prepared for the party, Chance realized Cassandra needed rest from her new job, so he aimed to ease her burdens by surprising her with the party. Brad ran to the shed and retrieved an old croquet set, adding another fun element to the backyard gathering. Gradually, the backyard filled with neighborhood kids, who helped themselves to punch and chips. Some of the parents also joined, introducing themselves to Lisa and Chance. One woman even mistook them as a married couple.

"Actually, this is my upstairs neighbor, Lisa," Chance clarified.

As the noise from the backyard entered Cassandra's consciousness, she slowly opened her eyes, surprised by the late hour. Gradually, her attention focused on the sounds and the enticing aroma of grilling food. Lazily making her way to her office, she observed with surprise as a dozen kids played in her backyard. "What's going on?" she wondered. Chance and Lisa caught her eye, engaged in conversation with a neighbor she had recently met. Chance playfully ruffled a boy's hair as he ran past, retrieving a stray frisbee before tossing it back to the kids. Yawning, Cassandra put on jeans and a light sweater, making her way out the porch door and into the backyard. Chance waved as she approached.

"This is Cassandra," he introduced her to a young couple.

"Nice to meet you," Janet, a neighbor, extended her hand for a friendly shake.

"My pleasure," Cassandra said, glancing slyly at a grinning Chance. "Honey, can I speak with you for a moment?" She led him to the side of the house. "Okay, what did I miss?" Laughing, Chance proceeded to explain everything that had transpired the night before. "You truly are everyone's Prince Charming, aren't you?"

Chance held Cassandra's hand as they walked over to greet their latest arrival. "Greg, I'd like you to meet Cassandra."

Surprised that Chance had invited an architect from the office, Cassandra greeted Greg politely. Instinctively, she sensed there was some hidden motive behind Chance's mischievous grin. She studied his face for clues, but he skillfully evaded her investigative gaze.

It wasn't until Chance said, "Greg, I'd like to introduce you to my upstairs neighbor, Lisa," that Cassandra realized his true intention.

"Nice to meet you," Greg said, shaking Lisa's hand. Clean-shaven with well-groomed black hair, he possessed a semi-athletic build and large hands. Lisa found him cute, and his polite demeanor only added to his charm.

"Something to drink?" Greg asked, following Lisa to a nearby picnic table. As he admired her figure, she felt a surge of attractiveness in her casual jeans and shirt.

"Ouch!" Chance winced when Cassandra playfully pinched his arm.

"Just one of Cupid's stray arrows, you sneak," Cassandra said, hugging him.

The afternoon was filled with grilling, games, and Peanuts joining in eagerly. Brad's neighbor, Billy, suggested a game of hide-and-seek, but Peanuts proved to be a cunning seeker, finding every hiding spot.

"Chance, I love the way your mind works," Cassandra remarked.

"What about my body?" he teased.

Leaning in close, she whispered into his ear, "I'll save that analysis for later."

Their playful exchanges were magnetic: Chance tweaked Cassandra's behind as she patted him back. Later, he hugged her while making iced tea, both eager for the party to wind down. As they helped clear away paper plates and cups, Lisa approached Cassandra. "Cassandra, do you think we could have a chat?"

"Of course," Cassandra replied.

"Brad is still having nightmares about Chance's brother. I know he's really troubled, but he doesn't want to admit it."

"I'd be happy to talk to him," Cassandra offered.

Relief washed over Lisa's face. "Let's keep this between ourselves. I know how bad Chance already feels about this whole situation."

Gradually, Brad's friends began to leave. "Thanks, Brad. See you at school on Monday," Billy said, giving him a high-five. Two girls giggled excitedly as they whispered to one another before running off. Brad felt like a new person, his confidence restored. He ran up to his mom, failing to notice the man standing next to her.

"That was so much fun," Brad said, his voice filled with joy.

"I'm talking with someone," Lisa lightly scolded him.

"Oops, sorry."

"Hi, Brad. I'm Greg Tracy. Your mom has been telling me all about you." A frisbee landed near Greg's feet and he picked it up. "She told me you can outrun Peanuts and catch a disc any day of the week."

As Greg held the frisbee ready, Brad sprinted into the yard at full speed, chasing after the long toss. The boy caught five tosses before Peanuts leaped into the air, intercepting a line drive.

"I think you've made a friend for life," Lisa smiled.

Turning to face her, Greg replied, "I certainly hope so."

* * *

The next morning, Cassandra called Brad, knowing that Lisa was filling in for an employee at work. She suggested they play a game of catch. Ten minutes later, they met outside and began tossing the ball back and forth, with Peanuts chasing after it. They eventually sat on the front stoop, lazily tossing the ball into the air. Cassandra asked

90

Brad about school and his Halloween costume plans for the upcoming weekend.

"I'm going as Darth Vader," Brad replied.

Cassandra lowered her voice, a mischievous twinkle in her eye. "It's the force, Luke." Sensing the right moment, Cassandra broached the subject she wanted to discuss. "Say, Brad, I've been having these nightmares about what happened last year with… Seth. I was wondering if I could talk to you about it? Sometimes it's good to talk with someone else, you know?"

Brad wore a pensive frown. He looked down at the ground and hesitated before responding. "You can tell me. We're friends," he assured her.

She gently placed her arm around his shoulder. "Well, one night about two weeks ago, it was dark, and I opened a utility drawer. I found a piece of rope in there, and it reminded me of Seth. I couldn't stop thinking about it. That night, I had a really bad nightmare. It's funny how something like that can trigger all the bad memories."

Brad paused, nodding in understanding. "I know what you mean. So, what are you going to do about it?"

"Well," Cassandra spoke slowly, "there are two things I could do. I can throw the rope away and try to move on with my life. Or I can try to forget about it. I'm not sure which option is best."

The conversation stalled momentarily as she waited for his reply. She was glad that her strategy of leading him into the conversation by focusing on her own concerns was working. Brad felt like he was genuinely helping her work through her issues, while unknowingly resolving his own.

"If it were me," he finally said, "I'd probably throw it away. Otherwise, you might never be able to forget about it."

"You're right, Brad. That's what I'm going to do." Her strategy halfway accomplished, she waited for him to continue.

"Yeah," he said, lost in thought. "That's probably a good idea. Even if it means letting go of something you really like."

"Have you been having nightmares too?" she asked, concerned.

"Well... some nights are just awful. My dad is always there to fix the problem, but then he disappears and I'm left holding the BB gun. But I can't shoot it. I want my dad to help me."

She waved to a passing neighbor, contemplating her response. "Do you want to get rid of the gun and stop seeing it?"

He held a few stones, letting them drop from his hand as he searched for an answer. "My dad gave it to me. He can't give me anything ever again."

"I understand your attachment to it. But maybe the nightmares are really about something else. Think for a moment about your dream. Your dad was there, right?"

"Yeah, but then he disappears, and I have to protect myself."

"But even when your dad wasn't physically there to protect you, you still shot the gun to protect Chance and me. If not for you, Chance wouldn't have gotten out of the basement. Brad, you were the hero who saved my life."

"You think so?" Brad asked, a glimmer of hope in his eyes.

"Of course. So does Chance, your mom, *and* your dad!" she exclaimed, pointing to his chest. "When someone passes away, they leave behind the things they taught us—values, morals, and their love."

"He showed me how to use the gun. He helped me remember it, didn't he?" Brad's finger pointed to his own heart. "I guess I did the right thing."

"Absolutely. You are my hero," she whispered, her voice filled with admiration.

Part II

As December approached, Cassandra marveled at how much time had passed since she moved in with Chance. *Six months already?* The entire neighborhood was adorned with Christmas decorations—reindeer, nativity scenes, Santas, and colorful lights adorned the houses. A festive atmosphere enveloped the community. On a cold and snowy Saturday morning, Chance answered the phone.

"This is Paul Smith, owner of Royal Catering. We have a small problem. Unfortunately, one of our servers won't be able to work tonight. Her daughter is home with a bad case of the flu. I've tried to find a replacement, but everyone is already booked for other parties." Concerned about the logistics for his office holiday party, which was to be held at his house that evening, Chance asked about their options. Paul said, "We might just have to make do."

Chance hung up the phone and informed Cassandra about the bad news. "We could really use an extra server. I want my staff to be pampered with attention."

Sipping her coffee, she offered a suggestion. "What if we ask Lisa to help? She could use the extra money."

"But we don't even know if they've talked on the phone since the barbecue," Chance mentioned, subtly steering the conversation toward Cassandra's underlying point.

"I know. But since Greg is going to be here, what better way to... you know... get them together again? Besides, Lisa has experience in the food service industry."

Within minutes of hanging up, Chance informed Cassandra that Paul Smith would be delighted to have a friend help out at the party. Excitedly, Cassandra called Lisa. "I know it's last minute, Lisa. Only if you can."

"Sure," Lisa replied enthusiastically. "I once helped cater a party for Charlton Heston."

"Great! The caterers will arrive at four," Cassandra said with a smile as she ended the call. "You see, every cloud does have a silver lining."

Chance gazed out of the living room window, watching the snowflakes gracefully descend. "Or a white lining. I hope everyone can make it in this weather. I wonder if Brad is up for a snowball fight?"

"And while he's out there, maybe you could both do some shoveling?" Cassandra suggested playfully.

"That sounds like a plan." Chance dialed the phone and soon received Brad's enthusiastic agreement to help. Once outside, Brad and Chance dove into the snow, digging and clearing the accumulated snow. Chance focused on the driveway while Brad tackled the walkway leading up to the house. As they shoveled, Chance waved to a passing snowplow battling the accumulating snow. When the walkways were cleared, Chance bent down and scooped up a handful of snow. He threw a snowball that whizzed past Brad's head. Brad dropped his shovel, tightly packed his own snowball, and threw it back.

"Missed me," Chance teased, sticking his tongue out.

"Not this time." Brad charged at him, exclaiming, "Got ya!" after a snowball landed on Chance's ankle.

Watching the lively fight from the living room window, Cassandra and Lisa giggled like teenagers. They quickly put on their boots and joined the battle.

"First floor against the second," Cassandra declared.

Suddenly, the front yard was a flurry of flying snow. Neighborhood children emerged and joined in the fun. "Go, Brad, go!" one of his friends shouted.

"Come on, Andy, help out!" Brad called, rallying his friend.

"Hey, that's not fair," Chance shouted. Cassandra invited two young girls to join their team, balancing the sides. The girls laughed and threw snowballs at Brad.

"Heads up!" Lisa warned as one of her throws accidentally hit her teammate. The boy turned to face her, holding a snowball, ready to retaliate. Backing off, she pleaded for mercy, but he let it fly, hitting her on the top of her head.

"Good thing you wore a hat," Cassandra laughed, coming to Lisa's rescue.

The battle continued, with playful shrieks filling the air. Eventually, Chance, covered in snow, raised his hands in defeat. "Truce. That's enough for me."

"Snowman!" someone exclaimed.

An ensemble of excited screams followed, and the group shifted their attention to building snowmen. Cassandra promised hot chocolate waiting for them when they finished. Later, as they sipped cocoa in the kitchen, Chance glanced out the window, admiring their snowy handiwork.

"By the way," Lisa said, gazing out the window, "thanks for the opportunity to work tonight."

"Who knows, maybe Greg will even be there," Chance said with a mischievous smile.

Lisa grinned at Cassandra. "Oh yeah, I remember him."

* * *

Later that afternoon, as the snow continued to fall, Chance welcomed the caterers into his home. They unloaded a van filled with supplies and two magnificent ice carvings. Together, he and Brad watched as two men carefully positioned a pair of stunning reindeer ice sculptures on either side of the entranceway. Paul, a large and imposing man, engaged in friendly banter with the young boy.

"They just followed me here," he quipped.

A crew of four caterers busied themselves inside, cooking, moving furniture, and creating an enchanting party atmosphere. Lisa arrived, listening attentively as the main server briefed her on her responsibilities. Gradually, guests started to arrive, many of them pausing to admire the ice carvings and the snowmen that Brad and his friends had crafted. Brad, dressed in his best suit, felt proud seeing his snow family standing proudly next to the majestic reindeer. At eight p.m., Greg arrived, surprised to see Lisa waiting to greet him.

"May I take this, please?" Lisa asked, reaching for his snow-covered jacket.

"Thank you. You look beautiful," Greg complimented her.

Lisa escorted him into the living room, their eyes locked in a shared moment. "Not like that old jeans I wore at the barbecue," she playfully replied.

Greg smiled warmly. "You looked great then too."

Lisa continued her duties, serving guests with poise and grace, offering stuffed mushrooms and chicken skewers while secretly stealing glances at Greg from the corner of her eye. Knowing he was watching her, she purposely avoided him while floating from guest to guest.

"Phew! Now we can relax," Chance remarked to Cassandra in the kitchen.

"Did you see the look on Greg's face when he saw Lisa? She looks stunning in her little server outfit," Cassandra observed.

The main course of seafood paella, vegetables, and salad was served at nine. Brad found himself engaged in a conversation with Chance's accountant as they stood in the buffet line.

"So, you carved those reindeer?" the man asked Brad.

"No, I made the snowmen," Brad clarified with a touch of pride.

"And how long have you been working for Chance?" Karen Bellows, Chance's assistant, playfully joined in.

Brad answered confidently, "As long as he wants," he said, drawing laughter.

Greg, standing in line, couldn't take his eyes off Lisa as she hurriedly walked past. "Lisa, can I talk to you for a moment?" he asked, leading her to the doorway of Cassandra's office where mistletoe hung. Taking her tray and placing it on the desk, he looked into her eyes and said, "Merry Christmas." Slowly, he approached her, and she placed her hands on his shoulders, closing her eyes in anticipation. Their lips met in a gentle, heartfelt kiss.

Cassandra, passing by her office, quickly darted away to find Chance. "Wait until you hear this," she exclaimed, explaining what she had witnessed.

"That's quite irregular, don't you think?" Chance comically sneered. "Imagine a server mingling with the guests. Maybe I should inform Chef Smith?"

She firmly grabbed his shoulder. "You'll do nothing of the kind!"

* * *

After a delightful dinner, the guests sipped on coffee and wine, marveling at the intricate architectural ornaments adorning the living room and dining room. Colorful paper cranes lined the windows and doorways, adding a touch of whimsy to the festive atmosphere. When the caterers brought out a cake shaped like one of Chance's firm's recent contemporary buildings, everyone claimed a slice, each vying for a specific part.

"I have dibs on the entranceway," one guest declared.

Someone else chimed in, "Dibs on the bathroom."

Brad, eager to join in the fun, proclaimed, "The roof is mine!" knowing it meant owning the icing. His clever wit brought smiles to the guests, showcasing his charm.

Later, Chance tapped his water glass to grab everyone's attention. "I would like to express my gratitude to each and every one of you for contributing to the successful growth of our company. We had a remarkable year, and tonight's celebration is just a small token of my appreciation. I am pleased to announce that this will be the first of regular annual bonuses." He gestured toward a table where envelopes awaited his employees. "Please help yourselves to one of the envelopes."

His loyal team expressed their gratitude, thanking Chance for his generosity. As guests began to bid their farewells, Brad slept peacefully on the couch, his mother gently covering him with a blanket.

Greg leaned in close to Lisa and whispered, "I'll pick you up at eleven tomorrow."

"I can't wait," Lisa replied, her eyes glowing with excitement.

After Greg left, Cassandra remarked, "Tomorrow at eleven? Sounds like you've done quite well for yourself."

Lisa laughed, her heart brimming with happiness. "He's taking us to the Omni show at the Museum of Science."

Lisa walked into Cassandra's office, took down the mistletoe, and placed it in her purse. "I know just where to put this," she said mischievously. She scooped up her sleeping son in her arms, his peaceful expression melting her heart.

Finally alone with her man, Cassandra called out, "Honey, could you please put on your boots and jacket? I want to show you something outside."

"More shoveling?" Chance said, recognizing her determined gaze. He instinctively complied with her request, slipping on his winter gear.

Once outside, Cassandra instructed him, "Spread your arms and legs and follow me."

She fell gracefully backward, landing safely in the soft blanket of snow. Chance followed suit, immersing himself in the snowy embrace. As they moved their arms and legs up and down, they dug themselves deeper into the snow, creating their own little paradise. Chance turned to watch Cassandra, her face radiant under the moonlit sky. They lay together, holding hands, as light snowflakes gently landed on their faces; their snow angels connected in perfect unison.

* * *

Chance glanced at his wristwatch, growing concerned about the late hour on that chilly March evening. He called Beth Israel Hospital and asked to speak with Cassandra Grey. As he waited on hold, he nervously tapped a pencil on Cassandra's desk. Peering out of her office window, he could barely make out the outline of Brad's tree fort in the darkness.

Finally, Cassandra's voice echoed across the phone lines. "Honey, it's me. I realize you're busy, but it's after nine and you didn't call."

Dreading another endless call from a patient or a barrage of administrative orders, Cassandra sighed with relief upon hearing his voice. "I probably won't be home for another hour. These counseling sessions are taking forever."

"Well, just imagine the hot bubble bath I'm going to draw for you when you return," Chance said, his voice filled with tenderness.

"I can't wait. But I have to go now. The sooner I finish here, the sooner I'll be home." She hung up, feeling fortunate to have such a caring and supportive man in her life. Work no longer felt like a tedious obligation.

Cassandra had been interning at the hospital for nine months, and her workload had exceeded anything she had experienced in New Jersey. Glancing at her watch, she marveled at how quickly time had flown. Taking a moment to absorb the bustling atmosphere of the hospital, she realized where all the time had gone. Doctors and nurses rushed by, attending to emergencies and shuttling patients to and from surgery. She checked her remaining appointments for the evening and made her way to the ward psychologist's wing.

Entering her office, she greeted her patient with a warm smile. "Hi, Andrew. I'm sorry to keep you waiting. Coffee?"

Andrew's head twitched nervously as Cassandra addressed him. "N... No, ma'am. Gives me the jitters."

Cassandra, you know better, she thought. *Wake up and remember who you're speaking to.* "So, how are you feeling today? You look relaxed," she remarked, trying to put him at ease. He bobbed his head

98

back and forth anxiously. "You know, Andrew, you've made incredible progress over the past few months, and I have an idea. How would you like to work part-time in the adolescent center, with some of the younger children staying at the hospital?"

His nervousness increased. "You mean babies and stuff?"

"No, not babies. Boys and girls between the ages of six and twelve. I believe they would enjoy your company. You'll be with several nurses from the hospital, so nothing bad could happen. Besides, your card tricks would bring them so much joy."

A glimmer of excitement appeared in Andrew's eyes as he removed his deck. "You really think they'd like me?"

"I think you're an incredible magician. Later you can show me that cool trick with the disappearing King," she laughed. "Right now we have other things to discuss."

Andrew obediently put away his cards, his head no longer twitching and his hands relaxed. Cassandra made a mental note of her session, pleased with the progress she was witnessing. The hour went by quickly. "I'll see you in two days, and we'll arrange for you to meet the children," she said, bidding him farewell.

Once he left, Cassandra turned in her chair, glancing out the window. She noticed that only six cars remained in the staff parking lot. *Will things ever slow down?* She gathered several patient files and placed them in her briefcase. The drive home was smooth, free of traffic.

Normally, Cassandra tried to leave work at the office, but tonight she had no choice but to bring some administrative work home. Reports on patients with psychological disorders and drug addictions awaited her attention. As one of four interns counseling seventy-five patients with various disorders, Cassandra felt the weight of her responsibilities. She had proven her abilities time and again, even organizing weekly brainstorming sessions with her fellow interns, categorizing each patient according to their specific treatment needs. While the administration often commended her efforts, she longed for tangible rewards such as extra time off or a small bonus. She smiled at the thought, focusing on her immediate desire to reach home.

Cassandra had sensed the competitive nature of one of her senior counselors, David Reynolds, who often downplayed her enthusiasm. Chance had offered her advice on how to navigate the tricky dynamics. She appreciated his guidance, even when it was unsolicited or occasionally misguided. As soon as she arrived home, he prepared a relaxing bath for her.

Chance lovingly scrubbed Cassandra's back, his touch soothing as hot water cascaded over her. "Feeling better?" he asked.

"I never want this to end," Cassandra sighed, savoring the moment.

"Do you see your workload easing up?" Chance inquired.

Cassandra reached for her wineglass. "It feels like things are only getting busier. Remember those weeks when you had to work late?"

Chance nodded, enjoying a lull between projects. "Those were project deadlines that I knew would eventually end."

Cassandra leaned back in the tub, the water enveloping her shoulders. "Patients are different. It's like peeling an onion. Each layer seems the same on the surface, but as you go deeper, you discover more complexities. I don't know when I'll ever reach the core of some of my patients."

Chance playfully scooped up a handful of bubbles and placed them on her head. "If I made onion soup for dinner, would that help?"

With her head crowned in bubbles, Cassandra chuckled. "Give it a try."

* * *

At eleven in the evening, Cassandra logged onto the Internet, a nightly ritual before bed. As the software loaded, she glanced at her wall calendar turned to June, marveling at how quickly time had flown. She had mixed feelings about the Internet—it provided immediate correspondence, but often meant more work. However, without it, she never would have met Chance. Her eyes wandered to the letters sent by doctors at the hospital. Suddenly, she noticed a familiar username.

My dearest AngelEyes,
I invite you to spend the next weekend with me at a secluded bed and breakfast in Cape Cod. I checked your calendar and saw no appointments or commitments. I hope you don't mind, but I went ahead and scheduled your mini vacation. I won't accept no for an answer because I have something very important to share with you.
Faithfully yours, Chance2

Cassandra's eyes filled with tears as she logged off, eager to join him. After a passionate evening with her man, her curiosity piqued. "So, what's this important thing you wanted to share with me?" she asked.

Chance turned off the light and kissed her goodnight with a subtle wink. As she lay there in silence, her mind danced with possibilities.

* * *

Cassandra and Chance sat down for dinner the following evening at home, but she couldn't help but bring her patient files to the table. "I wish I could peel away a few more layers of this man's onion," she sighed, her gaze fixed on Fred's file. Chance listened attentively, serving himself another helping of salad.

"Why do you think he despises his family?" Chance asked, genuinely curious.

"I'm not entirely sure. It seems he's resentful of his younger handicapped brother, who received most of their parents' attention. He finds pleasure in setting fires in abandoned buildings and has recently begun self-destructive behavior like pulling out his own hair and setting it on fire. I'm worried he'll end up hurting himself, and I don't know how he's been getting access to matches," she explained, concern evident in her voice.

As Cassandra spoke, Chance's mind drifted back in time. Her words became a distant murmur as memories flooded his thoughts. He remembered his tenth birthday party when he received the Lionel train set he had always wanted. However, the joy of the day quickly turned sour when Seth opened his present.

* * *

"Where is my chemistry set?" young Seth angrily pushed the fire truck aside.

"Are you going to ruin Chance's birthday too?" Kevin scolded. "Is this how you show your appreciation?"

Chance looked guiltily at his train set and then at his brother's firetruck. "Seth, do you want to trade?"

"I don't want your stupid present!" Seth ran upstairs in a fit of rage.

Kevin pounded his fist on the table. He poured himself a shot of whiskey. "That brat doesn't deserve a chemistry set!" Later, they smelled smoke and rushed upstairs.

Seth had set his bed on fire and stood in his room, admiring his handiwork. "You forgot to bring my firetruck!"

* * *

Interrupting Cassandra mid-sentence, Chance blurted out, "Maybe his family cares for him more than he realizes!"

Cassandra was taken aback by his outburst. She got up from the table and walked around to massage his shoulders, trying to offer comfort. He visibly relaxed under her touch.

"I'm sorry for snapping like that. We both need this trip to Cape Cod more than ever. It's still happening, right?" Chance asked, a hint of uncertainty in his voice.

"Absolutely!" Cassandra replied, leaning closer to his ear. "Are you sure you're okay?"

Taking a deep breath, Chance nodded that he was fine. They finished their meal in silence, cleaning up together but exchanging few words. Cassandra decided she wouldn't discuss such heavy topics with him for now. *He's thinking of Seth.*

* * *

They arrived at the Cape Cod bed and breakfast for a much-needed two-day escape. It was late on Friday, and both Cassandra and Chance were feeling the weight of exhaustion. Stepping into the mansion, they marveled at the grand foyer and the plush carpeted staircase leading to the second floor. Antique vases and lamps adorned the house, catching their attention. Chance's eyes were drawn to a grandfather clock in the hallway. He stood still, listening to the rhythmic ticking of the ancient timepiece.

"Breakfast is served between seven and nine," their hostess informed them, guiding them up the stairs. She opened the door to their room. "If there's anything you need, feel free to ask. Have a wonderful night."

Cassandra caught the scent of cedar woodwork mingled with the fragrant flowers from the hallway. She watched as Chance lowered his arms, ready to carry her across the threshold.

"You're such a romantic," she chuckled.

Chance lifted her into the air, stumbling with intentional clumsiness. She wrapped her arms around his neck, playfully tickling his cheek as he carried her. In his embrace, she seized the moment for a passionate kiss.

Taking in the interior of their room, Cassandra sighed with contentment. It was a beautiful space adorned with antique oak furniture and a queen-sized bed positioned near two windows overlooking the Atlantic. She ran her fingers across the silk curtains, relishing the luxurious feel. The vibrant quilt enticed Chance to plop onto the bed, and Cassandra joined him, savoring the tranquility of their surroundings. The room offered a picturesque view of the ocean, accompanied by the gentle sound of lapping waves and the salty aroma of the sea wafting through the window.

"Do you hear that?" Cassandra whispered. "The whispers of waves."

They cherished their evening of absolute privacy: no phones, faxes, or emails, just the blissful ocean breeze enveloping their senses. The following morning, as they enjoyed a continental breakfast, the sun beamed through the dining room windows, filling the space with warmth. Their hostess provided recommendations for local attractions.

"One of my favorite pastimes is walks along the beach," she mentioned after describing the nearby shops.

Later, as they strolled along the expansive beach, hand in hand, rows of perpetual waves kissed the shoreline. The Atlantic acted as a tranquil ensemble, presenting nature's soothing melody of solace. The warm, salty air reminded them of their need to escape from the bustling city life.

As she held his hand, Cassandra said, "You can smell the ocean from anywhere along this shore..."

"...and you can see for miles and miles to the distant land..." he said, glancing over the horizon.

"...and the gulls are welcoming us to their gorgeous beach..." she said, gazing upward.

Chance removed his sandals. "...with our toes feeling the warmth of the morning sun in the sand..."

"...and our hearts are at peace with the clean air we breathe..." she smiled, fighting her desire to laugh.

"...and our love knows no bounds like the world we see..."

She turned to face him. "...and our love knows no bounds like the world we see..."

They walked along the shore for a couple of miles before realizing how far down the beach they had travelled. As they turned back, she said, "This was such a great idea."

"There's more," he said in a mysterious tone.

"Oh, yes. The surprise," she winked.

* * *

Cassandra savored the last bite of her sumptuous entree, her taste buds tingling with delight. Pausing to take in the cozy ambiance of the restaurant, she admired the maritime antiques adorning the walls and ceiling. Chance had enthralled her with stories of the artifacts throughout their meal: antique sextants, rudders, and an array of fishing lures swaying gently in the sailboat rigging. Her eyes were drawn to the lobster traps and nets suspended above, a testament to Chance's profound knowledge of fishing and sailing. The tablecloth, fashioned from ship's sails, added to the enchanting atmosphere, while a lantern, once used to guide boats at night, cast a warm, inviting glow between them.

As their eyes locked, immersed in the blue flame of the lantern, Cassandra's heart skipped a beat when she noticed their waiter approaching. A surge of anticipation coursed through her, and she silently hoped her instincts were leading her down the right path.

In an orchestrated moment, two waiters wheeled out a magnificent ice sculpture, dazzling and grand. A heart-shaped carving with their initials meticulously etched in its center glistened before her eyes, capturing her breath. At the base of the sculpture, an exquisitely detailed open palm held a hidden treasure, unbeknownst to Cassandra. The soft melody of a violin filled the air, drawing attention from those around them. Cassandra blushed, feeling the gaze of diners upon her. Her eyes were fixed on the ethereal beauty of the ice sculpture, but her attention soon shifted to the small maroon felt box nestled in the open hand. Her hands trembled with anticipation as she reached for it. With a delicate touch, she gingerly opened the box, and gasped in awe at the sight before her.

A golden antique ring adorned with a circle of smaller diamonds encircling a breathtaking pear-shaped diamond sparkled within the box, casting a mesmerizing glow. As Chance descended to one knee, his hands resting on her lap, Cassandra's body quivered with excitement and emotion. She placed her trembling hands upon his shoulders, their eyes locked in an unbreakable connection.

In a voice filled with adoration, Chance uttered the words that danced upon her heart. "Cassandra, I love you with all my heart. Will you marry me?"

Tears of joy welled up in her eyes as she whispered, "Yes, yes, I will marry you." In a rush of euphoria, she sealed her answer with a passionate kiss, their promise celebrated by the cheers and applause of fellow diners.

Chance retrieved the ring from its delicate confines, a grin spreading across his face, mirroring Cassandra's joyous expression. As the diamond slipped onto her finger, Cassandra basked in the overwhelming realization that she was alive and in love, embracing this breathtaking chapter of her life. In that instance, she understood the profound impact Chance had on her soul, and she knew that their sentiment was boundless.

"What a nice way to end a beautiful chapter. Every woman's dream-to find the perfect man," Elizabeth said with a smile to the camera that captured her show.

"But as we know, a ghost from Chance's past still lurked in the background," Brad said, adding to the intrigue as he continued to describe more scenes from his novel.

"Indeed. I can see why Cassandra felt so concerned for their well-being. She must have tried hard to be supportive of Chance's complex family situation."

"Quite honestly, she was terrified, especially by what happens those years later. But I won't spoil the surprise. There's only so much I can tell our viewers."

"I'm most curious about Chance's relationship with Seth. Can you share this with our viewers?" Elizabeth said, leaning forward with anticipation.

"Things were going great for Chance and Cassandra," Brad began, "but they were always confronted by the prospect of Seth's inevitable release from jail. After all, as Chance learned, you can never hide from your past..."

Chapter 5

The Catholic church, adorned in an ethereal glow, seemed like a page plucked from a fairy tale. Cassandra's wedding unfolded with an air of love and commitment, surpassing her wildest dreams. Months of preparation had culminated in a display of brightly colored floral bouquets and flickering candles surrounding the wooden altar frame. As the sun filtered through the stained glass, casting a kaleidoscope of hues, the couple stood at the altar, their hearts entwined in the moment, savoring the priest's final words resonating throughout the sacred space.

"...and by the powers vested in me by the Commonwealth of Massachusetts, I now pronounce you man and wife. You may kiss the bride."

Chance's lips met Cassandra's, and her eyes sparkled with joy as his kiss bestowed upon her the promise of a lifetime. The applause of their family and friends echoed through the pews, but they were lost in each other, immersed in the celebration of their commitment to each other. Cassandra, radiant in her full-length, beaded wedding gown, and Chance, dashing in his black tuxedo, embarked on this new chapter of their lives together.

After greeting their guests in the receiving line, the couple retreated into the awaiting limousine, their hearts brimming with contentment. Cassandra nestled into Chance's shoulder, adored the serenity that surrounded them. Her words escaped in a soft whisper, "Chance, everything is just perfect."

He enveloped her in a tender embrace, his arms offering solace and protection. "You are perfect," he murmured, his voice laced with adoration. But amidst the joyous occasion, an unwelcome thought infiltrated Chance's mind—a pact made long ago with Seth, his troubled past resurfacing at the most unexpected moment.

In a hazy recollection, Chance remembered their childhood promise, forged with a knife and a mingling of blood. Seth's words reverberated in his mind, "Do you want me to be your best man someday? Don't you want to be mine?" The memory evoked conflicting emotions, a reminder of a bond forged in innocence and naivety. But Seth's ominous declaration, "Unless we decide to never get married," lingered like an unspoken shadow.

"Honey?" Cassandra's voice broke through Chance's reverie, and he returned his gaze to her, refocusing on the present. "You still there?"

He shifted his attention back to the limousine, his eyes meeting hers. "I can't believe we finally made it," he confessed, awe and gratitude coloring his voice.

Later, surrounded by the harmonious melodies of live music and the aroma of delectable food, Cassandra and Chance glowed in their reception. One hundred guests filled the space, eagerly sharing in their joy. Cassandra introduced her family to Chance's parents, intertwining the strands of their lives.

As Helen, Cassandra's friend and confidante, inquired about the man standing with Chance, Cassandra revealed, "That's my brother, Morgan. You met him once before, about a year ago."

Helen's surprise was evident as she replied, "Really? I don't recall." The momentary lapse puzzled her, given the multitude of guests in attendance.

Led by Cassandra, Helen ventured past the reception table, guided by the rhythmic melodies of the quintet, which played a diverse selection of music, ranging from jazz to pop. Chance indulged in the livelier tunes, acknowledging the desire for their guests to dance. Engaged in conversation with Morgan, Chance's attention abruptly shifted when he noticed Cassandra and Helen approaching.

"Morgan," Cassandra called out, unknowingly interrupting their conversation.

"What?" Morgan responded, raising his voice to be heard above the band's boisterous rhythm. "What did you say?"

She yelled, her voice carrying through the momentary lull in the music, "I said, this is my friend, Helen!" The sudden silence allowed everyone to hear her exclamation, resulting in a collective gaze toward the blushing bride. Sheepishly, Cassandra smiled at the singer, urging them to continue playing. Morgan chuckled at the comical turn of events, and as the music resumed, he extended his hand to Helen. "Nice to see you again, Helen. Care to dance?"

With a grateful nod, Helen accepted his invitation, and they gracefully moved to the rhythm of the music. Meanwhile, Chance, unable to resist the opportunity for mischief, approached from behind and playfully pinched his new bride.

"Ouch! Why did you do that?" Cassandra exclaimed, taken aback by the unexpected jolt.

"Just another one of Cupid's stray arrows," Chance quipped.

* * *

Two days later, the newlyweds found themselves basking on the warm sandy shores of Honolulu. The sun's gentle caress embraced them as they lounged on the beach, enjoying the idyllic surroundings. Amidst the tranquility, a serious and introspective expression crossed Chance's face. After a half-hour of internal debate, he summoned the courage to voice his thoughts. Cassandra turned to face him, shielding her eyes from the brilliant sun. He hesitated for a moment, his voice barely a whisper, as the words escaped his lips before he could retract them.

"I was wondering how your patient is doing," Chance said.

"Oh?" Cassandra said as she propped her head on her hand. "He's doing alright, I suppose. Still harboring resentment, but I believe I've managed to unravel a few more layers to his onion."

Curiosity brimming, Chance said, "Has his family attempted to reach out to him during his time at the hospital?"

Cassandra sighed, a tinge of sadness shadowing her features. "No, unfortunately not. They've mostly given up on him." A heavy silence settled between them, thick with unspoken emotions. *Why is he thinking of Seth now?* Sensing the weight of this conversation, Cassandra suggested they take a swim. "Come on, hunky hubby! It'll do us both good!"

She sprinted into the ocean, with Chance close behind.

* * *

As the alarm clock blared on the bureau back home, Cassandra reveled in dreams of their honeymoon, reliving each cherished moment. Oblivious to the urgency of time, she failed to hear its call. Chance, opening his eyes and realizing the late hour, gently shook her awake. Aware that she would be running late for work, she dashed off to the shower, her bare form a vision of natural beauty.

"I'll make coffee," Chance offered, rising from the bed. He prepared the elixir, savoring its rich aroma as it filled the room. A half-hour later, Cassandra downed two cups, hurriedly organizing her files before rushing out the door. "Kiss, kiss," she called out, her voice trailing behind her.

Chance, moving at a slower pace than usual on this first morning after their honeymoon, lingered over his coffee, lost in contemplation. His mind wandered back to his twin brother, whose presence loomed like a phantom shadow. For months, he had kept his thoughts about Seth to himself, choosing not to burden Cassandra with his inner turmoil. But lately, the weight of those unspoken emotions had begun to interfere with his ability to focus on work. "This is a battle between me and him," he whispered to himself, the resolve firm in his voice.

With Seth serving his ten-year sentence just a few miles away, Chance's thoughts turned to Cassandra's patient. Picking up the phone, he dialed the number to the corrections office, driven by a relentless desire to find a balance between his two relationships. Though worried about how Cassandra would react, he knew he needed to share his feelings with her. The officer provided him with visiting hours, and as Chance hung up, he resolved to have a heartfelt conversation with his new bride.

* * *

"You what?" Cassandra's voice quivered with anxiety and concern, her body tensing with unease.

"I need for you to understand why I have to see Seth," Chance pleaded, his voice filled with desperation.

The scrape of her chair against the floor echoed through the dining area as she pushed it back, rising to her feet. Each step she took towards the living room seemed measured, as if the weight of her thoughts mirrored the heaviness in her heart. Tears welled in her eyes as she closed them, refusing to succumb to the overwhelming flood of emotions threatening to engulf her. "You knew this day would come," she thought, her back turned towards Chance.

The soft melody of music drifted through the air, grating on Cassandra's nerves like sandpaper. With determined steps, she crossed the room, her hand reaching out to silence the noise, plunging the space into an abrupt silence. Meanwhile, Chance remained rooted to his seat at the table, his appetite forgotten in the wake of lingering tension. He laid his fork down, his gaze fixed on Cassandra's retreating form, a silent plea hanging in the air.

As Cassandra turned to face him, the weight of unspoken words hung heavy between them, suffocating in its intensity.

"My dear Chance, now I understand why you've been so curious about my patient. The tragic reality is that trying to reconnect with Seth is not only perilous for you and us, but it's also futile. Seth is not only physically dangerous, but he's emotionally and mentally unstable. He is incapable of feeling remorse for the pain he has caused others. As a psychologist, I have witnessed the aftermath of such encounters, and I implore you to seek alternative solutions. There are therapists who can help navigate these complexities. You are my husband, and I love you deeply. Please, let us find a path forward together, a path that ensures our safety and happiness."

Chance raised his head, anguish etched into every line on his face. "I still need to see him. It's as if a magnetic force is pulling me closer, and I can't ignore it."

Even though Cassandra had braced herself for this conversation, she realized in that moment that no amount of preparation could shield her from the flood of emotions that washed over her. She respected Chance's determination to find a compromise, to bridge the gap between his past and their present, but the haunting memories of the past resurfaced with force. The nightmares that had plagued her sleep were now threatening to invade their waking moments.

Unable to fully articulate her thoughts, she managed to utter, "I don't want to know when you visit him. Leave me out of it!" Her words were heavy with anguish and determination. Chance, understanding the weight of her pain, tried to draw her close with a kiss, but she instinctively held back. Seth had become a barrier between them, and he knew she had every right to harbor resentment towards his brother. As much as he wanted to believe he could forget about Seth, the undeniable bond of their twinhood exerted its pull. Amidst the conflict within him, he couldn't help but acknowledge Cassandra's words.

"Chance, he may be your twin brother, but more tragically, he's now my brother-in-law," Cassandra gasped.

* * *

"What visitor?" Seth's voice dripped with cynicism as he rose from his bunk, tucking in his shirt. He followed the guard through C Block, the clanging of steel doors and the imposing presence of armed guards lending an air of harsh reality to his surroundings. The blaring intercom relayed official announcements that Seth found oddly amusing.

"This way," the guard barked, leading him down a steel corridor towards the front of the prison.

The doors clanged shut, and Seth's eyes scanned the state-of-the-art surveillance system with curiosity and detachment. He hadn't traversed this path before. As they reached the visitor's booth, the unwelcome presence of a visitor loomed before him, an inconvenience he couldn't avoid. The guard punched in his access code, granting Seth entry into the booth.

"Get moving!" the guard snapped, pointing towards the booths. "Number six."

Seth entered the room, his gaze drifting over the friendly decor of blue wallpaper and small potted flowers that seemed out of place in this environment. "Just for our families. How nice," he thought cynically. The phoniness of the room grated on his nerves, and as he passed by several booths, he overheard snippets of conversations between prisoners and their loved ones. His thoughts lingered on booth four. "I smell you, brother," he muttered under his breath, before taking his place behind the chair at the sixth booth.

"Surprise, surprise," Seth muttered, his lips forming the words that Chance couldn't hear through the thick glass partition.

Chance sat across from him, hands resting calmly on the table, though his heart throbbed with anticipation. He tried to appear relaxed, to suppress the maelstrom of emotions swirling within him. His gaze locked onto Seth, separated by one-inch bulletproof glass, connected only by two phones. Chance picked up his phone, thinking, "This is ridiculous." Just as the guard approached, Seth pulled out the chair, sat down, and picked up the phone.

"Hello, little brother. How's life?" Seth's voice reverberated through the phone, his words laced with slyness and taunting familiarity.

Chance studied Seth's hardened features, fighting against the onslaught of emotions that threatened to overwhelm him. "I've been thinking about you lately and wanted to see how you were doing," he replied, his voice betraying a mixture of apprehension and genuine concern.

As Chance stared at Seth, frozen in time and imprisoned behind bars, he couldn't help but feel a profound sense of disconnect. Three years had passed since Seth's incarceration, and the toll was evident. Seth's unkempt hair and weathered beard made him appear older than his years. His face seemed gaunt and pale, devoid of visible scars or signs of abuse. Seth's words, carefully chosen and spoken slowly, struck Chance like a heavy blow.

"It's a regular picnic in here. I wish I could introduce you to my closest friends, but some of them are still recovering from recent injuries," Seth sneered, his voice dripping with both mockery and underlying bitterness.

Chance fought to steady himself, his emotions churning within him as he met Seth's hardened gaze. "I came because I thought it was time we talked," he said, mustering all the resolve he could find.

Seth leaned back in his chair, a calculated nonchalance emanating from his every movement. "Forgive and forget?" he suggested, a glimmer of mischief dancing in his eyes.

"No, Seth," Chance replied firmly. "But you're my brother."

Chance's eyes instinctively darted to his ring finger as Seth's gaze followed suit, a hint of a cruel smile tugging at his lips. "Where's your pretty wife? Doesn't she want to visit her new brother-in-law?" Seth taunted, his words designed to provoke.

Panic flashed across Chance's face as his expression turning serious. "I came here to talk about us, not about—" he began, only to be interrupted by Seth, who adopted a fake British accent.

"*Cassandra*," Seth sneered, emphasizing her name.

Suppressing the urge to react, Chance shifted the conversation. "It looks like you're being taken care of in here. That's good," he remarked, searching for common ground amidst the tumultuous sea of emotions.

Seth wasted no time with his cutting reply, his words dripping with sarcasm and bitterness. "Ah, the luxurious accommodations you've booked me into, dear brother. Such joy to revel in the delights of catered meals, unexpected laundry service, and midnight spot checks by the diligent maid. And let's not forget the culinary expertise of the cooks, graduates from the esteemed Homer Simpson school of cuisine. Oh, and the melodious symphony of farting toilets. The only thing missing now is that delightful home video of me and Cassandra to keep me company."

Incensed, Chance remained silent, refusing to fall into his rabbit hole.

Seth leaned back, his gaze shifting to a Norman Rockwell painting on the wall behind him. "You know, Chance, there's so much culture here that I never want to leave," he drawled, his voice laced with a hint of menace. Lowering his voice, he added, "Care to hear a few scandalous tales of prison lust?"

Frustration flickered across Chance's face, his attempt at levity overshadowed by the weight of their conversation. "Let's stay focused on us, Seth. Save the rest for your bestseller."

Seth's cold gaze bore into Chance's eyes, savoring his brother's unease. "I don't get many visitors, and I must say, you're as interesting as they come," he sneered.

As their time expired, the guard intervened, signaling the end of their visit. Seth hung up the phone, walking out of the visitors' area with an air of arrogance. Chance, still holding the phone in his hand, watched Seth disappear into the confines of his concrete prison. Minutes later, he emerged from the visitors' booth, his mind swirling with conflicting emotions. Following the guard through the prison, he couldn't help but long for the warmth of natural sunlight and fresh air, a stark contrast to the bleakness of his brother's existence. The clanging steel doors punctuated his thoughts, serving as a stark reminder of Seth's reality. As he walked through the jail, he cursed the judicial system while also praying for a glimmer of hope.

* * *

Cassandra observed Chance closely as they sat down at the dinner table, her heart fluttering with unease. She sensed that something had transpired, that he had visited Seth. Nervously pouring herself a glass of merlot, she tried to keep her composure. "Anything exciting happen at work?" she asked, attempting to divert his attention.

Chance struggled to meet her gaze, his eyes fixed on the untouched mound of mashed potatoes on his plate. After a lengthy pause, he mustered the courage to speak. "I visited Seth today," he admitted quietly.

114

Cassandra closed her eyes, summoning her strength. "And how is the monster?" she inquired, her voice tinged with apprehension.

"Fine, I guess," Chance sighed, his voice devoid of its usual warmth.

She bit her lip, fighting back her fears. The ensuing silence was suffocating, their unspoken thoughts hanging in the air. They had always been comfortable with their shared silence, but now it felt like an insurmountable chasm. "Are you going to see him again?" Cassandra finally asked, her voice trembling with vulnerability and concern.

Chance nodded slowly, fully aware of the weight of his decision. Before Cassandra could stop herself, she abruptly left the table, seeking solitude in the bathroom. Chance remained seated, his thoughts consumed by the strained atmosphere between them. He listened as the sound of running water filled the silence, her way of finding temporary respite. If she wanted to discuss it, he would be there to answer her questions. As the bathtub filled, he cleared the dining table, removing the remnants of their uneaten meal. He hoped that the soothing warmth of the water would calm her troubled spirit.

They climbed into bed without sharing a kiss or an embrace, the distance between them palpable. As Chance gazed at Cassandra's hair, he couldn't help but feel a pang of loneliness. Despite his efforts to understand her feelings, he sensed, for the first time, the absence of her support.

Cassandra lay in bed, immersed in her novel, while Chance attempted to focus on an article about a recent CAD upgrade. Their first significant conflict had surfaced, and she prayed that he shared her desire to find a resolution. Lowering her book, she switched off the light, the darkness enveloping them both. Soon, she succumbed to sleep, her soft snoring a stark contrast to the restlessness consuming Chance. He quietly slipped out of bed and made his way to the office, booting up his computer.

When they awoke the next morning, Chance attempted to offer his usual morning greeting, but Cassandra seemed distant, lost in her own thoughts as she retreated to the bathroom. He watched as she silently read a newspaper, avoiding eye contact. He knew that seeing his face—*Seth's face*—would only stir up more confusion in her mind. Despite her internal struggles, he loved her deeply, and he tried to draw strength from his understanding of Seth's disorder to guide him. But like a roller coaster careening out of control, their emotions seemed to have a will of their own, peaking and plunging without warning.

"I'm ok," she murmured with sadness in her eyes and distracted by work. "I'm expecting a letter from David Reynolds. I'll be right back," she announced, grabbing her coffee and fluffing Chance's hair before retreating into her office.

As she waited for her computer to boot up, she gazed out the window, reminiscing about the joyful moments they had shared in their backyard. A sense of guilt washed over her. *He doesn't deserve your cold shoulder*, she scolded herself. Once the internet chimed, she accessed her business mailbox, and her heart skipped a beat. It was her only letter, and it came from her best friend. Tears welled up in her eyes as she read Chance's sentiment.

"My Dearest Cassandra, My heart is always with you, wherever you are. As I walk through my day, I feel you so close to me. I long for those moments when we can make up with a simple kiss, bringing us to the heights of passion. Nothing can come between us. Your support during this time is vital to me, and I know how hard it is for you. All I desire is for you to experience the eternal happiness and comfort I feel when I am with you. Please know that I am devoted to you. You are my shining light, and I am your helpless little onion who only wants to strip away all the layers that surround my soul. My love to you forever and a day, Chance"

Cassandra reread his endearingly corny words, her hand pressed against her trembling lips. She printed the letter and filed it among the many others she cherished. Just as she was lost in her thoughts, Chance quietly entered her office, his voice tender as he called her name. Embarrassed, she brushed away the tears and stood up to greet him. No words were needed between them. He gathered her in his arms, carrying her through the house. Placing her on the bed, he untied her robe with deliberate slowness. Cassandra knew it was irresponsible, but in that moment, she was willing to be late for work.

* * *

Weeks passed with fewer discussions about Seth. Chance's business flourished, attracting new clients with each passing week. After winning a major contract from a pool of six competitors, he declared it to be a banner year. Cassandra, eager to be involved in their financial planning, spent hours reviewing their records with him. Their combined incomes allowed them to live comfortably, and she took it upon herself to open a retirement account and money market funds to secure their future. She began to envision the next phase of their marriage, filled with happiness and stability.

One evening, as they sat together reading in the living room, Cassandra broached the subject that had been on her mind. "I was thinking it would be nice to have a home all to ourselves. We can afford it now," she said casually, hoping he would understand the deeper desires hidden within her words. She couldn't help but feel a tinge of fear regarding Seth's potential return to their current home. "Don't get me wrong, I love this house and our upstairs neighbors, but... well, you know. I was just thinking out loud. We can drop it if you want," she added, returning her focus to her book while occasionally stealing glances at him.

Chance glanced up from his own book, a hint of confusion in his eyes. "Well," he began, "what if we rented out the downstairs? The market is tough to sell right now, but there are plenty of potential tenants out there."

"Really?" Cassandra's eyes sparkled with delight as she leaned forward, planting a kiss on his lips. He lowered his book, eager to welcome her affection. Time seemed to stand still as her fingers traced the contours of his jaw. In that moment, Cassandra knew how to show her appreciation and satisfy her own desires. Moments of shared intimacy passed, leaving Chance sighing with contentment.

Several months later, Chance and Cassandra sat in the office of their real estate agent, Todd Walker. Chance signed his name one final time, sealing the deal. Todd rose from his chair, extending his hand with a congratulatory smile. "Congratulations, Mr. and Mrs. Macklin. You are now the proud owners of a beautiful new home in West Newton."

Cassandra's excitement bubbled over as she imagined all the details she needed to attend to in preparation for the move. The large Victorian house with its spacious yard in a quiet part of town was a dream come true. The previous owner had taken care of major updates, including electrical wiring, plumbing, re-shingling and painting the exterior a sophisticated gun metal gray, and installing a more efficient boiler.

They had settled into their new home, carefully orchestrating the process while managing their additional commitments. Each night, they unpacked a little, making steady progress on weekends. Cassandra felt a sense of peace wash over her as she finally escaped the reminders of Seth that had haunted their previous house.

* * *

Seth stared forward, his gaze fixed on Chance, who held the phone beyond the glass barricade. Just like their previous visits, Chance patiently waited for Seth to pick up his phone. Seth couldn't help but silently admire his brother's well-tailored attire, contrasting sharply with his own inmate attire. With a smirk, he taunted Chance.

"Looks like married life has done you some good, Chance."

"Did you get my package?" Chance inquired.

"The cigarettes and magazines were a nice touch," Seth replied, acknowledging the gesture.

"I can get you anything you want. Within reason, of course."

Seth's eyes gleamed with mischief. "A hacksaw and file, perhaps?"

Chance clarified, "You know, books, puzzles, chocolate."

Intrigued by the offer, Seth paused for a moment. "The library here is dull. I could use some books on microbiology. You recall my petri experiment from years ago, right? The one you killed!"

"What?" Chance raised an eyebrow, unable to remember such an event. Nonetheless, he made a note of his brother's request.

"What else is new with you these days? You seem kind of... happy. What's it like being happy?" Seth inquired, trying to needle his brother. "And what about your loving wife? Remember how much she craved me when we first kissed?" Seth's biting words were laced with nostalgia and provocation, aimed squarely at Chance's heart.

Chance closed his eyes, taking a deep breath to steady himself. He changed the subject, refusing to let Seth get under his skin. "I come here with some bad news."

"Okay then, move it along," Seth said, feigning nonchalance. "I could use some cheering up right about now."

"It's about Grandpa. He passed away a couple of weeks ago," Chance revealed, knowing that Seth's confinement prevented him from attending the funeral.

Seth looked to his left, closed his eyes, and sighed. Glancing at the guard by the door, he focused on the conversation taking place nearby. When he turned back to his brother, there was a smile on his face. "It's about fucking time!"

Chance had debated whether to share the news, but Seth's reaction surprised him. "Is it because he punished you?"

Seth's words dripped with bitterness. "Dear Grandpa used to love me more than you will ever know," Seth replied with disdain and sarcasm.

As he felt Seth's sarcastic words, memories from their tumultuous adolescence flooded Chance's mind.

* * *

"What's wrong?" young Chance had asked, startled to find Seth in tears, curled up on his bed.

"Go away!" Seth sobbed, his voice filled with anguish.

Chance closed the cabin door, straining to hear his brother's cries. Uncertain of what to do, he descended the stairs to the kitchen, where their grandparents were.

"I haven't seen you for hours," Nana greeted him with a smile.

Chance adored his grandmother, not only because she spoiled them but also because she took an avid interest in their outdoor adventures, despite her advancing age. With her strong Irish accent, she baked traditional dishes, from soda bread to corned beef and cabbage. While both he and Seth weren't fans of bland potatoes or heavy bread, Nana always made up for it with her delicious cookies. Chance took a bite from a freshly baked one.

"These are delicious, Nana," he complimented her.

"Save your appetite," she responded, handing him another with a mischievous whisper, "One more couldn't hurt."

Chance glanced at his grandfather, his eyes filled with an unnerving intensity. Stop staring at me, he silently pleaded, unwilling to voice his thoughts. Grandpa always seemed grumpy and eccentric, though occasionally he would show them kindness. Engaging in small talk, Chance asked about the military ribbons displayed above the living room mantle.

Samuel Macklin's war years remained shrouded in silence. He rarely spoke about his time in the military, and only Nana knew about the numerous conflicts he had endured. It was she who had convinced him to display his service ribbons. But Chance remained oblivious to the dark and twisted history of his grandfather's service—a history marked by isolation, conflicts with fellow squad members, and a commanding officer who harbored an intense hatred for the young recruit.

Samuel's cold and sometimes demonic side had reached its peak during boot camp, where he was subjected to nightly runs around the compound, carrying a rifle high over his head. Through thick puddles of mud and heavy rain, other recruits would jeer at him from behind screen windows. But what Samuel tried to bury deep within his memories was the harrowing event that occurred two years later. Members of his own squad had attacked him, binding and gagging him before locking him in an isolation room, where an instructor lay in wait. Samuel had endured a brutal assault, a vicious violation that tore at his very soul. These memories clung to Samuel Macklin like a haunting obsession, one that he refused to share with anyone.

Chance, unaware of the torment that plagued his grandfather, asked Nana about the awards. But his gaze always returned to his grandpa.

Samuel took a noisy sip of his coffee and changed subjects. "It's uncanny how much you look like Seth!"

Caught off guard, Chance stumbled over his words. "Well... I..."

The ticking of the wall clock behind him reverberated in Chance's head, amplifying his discomfort. The suffocating silence engulfed him, and he yearned to escape the room, as if the air had grown too thin. Unable to bear it any longer, he excused himself from the table, casting a sheepish glance at his grandpa as he left.

Ascending the stairs, Chance made his way to Seth's room. As he entered, he found his brother still curled up in a ball, lost in a restless sleep. Seth began to toss and turn, trapped in the grip of a nightmare. Chance whispered his name, his voice growing louder until Seth abruptly woke, letting out a piercing scream that startled Chance. Sweat poured down Seth's face, his eyes wild with terror. Overwhelmed, he buried his face in his pillow, tears streaming down his cheeks.

"Where is Grandpa now?" Seth choked out between sobs.

"In the kitchen. Are you coming down?" Chance replied, concern etched across his face.

"I'm not hungry," Seth replied, fearing the consequences of not making an appearance.

Later at the dinner table, tensions ran high. Grandpa's gaze bore into Seth, who kept his eyes fixed on his plate. They shared a secret, that much was evident to Chance, though he couldn't fathom its depths.

"Please pass the peas," Chance said, attempting to diffuse the tension.

Nana obliged with a forced smile. "What did you boys do this afternoon?"

"Not much," Seth muttered under his breath.

"Speak up, boy!" Grandpa snapped, his voice dripping with confrontation.

Seth remained silent and froze like a statue, further infuriating Samuel. In a fit of rage, the old man slammed his fists on the table, causing Seth to jerk upright, his face drained of color. Panic gripped Seth, and he bolted from the table, rushing up the stairs.

"When I come up, you better explain yourself!" Grandpa shouted after him.

"Leave me alone!" Seth's voice echoed through the house.

The rest of the dinner descended into an unsettling silence, weighed down by an unspoken darkness. Time seemed to drag on as Chance sat with his hands folded, too afraid to ask for his own dismissal. His plate lay empty before him, a stark reminder of the unease that permeated the room.

"Run along," Grandpa finally said, his voice carrying a hint of exhaustion after exchanging glances with Chance.

Relieved, Chance hurriedly left the table, seeking refuge in the adjacent bedroom. He lay on his bed, fearful of the impending punishment. Moments later, he heard a knock on Seth's door.

"It's your grandfather," Samuel's voice resonated through the wall.

Chance pressed his ear against the wall, straining to hear their conversation. He caught snippets of Seth's whimpering, and his imagination filled in the rest. The sound of metal clanging reached his ears, signaling that Grandpa was removing his belt. Holding his breath, Chance kept his ear glued to the wall, but to his surprise, he heard Seth groaning rather than the sound of a whipping. The absence of physical punishment puzzled him.

* * *

"Wake up, sleepyhead. Are you in la la land again?" Seth's voice pierced through the phone in prison, snapping Chance out of his reflection.

"Sorry," Chance responded, his voice laced with a tense edge. "Didn't realize I was interrupting your pity party What was all that about Grandpa?"

"Mind your own fucking business!" Seth's biting reply stung, and he abruptly hung up the phone.

Bitterness seeped through the partition, causing the hair on the back of Chance's neck to stand on end. As always, Seth had closed the clamshell of his anger, leaving Chance with no choice but to watch his brother return to his prison cell.

* * *

As they sat down for dinner, the atmosphere was unusually quiet. Cassandra tried to capture Chance's attention, but his thoughts were consumed by one person—his grandfather. She served herself more salad, patiently waiting for him to share the details of his latest encounter with Seth.

"He really got to you this time, didn't he?" she probed.

"Seth's just so messed up. Both him and... my grandfather. There's something he remembers that I don't. It's complicated," Chance responded, dropping his fork onto the table.

Cassandra retreated to the living room, where she put on a CD of jazz ballads, hoping to infuse Chance's mind with a sense of peace.

"Does he know that we moved?" Cassandra inquired, unable to use the man's name.

"No," Chance replied, his mind still dwelling on their earlier conversation. "Somehow, he sensed my happiness. I tried to appear unaffected. But sometimes, when I visit him, I see him so clearly, as if I see myself. I feel a connection, not to his anger or meanness, but to his sense of loss. It's hard to explain what clicks between us, but it's happened multiple times. I find myself caught in flashes of the past during our conversations, suddenly remembering fragments. Bits

122

and pieces. I wonder how he remembers those events, if he remembers them at all, or if he even cares.”

He opened a window, letting in the cool evening air. “Prison must be hell for him. I know how much Seth misses the outdoors.” Cassandra observed him closely, unsure of how to respond. A part of her secretly reveled in Seth’s suffering, but she couldn’t bring herself to express it. Chance took another deep breath and continued. “He’s aware of my feelings. It’s eerie how he notices so many things, subtle glances, the way I dress. He reads it all. It’s as if he has a part of me inside him, trying to break free. Do you have any theories about why he is this way?”

Hesitantly, Cassandra replied, acknowledging that Seth was a complex and unusual case. “Honestly, I can’t offer an impartial opinion. Chance, we’re just starting to enjoy our life together. We’ve talked about starting a family, and we both feel ready. But the timing is crucial, and the thought of this troubled man coming between us is horrifying. If I dwell on it too much, it makes me sick to my stomach. I still have nightmares. Everything related to him is a part of you, and now it’s a part of me.”

“He’s not going to hurt you again,” Chance assured her, but his eyes betrayed his words.

“Don’t you see, he is like a drug addiction,” she said, with her heart pounding. “He’s in your blood and possibly in our children’s blood. He’s the reason why we have conflicts in our marriage. I can’t bear the thought of him exacting his revenge by watching our marriage crumble like burnt toast in his hands.” Her voice trembled with the weight of her fear.

Chance stared deeply into her eyes, his mouth slightly ajar. “Nothing is going to come between us!”

Cassandra wondered if she could transcend her anger, sift through years of experience, and uncover the truth. Could she honestly help a man who had tried to kill her? She possessed the ability to temper her own rage and the knowledge that could potentially change the situation, but Seth’s presence clawed at her. Stretching her hand across the table, she placed it gently on his.

“We’re in this together. I promise,” she declared.

* * *

"When is he moving in?" Cassandra asked, her curiosity piqued.

"Sometime next week," Chance replied. He had called her at work, informing her that Greg was interested in renting the vacant first-floor apartment.

Cassandra knew that Lisa, their upstairs neighbor, was excited about the prospect of Greg moving downstairs, especially since they had recently become romantically involved. When Chance's previous tenant had abruptly vacated due to a family death, he had to hastily find a replacement. With Cassandra's not-so-subtle encouragement, he had posted the rental information on the bulletin board at his office. To his surprise, but not Cassandra's, Greg had expressed interest.

"Lisa, you're the first person I called," Greg began, discussing the idea of him moving into the downstairs apartment. Days prior, Greg and Lisa had mulled over the idea, both recognizing that it would allow them to foster their blossoming relationship while maintaining their independence. Plus, Greg and Brad had formed a special bond, enjoying activities like playing catch, video games, and soccer together.

Brad was thrilled at the prospect, exclaiming, "Killer!" upon hearing the news.

Although Chance wanted to approach the situation as a business matter and not get too emotionally involved, he couldn't help but feel a surge of excitement. Cassandra fired questions at him during dinner, eager to know all the details.

"What did Lisa say?" she inquired.

Before he could answer, the ringing phone interrupted their conversation. Chance grabbed the receiver and answered, "Hello?"

"Hi, Chance. It's Lisa. I hope it's not too late," she said with an unusual tone in her voice. Chance hoped it had nothing to do with Greg's move.

"No, not at all. What's up?" he asked, sensing the underlying strangeness in her voice.

"I wanted to show you something Brad wrote for his English class. I think you'll get a kick out of it."

Chance glanced at Cassandra, who watched him intently as he spoke. "Sure, I'll be over in twenty minutes." He hung up, a mischievous grin forming on his face. "Lisa wants to chat about Brad."

"What? You never chat," Cassandra responded, perplexed. She tried to pry out more details, but Chance skillfully evaded her inquiries. Determined not to play into his hand, she remained on the couch.

Chance chuckled as he got into his car and drove to Framingham.

Upon entering Lisa's house, she whispered, "Brad's asleep. I don't want him to know I showed you this." She led him to the living room, where Chance settled into Brad's reading chair. "It's about you, Chance."

He stared at the title of Brad's essay: "Friends of All Ages." A smile spread across his face as he read the opening paragraph. Lisa observed his every expression, eagerly waiting for him to finish reading the four-hundred-word essay.

"I don't know what to say," Chance exclaimed.

"I do." Lisa reached over and hugged him tightly. "Thanks for being such a great friend."

"Can I share this with Cassandra? She won't take 'no' for an answer. I'll bring it back tomorrow."

"Of course," Lisa laughed, pride radiating from her.

As Chance left with Brad's story, Lisa settled back into the living room, sitting in Brad's chair and basking in the warmth of her son's heartfelt words. Meanwhile, Chance arrived home to the sound of Cassandra splashing in the bathtub—a clear signal that she wanted him to come in and share his secret. He estimated that she had been in the water for nearly an hour and was probably turning into a prune. Enjoying the suspense, he turned on the television, raising the volume. Cassandra cleared her throat loudly and splashed even more, determined to get his attention. Minutes ticked by as she fought against her curiosity.

"Chance, what's going on?" she finally demanded.

All she heard in response was the random selection of late-night channels. Her curiosity reached its boiling point, and she refused to succumb to his tactic of having her run out of the tub naked. Peering around the corner, he admired her frustration.

"How's the water?" he playfully asked.

Startled, Cassandra replied with feigned disinterest, "Fine. Thanks for asking." She sternly commanded, "Hold it right there," threatening him with a handful of suds poised and ready.

Chance chuckled. "Lisa wanted to share a story Brad wrote."

"Really? Read it to me," Cassandra eagerly requested.

"He calls it 'Friends of All Ages.'"

Cassandra sat upright, her eyes shining with excitement. "How wonderful."

"Friends of all ages, by Brad Genova. Friends of all ages are what I have. And as luck would have it, I have many. I have a dog named Peanuts, who spares no effort to involve himself in all my games. I have a mom who loves to play with me and my dog. I have mom's friends who come over and play catch or just sit around and talk. But there's one person in particular who stands out in my mind. Even though he's older than me, every day I learn something new from him and his wife—things like building a tree fort, cooking hamburgers and hot dogs, refinishing a room in his home, and how to be a good person no matter how sad I may feel inside. From him, I've learned how to be myself. No matter how sad I am, there are people in the world who are even sadder. Thinking about how I can help those people makes me happy, and I try harder every day. All because my friend inspires me to be the best person I can be. He is my teacher and my mentor. Whenever I'm mad or unhappy, I ask myself, 'What would Chance say or do?' There are a lot of people in this world, and I feel lucky to call him my best friend." Chance paused before continuing, glancing at Cassandra's beaming face.

"It's a story about us," Cassandra joked, her eyes sparkling with delight. Chance continued reading until the very end, his heart swelling with warmth. Cassandra sighed, moved by the heartfelt words. "You know, Chance, we should submit this for the writing contest in the Boston Globe."

"What contest?" Chance asked, intrigued.

"In the Sunday paper. It's in the other room," she explained.

Curiosity piqued, Chance returned and fumbled through the pages, eager to find mention of the contest. With Cassandra guiding him from the bath., he located the page. "I know the writer, Jim Sullivan, editor of the Family and Education section. We met last year at the unveiling of the high school auditorium. Maybe I should pay him a visit and submit this personally."

Cassandra cautioned, "We don't want him to show favoritism. It has to be fair."

Chance smirked playfully. "What do you think, I'm going to bribe the guy?"

"Call Lisa and ask for permission first," she suggested.

"Duh. Tell me something I don't know," he responded with a grin.

She spoke seductively, her voice dripping with allure. "I'll bet you don't know how to get into this tub."

Chance raised an eyebrow, his eyes meeting hers with a flirtatious gaze. "Give me two minutes to prove you wrong."

* * *

"Come in, Chance," Jim Sullivan invited warmly. "Please, have a seat."

Chance stepped into the office at the Boston Globe, taking in the behind-the-scenes atmosphere of a bustling newspaper. Earlier, he had been given a tour, marveling at the massive machinery used to produce thousands of issues per hour—giant paper cutters and rolling presses. Still slightly overwhelmed by the noise, he settled into the somewhat uncomfortable chair.

As they sipped their brew, Jim asked, "The high school must be thrilled with their new auditorium. Have you attended any concerts there yet?"

"I saw the holiday concert last year. The acoustics are incredible," Chance replied.

Cutting to the chase, Jim asked, "So, Chance, how can I help you?"

Chance leaned forward, earnestly meeting his gaze. "It's about the writing contest you're sponsoring. There's a young friend of mine who is just a few months shy of meeting the age requirements. What are the chances of making an exception? He's very talented."

Jim studied Chance's expression, contemplating his request. "Normally, I'd say no, but considering he's younger, I don't see a real problem in submitting it."

Chance handed him the sealed envelope. Understanding the rules of the contest, Jim said, "I'll put this in the pile with all the others."

For the rest of the afternoon, Chance felt like a proud parent. Win or lose, Brad deserved the opportunity to be heard.

* * *

"Greg, where do you want this box to go?" Brad asked, rearranging the boxes they had just unloaded into the new apartment.

Greg called from another room, "What does it say?"

"Kitchen," Brad replied.

"In that case, I guess it goes in the bedroom," Greg joked. As Lisa walked into the house, carrying two boxes at once, her eyes met Greg's, and they shared a secret kiss. She went back outside to help Chance and Cassandra unload more boxes from the rental van. Finally, confronted with piles of boxes that needed to be unpacked and organized, Greg let out a sigh. "Now the fun begins."

As they arranged the boxes out of the way, Chance found himself wandering aimlessly from room to room, unexpectedly overwhelmed by nostalgia. He reminisced about the day he had acquired his home and the hard work he had put into it, breathing life back into the old wood. He remembered designing the enclosed porch that served as Cassandra's home office, and the glow in her eyes when she had first seen it. He recalled the first time they had made love as husband and wife, creating cherished memories within these walls. Now, with Greg moving in, ready to occupy the space, Chance was hit by a wave of mixed emotions.

Cassandra, unaware of his personal reflection, chimed in, "I don't think we're needed here anymore."

Chance nodded his head, a playful smile forming. "Good luck. Greg, I'll see you on Monday." Brad saluted him as he left.

* * *

Chance picked up the receiver of his office phone, his heart pounding with anticipation as he recognized Jim Sullivan's voice. "Chance, I have some news. We have a winner!"

"You're kidding? You're not kidding!" Chance exclaimed, his voice filled with excitement.

"Brad won by a blind unanimous vote. The judges were particularly moved by the last paragraph, where he spoke of his father's passing and how you became his friend and father figure. His story will be published in this Sunday's Metro section. Who should I send the prize to?"

An idea formed in Chance's mind. "Send it to me. Brad's birthday is coming up, and it would make a wonderful addition to his collection of presents."

"So be it. Gotta run. Deadlines to meet," Jim replied before ending the call.

* * *

"You're kidding!" Brad exclaimed, his eyes widening in disbelief as Lisa held the newspaper in front of his face. He gazed with amazement at his very first published story. "I won? I can't believe it." Overwhelmed with emotion, Lisa hugged her son tightly, feeling his shaking body as he stared at the newsprint. "But... you...? Does Chance know?"

"Yup, he knows. We're all incredibly proud of you," Lisa replied, her voice brimming with pride.

A moment of shocked embarrassment crossed Brad's face. "How am I going to explain this at school?"

Lisa understood his ambivalence. She spoke with comforting reassurance, her voice filled with motherly wisdom. "Brad, it's a beautiful story. It's written straight from your heart, filled with genuine emotion. Never worry about what others may think. Write what you feel inside. Bear your soul. Tomorrow, you will be congratulated by your teachers and the boys and girls who are truly your friends. Nothing else matters. Okay?"

"I guess so," Brad replied, his confidence slowly returning.

"We're going out to celebrate tonight. Chance wants to treat you to dinner wherever you want."

Brad sat in his favorite chair, a wide grin spreading across his face as he read his published story from beginning to end. Seeing his own words in print filled him with inspiration. Without hesitation, he opened his notebook and began writing another story, pouring his heart and soul onto the pages.

* * *

As Brad walked into the living room, everyone yelled, "Surprise!" The room was adorned with colorful streamers and balloons. Brad couldn't believe his eyes as he took in the sight of his

129

friends and family gathered to celebrate his tenth birthday. "Wow! What the heck?" he exclaimed, his heart overflowing with joy. Lisa kissed his cheek, wishing him a happy birthday.

Throughout the day at school, Brad had wondered if anyone remembered his birthday, June twenty second. The anticipation had grown as he observed his friends and wondered if they were aware of the significance of the date. Even during Billy's birthday party two weeks ago, nobody had mentioned celebrating Brad's birthday. Yet, as he entered the room, his doubts were shattered, replaced by a sense of pure happiness and belonging.

Amy, one of Brad's closest friends, handed him a gift and said, "Open mine first."

His excitement grew as he unwrapped the present. "Wow! A new baseball," he exclaimed, leaning over to give Amy a quick kiss on the cheek.

"Cooties, you got cooties!" one of Amy's friends playfully teased, causing the girl to blush and rub her cheek.

Tommy eagerly presented his gift next. Brad tore open the wrapping paper to reveal a video game. "Sonic the Hedgehog! Thanks!"

As Cassandra watched the scene unfold in the living room, her thoughts turned to her own longing for a family of her own, where she could celebrate her children's birthdays with such joy. Glancing at Chance, she couldn't help but feel overwhelmed with emotion. Recognizing her sentimental expression, Chance wrapped his arm around her, offering her comfort and support. Lisa waited until the end before handing Brad her presents. He recognized the first box.

"A sweater, right?" he guessed, tearing it open to reveal a woolen garment. Laughter erupted in the room, agreeing that clothes should never count as real presents. Lisa then handed him a small envelope.

"Maybe it's money," one of the boys speculated, adding to the intrigue.

Brad pulled out the paper and read aloud, "The bearer of this coupon has been awarded ten free all-day passes to Holiday Land in New Hampshire." The room erupted in applause and cheers as Brad waved the coupon in the air. "But, where did it come from?"

"It's first prize for winning the writing contest. I'm so proud of you, Bradley," Lisa beamed, her heart swelling.

"Mom! Please," Brad whispered, feeling slightly embarrassed by his given name.

Overwhelmed with emotion, Cassandra interjected, her voice filled with sincere admiration. "Chance, you never cease to amaze me."

"Like Lisa said, he earned it all by himself," Chance replied modestly, though he couldn't deny the satisfaction of doing something special for his friend.

* * *

Chance walked through the prison compound, his gaze fixed on the beaming afternoon sun above. He inhaled deeply, savoring the fleeting moments of freedom that awaited him outside these suffocating walls. Each visit to the prison deepened his appreciation for the simple joys he had once taken for granted—the gentle breeze against his skin, the warmth of sunlight on his face, the exhilaration of pursuing his ambitions and dreams.

But as he stepped inside the prison, his senses were assaulted by the stark and lifeless atmosphere. The artificial glow of fluorescent lights and the harsh clang of metal doors reverberated through the air. It felt like entering a nightmare, a world stripped of vitality. Following the guard, he made his way to the visitors' waiting area, where he noticed a weary-looking woman with two children. He wondered how long they had been waiting and the toll this place took on their spirits. Settling into a chair, he thumbed through a magazine, resigned to the hours that lay ahead.

Finally, after what felt like an eternity, his name crackled through the intercom. He rose, his heart quickening with anticipation, and approached the security guard behind the bulletproof glass. "I'm Chance Macklin. I have a package to give to my brother."

The guard scrutinized Chance's attire, ensuring compliance with the strict dress code that prohibited layered clothing. After flipping through some pages, he inquired about the purpose of the visit. "Visiting Seth Macklin," Chance replied, his voice steady.

His gaze shifted to the package in Chance's hands, and he stood to examine his clothing more closely. Chance obligingly unbuttoned the top three buttons of his shirt. "I'll buzz you in and give you a

131

locker key. Take off all accessories—watches, rings, wallet—and remove your belt and socks. Any questions?"

Chance shook his head, having committed the drill to memory. The guard pressed a loud buzzer, and the steel door slid open, separating the visitors from the desolate prison grounds. He followed another guard to a changing room. "Number 18," the guard said, handing over a key. "We need to search the package." He took the box from Chance's hands.

"I feel like a prisoner myself in this place," Chance thought as he opened the locker, stowing away his personal items. Examining his appearance in the mirror, he slid his leather belt out of his pants and hung it up. Exiting the changing area, he waited patiently by the main door. Moments later, a guard emerged, holding the opened package in his hand. "We'll make sure he gets this later."

Chance followed the guard to the visitor booths, passing through a high-security metal detector. As always, he cleared the inspection, and another guard outside the booth conducted a quick search. "Turn your pockets inside out," he instructed before unlocking the visitor booth door. "Booth two."

Chance entered the booth and took a seat on the wooden chair. He glanced at the Norman Rockwell print adorning the prisoner's half of the room, contemplating Seth's biting sarcasm and the complex mix of irony and sympathy it evoked. Moments later, Seth appeared and took a seat across from him. Accustomed to the prolonged silences that characterized their conversations, Chance waited until Seth reached for the phone. Following suit, he picked up the receiver.

"It's been a while, little brother," Seth remarked, his voice tinged with detachment.

"Been busy lately. You look good," Chance replied, his voice void of emotion.

"Same old, same old." Seth paused, changing the subject. "By the way, I've got a secret. I found a way out of here. Looks like I'll be free soon." He relished the shock on his brother's face, his words carrying a sinister undertone. "Can't wait to visit you and... what's her name?"

Chance studied Seth's serious expression, a mix of concern and caution etched on his face. "I need to hear you say that you are going to leave me and my family alone."

Seth's voice dripped with derision. "You mean the little woman?"

"Haven't you tormented me enough?" Chance's plea hung in the air, a desperate call for mercy.

Chance recalled Cassandra's insight about Seth's influence on him. Seth, like a vampire, drained him of strength and self. As Seth spoke, Chance felt the weight of his own captivity, his brother's words echoing the bitterness of his heart. "Can you imagine what it's like," Seth's voice cut through, "sitting in these cells, abandoned and unforgiven? Who has that right?"

Chance knew he couldn't break through the walls that encased his brother's heart. The prison bars held Seth physically, but it was the shackles of his own bitterness and anger that truly confined him.

Seth's venomous words hung in the air, poisoning their already fractured relationship. As Chance blurted out his frustration, emotions battled within him. "What right do you have to torture my family?" he demanded, his voice tinged with anger and pain. Yet, he fought to maintain composure, adding calmly, "I come here as your brother, as someone who cares for you. And you spit at me."

Seth's retort came as a sharp rebuke, his words laced with bitterness. "Then stop acting like my fucking lawyer or guidance counselor. You're living in total denial about everything!"

Chance felt as though he were staring into a mirror of opposites, their hearts and minds pulled in opposing directions. "I will do everything in my power to protect Cassandra. I would protect you the same way, but you want nothing to do with me," he confessed, his voice filled with genuine sorrow.

Seth's demeanor remained defiant, his eyes gleaming with a twisted sense of satisfaction. "Chance, it's clear that these little visits are not helping you much, although they are doing wonders for me. The maids are starting to notice my happy face. The cooks are sneaking me real eggs. I am a king amongst the crooks. Like I said, you inspire me." He sensed the finality of their exchange, the conclusion of their bond.

"I'm serious, Seth. You've left me no choice!"

"Idle threats are beneath you, Chance. A little time here might toughen you up. Want to swap places so I can enjoy your wife's company? Doubt she'd even notice."

Chance's frustration simmered, but he remained composed. "You're delusional if you think you can manipulate me with your games."

Seth smirked, unfazed. "I'm just offering you a taste of reality, brother. You might find it refreshing."

Seth's cruel words crashed upon Chance, eroding the last vestiges of hope for reconciliation. In that moment, he realized that he needed to protect Cassandra at all costs. With a resounding slam, he hung up the phone, his gaze locked with Seth's. Seth mouthed the words "Good luck," and walked away.

The bonds of family that had once held them together dissolved in the face of Seth's darkness. The realization struck Chance with a bittersweet pang, for he had genuinely loved his twin, but now, he allowed himself to embrace the revelation that, for all the right reasons, he genuinely hated Seth. Getting into his car, he drove away, his eyes fixed on the road ahead, determined to cut Seth completely out of his mind for the sake of his beloved Cassandra. It pained him to accept the harsh truth that their enmity would endure forever.

* * *

Two weeks after his final encounter with Seth, Chance sat at his desk, sifting through his incoming business correspondences. The week had been busy, filled with relentless work, but the completion of several important deadlines had granted him a momentary respite. A laugh escaped his lips as he opened a peculiar letter addressed to him.

Dear Chance,
What's yellow, or pink, or sometimes blue?
Stop at the bakery to find your next clue.
Love, AngelEyes
P.S. Please stop by Adams' bakery at four and pick up the package waiting for you. But Do Not Open It!

Chance glanced at his schedule, grateful for the opportunity to indulge in his wife's mysterious request. Throughout the rest of the afternoon, he attempted to reach Cassandra, but was met with the hospital receptionist's message: "I'm sorry, Mrs. Macklin is unavailable for the rest of the day." Although curious, Chance focused on his routine, the enigmatic task lingering at the forefront of his thoughts.

At four o'clock, he arrived at Adams' bakery. Approaching the counter, he presented the ticket when the woman behind it requested number seven. "I'm here to pick up a package for Cassandra Macklin," he explained.

She recognized the name and handed him the prepaid package. "Excuse me, Mrs. Macklin wanted me to give you this." She handed him an envelope.

Curiosity surged through Chance as he tore open the envelope and read Cassandra's words.

Dear Chance,
Next door to this wonderful bakery of joy,
Is a florist who needs your presence, my boy.
A bouquet of flowers is yours at your leisure,
Your second ingredient to my secret treasure.
Love, AngelEyes

"Flowers? Treasure? She's always full of surprises," he mused, captivated by his wife's playful spirit. The interested glance of the woman behind the counter didn't go unnoticed. Thanking her, Chance made his way to the florist, carrying the box from the bakery, his mind filled with anticipation and confusion, yet certain that the clerk would reveal the next piece of the enchanting puzzle.

"We have a bouquet of flowers right here," the woman said with a knowing smile. Chance reached for his wallet, prepared to pay. "Nope, it's all paid for. She wanted me to give you this." She handed him another envelope.

With amusement and curiosity, Chance tore open the envelope to reveal Cassandra's words.

Dear Chance,
As you carry our flowers out this lovely door,
Please stop by Kappy's, our local liquor store.
Behind the counter, you will surely fine,
a prepaid bottle of tonight's celebration wine.
Love, AngelEyes

Chance chuckled at his wife's clever use of "fine" instead of "find" to maintain the rhyme. Expressing his gratitude to the woman for her participation in the unfolding mystery, he made his way to Kappy's, eager to see what awaited him.

Approaching the counter, Chance began to introduce himself. "Excuse me, my name is—"

The woman behind the counter interrupted him with a knowing smile. "Chance Macklin?" Two female cashiers nearby giggled, their eyes twinkling with the secret they all seemed to share. She handed him the package. "She said to tell you to pay the last dollar; something to do with a rhyme."

Chance handed her a dollar bill, his mind spinning with anticipation. "Yup, it's my fine," he grinned.

Pulling into the driveway, Chance's eyes searched for his wife's car, but it was nowhere to be seen. Nevertheless, he proceeded up the sidewalk, his arms full with the packages, his heart filled with desire. The drapes covering the living room window caught his attention, igniting a spark of curiosity within him. With his key in hand, he opened the front door and stepped inside, his gaze scanning the room. His breath hitched as he witnessed the sight before him.

Candles flickered, casting a warm and intimate glow through the house. The tantalizing aroma of food cooking in the kitchen filled the air, adding to the ambiance. "Cassandra?" he called out, his voice filled with excitement and tinge of apprehension.

As he made his way towards the dining room, he noticed the carefully set table, adorned with place settings and intriguing objects. Index cards with writing on them piqued his curiosity, drawing him closer. But it was what he saw reflected in the mirror that startled him—a glimpse of Seth's face staring back at him. The resemblance was uncanny, a chilling reminder of the darkness that once haunted their lives. Shaking off the eerie feeling, Chance refocused his attention on the table.

A small vase with a card awaited him, instructing him to put the flowers he had picked up earlier into it. Chance followed the instructions, his mind buzzing with anticipation. An ice bucket and another sign caught his attention. "Please put wine in here," it read. And finally, a rectangular serving dish with a sign that read, "Please put cake here. Do not open!"

Curiosity tugged at him, tempting him to peek inside the box, but he resisted, knowing that Cassandra had something special planned. He walked towards the kitchen door, its creaking sound heightening his sense of unease. Yet, he pushed forward, drawn by the enticing smell of food and the flickering candlelight that danced within.

Returning to the living room, his eyes fell upon the staircase, adorned with small candles illuminating every second step. His heart quickened as he realized this was the next clue in Cassandra's mysterious game. His gaze traveled up the stairs, and with excitement and nervousness, he picked up the black lace underwear resting on the bottom step. Holding it to his nose, he inhaled the intoxicating scent, whispering Cassandra's name. With the delicate fabric in hand, he began ascending the staircase, following the trail of candles.

On the second floor, the air was filled with the enchanting aroma of exotic incense, adding an air of mystery to the atmosphere. He discovered Cassandra's garter belt lying on the hallway carpet, a symbol of her sensuality and desire. Picking it up, he continued down the hallway, his heart pounding in his chest. He reached the bedroom door, hesitating for a moment before entering.

The room was bathed in the soft glow of candlelight and the lingering scent of incense. The silence hung heavy, building anticipation within Chance. He called out her name, his voice filled with longing and excitement. As the comforter at the head of the bed moved, his eyes widened, captivated by the sight that slowly revealed itself.

Cassandra unveiled herself, every delicate curve and unspoken desire illuminated in the flickering candlelight. As Chance's anxiety transformed into desire, he undressed, joining her in the bed. His lips worshipped her flesh, his touch gentle and passionate. Lost in each other's embrace, their bodies moved in perfect harmony, exploring the depths of their desire.

In the afterglow of their passionate union, they lay together, basking in the candlelit bedroom. Cassandra sighed contentedly, her heart overflowing. "Did you get everything?" she asked, her eyes sparkling with intrigue. Chance rolled to his side, fixing his gaze on her, eager for answers. "After dinner," she teased, a mischievous smile gracing her lips.

Like two eager kids, they slipped into their bathrobes and raced downstairs to the dining room. Cassandra served him potatoes, her excited glow igniting his curiosity.

"You got a raise?" he guessed, but she shook her head. "You won the lottery?" he tried again, hoping to solve the mystery.

"Dessert?" she said, diverting his attention.

Chance played along, his mind racing with anticipation. "Let me guess... cake?" His eyes fixed on the box sealed shut with a delicate string.

Cassandra placed the box on the table in front of him, maintaining her poker face with rehearsed style. She handed him a knife, eagerly awaiting the moment he would unveil the secret she held. He gently pulled the knife through the string, breaking the seal and lifting the lid. As he peered inside, his breath caught in his throat. Carved in icing were the words that made his heart soar.

Cassandra's heart raced as she watched his reaction, her own excitement finally shining through. Her pulse quickened, her breath catching in her throat, as she anticipated his response. The culmination of her treasure hunt had brought them to this moment, a testament to the depth of their connection.

Chance's eyes widened in disbelief as the inscribed words echoed in his mind: "Congratulations! You're going to be a daddy!" Unable to contain his excitement, Chance pulled her into a tight embrace as he tried to find the words. "Are you… Are we… You're pregnant?"

Cassandra nodded rapidly, her voice flowing with emotion. "We are! Chance, I wanted to bear your child from the first moment we met. It's a dream come true!" Their shared love and the miracle growing within her enveloped them in a cocoon of bliss.

Chance's eyes glistened with tears, his hands trembling. "Incredible! Wonderful! What do we call him?" he said amid his laughter.

A mischievous spark gleamed in Cassandra's reply: "What do we call *her*?" she said, teasing him with the possibilities.

Chance acquiesced, delighting in their playful banter. "Okay, what do we call them?"

Cassandra's gaze turned serious as they locked eyes. "Please, no twins!" She slowly leaned in, her voice barely above a whisper. "I know it's a girl. She'll be our little angel…"

"Brad, I feel I have come to know Seth a great deal more after reading this next chapter."

"Yes, Elizabeth, some important layers to Seth's onion are revealed. Unfortunately, though, he always kept his guilt to himself. It's a common occurrence with abused children."

"The images you convey are real and support Seth's troubled nature. How did you obtain the foundational material he experienced during his incarceration?"

"I had the opportunity to interview the prison psychiatrist, the priest who took him under his wing, and several prisoners who remembered Seth. I also had access to Seth's journal, which peeled away the most complex layers to his soul. Furthermore, I spoke at length with Cassandra, who is an excellent psychologist. Although she hesitated for her own personal reasons, she proved vital to my research. It was difficult for them both, but telling their story became a way of healing their own wounds... And my own."

"I'm sure our viewers are interested in obtaining deeper insights into our antagonist. Tell us what happens next."

"As you mentioned, this chapter is about Seth's life in prison."

Chapter 6

Part I

Seth jolted awake, his body drenched in sweat, his heart pounding in his chest. It was the same nightmare haunting him, suffocating in his subconscious depths. Gasping for air, Seth fought the twisted dream, feeling imprisoned within his brother's bed, watching Chance with Cassandra. Feeling trapped between mattress and box spring, overwhelmed him, as if the bed itself was his captor.

"Chance, get off! Let me breathe!" Seth gasped.

In the dim light of his prison cell, Seth's parade of images spun with a distorted hue, his thoughts flickering in and out of focus like shadows dancing on the walls. The scent of sandalwood incense filled his senses, mingling with the haunting melody of a Mozart sonata—a cruel reminder of the love and care that had always eluded him, showered upon his brother by fate. He screamed, his voice echoing in the depths of his nightmare, but his cries went unheard, lost in the abyss of his own torment.

As the intensity of his dream escalated, Seth felt the bed beneath him rock violently, as if it were a battering ram assaulting an impenetrable fortress, threatening to shatter his fragile reality. The mattress swallowed him deeper, its grip tightening, threatening to consume him entirely. And then, in a surreal twist, Seth dissolved into the essence of Chance, his brother's identity merging with his own. It was a warped form of justice, a sick satisfaction as he took possession of Chance's body, claiming Cassandra for himself.

"I fooled you, my pet," Seth sneered, relishing the horror that flashed across her face.

Meanwhile, Chance now gasped for air, trapped in the suffocating grip of the mattress. Seth reveled in the role reversal, savoring Chance's torment as his own.

The nightmare twisted further still, morphing Cassandra's face into that of their grandfather—a sinister figure from their past, haunting Seth's deepest fears. Seth recoiled, unable to confront the truth that lay buried within. The curmudgeon's presence taunted him, gloating about the depraved acts they had shared. Seth couldn't bear to look into those baggy eyes, the wicked grin that revealed the pleasure his grandfather had taken in their "special time" together. The air filled with the stench of his grandfather's foul pipe, overpowering Seth's senses, intensifying the horror of his night terror.

The sweet scent of sandalwood gave way to the acrid smell of burning flesh, flames engulfing the bedposts, casting eerie shadows on the walls. Seth, reduced to his childhood self, cried out for release, his voice echoing through the abyss as the bed descended into the depths like a sinister elevator. Surrounding him, curtains of darkness billowed, concealing the distant voices of his family, their echoes haunting him in the cavernous void. He saw Chance, a silent spectator at the edge of the bed, watching the unspeakable acts unfold without intervention. Seth's desperate pleas for help were drowned out by their laughter, their indifference.

"Chance, help me!"

* * *

Seth abruptly awoke, his body frozen in the reality of his prison cell. The echoes of clanging metal doors reverberated through the corridor, mingling with the sounds of an inmate's cries and the harsh reality of withdrawal, creating a cacophony of despair that enveloped the prison. Once again confined to the grey concrete walls, the feeble moonlight cast elongated shadows of the prison bars on the cold floor. The realization hit him like a blow—he was not Chance; he no longer had a twin brother. The bond they once shared had been severed, replaced by a deep-seated hatred and longing for revenge.

Amidst the darkness, one thought brought a smile to Seth's face: Cassandra. Panting heavily, he indulged in violent fantasies, relishing the terror he could inflict upon her from behind these bars. She was his sole source of entertainment, his only escape from the prison walls that surrounded him. Soon, the blaring horn would signal the start of another day for the inmates of C Block. The rows of fluorescent lights would illuminate their paths. Prisoners would rise obediently, their voices reciting their assigned numbers, a chilling reminder of their captive existence, trapped within the confines of their own fears.

Standing at the cell door, Seth eyed the book on human biology and genetics that Chance had brought him months earlier.. His thoughts swirled around his own bloodline, his DNA, as he contemplated his past and uncertain future. If only he could change it, trade it for something—anything but this. The irony of his dark humor brought a bitter end to his amusement. Crawling through a swamp as a reptile seemed more appealing than being trapped in this prison.

The horn blared and they all exited their cells. As the sound of the inmate to his left echoed through the corridor, Seth called out his own number, "Eighty-six," followed by the prisoner to his right, continuing the sequence. The blast of a whistle pierced the air, signaling for them to turn. Another sharp whistle resounded, and he advanced, watching the line of inmates trailing behind like obedient dogs responding to their masters. The sight amused him, but he longed for the day when he could turn the tables, when they would be forced to acknowledge his presence. They would have no choice but to see him.

Walking along with the chain of prisoners, Seth kept his gaze fixed on the coarse concrete beneath his feet. The repetitive morning drill echoed in his ears, snapping him back to the harsh reality of his surroundings. Rusty prison bars and century-old staircases were stark reminders of the lives that had come and gone within these walls, echoing with the whispers of forgotten souls. He couldn't bring himself to look at the other inmates, afraid of the reflection he might see staring back at him.

Entering the cafeteria, a wave of repulsive smells assaulted Seth's senses. Grease, disinfectant, burnt toast, and the artificial odor of freeze-dried eggs mingled in the air, threatening to turn his stomach. But hunger pushed aside his disgust, and he joined the line with an aluminum tray in hand. The chaotic scramble for food seemed futile, as the end result often led to nothing but discomfort. He observed as the cooks sloppily served the prisoners, slapping oatmeal into grimy bowls.

The pale grey color of the food matched the dreary cinder block walls, a grim reminder of their confined existence. Seth glanced up, catching a glimpse of sunlight streaming through small windows high above, a distant warmth that would never reach his cold body. Rows of flickering fluorescent bulbs cast a harsh light, nearing the end of their life expectancy.

Louis, the heavyset guard stationed near a concrete pillar, bellowed, "Hey, Macklin!" Seth kept moving in the food line, choosing to ignore the guard's call. He glanced towards the kitchen partition and caught sight of an assistant cook who seemed to be observing the interaction between him and Louis. "Get your ass over here," Louis demanded, his nightstick hitting his palm with a menacing thud. Seth reluctantly returned to the line, now the last to be served. The cook, aware of the situation, discreetly added something to Seth's bowl with a different ladle. With a dented spoon in hand, Seth knew he needed his strength, even if the taste was less than appetizing. The comparison to Pavlov's dog did little to improve his already waning appetite.

Balancing his tray, Seth scanned the rows of crowded tables, searching for an available seat. He felt the hungry gazes of fellow prisoners as he passed by. Desire for that which could never be his seemed to linger in their eyes. Moving between tables, Seth finally found a spot next to Abdul Faroukh, an imposing Iranian prisoner known as King Kong, his presence commanding respect and fear alike. Seth squeezed in beside him, the uncomfortable reality of life in prison pressing in on him once again.

Abdul, a convicted drug runner who commanded respect through physical intimidation, held sway over many inmates. He handpicked men to be part of his harem, exerting control with his imposing presence. Sporting a scruffy beard and long sideburns that added to his rough appearance, Abdul possessed massive hands and arms that could put most men to shame. Despite a slight limp, he could outrun anyone who dared challenge him. Seth had once been chosen as Abdul's target, but he had managed to turn the tables in his favor.

"Hey, Macklin," Abdul had called out from the shower years ago. Seth had known to be cautious, avoiding any unnecessary contact. "Nice white ass!"

Seth had sensed Abdul closing in from behind and turned off his shower, making his way into the changing area. Conversations halted as inmates took notice of Abdul's naked and aroused presence.

"I've got something for you," Abdul had taunted at the time, displaying his manhood.

At the time, Seth had refused to give in. He understood the consequences of succumbing to physical abuse and refused to be a victim. As he tried to leave, Abdul blocked his path, gripping Seth's arm tightly. Rage surged within Seth, his muscles tensing as adrenaline coursed through his veins. In that moment, he envisioned his grandfather, Samuel, restraining him. With a burst of strength, Seth broke free, surprising Abdul with his defiance. Seth moved closer, their faces mere inches apart, feeling Abdul's breath on his skin.

"Touch me again, and I *will* kill you," Seth had snarled. "I detest people with halitosis. You've ruined the mood."

The word "halitosis" carried a hidden meaning understood by the others, and laughter erupted at Abdul's expense. Fuming with anger, the giant turned his attention to them. As Seth calmly walked away, Abdul shouted, "Fuck off, Macklin!"

Since that incident in the shower, Seth had gained the respect of inmates who were forced to bow to Abdul's demands. For the time being, Abdul left him alone. Now, sitting in the cafeteria, Abdul glanced at Seth and grinned, engaging in banter with a fellow inmate, joking about halitosis.

"Love the aftershave," Abdul taunted, a smirk playing on his lips. With a deep exhale, Abdul expelled a sickening gust of pungent air toward Seth's face. Seth clenched his fist, adjusting his body weight as he resisted the urge to fight back. He sniffed his eggs, then caught a whiff of the putrid scent lingering around Abdul. Sensing Abdul's clenched fist, ready for a fight, Seth picked up his spoon and continued eating.

"The guards are starting to notice your stench too, dear Abby," Seth quipped.

Abdul glanced at Louis, who idly tapped his nightstick with his right hand. Seth wondered what had captured the guard's attention. As he ate, a sudden churn in his stomach gripped Seth, shifting from healthy pink to pale. He stared at the smiling guard, the realization sinking in that something was wrong. Panic surged through him as he realized he had consumed contaminated food. Nausea and dizziness overwhelmed him, his vision blurring in and out of focus. *Where am I?*

* * *

Visions of his childhood flickered in his mind. Memories of breakfasts with the family, gathered around the table on lazy Saturday mornings, invaded his thoughts. In the distorted flashback, Chance excitedly spoke about a girl he had a crush on, their father indulging in his enthusiasm. Seth struggled to control his anger and jealousy, resenting the attention lavished upon his brother. He glared at Chance, hating the girl's presence and the constant phone calls he received.

Days earlier, a phone call from Sheila had unknowingly sparked Seth's envy. She had asked, "Are you Chance or Seth?" Seth witnessed the disappointment on her face when he revealed his identity. "Sorry, I'm going to the movies with Carol."

Seth knew that Chance had spoken to Sheila about the movie they had watched, the same movie he had invited her to. Even if Chance was unaware of his involvement, it didn't matter. Chance had betrayed him. Kevin nudged Chance, playfully prodding him with an elbow tap and a wink.

"So, did you kiss her goodnight, Chance?"

Chance's face turned crimson, betraying his secret. Seth's stomach twisted into knots as he realized he had fallen in love with Sheila. The ache of loneliness gnawed at his heart, and he lost control, violently vomiting into his bowl. Oatmeal and saliva splattered across his face as he coughed up the contents of his stomach onto the table. Silence descended upon the table, and Seth avoided locking eyes with his father, aware of the anger that awaited him. He stumbled to clean up the mess, accidentally knocking his bowl to the floor. As his father reached for his belt, Seth darted away from the table, leaving the family meal in ruins.

* * *

Back at the prison, Abdul growled, "You disgusting pig," as Seth continued to retch. Seth, barely aware of his surroundings or the inmate beside him, felt a sense of detachment. For a fleeting moment, he was transported from the prison. In a daze induced by the chemicals coursing through his veins, he grabbed his bowl and hurled it at Abdul, covering him in a repulsive mixture of oatmeal and vomit. Abdul struggled to rise from his chair, colliding with the nearby inmate. Tempers flared as punches were thrown, some missing their mark while others landed with force. The guards swiftly intervened, and as quickly as the chaos had erupted, it came to an abrupt end.

"Get moving," Louis said angrily, pushing Seth toward the exit. Abdul followed closely behind, flanked by his own guards. Louis forcefully guided Seth toward the isolation ward. "Feeling a bit under the weather, are we?" he taunted, tripping Seth as they reached the front.

Seth collapsed onto the concrete floor, laughing. "You clueless idiot, Chance. Watch where you're going."

"What's wrong with this psycho?" Abdul sneered.

With the steel door slamming shut behind them, confining Seth to Isolation Ward B, Louis spat at his feet. "Seems like you don't appreciate the food we serve. I'll make sure you consume every last bite." The guards walked away, their footsteps echoing inside Seth's head.

* * *

At the crack of dawn, Louis, wielding a blinding flashlight, roused Seth from his fitful sleep. "Doc wants you," he grunted.

Seth, still reeling from yesterday's drugged meal, managed a wry retort, "Well, isn't this a delightful wake-up call." Struggling to steady himself, he added, "Thanks for yesterday's treat," a wry acknowledgment of the drugged food.

Louis dismissed Seth's comment as he shoved him out of the cell. Their footsteps echoed in the silent corridors, the guard's heavy boots thudding against the floor. Seth matched his steps instinctively until they reached the doctor's office.

"Here he is," Louis announced to the man behind the desk.

Dr. Percault rose, extending his hand. "Seth, come on in. Take a seat."

As Louis exited, Seth glanced around, his gaze landing on an oil painting. The leaves seemed to shimmer, caught in a breeze only they could feel. Dr. Percault observed Seth, noting his glazed eyes and dilated pupils. After a moment of scrutiny, he spoke, breaking the silence.

"Seth, how have you been?"

Seth laughed bitterly. "Peachy. And how's the wife and kids?" His words held a touch of coherence.

Dr. Percault leaned forward in his chair, reaching for a file on his desk. He flipped through numerous pages, and Seth crossed his legs, sinking into the chair's synthetic material. Finally, he closed the file and focused intently on Seth.

"It seems you're losing your grip on reality and channeling your inner aggression in dangerous ways," he said and paused. "Seth, you are remarkably calculating, intelligent, and even gifted. These

146

qualities could work in your favor if you channeled them more productively."

"You sound like my brother."

Dr. Percault opened another manila folder. "According to our records, your brother hasn't visited you in quite some time. In fact, aside from Chance, you haven't had any other visitors."

Seth glanced at his prison shirt, removing a dried piece of oatmeal from the fabric. "Yesterday's breakfast, the one I threw up. Why? Because of the tainted food this jail serves. If you want to be helpful, start by addressing that."

Dr. Percault walked toward a window overlooking the prison grounds. "For some time now, you've exhibited unusual and dangerous behavior. Yet, you persistently refuse to take the medication I've prescribed."

Seth shook his head, his tone turning aggressive. "You're just a damn shrink who knows nothing about my mind or body. You invade my privacy and expect me to be grateful?"

"Calm down," Dr. Percault urged, gesturing with his hands. "I prescribed Thorazine to help control your anger. But sudden withdrawal from the drug can be dangerous. If you stick to the prescribed schedule, it will benefit you."

"I don't want to become one of your mindless zombies! My mind is the only thing I have left for myself," Seth retorted vehemently.

Dr. Percault cleared his throat, leaning forward in his chair. "Tell me about your writing."

Seth let out a bitter laugh. "Oh, I meant to thank you for suggesting this meditative hobby. I've been exploring all sorts of ways to seek revenge against you, the guards, Abdul, and my beloved brother."

"That's not what I had hoped to hear," Dr. Percault replied grudgingly.

Seth locked eyes with the doctor, his gaze intense. "Any further invasion of my privacy, my food, my sleep, or my thoughts will unleash a rage you couldn't even fathom. Do we understand each other?"

Dr. Percault glanced at his desk, a hint of unease in his expression. "Why are you so angry?"

"Because they serve me contaminated food that makes me sick, I have to endure these damn sessions, and you want to drug my brain into oblivion. If I take your medication, I'll become so lethargic that Abdul will have his way with me. Right now, I'm just trying to protect myself." Seth's eyes burned with intensity as he challenged the doctor.

"If I can separate you from Abdul, will you cooperate?"

Ah, the good doctor cares, Seth thought sarcastically. *Diving deep into his prisoner's soul, acting like the wiser one while destroying the body with drugs.* "Just get me away from Abdul," he sternly replied.

"Very well. I will arrange for your transfer, and you will consider taking the medication. Louis!" Dr. Percault called, summoning the guard.

Once Seth was escorted out of the office, Dr. Percault picked up the phone, tapping a pencil on his desk as he waited for the warden to answer. "Macklin's hallucinations are getting worse, and Abdul is becoming a threat. We need to separate them."

Warden Platts's responded, "Faroukh is always a problem, but I'll make sure they're kept apart. Has Macklin agreed to be sedated? I'm tired of hearing complaints from the staff."

"If we can get him away from Faroukh, he might be more cooperative. No need to drug his meals." Dr. Percault hung up the phone, jotting down a few notes before locking Seth's file away with countless others.

* * *

In the middle of that same evening, Seth lay asleep in the isolation ward when he was abruptly jolted awake by two guards: Louis and Marcus. In the darkness, he heard the creaking of the metal door and felt the presence of the guards looming over his cot. His senses heightened, and he thought, *This is going to hurt.*

Louis swung his baton across Seth's thighs. "Wake up!"

Seth shot up, suppressing his pain. He scowled, the agony nearly unbearable. Louis yanked him up by the hair, their eyes locked in a fierce stare.

"The next time you're in the cafeteria, be prepared to do more than finish your meal. We expect you to dance for your fellow inmates! This is just the beginning," Louis sneered.

With a swift motion, he brought the steel baton crashing into Seth's groin. Seth gasped, the excruciating pain tearing through his insides. The other guard delivered a brutal kick to his abdomen with his steel-toed boots. Seth groaned, clutching his crotch. And just as quickly as they had appeared, the guards slammed the cell shut.

Wracked with pain, Seth crumpled onto the concrete floor. As if a curtain had fallen, he slipped into unconsciousness and found himself transported, not to jail, but to his bed at his grandparents' cottage.

* * *

"Go away, Chance!" Seth yelled from his bedroom, curling up into a ball, his voice filled with frustration and fear.

His gaze landed on the bureau in his room, where a picture of his grandparents smiling with the boys after a fishing trip hung on the wall. Anger and hatred replaced the happy memories of that outing. Seth hurled his pillow at the picture, knocking it off the wall. It crashed into the bureau, shattering the glass as it fell to the carpet. "I hate all of you!" he seethed, consumed by rage.

Lying on his side, he found his mind shrouded in a fog of uncertainty. The origins of the "secret games" eluded him, slipping through his grasp like smoke. Each attempt to remember only deepened the murkiness, threatening to drown his recollections. Yet, despite his desperate denial, the chilling truth seeped into his consciousness. This wasn't a mere dream. The torment he endured was all too real, etched into his very being. Fear gripped him tightly, whispering cruel warnings that if he dared to speak out, the punishment would be relentless. The mere thought of enduring those twisted events once more terrified him, igniting a burning desire to break free from the suffocating nightmare.

As the dinner table stretched before him, Seth absently prodded at the peas on his plate. The murmurs of conversation between his brother and grandparents grew faint, barely registering in his anxious mind. An urgent determination seized him: he had to escape this place, this suffocating web of secrets and torment. Amidst the muffled voices, he thought he caught a whisper of his name, a phantom echo of his grandfather's menacing tone.

Suddenly, Samuel Macklin's rage erupted like a thunderclap. His fist crashed upon the table, sending vibrations through the room and causing a fork to clatter to the floor. Seth's heart raced in his chest as his grandfather, consumed by fury, rose from his seat, his hands moving with an unsettling purpose. Seth knew he had to act, to flee from the impending danger that loomed before him. Without hesitation, he bolted from the table, his voice laced with desperation. "Leave me alone," he shouted, racing up the stairs. The bedroom door slammed shut behind him, a feeble barrier against the impending storm.

A half-hour crawled by, every agonizing second punctuated by the heavy thud of Samuel Macklin's ascending footsteps. Seth's instincts kicked into overdrive, his body propelled by a primal survival instinct. He snatched his baseball glove, gripping it tightly as he raced back to the safety of his bed. With a trembling hand, he closed his eyes, drawing a protective circle around himself, clutching the glove as if it were a lifeline.

At that moment, Samuel's voice, dripping with deceit, sliced through the silence like a venomous serpent. "Seth, it's your grandfather," he declared, his presence suffocating the room. He settled on the edge of the bed, his hand descending upon Seth's shoulder like a vise. The weight of his touch sent a shudder through Seth's entire being. Samuel's words twisted and slithered, a sickening reassurance that their wicked game was a shared secret, a pact of silence. The threat hung unspoken in the air: betraying this secret would invite an unfathomable punishment.

Seth fought against his grandfather's grasp, a futile struggle against the unyielding grip of a depraved predator. Samuel's smile, the embodiment of malice, offered a twisted sense of belonging, of being special. It was a sickening realization that Seth, in his grandfather's eyes, was favored above all others.

Seth squeezed his eyes shut, summoning an illusion of safety and innocence. He transported himself to the baseball field, where the crack of the bat and the thrill of the game drowned out the horrors of reality. In his mind, if he could just catch that ball, if he could prove himself, maybe his grandfather would release him from this grotesque dance. "Let's play catch, Grandpa," Seth pleaded, his voice tinged with a glimmer of hope. But his cries fell on deaf ears. Desperation laced his words as Seth declared, "I can really throw far," his fragile hope hanging by a thread.

With a chilling grin, the old man discarded Seth's pants, baring his vulnerability to the abyss. His words, laced with sadistic amusement, assigned twisted roles to Seth's own body. The game of baseball they once shared morphed into an unspeakable horror. Seth's mind recoiled, slipping in and out of consciousness as he felt the assault against his body. With each futile struggle, his body betrayed him, responding in ways that terrorized him to his core. The pleas for mercy faded into an unintelligible murmur as Seth desperately sought to escape the horrifying reality that enveloped him.

* * *

Seth's eyes snapped open, his prison surroundings a disorienting blur. As he regained his bearings within the desolate isolation ward, a surge of pain shot through his body, a tangible reminder of the guards' torment intertwining with the deeper wounds etched into his soul. Sitting upright, he sifted through the fragments of his past, desperate to comprehend his role as the hapless victim, while his brother remained blissfully ignorant of the abuse.

Returning to his cell that afternoon, Seth reached beneath his bed, his fingers curling around a thick composition book. Flipping it open to the last page, he meticulously transcribed his most recent dream, resurrecting the images of his grandfather. He twisted the narrative to suit his desires, rewriting the details with himself as the triumphant victor, vanquishing his oppressors, the bosses, his own brother. Following the bizarre advice of the doctor, Seth found solace in rewriting history, discovering a fleeting respite within his words, a temporary balm that nourished his inner strength. Enjoy baseball, Grandpa? Behold this bat! Does the crushing of your skull bring you pain? How about the sensation of shoving this ball up your decrepit ass? Are you familiar with the concept of justifiable homicide?

An hour passed, and Seth's fabricated moments of glory found their place among hundreds of others, filling the five-hundred-page notebook halfway. Flashbacks from his youth, all culminating in a similar vein of revenge. Thoughts of Chance and Cassandra consumed him. He was just a heartbeat away.

* * *

One fateful morning, the prison's harsh intercom blared, commanding the prisoners to exit their cells. They formed single-file lines, some clutching books, others toting balls and frisbees, as they

151

filtered into the grim prison yard. Seth carried nothing with him, harboring no interest in games or distractions from his relentless contemplations. Stepping out into the warmth of the afternoon sun, he cast a piercing gaze upon his surroundings. A double row of barbed wire loomed, a stark reminder of the prison's inescapable grip. The beige dirt and dust matched the decay of the mortar and bricks. Inmates played catch with gloves clinging desperately to the remnants of their former glory. Mud puddles scattered across the yard, remnants of earlier rain.

Seth sat alone in the prison yard, eyes shut tight, soaking in the unforgiving sun. The cacophony of baseballs meeting leather gloves assaulted his ears, but he paid it no mind. His stomach churned as he struggled to banish the haunting images conjured by the game. "If only I had brought my revenge journal," he mused, as a particularly twisted scenario involving Chance's demise took hold of his mind. Shutting his eyes, he focused on the vivid mental image of his brother, subject to the brutality of four enraged inmates dressed in preppy attire.

A jarring squawk pierced through the air, forcing Seth's eyes open. He witnessed a winged guest tilting its head sideways, its pitch-black eyes fixated upon him. "Hello there," he said, greeting the crow. "Just another jailbird, I suppose."

With partially spread wings, the bird swayed its head from side to side, reminiscent of an injured bird Seth had encountered during a summer camp long ago. He had named it "Freebird," after the Lynyrd Skynyrd song. The crow squawked and hopped closer to Seth, pecking at the ground in search of sustenance. It gazed at him, then turned its head, pecking once more.

"Welcome to the monotonous life of prison. Repetition without reward," Seth murmured, his words laced with resignation.

"Got yourself a new buddy, huh?" a tattooed inmate remarked, nodding at the crow perched nearby.

Seth extended his hand as the bird hopped closer. "Seems like it," he replied, a hint of warmth in his voice.

In a matter of seconds, the bird took flight, vanishing beyond the prison grounds. Seth's thoughts returned to the injured sparrow from his youth. *Mustn't forget the loyalty of others.* His deep affection for animals had always confounded his parents, who failed to comprehend why this tender aspect of his personality was never extended to his own kin. They had even permitted Seth to nurse an injured mouse, nearly claimed by a stray cat, hoping that his compassion for animals would somehow transfer to his human interactions.

The air carried the faint strains of a melancholic melody, drifting through the prison yard. A prisoner, lost in the soulful tunes of his harmonica, momentarily brought a semblance of peace and humanity to Seth's world—a fleeting respite that always evaporated too quickly. He offered a smile to the musician, who improvised with a skillful touch, extending the blues progression over several choruses.

The abrupt thud of a glove and ball hitting the ground pierced the air as another inmate shouted, "Here they come!"

Seth jolted awake at the sound of raucous cheers from the prisoners.. They lined the perimeter, hailing the approaching bus carrying new inmates. To Seth, it seemed as if the population reveled in a sordid spectacle, akin to a low-class burlesque house, their hands clutching dollar bills to tip the evening's entertainment.

As the newcomers stepped off the bus, Louis and several guards brandished their guns, a silent warning that did little to stifle the jeers and cheers. Like helpless fish awaiting their fate in a frying pan, the convicted men entered a world that would soon become their dreaded home. The guards remained impervious to the taunts, and this callous indifference disgusted Seth the most. Human flesh, tossed around like baseballs in a twisted game played by amateurs.

The intercom blared multiple commands. "Face the wall! Arms by your sides! Silence!"

Seth's gaze shifted to the tower, where three armed guards with rifles perched, prepared for any signs of unrest. Warden Platts, a stocky man in his mid-fifties, made his customary appearance in the yard.

"Listen up!" he bellowed, pausing to command their attention. The Warden's eyes flicked to Louis, who fired three shots into the air. When silence descended upon the compound, Platts continued addressing the new inmates. "Respect is the cornerstone here. With it, you will survive. Within these walls, you will grow up quickly." He scrutinized the current prisoners with a hunger resembling a pack of wild dogs calculating their next kill. He ordered Louis to escort the newcomers to their cells.

The prisoners chanted lewd comments like "Hey cutie" and "Lover boy, I want you," summoning their power over the fresh arrivals. Seth had witnessed it all when he first stepped off that very same bus years ago. He knew the routine by heart, but the silence of one's cell never lasted for the newbies. He knew that mere seconds after the "lights out" command, the relentless taunting from inmates would commence.

"Let's go, Macklin," Thomas, a seasoned guard, said as the new inmates were herded into C Block. "You've been reassigned to D Block."

Part II

Months blurred, amounting to five years since Chance's betrayal led to Seth's incarceration. Over time, Seth started revealing his skills in mechanics and physics. A few weeks ago, several prison dryers malfunctioned. During a brief conversation, Seth casually offered his interpretation of the issue to the supervisor, Chauncy.

"Where does the vent for this row of dryers lead?" Seth inquired.

Chauncey, his head covered in dust, turned to face Seth. "I didn't design this damn thing!" He pounded the machine in frustration.

The prison laundry boasted twelve industrial washers and dryers, each connected to different ventilation systems. Seth had walked by the laundry countless times on his way to the library. On a previous occasion, he even volunteered for laundry duty, if only to escape the monotony.

"Hell, no," Louis had sneered, rejecting his request. "That detail is reserved for the privileged inmates with *real* money!"

Seth laughed at the irony of paying for the privilege of working. *Twisted, just like everything else in this wretched place.* On this particular day, as he passed by the laundry, his curiosity piqued by Chauncey's conversation about the dryer issue, Seth examined the grime and dirt adorning the mechanic's hair.

"You're wearing both the problem and the solution," Seth remarked.

"Who asked for your help?" Chauncey snapped, annoyed.

He glanced at his own grimy attire, noticing the dirt and grime adorning it. "I do have a vested interest. My fellow inmates are starting to offend me."

Laughter erupted from Chauncey's assistants, but he silenced them with a glare. "Oh, you think this guy's a comedian?" He turned to Seth, wiping his hands on a greasy rag. "Alright, genius, what's your brilliant idea?"

Kneeling beside Chauncey, Seth spoke in a hushed tone. "Your machines are clogging because of the new air conditioning system installed for the higher-ups in this joint. The vents for the dryers and air conditioners have crossed paths. Instead of blowing air out, the dryers are sucking in dirt from the outside. Check the blueprints."

Four days later, the machines were up and running again. Chauncey made no mention of Seth's contribution, but word had leaked out from his assistants. Soon, Seth found himself consulted for various mechanical problems within the prison. He also spent much of his free time in the prison library, devouring books on biology, mathematics, and political science. Some nights, he drifted off to sleep at a table near the window overlooking the compound, his revenge journal never far from his reach.

* * *

The medical schedule prescribed by the doctor had become Seth's routine since his transfer. One night, alone in his cell after dinner, Seth felt a strange churning in his stomach. He was suddenly reminded of his teenage years when he had impersonated Chance to date Barbara Connors. Lost in the memory, Seth mixed up his own role in the past, repeating the words Chance had once said. Overwhelmed, he cried out, "I'll kill you, Seth!"

The adjacent inmates grew agitated, their angry complaints fueling Seth's growing distress. One voice shouted, "Shut the fuck up!" followed by another, who banged a coffee cup against the steel bars, chanting, "Psycho Macklin! Psycho Macklin!"

Moments later, guards converged upon his cell, accompanied by Dr. Percault. Seth tore books from their spines, threatening anyone who dared approach.

"Calm down, Macklin," one guard demanded.

"Kill the psycho!" an inmate bellowed, lashing out against the bars with a plastic cup.

Suddenly, the noise in D Block erupted into a storm of screams and chants. The chemicals from the drugs now mingled with his rage, propelling him downstream like a rogue canoe hurtling toward an impenetrable boulder. *Kill Seth. Kill Chance. No more baseballs to throw or catch!*

"Seth, tell Grandpa you didn't mean to cause such trouble," he muttered incoherently.

"What's his problem?" the guard asked, perplexed.

Dr. Percault harbored suspicions. "He believes he's his brother. He's dangerous in this state."

Seth continued his tirade, shouting his name, his brother's name, his grandfather's name as he tore apart his cell. A guard cautiously

156

unlocked the door, and four others rushed in, swiftly subduing him. In the chaos, Dr. Percault injected him with a sedative.

As his mind blurred into oblivion, Seth murmured, "You finally got your way, Chance," and crumpled to the ground.

The uproar of prisoners persisted as the guards carried Seth to a lower level. Dr. Percault knew he had to increase Seth's medication. Over the following months, as he recklessly experimented with doses of Thorazine, Seth oscillated between ferocious aggression one day and a motionless vegetable-like state the next. Throughout it all, Seth retreated into his mind, the scars of his past widening rather than healing.

* * *

Another year slipped by, and Seth's hatred for Chance intensified within the confines of his prison cell. *Six years spent in this putrid place!* How many more were yet to come? His lengthy and detailed revenge journal became his only companion, a constant reminder that soon he would live out the stories he had penned. After yet another violent breakdown, he was overpowered and locked away in the isolation ward. *Must I starve myself to elude your manipulations, Percault?* On this particular day, he had lost all sense of time; the drugs forced upon him blurred the delicate line between reality and fantasy.

His sentences blended together as he wrote, "And he hated me as I loved him. And I hated him as he loved me. And he hit me, feeling my pain. And I hit him, feeling his pain. We fought, and it hurt us both. We fought again, and this time the pain was gone. I am here, and he forgot me. He is there, and that I will never forget. Don't swim those waters. Don't even think..."

An announcement echoed outside his cell. "Macklin! Your time has come!"

Seth's weary eyes rolled with fatigue. He glanced at his journal, scribbling one more word before closing the book—Chance!

Louis chuckled as Seth struggled to his feet. "Feels good, doesn't it?" he taunted, pushing Seth forward.

Seth blindly navigated the corridor, entering an unfamiliar area of the prison. The guard led him into a large rectangular room where six well-dressed individuals sat behind a table—four men and two

157

women—reviewing inmate files. Now eligible for parole, Seth sank into a wooden chair, listening with vacant eyes. A woman's sharp voice cut through the air as she read from a file labeled with Seth's name. His mind dulled, comprehension slipping away like sand through his fingers. Eyelids heavy, the woman's voice faded into a distant hum, akin to a persistent insect buzzing past his ear. The man beside her spoke.

"Seth Macklin, you have been incarcerated for six years. Do you have anything to say in your defense?" Seth's head slumped onto his chest, succumbing to sleep. "Does he even understand what I'm saying?"

"He understands," Louis replied, shaking Seth's slumbering form. "We had to sedate him."

Seth raised his head, but his mind was elsewhere, his gaze fixed on the parole board members. In his distorted perception, only two figures stood before him—his grandfather and Chance—urging him to unleash his fury. You have to kill them, Seth. Don't let Grandpa or Chance deceive you. *Do it!* With a feeble lunge towards the table, he screamed, "I'll kill you all!"

Before Seth could reach the table, Louis swiftly grabbed hold of him, restraining him with an iron grip. The members of the parole board recoiled, exchanging knowing glances. Without hesitation, Seth's fate was sealed as the woman stamped his file: parole denied.

As Seth stood there, the man from the board spoke with a stern expression, "It is prisoners like yourself that cause the system to fail." He issued a challenge, his words heavy with gravity, "Prove me wrong."

Back in his cell, Seth replayed the only words he had heard, "Prove me wrong." His mind was consumed by the challenge.

* * *

Over the next several months, Seth underwent a noticeable change in outward demeanor. Some guards speculated that he had finally broken, as he displayed an uncommon respect for authority. His body had grown accustomed to Dr. Percault's drugs, allowing him to control his outbursts by channeling his aggression into his journal.

One Sunday morning, Seth devised his next strategy to win the trust of those in power. He ventured towards an area of the prison he never visited—the interfaith chapel, located on the opposite wing of the library. The chapel attracted inmates of various religions, offering a reading area where seminary materials were available for studying specific faiths. Inmates who participated in chapel activities were exempted from conflicting work details.

Seth stood outside the chapel door, deep in thought. He opened the door and casually peeked inside. The spacious room featured an aisle dividing two groups of pews. His gaze landed on a middle-aged pastor with graying hair, delivering a sermon to a dozen Christian inmates, who dutifully followed along in their Bibles. Seth watched, hoping to catch the pastor's attention. At one point, the pastor motioned for Seth to enter. Feigning shyness and misguidedness, Seth averted his gaze and turned to leave, thinking, *Your stray sheep will return next week.*

The following Sunday, Father Joseph once again spotted Seth standing outside the chapel door. Mid-sermon, he paused and approached the entrance. "Come in, my son, come in," the pastor welcomed with open hands. "God welcomes all into His home."

"Thank you," Seth replied humbly.

He took a seat in the back pew, listening as the pastor spoke about the significance of honesty within oneself and in relationships with others. Although the lesson held little meaning for Seth, he maintained a facade of sincerity. God will show me the way out of here, he silently convinced himself.

In the weeks that followed, Seth began actively participating in the chapel activities, claiming to have discovered the importance of religion in his life. He gained the pastor's trust, who embraced Seth as a lost soul in need of guidance and support.

One Sunday, after sweeping the aisle between the pews, Seth set his broom aside and knelt in the front pew, his thoughts consumed by his new plan. From the corner of his eye, he noticed Pastor Joseph observing him, fueling his deceptive ploy. He pressed his hands together, closed his eyes, and silently prayed. Please, Lord, let Pastor Joseph believe I have found redemption through his guidance. *Let him hear my words.*

His prayers seemingly answered, Seth opened his eyes and greeted Pastor Joseph with a warm smile. "I should return to my cleaning. I didn't mean to disturb you."

"No, no," Joseph reassured him. "You are always welcome."

Seth resumed his seat, bowing his head. "I know I have sinned, and I know the Lord forgives me. But I struggle with feelings of anger."

Taking a seat beside him, Joseph placed a comforting hand on Seth's shoulder. "I can sense your desire to turn your life around."

Seth responded with the practiced words of a seasoned liar. "I can only hope that He forgives my sins as you have forgiven me."

"We are all guided by the Almighty. He will not forsake you."

With clasped hands, Seth expressed his gratitude. "Bless you, Father." As they engaged in deeper conversation, he felt their connection strengthen.

"I've been meaning to ask you," Joseph began, leaning closer. "What sin has led you to this house of rehabilitation?"

Seth let out a sigh, dredging up deep personal pain. "My family betrayed me, and in response, I unleashed my aggression on society. I was caught in the act of robbery." His gaze scanned the chapel, noting the absence of familiar rows of candles and the stained glass windows that had captivated him during his Catholic upbringing. "My anger is primarily directed at my twin brother, not my parents."

"Twins often share a profound connection, for better or worse. I have witnessed this dynamic many times," Joseph acknowledged.

"Chance envied my success and friends. Can you believe he even pretended to be me to steal my girlfriend?" Seth lamented.

Joseph nodded knowingly. "The Bible recounts such character traits that plague siblings in competitive families. I understand you much better now, my son. You lost your way in life, and I hope to guide you back."

The pastor paused, his fingers tracing the gold cross around his neck. "You mentioned being born and raised in the Catholic Church. Were you also an altar boy when you were younger?"

"Why, yes, I was," Seth replied, as he skillfully reversed the roles of himself and his brother in his mind. A sudden flashback catapulted him to church with his family.

* * *

Maggie tightly gripped her twelve-year-old son's hand. "Seth, behave yourself!" She glanced at her husband, Kevin, a silent plea for help. Kevin closed his eyes, trying to dismiss his son's disruptive behavior.

Ignoring his parents, Seth kicked the pew in front of him, causing a young couple to turn and politely request that he stop. "Didn't know anyone was listening to this crap," he muttered.

The woman stared at Seth's mother in disbelief. The hour-long sermon was only halfway through, and Seth continued to curse silently at Chance, who sat behind the pastor, donned in his altar-boy outfit. *All prim and proper, aren't you, Chance?* As the congregation rose and sang a psalm, Seth's gaze drifted into space, fixated on his brother's performance. Despite the continuous motions of sitting, standing, kneeling, and sitting again, Seth remained seated. His mother hissed in frustration.

"Do you really want a public spanking?" she whispered angrily.

"Anything to get me outta here," Seth replied with such volume that the couple in front shook their heads in disgust.

Kevin interjected, his voice laced with warning, "One more word, and you'll be grounded for a month with a bruise on your butt you'll never forget!"

Seth remained motionless, enduring a lengthy, ironically relevant passage from the Bible. "Many of us are familiar with the story of Jacob and Esau," the preacher said. "We know how Jacob defended his father's birthright, with his brother Esau attempting to deceive their father into believing he was Jacob. The Bible teaches us other similar lessons."

Seth glanced at his mother, grunting silently, knowing all too well that he was not the favored child. Tell that to my damn parents, God. They can't hear me, but I imagine they'd hear you. Give it a shot. *I dare you.* He looked up at the ceiling fan whirling above him. "Just as I thought," he muttered.

Throughout the service, Seth sneered and made snide faces at his brother. Chance attempted to ignore Seth's antics but found himself unable to look away. At one point, Seth began picking his nose, deliberately aiming his actions at his brother. He even stuck his finger into his mouth. Chance gasped, drawing the attention of the entire congregation. Embarrassed, Chance cowered apologetically. The priest halted his reading, shocked by the altar boy's lack of decorum. He turned and stared at the boy, then faced the congregation and resumed the interrupted passage. The whispers rippled through the pews, distracting from the sermon. Mr. and Mrs. Macklin were mortified. Meanwhile, Seth grinned, relishing in his brother's humiliation, an experience he wished would never end.

Later, as they approached the family car, Kevin demanded, "How dare you act so disrespectfully in the presence of God!" He grabbed Chance's arm, pulling him forcefully.

Seth adeptly assumed the role of the well-behaved son, though his heart brimmed with twisted pleasure. From the back seat, Chance sobbed while Seth remained silent. After a few moments, he inserted his finger into his nose, directing his gaze at Chance.

"Stop it!" Chance snapped.

Kevin's eyes blazed in the rearview mirror. "I don't want to hear another word!" Upon arriving home, he commanded, "Go to your room and stay there!" Chance dashed into the house, tears streaming down his face.

Seth, puzzled by the lenient punishment, questioned, "Aren't you going to spank him?"

"No. Chance has learned his lesson," Kevin replied firmly.

"That's not fair!"

"Don't start with me!"

Seth stood alone by the car, seething with anger at the absence of punishment for his brother's misbehavior.

* * *

As the memory faded, Seth struggled to compose himself, his hands trembling as he gazed sadly at Father Joseph. The room felt suffocating, memories clawing at the edges of his consciousness. "When Chance and I grew apart, I lost all faith in God. But after meeting and talking with you, Father, I feel like I've found my way back." With a respectful tone, he added, "I should get going."

"Remember, you're always welcome here," the priest replied, extending his hand.

"Thanks, Father," Seth said, shaking his hand before leaving.

* * *

Seth spent hours in the chapel, fixing squeaky doors and malfunctioning lights. He enjoyed the sense of freedom it brought

162

him, a brief respite from the monotony of prison life. One day, Smitty, the prison mechanic, sought Seth's advice on fixing the old prison bus. Seth analyzed the problem and suggested a solution—a new distributor.

As Smitty took a drag from a joint, Seth's mind wandered back to the days when drugs offered temporary escape. He hesitated for a moment, the aroma triggering memories of hazy nights and poor decisions. With a heavy heart, he declined, the taste of regret lingering on his tongue.

"I'm done with that stuff."

"What?" Smitty said, exhaling with a cough. "This stuff is like gold around here. What's gotten into you, Macklin?"

Deep down, Seth yearned for the temporary escape. "The drugs they've forced upon me in this hellhole have taken a toll on more brain cells than I'd care to admit."

Smitty took another drag. "Alright then, what's wrong with this piece of junk?" he asked, kicking the rusted sedan's front tires.

Seth patted Smitty on the shoulder. "I honestly don't have a clue. Sometimes there's only so much you can do to salvage a relic like this. Wish I could help." He began walking away.

Exhaling loudly, Smitty said, "Thanks for nothing, Macklin."

Seth noticed an approaching guard, pointing it out to Smitty, who quickly disposed of the joint and resumed his work.

* * *

As darkness enveloped the corridor, Seth made his way back to his cell from the laundry. Working with the maintenance staff three nights a week gave him a respite, allowing him to tinker with old machinery. He washed his hands, tossed a dirty towel into a hamper, and embarked on his usual route. He motioned for the guard at Access Level 1, gained admittance, and ascended two flights of stairs. Buzzing for access into D Block, he passed fifteen cells before reaching his own.

However, tonight was different. As he approached the library, he detected a faint sound from within. Seth halted, straining his ears, but the noise ceased. He noticed that the library entrance door was unlocked. A book fell to the floor, catching his attention. Inside the dimly lit room, he sensed an eerie presence. Proceeding cautiously, he approached the exit when a textbook slid past his feet, stopping in front of him. Several shadowy figures emerged, and panic surged within him. Seth made a dash toward the laundry, but someone tripped him, sending him crashing to the floor. He attempted to crawl forward, only to collide with another man. Before he could react, a blow landed on his back. Seth screamed, aware that he was trapped.

"Do try to keep quiet," one of the men sneered, gripping his arm tightly. "Remember, this is a library."

Four prisoners seized Seth from both sides, forcibly silencing him. A cold, clammy hand covered his mouth, scraping against his face with rough calluses. He struggled to break free, but the assailants delivered swift kicks to his legs, causing his knees to buckle. A rag reeking of kerosene was stuffed into his mouth, making him gag at the repulsive taste. They yanked his hair, jerking his head back forcefully. And then, he found himself staring into the eyes of his archenemy.

"You think I forgot about you?" Abdul bellowed. "This place suits you, doesn't it? Surrounded by books like a pathetic little scholar." He grabbed a heavy textbook and viciously slammed it into Seth's stomach, causing him to double over in excruciating pain. Abdul nodded to his men. "Put him on the table. I'm going to savor every moment of torturing this bastard!"

Seth collapsed with the rush of adrenaline as they ripped his pants from his body. Abdul's men forced him toward a reading table. He struggled, but within seconds, all of his clothes were torn from his body. They laid him face down on the table, his legs spread. Seth's eyes bulged at the rows of books resting on their shelves. The smell of library glue and kerosene on the rag in his mouth, combined with the putrid odor of the inmate, caused him to lose his sense of reality. He felt the penetration and gasped in horror and pain. They rammed the cloth deeper into his throat, silencing his muffled cries.

As Abdul's thrusts intensified, the table slid forward until it stopped against the bookshelf. Seth's anger rose within, but his agony only produced more laughter from his attackers. Abdul slammed the table into the bookshelf, causing books to fall next to Seth's head. He focused on the title of one that stared him in the face—something his grandpa used to read to him. *No. It can't be!* Seth's mind whirled through time, back to an incident he hoped he had buried forever. Within his thoughts, he yelled, "Stop it!"

              * * *

"I felt a bite," eight-year-old Chance said, holding his fishing pole.

They were casting lures from their aluminum canoe and could see Nana hanging laundry on a makeshift line. Seth glanced at Grandpa, who sat in a chair rereading his favorite novel, Herman Melville's Moby Dick.

Seth loved the story about the white whale, although he found it difficult to read the words of the great writer. "Let me read it to you at night," his grandpa had said the day before. Chance was not interested in hearing the story, opting instead to read comic books. The games, as his grandpa had called them, had begun innocently enough with Seth laying in his bed, listening to his grandpa say in a bellowing voice, "Call me Ishmael." Samuel had told him that they were the three most famous opening words of any novel.

As he fished from their canoe, Seth swallowed hard, remembering what had happened when Grandpa first started to read the story—the old man's hand resting innocently on his leg, then slowly caressing his thigh. Seth tried but could not speak. "Shh," his grandfather had said, continuing to explore his body as he read aloud.

As he finished the first page, Samuel reached his hand under the blanket, touching the boy's flesh. Goose bumps traversed Seth's body. He tried to inch himself away, but Samuel nudged him back. Seth froze, hearing only fragments of the words his grandpa spoke.

He remembered his grandfather crawling with his fingers like a spider up his thigh, stopping on his underwear. He felt Seth's crotch. The boy rolled his body, trying to free himself, but he could not. Because his body was so tense, it hurt for him to move. *Why is Grandpa touching me down there?*

"Grandpa," Seth begged during his struggle, "I'm not supposed to touch myself like that."

"But it's okay for me to."

His senses focused on the strong pipe smell coming from his grandpa's breath; he became nauseous and started to vomit into his mouth. He forced himself to swallow, afraid the strange punishment would get worse.

Seth started rocking back and forth in the canoe, trying to free himself. Grandpa glanced up from his novel and winked. He gasped, dropping his pole into the lake. Chance turned in shock.

"Stop rocking, wacko!"

But Seth could not stop. Staring at his grandpa's face sickened him. He rocked even harder, searching for escape. Suddenly, the canoe turned over, and the boys tumbled into the lake, their poles and tackle sinking to the bottom. Grandpa stood, throwing his book to the ground.

"Seth, get back here!"

He quickly swam away. "Stop it!"

* * *

"Stop it!" Seth yelled during Abdul's assault.

A guard switched on the library lights. Several others hosed the prisoners down with cold water. They grabbed Abdul, pulled him off, and threw him onto the concrete.

"Had enough, Macklin?" Abdul taunted.

"Shut the fuck up!" a guard said, disgusted by what he had seen.

Louis and the others waited for Seth to regain perspective. Seth glanced at the table with the scattered books and Moby Dick staring him in the face. Enraged, he threw it off the table, screaming. The guards led him to the infirmary, where the doctor gave him Valium.

This time, Seth gladly swallowed it, hoping for peaceful sleep to ease his pain. Yet his rage reminded him that no such pill existed.

* * *

The following morning, Seth found himself seated in Dr. Percault's office. As the doctor read through the file detailing the recent incident, Seth observed him with a hint of disdain. "What's it like to fail in your profession?" he taunted, leaning forward on his elbows.

Dr. Percault maintained his composure. "Seth, I'm here to help you."

Laughing bitterly, Seth replied, "Your medication made it impossible for me to defend myself. Add violent rape to your file!"

Though Dr. Percault stood before him, Seth's distorted vision replaced the doctor with the image of his grandfather. He closed his eyes, attempting to banish the haunting vision. Sensing the internal struggle within Seth, the doctor knew that if he could find a way to make him confront his past, the healing process could begin. With unwavering certainty, he decided to wean Seth off the medications immediately, believing that freedom from their grasp was crucial.

* * *

Seth navigated his prison routine with minimal emotion, interacting sparingly with other inmates, his focus fixed on revenge against one person. The prison library, once a haven of knowledge that fascinated him, now held no allure. The mere sight of books triggered a tightening in his stomach and waves of nausea. Only one book brought him any semblance of pleasure—his revenge journal.

One afternoon, as Seth returned to his cell, he opened his journal to the last page and began to write: We've reached a crossroads, my younger twin... This battle may be yours, but the war I will win... On this plane, parallel lines don't meet... Yet I overlap same, and my life is complete... Mark my words as you run and hide, Grandpa touched you and you have lied. Like all boys, we played games as kids, but I never did learn where it was that you hid.

Closing the journal with a self-satisfied smile, Seth knew that soon his brother would no longer be able to hide from him. His monthly visits with Dr. Percault had become weekly now.

"Is reducing your medication helping to clear your mind?" he inquired.

"Better," Seth responded.

Dr. Percault noticed the difference. Though Seth still harbored deep trust issues, he was starting to believe that Percault genuinely wanted to help him. Throughout their weekly sessions, Seth avoided admitting to the childhood abuse, but Dr. Percault had his suspicions. In one session, he felt Seth drawing close to revealing his past, only to witness the steel door of Seth's memories slam shut, concealing everything. Seth Macklin was an enigmatic case study—a highly intelligent man with natural mechanical aptitude and a keen analytical mind. But even the doctor struggled to penetrate Seth's layers of anger and guilt. Seth remained in control, shielding his innermost thoughts from detection. With Thorazine no longer clouding his mind, Seth's purpose became clear.

* * *

Louis loomed over Seth's slumbering body, barking, "Macklin, get up! You've got a new work detail." Seth's eyes flew open, and he hesitated before slipping on his shoes. "You must have kissed some serious ass to get this job," he muttered.

Louis ushered him along the steel floors of D Block, their footsteps echoing in the corridor. Seth moved swiftly, guessing it was around three in the morning. As they entered the kitchen, Louis taunted Claudio, the rotund Italian cook notorious for his volatile temper. Seth had always found Claudio to be a mystery. He remembered seeing him barking orders and maintaining strict discipline in front of the guards, but also sharing jokes with fellow inmates when no one was watching. He kept his silence as he was introduced to the prison cook.

"A troublemaker, huh?" Claudio looked at Seth with force. "Welcome to my den of fools!"

Dressed in a stained apron, Claudio scratched his thick sideburns and stubbly double chin, waiting for a response. Seth matched his silence, engaging in a waiting game.

"His name's Seth, but you can call him whatever the hell you want," Louis interjected.

"Hello, spignoli breath." Claudio's hearty laughter filled the kitchen. "Over here!"

As Louis left, the energy in the room shifted. Claudio placed his hand on Seth's shoulder. "Welcome to kitchen detail, Seth. The work sucks, the hours are long, it's hotter than hell in here, and I'm one mean son-of-a-bitch when the guards are around. The good news is we eat well, and when no one's looking, I can be a pretty nice guy. But when Louis is around, don't even think of talking to me. I hate that guard more than any of the others."

"Let's do it," Seth agreed, ready to tackle his new assignment.

"First, we feast on real eggs and bacon," Claudio declared, leading Seth to a large grill. "This is where I work my magic! You've come to savor my culinary delights, haven't you?" Claudio chuckled as Seth's shock turned to anticipation. "Ah, a food critic," he continued. In a flurry of activity, Claudio scrambled eggs in a mixing bowl, adding pieces of ham, cheese, onions, and peppers. Within minutes, a mouthwatering omelet was plated before Seth.

Eagerly delving into his breakfast, Seth savored the simple pleasure of real food. "These eggs aren't like the ones I've eaten for two thousand days,' he remarked with nostalgia."

"Damn right! You guys get fed garbage. But today, you're the king of this hill."

"So, Claudio, what are you in for?"

Claudio replied with a smirk, "I'm innocent."

Seth chuckled. "None of my business."

"I'll tell you anyway," Claudio said, frying onions on the stove. "I opened a restaurant with a friend, but being a poor bookkeeper, I didn't notice when he embezzled eighty thousand dollars."

Curiosity piqued, Seth asked, "So why isn't he here instead of you?"

"He's still in the hospital, recovering. And don't even think about trying anything behind my back, Macklin." Claudio held a large knife, attempting to look menacing. After a few minutes of cleanup, he announced, "Time to prepare the crap. You're in charge of the eggs."

Glancing at the metal mixing bowl and boxes of ready-mix eggs, Seth grabbed the first box labeled "Reconstituted Eggs," studying the list of artificial ingredients with disdain. Claudio tossed chopped onions onto the grill, claiming they masked the phony taste. Seth observed the powdered substances on the counter, shaking his head in disgust. Then, he spotted several coolers stocked with real food. He opened one, retrieved a plastic bottle, and poured himself a glass of orange juice. Claudio handed him a mug of coffee.

"You see, it's good to be a cook," Claudio remarked.

Seth scrutinized the cardboard box, contemplating more suitable variations for the distasteful fare. Claudio, impressed with Seth's culinary skills, enjoyed a brief respite with him before lunch detail began. Jose and Ronald, two of Claudio's assistants, arrived to lend a hand. Later, during dinner service, as Louis made his usual rounds to inspect the evening menu, Seth witnessed his constant torment of Claudio—mocking his excessive weight and perpetual perspiration.

Tapping his nightstick, Louis said with disdain, "Hey, fatso, I expect two helpings of dinner. Make it hot, with plenty of bread. You got that, sweathog?"

"Yes, boss," Claudio responded meekly.

Seth spent two weeks on kitchen detail, enjoying Claudio's company and exchanging stories about life behind bars. His respect for Claudio grew steadily, recognizing him as an important mentor—*a mind as sharp as his gut, and a heart twice the size.*

One night, before serving the guards in an isolated section of the cafeteria, Louis mercilessly taunted Claudio. He stuck out his foot, causing Claudio to trip and crash onto the concrete floor. Blood gushed from his forehead, dishes shattered. Seth rushed to assist his friend.

"Freeze, Macklin!" Louis barked. "Touch him, and you're off detail, back to the general population." He kicked Claudio in the side, rousing him. "Get up, slob. I want to eat!"

Claudio slowly regained consciousness, summoning the strength to rise. His matted hair was stained with blood. Louis pushed him toward the kitchen.

"I want a plate of that famous stew of yours. Get it now!"

While Louis engrossed himself in reading the newspaper, his hand caressed the black handle of his nightstick. Claudio seethed with anger. Seth noticed the cook's blood-stained uniform and how unsteady he seemed. Claudio had done nothing to deserve such mistreatment, yet injustice prevailed within the prison walls. Claudio wiped his bleeding forehead with a wet towel, his face turning black and blue, his eyebrow swelling.

"It's time to pay that son-of-a-bitch back. Get the stew from the cooler," Claudio commanded.

Seth retrieved the large pot, pushing the cooler door closed. But Claudio gestured for him to wait.

"In the back, there's a red coffee can. Bring it here," Claudio instructed.

Seth opened the cooler door again and scanned the wire shelves until he found the can. He removed it and opened the lid, only to be assaulted by a foul stench. "What the hell is this?" Seth exclaimed, recoiling in disgust.

"My science experiment," Claudio laughed, clutching the can. "Now I'll show you the privileges we earn for taking a beating." He poured the stew into the pot on the stove. Opening the coffee can, he scooped out a spoonful, stirring it into the stew until it blended completely. "I'm going to make Louis regret every bite."

As Claudio served the laced stew to Louis, Seth grinned, his mind drifting back to a science experiment from his past, while the guard took the first mouthful.

* * *

"Class, does anyone know what happens when these two chemicals are combined?" Mrs. Miller asked, pointing to young Seth, who eagerly raised his hand.

"The color changes to red, and the chemical becomes toxic," Seth answered confidently.

"Excellent! Your understanding of biology and chemistry is remarkable," Mrs. Miller praised, peering over her glasses. "I see on our calendar that your biology experiments are due this Monday. They contribute significantly to your grade. No exceptions. Understood?"

"Yes, Mrs. Miller," the class replied in unison.

Filled with excitement from being the star pupil, Seth raced home, eager to share his news. Bursting through the front door, he exclaimed, "Mom, Dad, guess what I—"

"Quiet," his father interrupted. "Your brother was just telling us about his soccer goal today. Go on, Chance."

Seth froze, mid-sentence, as he watched his parents shower praise upon Chance. Feeling invisible and unheard, he slammed the front door in a desperate attempt to gain their attention.

"What is it?" Chance asked, concerned.

Seth's crestfallen face turned toward his father. "I had something to share from class today, and—"

"Seth!" his father sternly reprimanded. "Wait your turn." Instead, Seth ran up the stairs, his dad bellowing, "You're leaving in an hour, Seth. I expect you to be ready to go!"

Later, Chance knocked on his brother's door. "Seth, can I come in?" He entered the room, noticing Seth's bags packed for the overnight Scout trip. "What happened today?"

"Nothing," Seth responded listlessly, making his way to the bookshelf. "Chance, I need you to do me a favor while I'm away. I've been working on this biology experiment, and I need you to place it by the window twice a day for one hour each time. My grade depends on it. Can you help?"

"Of course," Chance replied, glancing at the three petri dishes. "Just write down the instructions."

Seth's face lit up. "I'll be back on Sunday night, okay?" He quickly jotted down the simple guidelines for Chance to follow.

Their father's voice echoed from downstairs, "Seth, they're here. Come on!"

"I'll ace biology with this experiment," Seth said before rushing downstairs. Once outside, he glanced up at the second-floor window, waving to Chance. The weekend passed swiftly, with Seth eagerly anticipating his return home to check on his experiment. Carrying his sleeping bag and backpack up the steps, he couldn't wait to share stories of his trip with his family. But as he entered the living room, he noticed his father's solemn expression.

"What's wrong?" Seth inquired anxiously.

"I have bad news. Chance accidentally left your experiment by the window all day yesterday. The petri dishes turned brown. He's in his room, upset over what happened," his father revealed.

"But he promised to take care of them!" Seth protested.

"It was an accident. Chance had a soccer game on Saturday and simply forgot," his father explained. Seth fell to the living room floor, his fists clenching the thick carpet. "It's just one experiment. You'll have plenty more."

Looking up at his father through tear-filled eyes, Seth cried out, "This is the only thing I'm good at, and none of you even care! I hate all of you!"

Kevin tried to restrain Seth's flailing arms, but Seth struck him. "Don't you ever do that again!" He retaliated, twisting Seth's arm behind his back.

Seth begged for mercy, his voice filled with desperation. "I just wanted to get good grades. To make you proud!"

* * *

"Chance, you bastard," Seth muttered under his breath in the prison kitchen.

"What did you say?" Claudio turned and asked, catching Seth off guard.

"Nothing. Did Louis finish eating that crap?" Seth replied, trying to divert attention.

Claudio proudly displayed the empty bowl. "Now the real fun begins. Soon, you'll see him sprinting to the crapper."

As Seth cleaned up, he observed Louis, the sole victim consuming the tainted food. Later, clutching his stomach and grimacing in pain, the guard hastily rushed towards the bathroom. Claudio smiled, his eye still bearing the mark of their earlier encounter. "Paybacks are a bitch," he remarked with satisfaction.

* * *

During Seth's second parole board meeting, he was escorted into the room where the same individuals from the previous year were gathered. His past record was recited aloud, but this time, it was supplemented with letters from Pastor Joseph and Dr. Percault.

The man who had spoken to him before said, "Based on what I've read, it seems you've taken my advice to heart."

Seth responded with a respectful tone, "It's been a difficult journey, but my ride is nearing its end. I have embraced honesty, religion, and discipline. If given the opportunity, I will work positively to contribute to society and further my career in biology." Seth leaned back in his chair, maintaining a composed demeanor.

The woman from the previous year scrutinized his every move, searching for any sign of deception. Engaging in a private group discussion, she occasionally glanced at Seth, sensing there might be more to him than meets the eye. Determined to portray the image of a reformed man, Seth merely smiled, exuding an air of regret for his past actions. Moments later, the decision was made. Parole was granted with a majority vote of five to one, the older woman being the sole dissenter.

"Thank you. I won't betray your faith," Seth acknowledged, nodding at the woman.

His words masked his true intentions, as he relished the role of a skilled manipulator, eager for the day when he could enact the stories within his journal. The following morning, he was led past the cells of his fellow inmates in D Block, receiving envy-filled cheers. Spotting Abdul and his gang, Seth remained silent as he walked out of the main door and into the embrace of the outside world. He inhaled deeply, savoring the taste of freedom and gazing out at the vast expanse before him.

He was back, two years ahead of schedule and liberated to pursue his own agenda.

* * *

After disembarking from a commuter bus in the heart of Boston, Seth paused to take in the sights at Park Street. Couples with children entered and exited the station, while people enjoyed outdoor activities in the nearby park. Boarding a Green Line train to the Kenmore Station, he observed the diverse gathering of individuals in the carriage, absorbing the ambiance of a warm evening. Stepping out of the underground station, he cast his eyes upon passersby who seemingly took their freedom for granted. Adding to the satisfaction of his freedom, he strolled past Fenway Stadium, reminiscing about past ball games with family and friends, including his grandfather.

Continuing along, he approached Boylston Street. The year was 2002, and Seth had yet to grasp the changes brought forth by the new millennium. Time had held no meaning behind bars, rendering progress irrelevant. After hailing a cab, he instructed the driver, "Just drive." Boston appeared unfamiliar to Seth, as he marveled at the imposing suspension bridge that graced the downtown area, adjacent to the new Fleet Center. The cabbie grumbled about the inconveniences caused by all the ongoing construction, but Seth paid little attention, lost in his own fantasies of encountering Chance and Cassandra at any moment. He had longed for this day, and now time was finally on his side.

As they drove through Cambridge, Seth's attention was captivated by a neighborhood park. "Stop here," he commanded, handing the cabbie his fare and a small tip. Stepping out of the cab, he observed boys and girls engrossed in play on swings and merry-go-rounds. His gaze sharpened as he fixated on a little boy darting about with a friend in pursuit. Their joyful antics served as a haunting reminder of bygone days when Seth and Chance reveled in the thrill of hide-and-seek.

Seth surveyed the surroundings, his mind teeming with the possibility of spotting Chance and Cassandra watching over their own children. "You're close, dear brother. Can you sense my presence?"

Acknowledging the vast passage of time, he contemplated the likelihood that Chance could now be among those parents. His eyes

174

followed the boy's gleeful descent down the slide, a soft landing on the cushioning sand below. The child eagerly climbed the ladder, ready for another exhilarating ride. However, his excitement quickly turned to fear as things immediately went awry when he started to slide. Seth's instincts kicked in, and he reached out, adjusting him just in time to prevent the boy from falling off the slide. Startled by the unexpected assistance, the boy expressed gratitude to the stranger who had helped him regain his balance. Seth scanned the park, but the child's parents eluded his gaze. It became apparent that his presence had gone unnoticed, rendering him invisible. A familiar smile curled upon his lips.

Clutching his revenge journal, he departed the park, observing the carefree children frolicking in delight. Just like the unburdened boy on the slide, Seth recognized the freedom to explore any playground he desired.

No one could halt his pursuit.

No one.

"Brad, it's too bad Seth didn't share his abuse with his parents. They might have been able to help him," Elizabeth said, as she continued hosting her show.

"Unfortunately, we'll never know. But, with every dark cloud there is that ray of sunshine. Chance and Cassandra's ray of sunshine soon became all they could think about."

"Their little bundle of joy. And yet, as I read this final chapter, I couldn't help but think about Seth lurking in the background."

"The suspense always surrounded Chance and Cassandra. They just didn't recognize it before it was almost too late."

"The show is 'Topics Above The Line' and I'm speaking with Brad Genova, author of Twin Crossing. Any last comments?"

"I'd like to conclude by saying how much I've enjoyed being on your show, Elizabeth. Perhaps, when I have finished my sequel to this story, you might ask me back."

"Indeed..."

Chapter 7

Part I

"Whee, Mommy! Catch me if you can." The four-and-a-half-year-old girl giggled with delight as she slid down the towering slide at their neighborhood park in West Newton. Her mother caught her at the bottom, their eyes sparkling with joy.

"Again, pleeease!" the girl pleaded.

Cassandra stole a glance at Chance, who sat nearby, sketching in his notebook, soaking in the tranquil Saturday afternoon in early October. Realizing they were running late, he pointed to his watch, conveying the need to leave.

"Angel, we have to go. Daddy's waiting for us," Cassandra informed her daughter.

Angel pouted, attempting to sway them with contrived sadness. "Please?"

"Okay, one more fast one, but you have to hurry."

Chance laughed as Angel bounded up the ladder. Just like her mother, he thought. After her final exhilarating ride, she rushed to hug her father.

"Daddy, did you see me on the big slide?" she asked, her eyes glowing with excitement.

"Yes, I did. Weren't you scared?" Chance replied.

Angel beamed with bravery. "Nope. Wanna see me do it again?"

"No, no, not now," he quickly added. "We don't want to be late for the concert. Plus, you want to play with Brad, right?"

Angel grinned at the thought of being with her favorite babysitter. Cassandra zipped up Angel's jacket, inquiring about the time they were supposed to meet.

"Four o'clock. Less than an hour," Chance answered, winking at Angel.

During the drive home, the young girl's mind buzzed with questions. "Are the Tracys going too?"

Chance nodded, explaining that they were all going out for dinner and to the symphony. "Brad really enjoys babysitting. He says you're very entertaining."

Her hair cascaded to the side as she asked, "What does entertaining mean?"

Glancing at Cassandra, Chance replied, "Entertaining means you're very funny."

Kicking her feet against the back of the front seat, Angel declared, "Brad's entertaining too!"

* * *

Now fifteen years old, Brad had become popular and active in high school. He played right wing for the soccer team and excelled academically without boasting about his achievements. Everyone, especially Angel, adored the young man he had become.

As they arrived home, Angel anxiously peered out the window, eagerly anticipating their arrival.

"They're here!" she exclaimed.

"Open the door," Cassandra called, descending the stairs.

"It's stuck," Angel replied, struggling to open it. Laughter emanated from outside as the guests arrived.

"Anybody home?" Greg called out.

With the door finally opened, Brad exclaimed, "Surprise!"

"Wow! What's this?" Angel glowed as she observed what he held.

"It's a bear," Brad said.

"It's a funny-looking bear, isn't it, Brad?" Angel queried, looking at her mom.

"It's a special kind called a panda bear," Brad explained, imparting just enough information for the little girl to grasp. He playfully tickled her tummy, evoking delightful giggles.

Chance made his way downstairs, saying, "What's all the commotion?"

"Daddy, it's a panda bear. Brad got it for me," Angel eagerly shared.

"You are a lucky girl." Chance turned to Greg and Lisa. "Can I offer you anything before we go?"

Cassandra immediately intervened. "No! We have dinner reservations in twenty minutes," she asserted, giving Chance a stern look then smiled at Brad. "We'll be home just after eleven. I left the phone number of the restaurant in the living room. Both your dinners are in the fridge and can be heated up in the microwave. Angel needs to be in bed by eight, and..." She paused, realizing that Brad was well aware of the responsibilities. She kissed them both good night.

"Have fun," Brad waved as the adults departed.

"Have fun," Angel echoed.

As Brad locked the door, excitement filled his voice. "Speaking of fun, Angel, we're gonna have some right here!"

"What do we do first?" Angel asked, her eyes brimming with anticipation.

"How about hide and seek?"

Her eyes lit up. "You're it!"

"I'll count to twenty, and then here I come," Brad declared, closing his eyes as Angel scampered away, her tiny footsteps ascending the stairs.

"Ready or not, here I come!" Brad's voice echoed through the house as he playfully narrated his search. Although he knew she had hidden on the second floor, he pretended to check the downstairs. "Are you behind the drapes? Behind the TV? You're quite the little hider, aren't you?" He stomped up the stairs, giving away his position. "Hmm, in your parents' room?" He entered and began searching earnestly, looking through closets and under the bed.

Slowly opening Angel's bedroom door, which was adorned with dolls and toys, he surveyed the room. The new panda bear sat proudly atop her pillow. Brad examined the dollhouse, peering under Barbie's bedspread. "Nope, not inside Barbie's bed. But I think I'm getting warmer." Muffled laughter emerged from the closet. "Gosh, I just don't know where that little girl is. Barbie, do you know where she is?"

Suddenly, the closet door burst open, and Angel leapt forward, attempting to surprise him. "Here I am!" She landed on her bed, bouncing up and down as if it were a trampoline. "Watch this!"

Brad laughed as she jumped higher and higher, bouncing from one end of the bed to the other. "Be careful," he cautioned.

"It's... O... kay... Mom... lets... me... do... this... all... the... time," she said, each syllable aligning with her bounces.

With each successive bounce, Brad interjected, "I... think... you... should... stop." Angel soared into the air, landing flat on her stomach. He sat beside her on the bed, observing her room.

"Can I show you my new Barbie dolls?" Angel asked, gripping his hand tightly and leading him to a meticulously arranged display. "This is Barbie, and this is Ken," she stated the obvious with care.

"And who's this?" Brad inquired, pointing to another doll.

"That's also Barbie, silly boy."

"I thought they were twins or something."

"No, Barbie has no brother or sister. And neither does Ken."

Brad was impressed by her authoritative tone, even if she might be incorrect. "But, isn't Skipper Barbie's sister?"

Angel suddenly realized she wasn't sure. She furrowed her brow, frowning as she attempted to figure out the answer. "Skipper?" Her attention was diverted by another part of her playhouse, and she shared another prized possession. "Look, it's their bright red car." Placing it back on her dresser, she rearranged her dolls. They left the bedroom and descended the stairs to play.

Later, she asked, "What concert did they go see at Sympathy Hall?"

Brad laughed at her mispronunciation. "It's Symphony, Angel. Can you say Symphony?"

She mouthed the unfamiliar word. "Simfony!"

"They went to hear a concert of Beethoven's 'Ninth Symphony.'"

Her excitement grew. "What about the other eight? Don't they have to hear them first?" Brad chuckled. "What's so funny?" she pouted.

"You crack me up." He proceeded to explain the fundamentals of a symphony. Recalling a recent music class, Brad suggested, "Maybe we'll go hear Mahler's 'First Symphony' when you're older."

Confusion clouded her face. "What's a Mahler?"

"It's the name of a man who wrote lots of symphonies."

"Daddy talked about his Mahler. He caught it on a big boat he went on. Is it the same Mahler?"

This time, Brad burst into laughter. "No, Angel, that Marlin is a fish. The other Mahler is a man who wrote lots of music. But not the one Daddy and Mommy went to see. Do you understand now?"

She shook her head, and Brad, eager to change the subject, came up with a clever idea. "How about we heat up some dinner, eat in front of the TV, and watch your favorite movie?"

Angel nodded eagerly. "The Lion King!"

* * *

"Can I offer you some coffee and dessert?" the waitress asked at a Thai restaurant near Symphony Hall.

Chance spoke up. "Four coffees, please."

"I'd love some coconut ice cream," Greg replied.

Cassandra and Lisa grinned. "I guess we'll have four servings," Cassandra said, half-dreading the extra exercise she would need to compensate.

"Have you ever heard the 'Ninth' performed live?" Greg inquired.

"No, but we have the CD at home. Chance gets a lot of energy from the 'Ninth,' don't you, Chance?" Cassandra's eyes met her husband's, momentarily erasing Lisa and Greg from existence.

Later, the two couples stepped into the grandeur of Symphony Hall, nestled in Boston's historic Back Bay. Lisa's eyes widened in awe as she took in the breathtaking interior adorned with majestic white pillars and lofty ceilings. A sea of elegantly attired art enthusiasts gracefully floated past, adding an air of enchantment to the atmosphere. The hall shimmered with a fusion of opulent decorations and resplendent chandeliers, while attendees showcased gowns as magnificent as the hall itself. Some opted for a more relaxed attire, and Chance couldn't help but feel slightly overdressed in his sleek black suit. However, stealing a glance at Cassandra, he was reminded of the reason he had dressed to the nines—to be the object of his wife's admiration.

Lisa found herself entranced by the rows of golden cherubs adorning the balconies, their ethereal presence complementing the deep red velvet curtains and luxurious white marble stairs. As they entered the performance hall, her breath caught in her throat at the sheer expanse of the room. Its length seemed to stretch on forever, embellished with ornate gold-trimmed ceiling ornaments and delicate figurines. The upper balcony spanned the entirety of the hall, its continuous banister crafted from the finest stained cherry wood. Onstage, musicians were preparing their strings and horns, their warm-up melodies drifting through the air. From the back row, a percussionist fine-tuned the timpani, while another adjusted the grip of a pair of crash cymbals.

"I can hardly contain my excitement," Lisa whispered, her hand nestled in Greg's arm.

They found their seats in the twelfth row, eagerly anticipating the moment when the rest of the musicians would take the stage and the conductor would make his grand entrance.

"I've always dreamed of seeing John Williams in person," Lisa confessed, her eyes filled with wonder.

Cassandra, eager to share her knowledge of the upcoming performance, chimed in, "I adore the timpani part in the second movement." Lisa scanned the percussion section, her finger pointing at the large brass drums stationed at the back.

Chance shot his wife a mischievous glance, recalling the passion they had shared during the second movement—a percussion part Cassandra had hardly noticed until they met. Now, as the piece unfolded, her closed her eyes, immersing herself in every note, her refined and passionate ears absorbing each sound. She reached forward, entwining her fingers with her husband's.

"It's wonderful," Cassandra murmured, her voice filled with emotion.

* * *

"Bradley, it's time to wake up," Lisa whispered when they arrived back at the Macklin's house.

Finding Brad fast asleep on the couch, the television casting the evening news to an empty room, he groggily opened his eyes. "I hate that name," he mumbled.

"Did everything go well?" Cassandra inquired, her voice warm and caring.

"Yup," he yawned, stretching his tired limbs. "Angel's asleep upstairs."

"Did you two have a good time?" she asked.

Brad sat upright, rubbing the sleep from his eyes as he nodded his head. Cassandra handed him an envelope, a twenty-dollar bill nestled within. "Here you are, Brad, and thank you."

He slipped on his shoes and jacket, standing by the door in a drowsy haze. Cassandra walked over to the entertainment console, selecting a CD and quietly passing it to Lisa. "Here it is," she whispered, her voice barely audible.

"Thank you," Lisa murmured, lightly tapping Greg on the shoulder as he conversed with Chance. "I believe it's time for us to depart." Greg and Lisa bid farewell as they left.

Now alone, Chance couldn't help but ask about the private conversation Cassandra and Lisa had shared during the intermission.

"I may have mentioned how Beethoven drives you to the brink of madness," she teased.

"You didn't! Tell me you didn't," Chance blushed, surprised to learn that their secret had been revealed, and she had even loaned Lisa the CD. He followed her up the stairs, anticipation growing within him. "Cassandra, you'll pay for this," he laughed.

"You'll have to catch me first," she retorted, disappearing into the bedroom, her clothes hastily discarded.

* * *

Several weeks passed, and the first snowfall gracefully descended after the Thanksgiving break. With the holiday season approaching, Chance seized every moment to fulfill his shopping duties, carefully selecting presents for his beloved wife and daughter, Greg and Lisa, and, of course, his buddy, Brad. And as the magical day of Christmas drew near, Chance could hardly contain his excitement.

"Brad, hurry up! We'll be late for church," Lisa called out, her voice filled with urgency and anticipation.

Bounding down the stairs of their home on Haywood Knolls Drive—the home Chance had sold to the Tracy's two years ago after Greg and Lisa's wedding—Brad couldn't help but notice his Mom's playful expression.

"What's wrong?" Brad inquired, adjusting the red and blue tie he wore on special occasions. Lisa straightened his collar, her hand grazing his cheek. "Are we going to meet the Macklin's at church?"

"Yes. Then we'll return home for breakfast."

"Do I have to wear this suit all day?" Brad questioned, brushing off his jacket. "I do feel like James Bond." They made their way to the church, and as Brad caught sight of Angel in the parking lot, he couldn't help but utter, "Hello, Angel Eyes."

Cassandra's mind flooded with memories, her internet sign-on name resurfacing in her thoughts. "What did you say?" she inquired, her curiosity piqued.

"Angel Eyes," Brad repeated, his voice filled with innocence. "I can see little angels in her eyes."

Catching Cassandra's eye, Chance remarked, "The power of the church."

She followed the rest of the group into the service, whispering softly, "Pretty powerful church."

* * *

After they arrived back at Lisa's home, Lisa asked, "Eggnog or coffee?" The adults raised their hands for coffee, while Brad and Angel opted for eggnog.

"Who goes first?" Greg asked, eyeing the pile of presents under the tree.

Brad handed Angel a wrapped package, and she quickly tore it open. "Wow! A Barbie Beach Buggy! Thanks, Brad." She leaned in and kissed his cheek.

Peanuts, their beloved furry companion, scampered around the house, barking with delight as they engaged in a game of fetch, his paws dancing across the floor, occasionally sending bundles of wrapping paper through the air. As the afternoon sun wafted through the cool air, they embarked on a drive to the Macklin house.

Back at her own home, Cassandra had adorned every corner with delicate glass and porcelain Christmas ornaments. The living room had become a magical haven, with rows of colored lights tracing the perimeter and casting a soft, enchanting glow. The air was imbued with the alluring scent of sandalwood incense, its sweet and comforting aroma embracing the room like a warm blanket.

"This is beautiful," Lisa said, admiring the fireplace. Hanging from the mantle were red Christmas stockings, brimming with toys and candy. Each stocking had a name sewn into the fabric.

Angel pointed proudly to her stocking. "Mine's the biggest."

"It sure is," Lisa replied, patting Angel's golden hair.

Cassandra had arranged a cherished antique porcelain nativity scene on the mantle, placing each figurine amidst a bed of real hay. The scene came alive with the story of the birth of Jesus, capturing the hearts of all who beheld it. Lisa's eyes glimmered as she took in the intricate details, her fingertips adjusting the position of a small camel figurine, ensuring its place was just right.

184

Meanwhile, Angel, full of excitement and anticipation, couldn't contain her enthusiasm any longer. Tugging at Brad's arm with a mischievous glimmer in her eyes, she whispered in a hushed tone, promising him a delightful surprise.

"Close your eyes," she instructed, leading him toward the brightly lit Christmas tree. "Surprise!"

Confused, Brad opened his eyes and asked, "Surprise? What surprise?"

"My tree is your tree," Angel giggled.

"She really takes after her mother, doesn't she?" Brad chuckled.

"I really take after my mom, don't I?" Angel danced around the living room, her joy infectious. She handed Brad a large, haphazardly wrapped box held together with multiple layers of tape. "I wrapped it myself."

"I can tell," Brad laughed, pulling at the tape to reveal a leather soccer ball. "Thanks, Angel Eyes."

Just then, the phone rang. Chance got up to answer it. "It's Morgan," he announced, passing the receiver to Cassandra to talk to her brother.

"Perfect timing," Cassandra said, pointing for Brad to give Angel the present from her uncle. "She's opening it now, Morgan."

Angel unwrapped the gift, puzzled. "What are these?"

"Cool," Brad gasped. "Walkie-talkies!"

"Morgan, that's great," Cassandra said into the phone.

"Do you remember the ones we had? When you got lost in the park, and I used them to guide you home?" Morgan asked through the phone.

"I do," Cassandra reminisced. "I was really scared. Our presents for you and Mom are under her tree." She watched as the kids inserted batteries into the walkie-talkies. "Just a second. They're about to try them out."

Brad ran up the stairs with his walkie-talkie in hand, and Angel's confusion turned to excitement.

"Come in, Angel. This is Brad. Your number one secret spy," he said through the device

Amazed to hear his voice, Angel pushed the button and replied, "Brad, are you there?"

"Yup. Loud and clear," he bellowed through the speaker.

Her eyes widened with wonder. "Mommy, he heard me!"

Cassandra waved to her daughter. "You made her day, Morgan. Mine too!"

"Don't forget to make those snow angels," Morgan reminded her.

"I won't. Talk to you later," Cassandra replied, hanging up the phone.

Soon, Cassandra and Lisa began preparing dinner. She invited Angel to say grace. Blushing with pride, Angel looked at Brad and said, "Thank you for all my cool presents and for the delicious food. Thank you for Mommy and Daddy, Greg and Lisa, and Peanuts. And most of all, thank you for my bestest friend, Brad. How was that, Mommy?"

"Perfect," Cassandra whispered, her eyes moist with emotion. It was the first time Angel had said grace.

"Merry Christmas," Chance raised his glass, toasting to the occasion.

Angel held her glass of milk with both hands, a shy smile on her face as she looked at Brad. "And a happy new year!"

* * *

The following year unfolded with promising opportunities and new ventures for Chance's thriving architectural firm. With a dedicated team of fourteen employees, both full-time and part-time, he found himself blessed with more time to devote to his cherished family. Greg's exceptional skills and commitment had earned him a well-deserved promotion to the position of Design Supervisor, further fueling the firm's success. Projects progressed seamlessly, leaving satisfied clients in their wake, as the company soared to new heights.

Greg and Lisa's hard work and prudence bore fruit, improving their financial stability and enabling them to set aside funds for Brad's future college endeavors. This newfound stability allowed them to indulge in occasional weekend getaways, creating precious memories as they explored new destinations and reveled in each other's company. And whenever Brad's parents were away, Chance and Cassandra lovingly opened their doors, welcoming him into their home, fully aware of the cherished bond shared with Angel.

In the wake of Angel's birth, Cassandra had made a conscious decision to scale back her work hours at the hospital, prioritizing her role as a devoted mother. She now dedicated two days a week to her profession, balancing her responsibilities while also ensuring Angel's well-being. The hospital's daycare center became Angel's second home during those days, where she charmed the other children with her infectious joy and playful spirit. However, there were occasional moments when the vigilant teacher had to guide Angel on appropriate behavior, a gentle reminder to help her navigate the world around her with grace and consideration.

"Angel is very sweet," the teacher had said a few weeks ago. "But sometimes, she doesn't want to share her toys."

Cassandra watched Angel playing and motioned for her to come over. "Angel, we've talked about sharing," she said gently. Angel pouted in response. "Remember, these toys don't belong to you. You should thank the teacher and the children for letting you play with them."

Angel looked up at her mother, then glanced at her teacher. I'm sorry, Mrs. Patterson. Thank you for letting me play with your toys," she said, lowering her head before walking away.

Cassandra's home had a spacious downstairs area where she could meet with her outpatient clients. She also started establishing her own private practice. While she worked, Angel played upstairs with her many toys. When Brad visited, they often played with a tape recorder that Chance had given Angel. She admired the sound of her own voice and enjoyed playing recording games with Brad. Sometimes, she would pretend to be an interviewer while Brad played the role of a famous baseball star. She spoke clearly into the microphone.

"Tell us about how you won the baseball game, Mr. Genova," Angel said.

Brad cleared his throat, playing along. "Well, it was a fast ball, but I was even faster. It was a hard-to-hit ball, but I hit it even harder. It was a fly ball, and I made it soar all the way over center field. They didn't stand a chance. Not a single chance."

Angel laughed. "Hey, that's my Daddy's name," she said, realizing her interruption. "Excuse me, I mean, that was really cool, Mr. Genova. I hope you can do it again." She rewound the tape and listened to her interview.

"You're really good at this," Brad grinned.

Pausing the recording, she said proudly, "Yes, I am."

* * *

Winter gradually transformed into spring. Trees blossomed with leaves, flowers emerged from their buds, and warm breezes replaced the cold snow. On the first day of April, Chance logged onto the computer and came across an unsolicited letter that caught his attention.

Dear lonely soul,
What is like a flower which casts no reflection on a cloudy day?
Or a mirror that portrays the images you cannot see?
As you travel through life, reaping rewards you hide away,
Burying the past, knowing you'll never be free.
Signed, Anonymous

Chance was taken aback by the cryptic poem, his curiosity ignited by the sender's sign-on name, FrgtnGhst. As he mulled over the possibilities, a nagging thought tugged at him—could Cassandra be orchestrating yet another one of her playful riddles? However, deep within his heart, he knew that these strange words couldn't possibly be her creation. He printed the letter, tucking it into his pocket, realizing that his business web page openly displayed his email address, making it accessible to anyone who wished to contact him.

Later that evening, as Cassandra sorted through the laundry, she stumbled upon the folded paper tucked within his pants. Curiosity flickered in her eyes as she held it up, a questioning expression gracing her face.

"Honey, what's this?" she asked.

"Just some joker," Chance replied, reaching for the letter. But it was too late. She had already read it.

"It's strange, but kind of pretty. Do you have any idea who sent it?" Cassandra asked.

Chance crumpled the letter and tossed it into the trash. "Junk mail," he said, heading into the bathroom to brush his teeth.

Later, as they lay in bed, Cassandra couldn't shake off the thoughts of the note. "It doesn't sound like anyone I know," she mused.

Within half an hour, Cassandra succumbed to the embrace of slumber, her breathing gentle and tranquil. In stark contrast, Chance found himself restlessly seated upright, his mind a whirlwind of thoughts and emotions. Seeking solace in the living room, he descended the stairs, allowing the soft glow of the television to cast its flickering light upon his troubled countenance.

Absently, he navigated through various channels, finding temporary refuge in the classic charm of an episode of "The Munsters." Yet, despite the lighthearted antics playing out before him, his mind remained consumed by the enigma surrounding his brother. Rationality battled with doubt as he tried to convince himself that Seth couldn't be the mysterious sender. Eventually, he switched off the television, the room plunging into stillness, and returned to the comfort of their shared bed. However, even amidst the hushed darkness, his eyes remained transfixed upon the clock, each passing second amplifying the relentless pace of his racing thoughts.

The following morning, while Cassandra sought renewal in the shower, Chance seized the opportunity to quell his curiosity. He settled in front of his computer, its soft hum filling the room as he logged in, anxious anticipation building within him. With a blend of trepidation and curiosity, he discovered a second letter awaiting him in his inbox, with the anonymous sender unveiling yet another layer of this strange drama.

Dear lonely soul,
Ours is not to reason why, ours is but to do or...?
Signed, anonymous

"What the hell is going on?" Chance muttered to himself, his anger simmering as his mind raced to comprehend the intrusion. He wasted no time in preparing a reply.

I don't know who you are, and I suspect you don't know who I am. Stop sending me emails!
Signed, Dead Serious

The next morning, as Chance logged onto his computer at work, he discovered a third letter from FrgtnGhst.

Dear Dead Serious,

I know full well who you are, and I'm certain you're slowly realizing who I am. If my poetry doesn't help solve your riddle, perhaps you should open your office mail. Sometimes, Forgotten Ghosts need to materialize!

Signed, Less than anonymous

"Shit!" Chance gasped, feeling a chill run down his spine. As Chance's disturbed exclamation escaped his lips, Karen, his office assistant, happened to pass by his open door. Concern etched upon her face, she couldn't help but inquire, "Is everything alright?"

Sensing his distress, Chance's voice trembled slightly as he asked if the morning mail had arrived. Understanding the urgency in his tone, Karen swiftly replied, "Not yet. But I'll bring it to you as soon as it's here."

Closing his office door, Chance found himself immersed in deep contemplation, his thoughts consumed by the unsettling implications of the third anonymous letter. The weight of the situation hung heavy upon him, urging him to seek answers amidst the shadows of uncertainty.

Later that morning, Karen handed him a stack of routine business correspondences. Nestled among them lay a typed envelope, devoid of any return address, its postmark indicating it had originated from Boston. Anger coursed through his veins as he tore open the envelope, his eyes scanning the contents that lay within.

"Chance2? Chance to do what?" he read aloud, the words echoing with an unsettling air of mystery.

An insidious suspicion began to take root within him, hinting at the possibility that Seth, the enigmatic sender, was orchestrating an intricate mind game. Driven by a resolute need for answers, Chance's hand instinctively reached for the phone, dialing the information line. He requested the contact information for Boston Corrections and dialed the provided number, his heart pounding within his chest as he awaited a response.

"I'd like to inquire about a prisoner named Seth Macklin," he spoke, his voice betraying the anxious tension that gripped him.

Providing the officer with Seth's prison number and the expected release date in March 2005, Chance held his breath as the officer placed him on hold. Each passing minute felt like an eternity, the lyrics of a Frank Sinatra medley permeating the background, its songs of

"Strangers in the Night" and "My Way" seemingly mocking him, adding to the mounting irony that engulfed his thoughts. With bated breath, Chance held the phone away from his ear, anxiously awaiting the officer's response.

"Seth Macklin became eligible for parole two months ago. He was released in March."

As Chance lowered the phone, a heavy silence settled within his office. His mind whirled with emotion, fixated on the realization that Seth, the enigmatic twin from his past, was out there in the bustling city of Boston.

Interrupting the silence, the ringing of the phone suddenly filled the room, jolting Chance out of his daze. Ignoring the persistent clamor, he shifted his focus, his gaze now fixed upon the computer screen before him. With determination, he logged into his computer, his fingers poised above the keyboard, ready to compose a reply that would reflect his newfound resolve.

As the words formed on the screen, each keystroke carried a sense of urgency, a clear intent to confront the unknown forces at play. The mysterious game set in motion by Seth would no longer be met with passive acceptance. It was time to take control of the situation and forge his own path towards resolution.

Seth,

So you're free. That is good. I hope you can move on with your life. I wish you well, and perhaps someday we can reconcile. But for now, I ask that you leave me and my family alone.

Sincerely, your brother

That evening, as Cassandra noticed Chance's preoccupation at home, she couldn't help but ask, "Everything all right?"

"Of course," he replied, trying to dismiss her concerns.

"Sweetie, you can't hide anything from me. This is Cassandra, remember?" She leaned forward on the couch, gently running her fingers through his hair.

He had devised a plan earlier in the day, and now he needed to introduce the idea gradually. "I was just thinking that with spring in the air, it might be nice to spend some quiet time alone at the cottage. We haven't been there for three summers."

Her eyes lit up with curiosity. "Can you get away from work?"

“No, I can’t. But there’s no reason why the three of you can’t go. Hey, maybe Morgan would like to join as well? He’s between jobs, and you still have a week of vacation from last year.”

“But I was hoping to spend that time with you,” she expressed.

He caressed her hair, speaking slowly and casually. “This is our busy season, and I don’t see things slowing down anytime soon.”

Cassandra realized it was a good opportunity to catch up with Morgan, whom she had seen little of since moving to Boston. “Are you sure you wouldn’t mind?”

“Mind? It was my idea,” he reassured her, knowing that he needed a private meeting with Seth, if only to understand his brother’s intentions.

“Okay, why not!”

Later, Chance entered her home office, eager to hear her update. “Morgan’s on board. Chance, what a great idea!”

Part II

"This is so exciting," Cassandra exclaimed, embracing Chance as Morgan, Brad, and Angel finished packing the car. She kissed Chance and sat in the passenger seat with Morgan behind the wheel.

As they drove north on Route 95, a sense of anticipation filled the car. Angel's innocent question broke the silence, "Are we almost there?"

Cassandra turned and laughed. "Just another half-hour or so."

"How long's that?" Angel pressed.

"Real soon," Cassandra assured her.

"Brad, you ever been to the lake?" Angel asked.

"Nope, first time. How about you?"

"I think so, right Mommy?"

"Yes, but you were quite young then," Cassandra answered, reminiscing.

"I'm almost grown up now," Angel declared, raising herself higher in her seat. "Almost as big as Brad." He tickled her stomach, causing her to squirm with laughter.

"Shh, listen," Morgan turned up the volume for the weather report.

Cassandra caught fragments of the thunderstorm warning. "Was that for tonight?"

"We should be able to get a couple of hours of sun," Morgan said, his gaze fixed on the distant thunderheads.

Unable to resist her curiosity about her brother's love life, Cassandra asked how things were going with Helen.

"Things are great. Helen could be the one," Morgan replied, a hint of excitement in his voice.

Cassandra smiled, proud of her matchmaking skills. "I spoke with her the other day. She really likes you, Morgan. You'd better not break her heart."

"She'd better not break mine," Morgan retorted.

The lightheartedness of their conversation added an extra layer of warmth to their journey, as they continued to draw closer to their destination. Her mind, now focused on the final stretch, retraced the directions she had memorized. "Turn right up here, then take your next left. The cottage will be on the right."

Morgan turned into the long gravel driveway that meandered its way towards the secluded summer home. As the vehicle drew closer, anticipation filled the air, palpable in the wide-eyed excitement that illuminated Brad's face. The possibilities and adventures awaiting them ignited a spark of exhilaration within him. Unable to contain their eagerness when they arrived, Brad and Angel practically leaped out of the car, their energy propelling them towards the inviting expanse of the nearby lake.

"Hold it!" Cassandra called out, bringing their playtime to a halt. "First we unload, then we can play."

"Aw, what a gyp," Brad said, winking at Angel. "Yeah, what a gyp." They exchanged mischievous smiles, sensing Cassandra's serious tone.

"Come on, Angel, let's unpack," Brad said. "Then we can play with the walkie-talkies."

"Yippee!" Angel exclaimed, rushing to grab her small suitcase.

As the group stepped through the threshold of the cottage, a sense of nostalgia washed over Cassandra. The summer home had undergone a major transformation since their previous stays. Once the proud Macklin family house, time and decay had led to its unfortunate demise, eventually replaced by a simpler single-floor vacation residence.

Cassandra placed her suitcase near the entrance, her eyes surveying the interior. A lingering stillness hung in the air, as if time had momentarily frozen in this tranquil retreat. She couldn't help but notice the faint touch of stale air that clung to the space, a testament to its prolonged vacancy. But beneath that stillness and the hushed whispers of forgotten memories, Cassandra felt a glimmer of excitement. The cottage held the potential to once again be filled with life, laughter, and the creation of new memories.

As she began to open windows, allowing the warm breeze to breathe life back into the cottage, Cassandra embraced the opportunity to infuse the space with the vibrancy of their presence once more. Eager to settle in fully, she turned on the faucet; however, brown water sputtered out in feeble spurts, tumbling into the sink. Cassandra took a deep breath, reminding herself of the challenges that could arise when returning to a place left unattended for an extended period.

The quaint cabin boasted an open living room, dining room, and kitchen area. Two bedrooms were tucked away to the side, and an outhouse stood at the back. A well provided plenty of water, which they would filter for drinking.

"I have to go," Angel announced, crossing her legs. "Where?"

Cassandra smiled, anticipating her daughter's urgency. "The bathroom is outside in the little cabin just behind this one. Morgan will show you how it works." Angel's confused expression diverted her attention. "It'll be okay. It's called an outhouse," she reassured her, recollecting the location of the necessary supplies.

As Cassandra went into a storage closet, she overheard Angel's perplexed question, "Outhouse?"

Brad laughed. "We call it a nature call."

"Really? And does nature come?" Angel asked innocently.

Morgan took her hand. "Let's go find out. See if you can show me where this house is."

Moments later, Angel burst back into the cabin. "I did it, Mommy. It was fun!" She dashed into one of the bedrooms, declaring it as her own. "Mine!"

"Angel, you'll be sleeping in my room," Cassandra corrected her gently, wiping the kitchen counters. With a more serious tone, she added, "Come here, please." Angel reluctantly left the bedroom, wearing a frown. "Morgan gets the other room," Cassandra continued, uncovering furniture with fresh sheets. "And Brad will sleep on the pullout couch."

Brad inspected his designated bed. "This is a pullout?" he questioned, flipping over a cushion.

"If it's uncomfortable, just pull the mattress off and put it on the floor," Cassandra suggested, trying to make it more accommodating. She picked up the telephone in the corner of the living room. Hearing the dial tone, she said, "Good job, Chance." She dialed his office number back in Boston. "Hi, Honey. We made it okay. How are you?" She listened intently. "The kids are having a great time. Right now, they're all cleaning inside."

With a broom in hand, Angel approached her mother, sternly reminding her, "Daddy, Mommy has to help. So hang up and let her get back to work."

Cassandra laughed. "I should go. Give us a call later. Good luck with your meeting. Love you, bye." Reluctantly, she hung up the phone. "Angel, you sweep, and I'll hold the dustpan."

Later, Cassandra admired the results of their cooperative efforts. The furniture had been dusted and cleaned, the floor swept, windows washed, and the bedrooms all made up. "Looks like a home, after all," she declared with satisfaction. "Time to move this party outside."

As they strolled outside, Morgan asked, "How close are your neighbors?"

"About a hundred yards in each direction. It's like a different world here," Cassandra replied, inhaling deeply. "Smell those pine trees, Morgan."

He glanced skyward, noticing the approaching thunderheads. "Storm's creeping in. But we have some time."

Suddenly, Angel came running back, tears streaming down her face as she held her hand. "Mommy, something bit me. It hurts."

Cassandra inspected her daughter's hand, reassuring her, "It's just a mosquito. We'll put some lotion on it."

"Hey, what's that over there?" Brad yelled excitedly, pointing towards a house by the shore.

Angel turned and saw his gesture. "I have to go," she said, running towards him, momentarily forgetting the small bite on her hand.

"That's a boathouse," Cassandra yelled after them. "You two go ahead. We'll catch up, but be careful."

"Race you there," Brad challenged, darting forward.

"No fair!" Angel protested, tracing his steps at a slower pace.

"So, you have a boathouse?" Morgan inquired, intrigued by the lakefront property.

"A motorboat and canoe," Cassandra confirmed, leading Morgan past a big oak tree that marked the beginning of the dirt path to the boathouse. However, Morgan stumbled on a clump of weeds and grass, momentarily throwing him off balance.

"I guess the gardener forgot to clean out here, too," Cassandra joked, picking up a branch from the path and tossing it into the woods. "One day, we'll develop the land."

"I'd leave it," Morgan said. "That's part of the magic and mystery. Imagine how creepy it would be at night, playing tag or hide-and-seek in the woods."

"No thanks. You can play with Brad tonight. Angel and I will watch from the cabin, sipping hot chocolate," Cassandra replied.

As they arrived at the edge of the glistening lake, Morgan's feet found purchase on a weathered wooden dock that stretched fifteen feet into the tranquil water. However, his confidence was short-lived; after taking merely three steps onto the aged structure, he felt it unsettling beneath his weight.

The weathered boathouse stood as a testament to the passage of time and the dance of neglect. A relic from yesteryears, this once-vibrant structure now wore the cloak of abandonment. The building, nestled between a thicket of ancient pines and the shimmering expanse of the lake, bore the brunt of ruthless winters and tempestuous waves, revealing its tale through every crack and peeling paint chip.

While its foundation remained steadfast, the facade whispered stories of disrepair. Panels of wood, once tightly bound, now sagged wearily, yearning for the touch of the owner's hand to mend their fractures. The vestiges of paint clung to the walls. The roof, though venerable in its traditional craftsmanship, bore the scars of countless storms, acting as a sieve for raindrops to perform their rhythmic dance.

"Make sure the kids don't play out on the dock," Morgan said as he stepped back onto the shore.

Cassandra let out a sigh. "I remember diving off this only a few years ago. Just one more thing to repair, I guess."

"That's the price one pays for owning property on a lake," Morgan mused. He heard the children's laughter emanating from the boathouse, which was located ten feet to the left of the dock. Tapping the wall, he commented, "Feels solid."

Brad responded to the echoing sound, his voice filled with anticipation, "I'm gonna get you, Angel!"

"Mommy! There's a monster in here," Angel exclaimed.

"It's only Morgan," Cassandra reassured her.

"Very funny, Uncle Morgan." Angel playfully pounded the wall. "See, I can be a monster too."

"You sure can," Morgan teased.

Cassandra playfully slapped her brother's arm. "Watch it, bud."

Brad explored the area inside the boathouse, strolling along the plankway that led to the motorboat. "How did these boats get here?"

"Chance took care of that too," Cassandra explained. "They were in storage, and with a simple phone call, here they are."

"He's clever," Morgan remarked with a laugh. "Managed to kick us all out so he could have some peace and quiet at home."

"Hey," Angel interjected. "Be nice, or else."

"Angel!" Cassandra scolded, giving her daughter a stern look. Then, looking at Angel's smiling face, she softened. "You tell him."

Morgan shook his head, amused. "What a team."

"Do these boats really live here?" Angel asked, her eyes filled with curiosity.

"That's why it's called a boathouse," Brad explained, tapping the side of the aluminum canoe. His imagination sparked with ideas for fun. Glancing upwards, he noticed the rafters. "Can we climb up there?"

"No way," Cassandra responded firmly, her gaze fixed on Angel. "Also, no going out on the dock, understand?"

Both Brad and Angel nodded in agreement. As they examined the boathouse further, Brad inquired, "What kind of wood is this?"

"Cedar," Cassandra replied.

"Like apple cedar?" Angel asked, her mind wandering.

Cassandra chuckled. "No, honey. Cedar is a type of wood that lasts a long time. You're thinking of apple cider, the drink."

"Can I have some?" Angel requested.

"What?" Cassandra was momentarily confused.

"Apple cedar," Brad laughed, recalling an earlier discussion about symphonies. "With a Mahler sandwich, right Angel?"

"That's Marlin," Angel corrected, proud to have remembered the name of the fish.

Now Cassandra was perplexed. "We're having turkey."

Upon hearing this, Brad dashed out of the boathouse. "Last one there is a turkey!"

"Hey, wait for me!" Angel called out as she chased after him.

* * *

Chance closed the session on his home computer, his eyes darting between the screen and his silent phone, still awaiting a response from his brother. Determined, he made his way to his car, intending to send another letter from the office.

At two-fifty, he logged onto his computer, hope flickering within him as he anticipated a reply. However, he found no new message. In the face of this silence, he couldn't help but contemplate the diminishing options, his heartbeat quickening as he searched for alternative paths to unravel the enigma that had consumed his thoughts.

"Chance, you have a meeting in ten minutes with the library administrators," Karen reminded him.

"Got it," Chance said, his voice tight. While gathering sketch revisions on his desk, his mind wandered elsewhere, his palms growing clammy with each passing moment.

"Did you see the note I left you about Cassandra's high school friend?" Karen asked casually.

Chance searched his desk. "No. Who was it?"

"He called this morning. I gave him your number."

"Nobody called," Chance replied, fear gripping him tightly as the walls seemed to close around him. "What did you tell him?"

"I told him she and Angel were up north and that he should talk to you," Karen explained, realizing her mistake. "I'm really sorry. He seemed to know who she was and about the property in New Hampshire."

Panic overwhelmed Chance. "What did he say?"

"N...Nothing. He just said thanks and hung up," Karen replied, her heart pounding. "Is everything all right?"

Chance checked the time. "Stall the meeting. Do anything!" He hurriedly ushered Karen out of the office and closed the door behind her. Once alone, he dialed information, requesting the number for the Loon Mountain Police in New Hampshire. Scribbling down the number, he heard a knock at the door.

"I'm sorry, Chance, but they're here early," Karen informed him.

"Five minutes!" he exclaimed. Karen nodded and hurried away, her face flushed with concern. Chance dialed the number he had just obtained. "This is Chance Macklin," he said urgently. "I own a cottage on Wilderness Way. My family is up there now, and they're in danger. Please send a patrol car right away."

"Is this an emergency?" the dispatcher asked.

"Yes, hurry," Chance pleaded, desperation creeping into his voice.

The sergeant assured him that a car would be dispatched immediately. Chance then dialed the number for the cottage, his heart pounding in his chest. "Come on! Answer the damn phone!" he muttered, frustration mounting as it rang and rang with no answering machine.

Karen appeared by his doorway. "I know, I'm coming!" He slammed the phone down, his mind filled with worry. After gathering his files, he said, "Could you ask Greg to come into my office?"

Moments later, Greg knocked on the door. As he entered, he immediately noticed the serious expression on Chance's face. "What's wrong?"

Hoping to hide his deep concern, Chance replied, "Greg, I need you to run this meeting for me. I have something urgent to attend to."

Greg agreed, but the visible relief on Chance's face alarmed him. "Does this have anything to do with—"

"Not now!" Chance interrupted, his voice strained as he handed over the relevant paperwork. He tossed his phone into a bag and exited his office, with Greg following closely behind.

Three individuals anxiously awaited Chance's arrival in the meeting room. Present were Mr. Sarter, a representative from the National Bank and Trust, Mrs. Williams, a member of the Planning Board, and Mr. Agrapate, an associate from an investment firm.

"Your staff gave us the nickel tour," Mr. Sarter commented.

"Good. I'd like you to meet Greg Tracy, my second in command. Unfortunately, I have a small family matter and won't be able to attend our meeting. But rest assured, Greg has studied the blueprints and can answer all your questions," Chance assured them, though Mr. Sarter seemed disappointed.

Greg shot a glance at Chance, his stomach tightening at the agitated tone in his voice and the unsettling feeling of being kept in the dark. "What is it, Chance?"

Chance felt the pressure of the situation and began to sweat, his throat constricting with each passing second. "You're in good hands, Mr. Sarter," he said in a calm voice that betrayed his inner turmoil. He shook the man's hand again and turned to his confused associate. "Greg, I need to brief you on one item." He motioned for Greg to follow him into his office. Attempting to appear composed, Chance said, "Everything is fine. I just can't explain right now." As he started to leave, he added, "I'll call later tonight."

"If not by sunset, I'm calling you!" Greg stated firmly, his eyes fixed on Chance's retreating figure.

In his car, Chance encountered the slow-moving rush-hour traffic on Storrow Drive. "Come on!" he yelled, his frustration mounting. It felt like an eternity before he spotted the sign for I-95 North.

“Finally,” he muttered, his foot pressing harder on the accelerator.

* * *

Earlier that afternoon, Brad and Angel had gone swimming in the cool lake. Cassandra and Morgan were quietly paddling in the aluminum canoe along the water’s edge.

“Hey, Morgan, paddle over here,” Brad called, floating alongside the shore.

Angel, wearing a pink swimsuit adorned with little fish, waded nearby, inflatable swim bubbles clinging to her arms. She chuckled, recognizing Brad’s mischievous voice.

“What, and let you splash us?” Morgan deduced.

“Do it, uncle,” Angel urged.

“I won’t, I promise.” Brad winked at Angel, a sly plan forming in his mind.

Cassandra turned from the bow of the boat. “Don’t take the bait.”

“Really, I’ll behave,” Brad assured them, noticing their hesitation. “Look out, here I come!” With that, he dove underwater, kicking his legs vigorously towards the canoe, its sleek form glistening beneath the surface. Cassandra and Morgan quickly paddled away, evading the oncoming attack.

“Go, Brad, go!” Angel cheered from the shore.

Cassandra hollered back, “Whose side are you on anyway?”

“Go, Mom, go!” Angel replied, her excitement growing.

Brad emerged from the water, splashing a layer of water onto Morgan’s back. “Gotcha!”

Cassandra laughed, enjoying the playful moment. Morgan, grimacing from the water, retaliated by splashing Cassandra with his paddle, causing the canoe to spin in a swirling circle right in front of Angel.

“Stop!” Cassandra called out, but her words only fueled Morgan’s assault.

“Go, go, go!” Angel cheered enthusiastically, torn between deciding whom to support.

Drenched in water, Morgan felt the heaviness of his soaked attire and the mild chill of the lake. It seemed only fair that his sister should share in the full experience as well. Cassandra, with a mischievous sparkle in her eyes, began rocking the canoe back and forth. As

Morgan's grip on the paddle loosened, it slipped from his grasp and splashed into the water. In an unexpected turn of events, Cassandra's maneuver caused the canoe to overturn, submerging them both into the chilly depths.

"That's what you get for rocking the boat," Cassandra laughed, her voice filled with amusement.

In the shallows, Morgan and Cassandra engaged in a spirited and playful water battle, their laughter carrying across the glistening surface. From the shore, Brad and Angel observed the scene, Angel's youthful eyes filled with awe and curiosity. After an exhilarating exchange, Morgan, now exhausted, swam towards the shore with a wide grin on his face.

"You were funny, Uncle Morgan," Angel said, a playful twinkle in her eyes.

He crawled next to her, his clothes clinging to his body. "Do you wanna go in?"

She stepped back cautiously. "Don't."

Morgan laughed. "You kids go ahead and play. I need to change out of these wet clothes. Besides, do you see that?" He pointed upwards towards the gathering storm clouds. "It's getting close. Are you coming, Sis?"

"I have my swimsuit on underneath," Cassandra replied, swimming by the half-sunken canoe. She tossed her shirt and pants to the shore. "See ya, sucker," she said with a smirk.

"See ya, sucker," Angel mimicked, her young voice echoing with innocence.

Cassandra couldn't help but roll her eyes playfully at her daughter, her attention momentarily shifting to the submerged canoe gently bobbing in the water. "Hey, you two. Come over here," she called out, settling herself comfortably into the partially submerged canoe. With an inviting gesture, she encouraged them to join her. "Come on, Angel. You've got this," she said, her voice filled with encouragement. Cassandra watched with delight and pride as her daughter approached the water's edge, cautiously easing herself into the refreshing embrace of the lake.

"It's cold," Angel frowned, her small hands clenched tightly as she shivered.

Brad swam towards her. "I'll go with you."

"Okay, Brad. But no tricks," Angel warned.

Together, they paddled their hands in the partially submerged canoe. Angel asked how the canoe stayed afloat, his curiosity piqued.

"It's filled with foam in the bow and stern," Cassandra explained, the water reaching up to her shoulders. "This is called canoe dumping. We used to do it at summer camp. Believe it or not," she added with a mysterious tone, "this is how I met your daddy."

"No way!" the girl exclaimed, her eyes wide with astonishment.

"Yes way. Chance also likes canoe dumping, and, well... any man I date has to appreciate this hobby. I married your father because of his great canoe dumping abilities."

Brad winked at Angel. "How romantic."

Cassandra playfully splashed the water. "You two are a couple of dingalings."

Angel smiled and joined in the fun. "Dingaling, dingaling, dingaling." She dove into the water, resurfacing and grabbing onto the canoe. She spat out a mouthful of water.

"You're a little fish," Brad chimed in.

"One fish. Blue fish. Red fish. Glue fish," Angel replied, mixing up the words to the Dr. Seuss classic.

* * *

As Morgan followed the winding path back to the cottage, he heard the excited yells of the children echoing through the trees. Pausing to remove his soaking tennis shoes, he squeezed out the water from the old canvas material, wondering how long it would take for them to dry. Carrying his wet shoes, he continued his journey up the path. As he approached the large oak tree near the cabin, he heard a rustling noise in the woods. His senses heightened, he stopped and listened intently, but the silence was deafening. He glanced back down the path, questioning whether he had heard the sound of a rabbit or a deer. Shaking off the feeling of unease, he took another step forward, only to hear the rustling noise once again.

"Who's there?" Morgan's voice trembled, his instincts alert.

The wind whipped through the trees, adding an eerie backdrop to the unfolding scene. Dark storm clouds loomed overhead, casting a foreboding shadow. Morgan glanced towards the boathouse, where the others were still playing. Taking a step towards the safety of the cabin, he halted abruptly, a sense of urgency overtaking him.

"Who is it?" Morgan demanded, his voice tinged with a growing certainty that the source of the noise was not natural.

He stood before the imposing oak tree, his gaze fixed on movement from behind. With caution, he veered off the path, moving closer to the tree. As he peered around its trunk, a sudden rush of sound startled him, and he swiftly turned, only to meet a clenched fist slamming into his face. The force of the blow sent him sprawling to the ground, his shoes slipping from his grasp. Reacting instinctively, he aimed his kicks at his attacker's feet, but a sharp strike to his groin brought him to his knees. Overwhelmed by excruciating pain, darkness swallowed him whole.

While his victim remained unconscious, Seth took swift action, binding the man's hands with nylon rope. He dragged him into the cabin, their movements shrouded in secrecy. Within one of the empty bedrooms, Seth secured the man's limbs to the bed, ensuring he couldn't escape. He also employed duct tape to attach a gag to his mouth. Satisfied with his handiwork, Seth wiped his hands clean, a smile playing on his lips. Delving into the man's pocket, he searched for clues about his identity. The distant laughter of the children echoed through the forest, adding an unsettling contrast to the tense atmosphere. Knowing he had ample time, Seth slipped back outside, his mind consumed by his malicious plans.

He headed deeper into the woods.

* * *

"That was fun, Cassandra. Can we do it again?" Brad's excitement was palpable as they secured the canoe in the boathouse, their exhilarating adventure leaving them craving more.

"Tomorrow, Brad. I need a break," Cassandra replied, her voice carrying a tinge of weariness. As they neared the cabin, the ringing phone caught her attention, igniting a surge of anticipation. "Maybe it's Daddy," she mused.

"Hurry, Mommy. Before he hangs up," Angel urged, her small legs carrying her as fast as they could.

Cassandra opened the front door and quickly grabbed the phone. "Hi, Daddy," Angel exclaimed, her voice filled with childlike innocence, hoping to hear her father's voice.

"Chance, I was wondering when you were going to—" Cassandra's voice trailed off, her smile fading into concern and alarm.

Chance's voice reached her, his words weighted with tension. "Listen to me very carefully. I'm on my way there," he paused, his next words catching in his throat. "Seth is free."

Cassandra sank into the chair, her grip on the phone tightening. Panic welled up within her, but she fought to conceal it, aware of Angel's confused gaze upon her. Her mind raced, thoughts spinning in a whirlwind of fear and uncertainty. "Morgan?" she whispered into the phone, desperation creeping into her voice. She scanned the room, her eyes searching for any sign. "He's not here!"

"Are the police there yet?" Chance asked.

"No," Cassandra responded, her hand reaching out to hold Angel's arm, her touch trembling.

"What's wrong?" Angel's innocent question pierced the tense atmosphere.

"They should have sent a car by now," Chance continued. "But I don't want you to wait for them. Do exactly as I say."

"Mommy, let go," Angel protested, feeling her mother's grip tighten.

Cassandra released her hold, her fingers running through Angel's hair as she listened intently to Chance's instructions.

"Is mom okay?" Angel asked, her concern evident.

"Maybe it's a game," Brad suggested, his concern growing.

"Yeah, Daddy is playing a trick on us," Angel chimed in, trying to find a sense of normalcy in the face of uncertainty.

Cassandra listened to Chance's plan, her mind racing with the peril of their situation. "Brad, Angel, come here," she beckoned them, her voice carrying a mix of determination and forced cheerfulness. "We're going to play hide and seek. Daddy is coming up soon to find us. Won't that be fun?" she added, hanging up.

"This doesn't sound right," Brad voiced his concern, his worry overshadowing any desire for a game.

"Please, Brad, just trust me and do as I ask!" Cassandra peered out of the window, her senses on high alert, taking in the immediate surroundings. The rustling of the trees in the wind and the darkening sky hinted at an impending storm. Distant thunder added an ominous backdrop to the scene.

"Brad, you need to go first, and then help Angel," she commanded, her tone firm yet tinged with concern.

Confusion etched Brad's face as he questioned, "Through the back window? Why?" Nonetheless, Cassandra's intense gaze left him no choice but to comply. "Alright, I'll do it," he relented. Taking a step on a nearby chair, he opened the back window, carefully lowering himself down about four feet to the ground. Cassandra, speaking in hushed tones, assisted Angel through the window, ensuring her safety.

"Mom, you look afraid," Angel observed, her leg dangling through the window. "Is this part of the game?"

"Yes, but you must be quiet," Cassandra whispered, guiding Angel to the ground. She handed Brad the walkie-talkies.

Brad attached the devices to his belt. "You see, Angel? We can play with these too."

"I guess so," Angel replied, her uncertainty evident.

Cassandra grabbed a small blanket, tossing it out of the window before joining the children outside. "Follow me, but remember, we must remain silent," she whispered urgently, gripping their hands tightly. Leading them towards the far side of the house, she pointed out a specific location, her finger indicating where they needed to go.

"What's going on?" Brad couldn't contain his curiosity any longer.

"Not now, Brad!" Cassandra snapped, her attention diverted by a crack of thunder. "Hurry, before the rain starts."

Part III

With the children in tow, Cassandra led them approximately twenty feet away from their previous location. Her gaze fixed upon an aged and abandoned natural gas tank that loomed before them like a sentinel of the past. Its sturdy steel legs supported a robust structure, weathered by years of neglect. The tank, resembling a colossal pill lying on its side, cast a shadow over the surrounding area. Its surface, coated in a deep shade of mossy green, bore patches of rust and faded paint, serving as a poignant reminder of its former purpose of heating the house. As they approached, a faint scent of oil and metal lingered in the air, mingling with the soft hum of insects and the distant rustle of leaves.

Cassandra recognized that hiding inside the tank would be a tight fit, but she remained undeterred. She circled the tank, her eyes scanning the surroundings with a sharp focus. To her relief, she spotted a discreetly arranged pile of birch logs nearby, remnants from a time when Chance had concealed a hidden opening to play hide-and-seek with Seth. Though weathered by time, Cassandra swiftly removed the decaying logs, unveiling a pathway to the secret entrance.

"Mommy, I'm cold," Angel shivered.

"It will be warm and dry inside," Cassandra assured her. She crouched down and pushed at the steel door that Chance had ingeniously fashioned. "Brad," she motioned for him to enter.

Peering inside, Brad hesitated. "It's dark and smells moldy."

"This tank hasn't been used for decades. There's no danger. Chance used to hide in here all the time when he played hide-and-seek." Cassandra handed him a small flashlight.

Brad aimed the light into the tank. "I bet there are weird bugs inside."

"Get inside now!" Cassandra's urgency resonated in her voice.

"Alright," Brad relented, brushing cobwebs off his face. He crawled inside, feeling his way along the metal until he reached the end of the tank. "Angel, can you see me?" he asked, shining the light on his face. "Come sit with me. I promise there are no bugs."

"Coming, Brad." Angel crawled on her hands and knees, guided by his voice. She nestled herself in his lap. "I'm glad we get to hide together. I hope daddy can find us," she said, her soft voice reverberating.

Cassandra scanned the property once more, ensuring they hadn't been followed, before entering the metal tank herself. As she stepped inside, the cool darkness enveloped them. Taking a moment to orient herself, she located the mechanism to secure the lid from within, sealing their hiding spot.

She turned to Angel, handing her the blanket and whispering softly, "Daddy will find us soon. You watch." Cassandra's words carried a mixture of reassurance and determination, comforting her young daughter in the darkness. They settled in, waiting patiently for their rescue, the blanket providing a small sense of comfort amidst the uncertainty.

"I'm not worried." Angel held onto Brad's arm, her small voice filled with trust.

* * *

After surveying the surrounding area and ensuring their closest neighbors were not present, Seth moved stealthily along the left side of the cabin, his senses heightened for any signs of unusual activity. The crackling of branches under his feet no longer worried him, as he was no longer concerned with concealing his presence.

Reaching the side of the cabin, Seth pressed his ear against the weathered wall, listening intently for any sounds from within. To his surprise, he was met with an eerie silence. However, as he leaned in closer, he detected the faint ringing sound coming from inside the cabin.

"When did he install that?" Seth muttered under his breath, realizing that Chance must have alerted them to his presence. "Can't escape the stinking grind, can you, Chance?" The scent of rain filled the air as storm clouds loomed overhead.

"Cassandra, it's me, Chance. I'm here!" Seth's voice echoed as he yelled, circling the cabin and searching the surrounding foliage. "Angel, it's Daddy. I brought you candy and toys. Come out, come out, wherever you are."

Inside the tank, Cassandra and the children heard Seth's voice growing louder as he approached, and then passing by their hiding place.

"It's Daddy," Angel whispered excitedly. "He's here."

"Shh! That's not Daddy," Cassandra whispered back, gently covering Angel's mouth. "It just sounds like him."

Brad aimed the flashlight at Cassandra, his eyes filled with concern. "It's Seth, isn't it?"

Cassandra clutched Brad's arm tightly, fear flickering in her eyes.

"Who's Seth?" Angel innocently asked, but her question went unanswered.

Brad curled up, haunted by memories of the past. "I wish I had my BB gun," he muttered.

"Quiet," Cassandra said, patting Brad's shoulder apologetically.

Seth continued his taunting, scouring the area. "Cassandra? Where are you? I want to go swimming with you and the kids."

Cassandra's ears perked up at the sound of tires grinding on the gravel driveway. She also overheard Seth muttering, "Cops gotta spoil everything!"

As a police officer stepped out of his car, his voice boomed through the air. "Anybody here?"

Cassandra's voice cut through the tension, her whisper carrying relief and caution. "It's the police."

"Police? Mommy, is Daddy okay?" Angel's voice trembled.

"Daddy's fine. He still wants to play," Cassandra assured her, gently pushing open the trap door of the tank. "I'm going outside to check. Stay here and be brave, my Angel," she said, giving Brad's hand a reassuring squeeze.

* * *

While stepping deeper into the woods, the officer heard footsteps approaching. "Who's there?"

"Hello, officer," Seth's voice greeted him, emerging from the shadows. "Sorry, I didn't hear you. I was doing some bird-watching and spotted a blue heron."

The officer nodded, casting a glance at the darkening sky. "Yeah, herons love this lake. But with the storm coming, even they would be seeking cover."

Suppressing his anger, Seth moved closer to the unsuspecting cop. The officer paused for a moment, studying Seth intently. "Chance, is that you?"

"Yes, it is," Seth played along, feigning surprise. "I'm sorry, I forgot your name."

"Bill Grainger. We played soccer together in high school," the officer replied.

"Of course, Bill. How could I forget?" Seth extended his hand.

"Must be the uniform," Bill remarked, shaking Seth's hand.

Cassandra's heart sank as she covertly watched Seth and the officer exchange friendly greetings.

"How long have you been on the force?" Seth asked, comfortably slipping into his role as Chance.

"A couple of years now. And you?"

"I'm an architect in Boston, running my own business."

"Great. Say, we got a call about a potential danger here. Have you noticed anything suspicious?" Bill inquired.

Playing the role of an unsuspecting homeowner, Seth adopted a calm demeanor as he spoke to Bill. "I heard some kids drinking last night, but apart from a few beer bottles, everything seems normal. Take a look," he said, gesturing towards the property, purposely diverting Bill's attention away from Morgan's abandoned tennis shoes near the oak tree. The first droplets of rain began to fall, signaling the onset of a storm.

Bill adjusted his jacket collar, raindrops glistening on his shoulders. As they approached the front of the cottage, he inquired, "Do you have any kids?"

Seth, his gaze fixed on the ground near the oak tree, skillfully trying to steer their path away from it, replied, "Just a little girl." Sensing the intensifying rain, he suggested, "It's pouring now. Perhaps we should take cover in the cabin and continue later."

"No, I don't think the rain will let up anytime soon. We'll be quick," Bill insisted, unaware of Seth's hidden intentions.

The officer approached the oak tree, noticing the abandoned sneakers and the disturbed ground—a clear indication of a struggle. Bill turned to face Seth, his eyes demanding an explanation. Caught off guard, Bill gasped for breath as Seth's fist struck his stomach. Doubled over in pain, Bill instinctively reached for his nightstick, but Seth swiftly delivered a powerful kick to his stomach, sending him sprawling onto his back, struggling to breathe. Taking advantage of the officer's vulnerability, Seth seized the nightstick and struck Bill, rendering him unconscious, just as he had done to Morgan.

"I love this old tree," Seth muttered to himself, a sinister smile twisting his lips like gnarled branches. Drawing upon all his strength once more, he hauled the unconscious officer into the cabin, securing him to the same bed where Morgan lay captive. As he observed the two helpless figures, tightly bound and gagged, a chilling satisfaction coursed through him, sending shivers down his spine. Seth's grin widened into a grotesque mask of triumph. "Two concussions are better than one."

* * *

"I'm scared," Angel whispered, her voice trembling as she tightly clutched Brad's hand from inside the tank. Tears streamed down her face, and she struggled to find her words amidst the sobs. "I don't know how to be brave. It's dark and scary. I think something bit me."

"I'll protect you, Angel," Brad responded, his voice steady despite the fear that gnawed at him. He chose not to reveal his own apprehension about what lay ahead. "You know, being brave doesn't mean you're never scared."

Angel pondered his words, her determination gradually overtaking her fear. With a newfound resolve, she spoke with a stronger tone, "Then let's go help Mom and Dad. They need us!"

Brad squeezed her hand tighter, his own inner terror masked by admiration for Angel's defiance and unwavering determination to fight back. "We will," he reassured her, his voice filled with conviction. "But remember, your Mom told us to stay hidden for a little while longer. We're playing hide and seek, just like that time when our parents went to the symphony. You hid so well in your closet, and I couldn't find you. Now, we'll hide together, and the bad man won't find us either."

Angel nodded, her voice barely above a whisper. "Okay," she agreed. "It's better when we're brave together." She nestled closer to Brad, feeling a sense of security enveloping her as her breathing steadied, and she began to relax.

Moments later, Cassandra returned and quietly slipped into the hiding place, reuniting with the children.

* * *

Two hours after leaving Boston, Chance turned onto Wilderness Way, the road that led to the Macklin cottage. Filled with anticipation and anxiety, he muttered to himself, "There better be a cop here." As he parked his car just beyond the driveway, a surge of relief washed over him when he spotted the patrol car positioned halfway up the hill. Moving cautiously, he scanned the surroundings, alert for any signs of danger.

To his surprise, the driver's side door of the patrol car was open, and the voices from the dispatch radio filled the air, discussing official police matters. But then, amidst the familiar chatter, a voice made Chance's blood run cold. "Cassandra, my love. I need you."

Taking cover behind the open car door, Chance watched in disbelief as Seth emerged from the cabin, calling out for his wife. Peering around the door, he observed Seth continuing down the path, unaware that Cassandra and the children were safe in their hiding place. Realizing that the officer had likely fallen victim to Seth's wrath, Chance's eyes fell upon a rifle secured inside the patrol car. Seizing the opportunity, he reached inside, unlocked the weapon, and withdrew it from its holster.

Hoping to divert Seth's attention, Chance increased the volume of the radio, the blaring sound echoing through the woods. Stepping out of the car, he positioned himself behind a maple tree next to the driver's side door, tightly gripping the gun and silently waiting.

As Seth continued his search, the blaring police car radio caught his attention. Intrigued, he made his way up the hill, the distorted sound growing louder. Entering the car, he forcefully yanked the handset out of the radio, tossing it out the window. With a swift kick, he dislodged the radio from its bracket, relishing the sound of its destruction on the car's floor. Stepping out, he stretched his back, catching a glimpse of Chance's reflection in the chrome side view mirror. Turning to face his brother, he let out a chilling laugh.

"One shot, dear brother."

Reacting swiftly, Chance raised the shotgun, but Seth deftly grabbed the barrel, redirecting its aim. "Tsk, tsk, tsk! Stealing police property," Seth taunted. Chance lunged forward, attempting to push the barrel towards Seth's stomach, but Seth skillfully moved it aside, causing the gun to discharge harmlessly into the woods. "Careful, Chance. You could hurt yourself," Seth mocked, snatching the gun from his brother's grasp and hurling it into the squad car.

Adrenaline surged through Chance's veins as he forced Seth into the car, launching himself on top of him, delivering blow after blow. But Seth's laughter persisted, mocking Chance's futile efforts.

"Don't waste your energy," Seth jeered, his laughter ringing in Chance's ears.

* * *

"What's happening?" Brad asked, his voice reverberating from inside their hiding place. "I heard a gunshot."

Cassandra knew something was terribly wrong. "I have to go out again. Give me a walkie-talkie. Only respond if you hear my voice. Understand?"

Brad nodded, handing her the device. "Be careful."

"Mommy, please don't go," Angel pleaded, her voice filled with fear.

"It's okay. Brad will stay with you. The next time you see me, Daddy will be with me." Cassandra eased her way out of the trapdoor, ensuring it was secured, and silently crept alongside the cottage. Her eyes fixed on the police car parked up the hill.

"Chance!" she called out, her voice filled with urgency.

Seth smiled, restraining his brother. "Sounds like my true love."

Chance lunged for the gear and shifted it into neutral. However, Seth remained on top of him, laughing triumphantly at his brother's futile attempt. As the car began to roll downhill, its path now directed towards the gas tank where the children were hiding, panic surged through Chance's veins.

Desperately reaching for the steering wheel, Chance strained against Seth's weight, trying to alter the car's course. Cassandra, standing by the side of the cabin, screamed in horror as she saw the car picking up speed, hurtling towards her and the cabin itself. Fear gripped her heart, and she narrowly managed to evade the vehicle's path, her cry for Chance ringing through the chaotic scene.

"My wife wants you gone," Seth taunted, fully embracing his twisted role. "Have you been fooling around with her?"

The car raced towards Cassandra as the tense air thickened with danger. "Chance!" she yelled, her voice filled with desperation and fear. The car crashed through the side of the cabin, colliding with the couch and coffee table in the living room, causing a violent crash and

213

scattering debris across the room. The impact left an eerie silence in its wake as the dust settled.

* * *

The impact jolted the children. "What was that?" Angel gasped, her body tensing up like a tightly wound knot as they heard the loud crashing noise.

Lost in a daze of confusion and fear, Brad struggled to make sense of the situation. "Well," he began, his words cautious and deliberate, "That sounds like thunder. You know, when it rains, sometimes thunder and lightning come along too. It can be loud and scary, but it's just nature doing its thing."

"Are you sure?" she asked tentatively, seeking reassurance. "I think I can be brave now. Let's call Mommy on the phone," she said, reaching for the walkie-talkie.

"No, we have to wait for her to call us," Brad explained, weighing the options in his mind. "You know who else is brave?" he quickly interjected, trying to divert her attention. "Barbie and Ken. They have to be brave all the time, always smiling, always ready for adventures. Let's pretend you're Barbie, and I'm Ken, and we're in Barbie's special submarine, exploring an underwater world. You're so good at being a brave Barbie, and I'm learning how to be brave like Ken."

She cried, her voice tinged with vulnerability and fear. "I'm not brave, Brad. I'm scared, and I don't want to be alone."

"Angel," he said, swallowing his own fear and mustering strength in his voice. "I'm always here for you. Always ready to protect you. After all, I'm your babysitter, and that's part of my job."

Angel clung to him, wrapping her arms around his waist. "But what if she doesn't come back?"

Brad gently caressed Angel's hair, his senses on high alert, as he strained to listen for any sounds of danger. After a moment of contemplation, he reached for his walkie-talkie and pressed the button. "Cassandra, what happened?"

* * *

Startled by the sound, she pressed the button on the walkie-talkie to respond. "Stay put and don't call me again!" Her finger released from the device, and in the midst of the chaos, she heard Angel's small voice say, "I love you, Mommy." Determined, Cassandra cautiously approached the mangled squad car, which was now partially lodged inside the cabin.

The ominous silence settled over the scene, a stark contrast to the havoc that had unfolded mere seconds ago. Cassandra made her way around the car, discovering an opening in the cabin's damaged wall. She entered the shattered remains of the structure, carefully moving toward the passenger side of the car. Shifting the displaced sofa out of the way, she struggled to open the car door. Peering through the window, she called out Chance's name, her eyes falling upon two lifeless bodies intertwined in the front seat. With great effort, she managed to pry the door open.

"Chance, are you okay?" Inches away from the motionless figures, she couldn't distinguish between them.

"Don't you care about me?" Seth's voice cut through the air as his grip tightened around her arm. Cassandra let out a cry, struggling to break free from his grasp. Seth crawled out of the car, taunting her. "How I've missed you, my love."

Realizing that screaming would only frighten the children, she pleaded, "Seth, don't do it."

Chance began to regain consciousness, a gash on his forehead oozing blood down his face.

"Glad you could join our family reunion," Seth laughed. "Now all we need are the kids." His gaze locked onto Cassandra, a silent demand for her compliance burning in his eyes.

"Never!"

In a swift motion, Seth's hand struck her across the face, sending her sprawling onto the shattered planks of wood. He reached for the shotgun, leveling it at his two captive prizes. Chance attempted to move, but froze as he stared down the barrel. Weakened by his head injury, his vision blurred, opening and closing.

Seth's laughter reverberated through the room. He spread his arms wide, showcasing the destruction of their once-beloved summer home. "Now, if you would both kindly take a seat."

Part IV

Seth lightly slapped his semi-conscious brother, his sadistic amusement evident.

"Wake up, Chance. The fun is just beginning."

Chance's eyes fluttered open, only to find himself bound to a wooden chair. The dim glow of kerosene lamps illuminated the remnants of the living room. The mangled police car loomed less than ten feet away, its collision with the cabin wall leaving a gaping hole. Rain pounded relentlessly on the cabin roof and the exposed trunk of the police car protruding into the outside. He turned his head to the right, taking in the shattered remnants of a sofa bed, a broken dining room table, and broken chairs. Turning left, he felt a sense of relief seeing Cassandra bound beside him, unharmed yet imprisoned. The rain intensified, large drops crashing against the car trunk.

Cassandra studied Seth's features, a chilling realization dawning upon her. Despite spending seven years in jail, he still bore an uncanny resemblance to Chance—the same build, facial features, hair color, and even their voices matched. She closed her eyes, fighting back the memories. Glancing at Chance, she noticed the trickle of blood running down his forehead.

"Chance, are you okay?"

A blinding bolt of lightning struck a nearby tree, the thunderous crack causing her to sit upright. Seth nonchalantly pointed the shotgun at her.

"You look lovely, Cassandra. It's been far too long."

The storm reached its peak, bolts followed by deafening thunderclaps reverberating over the lake. Seth approached the wreckage of the police car, admiring how rain pelted against the exposed trunk that served as a macabre centerpiece amidst the chaos.

"Where is my brother?" Cassandra pleaded, desperation lacing her voice.

"In the bedroom with the pig."

"Can I talk to him?"

Seth laughed. "We'll just wait here for the kids to come running back to Mommy and Daddy. Then we can all catch up." He clapped his hands together, his enthusiasm mirroring that of an eager child ready to play. "We'll have a little picnic in the rain. How does that sound?"

"You do realize that the police will investigate their missing car," Chance reasoned, grasping for any glimmer of hope.

"Nice try," Seth scoffed, anticipating his brother's potential moves. "And if you're thinking of using your home phone, forget it! Turns out it's now grossly defective. So, we have the night all to ourselves, with only the rain and thunder to keep us company." He sighed wistfully. "I know your little Angel would love to meet her long-lost Uncle Seth. It's not very nice of you to keep me from her. What kind of parents are you, anyway, leaving your daughter out in the cold rain?" Seth taunted. "Where are they?"

"I'd rather die than tell you," Chance retorted, a steely resolve in his voice.

As Seth slowly rose from his chair, a flicker of anticipation passed between the two prisoners. Their eyes locked, silently communicating their shared determination. In that fleeting moment, Cassandra made a bold decision. She would disclose a critical piece of information, hoping it would sway Seth's actions.

"I know you wouldn't really harm them. It's my profession to understand how people think," she said, hoping to appeal to his sense of reason.

Seth sat on the hood of the mangled car, intrigued by her words.

"Shrink talk, huh?" Seth laughed mockingly. "I wish my good friend, Dr. Percault, was here now. You two would have a field day arguing your theories about my condition and what levels of Thorazine to prescribe. I can hear it now, 'Give him the red pills. No, give him the green ones. No, the blue ones, they make him happy.'"

Seth grabbed the walkie-talkie. Holding it tauntingly in front of them, he extended the antenna. Pushing the button, he spoke into the device.

"Ground control to Major Tom. Can you hear me, Major Tom?" He released the button, the static caused by the storm filling the air.

"You see," Chance interjected. "They won't work in this storm."

Seth turned up the volume and pressed the button again. "Come in, Major Tom."

Just as Chance spoke, a distorted voice echoed back, "Major who? Chance, is that you?"

"Bingo!" Seth said and pressed the button to speak. "Yes, this is Chance. Brad, you and Angel can come back into the cabin now." He released the button just as Chance yelled, "Don't listen to him!" Seth pointed the shotgun at Cassandra's head.

Brad's voice crackled through the walkie-talkie, filled with uncertainty. "What's going on?"

Pressing the button, Seth said, "We caught Seth. You and Angel must be cold and hungry."

Cassandra turned to Chance, whispering, "He won't come."

Seconds passed, feeling like an eternity, before Brad's voice came through resolutely. "If this is really you, then you can come and get us. Otherwise, no way!"

Seth pressed the button and spoke calmly. "Brad, I would come, but I've broken my leg."

Time seemed to stand still as seconds ticked away. "Hell no, Seth. Signing off!"

"Brad? Brad!" Seth yelled into the device. "I need you."

No further words came through the walkie-talkie. Seth rubbed his forehead, attempting to alleviate the pain, trying to fight off fragments of haunting memories—his grandpa's agonizing touch, his father's abuse, his brother's indifference. Reality blurred with fantasy, causing dizziness that made him stumble into the edge of the kitchen counter. The searing pain in his stomach jolted him back to the present, shattering the images in his mind. Enraged, he hurled the walkie-talkie against the side of the house, breaking it into pieces. He spoke slowly, his exhaustion palpable.

"Round one to the kids."

* * *

Lumbering into the kitchen, Seth breathed heavily. His mind was filled with turmoil as he contemplated his next move, desperately attempting to banish the haunting images that this home inspired. He muttered to himself, accusing young Chance of hearing the abuse from the adjacent bedroom but choosing to do nothing to stop their grandfather. He even imagined Chance laughing because Seth had received what he deserved.

Chance and Cassandra exchanged a fearful glance, aware that Seth's dangerously unstable state of mind could lead to uncontrollable violence. They instinctively chose silence, recognizing that words might only further provoke his volatile nature.

Seth examined his hands, turning them over and over as if they were foreign objects. In his mind, he saw himself as an eight-year-old boy with the same adult hands, overpowering and beating his grandfather to death, just as he had fantasized in his revenge journal. He clenched his fists, feeling the surge of blood turning his knuckles white. Regaining his composure, he turned to face his captives and smiled.

With deliberate noise, he opened a kitchen drawer and surveyed its contents. Grasping a large knife, he held it adoringly, relishing the silver gleam of the blade and the comforting weight of the wooden handle. He approached Chance and ran the dull end of the blade along his cheek, taunting and tormenting them both.

"What does this remind you of, Cassandra?" Seth playfully danced the sharp edge of the knife in front of his brother's face and chest. "I will ask once more. Where are they?"

"The neighbors have them in town," Cassandra blurted out, hoping to appease him.

Seth pressed the knife against Chance's throat. "Where are the brats?" He lowered the blade to Chance's face, a thin trail of blood trickling down his cheek.

"I'll tell you where. Just don't hurt them," she pleaded desperately.

"Cassandra, don't," Chance interjected. "He wouldn't hurt me."

Seth slapped Chance across the face. "She knows damn well I would hurt you. Why should I stop now?"

"They're in the boathouse," she said.

"Boathouse?" Seth paused. "Could this be a diversion? Try again, my pet."

"They're in the rafters. Just don't hurt them," Cassandra pleaded, hoping he would believe her.

Seth studied Chance's subdued reaction. "Why aren't you yelling at your wife, little brother? Don't you care about your daughter?"

"We have no choice. Go see for yourself, but bring them back safely," Chance responded, resigned to their predicament.

"If they're not there, I am going to remove both of your ears, Chance. With a few scars, people will finally be able to tell us apart."

"Fine. Just go," Chance acquiesced, his voice filled with fear and resignation.

* * *

As Seth placed the knife on the kitchen counter and buttoned his coat, the atmosphere in the cabin grew increasingly tense. Rain pounded against the cabin, matching the rhythm of Chance's pounding heart. He strained against his restraints, feeling the weight of desperation pressing down on him.

"Looks like we pissed off that bitch, Mother Nature. Really adds to the drama, don't you think?" Seth's words echoed in the confined space, his casual demeanor contrasting sharply with the gravity of the situation. The broken cabin wall loomed like a gaping wound, a stark reminder of their vulnerability in the face of both human malice and the unforgiving elements outside.

As Seth left, his humming of "Singing in the Rain" grated on Chance's nerves, a macabre soundtrack to their ordeal. The storm raged on outside, its fury seeming to mirror the fear and uncertainty swirling within the cabin.

Alone in the dimly lit room, Chance fought against his bonds, his muscles screaming in protest. Every second felt like an eternity as he struggled, his mind racing with thoughts of escape and survival. But his efforts were in vain, his strength waning with each futile struggle.

"Cassandra, can you reach the knife on the counter?" Chance's voice was strained with urgency, his eyes pleading with Cassandra to act swiftly.

Cassandra began to bounce her chair along the wooden floor, the noise echoing through the cabin like a frantic heartbeat. Each creak of the floorboards seemed to reverberate with the weight of their fear, amplifying the sense of impending danger.

"Hurry!" Chance's words were a desperate plea, his gaze darting anxiously between Cassandra and the kitchen counter. Time was running out, and their only hope lay in reaching the knife before Seth returned.

Cassandra's heart raced with adrenaline as she focused intently on the gleaming blade before her. Each hop toward the counter felt like an eternity, her movements slow and deliberate as if every step brought her closer to the precipice of danger.

Once she reached the counter, Cassandra's pulse quickened. With painstaking precision, she used her chin to nudge the blade so that the handle dangled just beyond her reach. With each inch gained, the weight of their predicament bore down on her, a suffocating blanket of fear.

Carefully, she turned herself around, the ropes digging into her skin as she twisted and contorted in her seat. Her fingertips grazed the handle of the knife, tantalizingly close yet agonizingly out of reach. With each breath, she willed herself to remain calm, to focus on the task at hand despite the mounting terror threatening to consume her.

Slowly, she inched her fingers closer, regulating her breathing to relax. Finally, after what felt like an eternity, Cassandra felt the knife beneath her fingertips. A surge of relief washed over her as she grasped the handle with her index finger and thumb, her hands trembling with exertion and emotion.

"Got it!" Cassandra's whisper echoed through the tense air.

"Come back and cut me free," Chance urged.

As Cassandra bounced her chair back, a light shone up the path, signaling Seth's return. Panic surged through her veins, driving her to accelerate, to hop feverishly along the floor in a desperate race against time.

Within seconds, she positioned the back of her chair against Chance's, their bodies pressed close together in a desperate bid for freedom. Cassandra began cutting through the ropes with the blade, her hands trembling with exertion and fear. With each slice, the fibers of the rope curled and gave way, the sound of their release a symphony of salvation in the stifling darkness of their confinement.

"Ouch! Keep going. I don't care if you cut my hand off," Chance gritted through the pain, his voice a hoarse whisper. Blood welled from the cuts in his skin, mingling with the warmth of Cassandra's hands as she worked to free him.

In the distance, they heard the sound of a police siren approaching, a beacon of hope cutting through the darkness. Chance closed his eyes, the pain radiating through his body, but his spirit unbroken.

"You're almost there!" he encouraged, his words a lifeline in the tumultuous sea of their ordeal.

* * *

"Foul-mouthed liar," Seth seethed, his anger intensifying as he stormed back toward the cabin. He cursed his brother and wife for their deceitful diversion, feeling the weight of betrayal heavy on his shoulders. Suddenly, the sound of a police siren and the approaching headlights caught his attention, diverting his focus.

Thinking quickly, Seth switched off his flashlight and stealthily positioned himself alongside the car as it entered the property. A sweeping search beam pierced through the relentless rain, illuminating the surroundings. The rhythmic movements of the windshield wipers battled the downpour, creating a hazy backdrop as Seth silently trailed the approaching vehicle.

As Seth tightened his grip around a sturdy birch limb, poised for action, the squad car continued its cautious descent, its headlights freezing on the protruding vehicle lodged in the cabin. Seizing the opportune moment, Seth swung the hefty limb with force, smashing it through the driver's side window. The glass shattered, causing shards to rain down as the impact sent the officer sprawling unconscious onto the steering wheel.

"I thought I smelled a pig," Seth remarked with a grin, reveling in his perverse satisfaction at the sight of his latest victim.

With callous indifference, he reached inside the squad car, forcefully pushing the unconscious officer aside. His hand darted to the radio, ripping the handset from its mount and tossing it out the window, where it landed in a puddle. Seth used the handcuffs of the cop to secure him to the steering wheel.

Seth's attention shifted back to the cabin, his eyes gleaming with anticipation as the glow of kerosene lanterns radiated from within. The beam of his flashlight traced the path ahead, now transformed into a meandering river under the torrential rain.

Suddenly, Grandpa materialized before Seth's eyes. Memories of the evil that had taken place here flooded his mind. This was where it had all begun, the same spot where Grandpa had once molested him. Rage and fear consumed him, causing his body to tremble.

* * *

Cassandra and Chance huddled together tightly, their bodies pressed against the old gas tank as rain pelted down. In the dim light of the storm, Chance's wrist stood out starkly, wrapped in a white Ace bandage, the result of her desperate attempt to free him from his restraints.

222

"Brad, Angel, can you hear me?" Cassandra's voice called out amidst the raging storm.

"Mommy, I knew you'd come back," Angel's voice echoed back, filled with relief and trust.

"Can we come out now?" Brad asked, his anxiety evident.

"Not yet. Open the bottom hatch, Brad. Chance will hand you some food," Cassandra instructed, guiding them through their plan.

"Are you sure it's Chance?" Brad hesitated, seeking reassurance.

"Shave and a Hair Cut," Chance responded, utilizing their secret signal to confirm his identity.

Brad removed the false bottom, allowing access to the supplies. "What's Seth up to?" he asked, reaching for the food.

"Don't come out unless you hear Cassandra's voice. Do you understand? Not my voice, but Cassandra's," Chance cautioned, emphasizing the importance of their safety.

"Yes, I understand," Brad echoed, grasping the gravity of the situation. "What happened to your hand?" he inquired, but received no immediate answer.

Just then, Angel popped her head out of the tank, determined to help her parents. Seeing them standing in the rain, she exclaimed, "I'll help you," and thrust her hands into the mud.

Brad attempted to pull Angel back inside, reminding her of the need to hide from the dangerous man. "We have to hide from the bad man. Remember?" he urged, his concern for their safety evident.

Reluctantly, Angel removed her muddy hands and crawled back into the tank, obediently following Brad's instructions. Cassandra reached down, hoping to feel her daughter's hand, but Angel had vanished back inside, swallowed by the darkness within the tank. Overwhelmed by fear and the storm's fury, Cassandra turned to Chance.

"What now?" she asked, her voice colored with apprehension and determination.

Chance gently brushed the rainwater from her face, offering her a reassuring smile. "We end this madness ourselves," he said resolutely, tightening the Ace bandage around his hand and preparing for the impending battle.

* * *

Slipping and sliding through the treacherous mud and rain, Chance and Cassandra carefully made their way to the opposite side of the cabin. Peering through a window, they witnessed Seth thrashing about, wreaking havoc on the interior in a fit of uncontrollable rage. At first, Chance struggled to comprehend what was happening to his brother.

Seth kicked and cursed, his voice filled with anguish. "He took my kids. My Angel. Seth, what did you do to my kids? You want your revenge? Well, come and get it!" he bellowed, consumed by his own torment and desperate for answers.

Chance's mind raced as he recalled the unsettling ways in which Seth had impersonated him in the past, manipulating situations to his advantage. Now, as he witnessed Seth's unstable state, with hallucinations coming and going like a flickering switch, Chance saw a potential psychological advantage. An opportunity to gain an edge in their precarious situation emerged.

Gently, he whispered to Cassandra, his voice barely audible over the pounding rain, "Do you see what's happening? Seth thinks he's me. This just might work." Intrigued, Cassandra leaned in, her eyes reflecting both curiosity and caution, eager to hear his plan.

Chance outlined his strategy, carefully considering every detail. The plan hinged on keeping the switch of Seth's delusion turned on, delicately fueling his mistaken belief without triggering his volatile rage. It was a risky gambit, but it held the potential to turn the tables in their favor.

Part V

Cassandra found herself caught in a moment of hesitation, fully aware of the risks that lay ahead. The deranged state in which Seth currently found himself was a stark reminder of the dangers that could unfold. However, amidst the uncertainty, her background as a psychologist lent her a unique perspective. She understood the potential effectiveness of the plan that had taken shape in her mind, a plan that, if executed with care and precision, held the promise of success.

Chance took charge: "Go back and tell Angel and Brad to ignore everything I say or do."

She kissed him before retracing her steps back to the gas tank where the kids hid.

Chance began to yell, "Angel, where are you? This is your Uncle Seth! I have candy and treats for you." He glanced at the cabin before descending the path leading to the lake. A few steps later, he found a sturdy piece of wood and tested its weight and balance. "Angel, where are you?"

Gazing out from the kitchen window, Seth's eyes lit up with a smile as he spotted Chance. Hearing his brother's voice shattered the mirage of haunting relatives, grounding him in a new reality. "I'll be your little angel," he muttered, gripping the shotgun tightly and stepping outside, rain pouring down on him unabated.

"That's right, keep coming, you psycho," Chance taunted, his words laced with bravado and determination.

Meanwhile, back at the tank, Angel's innocent voice broke the tension. "Daddy wants me to come out," she whispered, her words tinged with curiosity and fear.

"No," Cassandra replied swiftly, her voice filled with urgency. "Remember, we're trying to trick the bad man. I have to go soon. Brad, promise me you'll stay put!"

"We will. Be careful," Brad assured her.

* * *

As Chance navigated the slippery pathway toward the boathouse, each step was a struggle against the rain-soaked ground. Thunder roared overhead, momentarily breaking his focus. Despite the distraction, he pressed on, entering the boathouse and positioning himself near the fifteen-foot motorboat.

Unaware of the thunder and lightning, Seth stepped into the boathouse, surveying the interior with confusion and delusion. Moving along the plank, he gradually made his way toward the bow of the motorboat, engaging in a perplexing monologue. His words both confused Chance and affirmed the viability of their plan.

"Did you find your precious Angel, Uncle Seth?" the deranged twin sneered, his voice tinged with a disturbing familiarity. "You've been acting strangely, you know. You should have kept taking your medication. Percault warned you about the withdrawals, the hallucinations, the nightmares. As your younger twin brother, I just want to help you. I'm sorry I stopped visiting you in jail. I couldn't bear to see you anymore. I'm sorry I erased all memories of you from my mind. I'm sorry your soul has withered away."

Chance remained motionless, absorbing Seth's emotional confession, waiting for Cassandra's signal. Meanwhile, Cassandra cautiously made her way down the path toward the lake. Approaching the entrance of the boathouse, her expression was warm and reassuring as she looked at Seth.

"Chance, are you alright? Thank God you have the gun. Seth will be here any minute," she said, projecting relief upon seeing him.

Seth's eyes locked onto Cassandra, studying her expression. The sincerity emanating from her gaze, her genuine concern for his well-being, began to penetrate the haze of his deranged state. Slowly, he lowered the shotgun to his side, the threatening presence of the weapon diminished as his demeanor shifted, if only for a fleeting moment.

A melancholic tone laced his voice, revealing a vulnerability beneath his unsettling facade. "My dear, I... I wondered where you had gone," he said, his words carrying a hint of longing. With a somber tenderness, he continued, "I was so worried that Seth had harmed you. But please, don't be afraid. I have the gun, and I will protect you with my life."

Cassandra's heart ached as she witnessed the depths of Seth's delusion and the love he mistakenly associated with his twisted actions. Her compassion swelled within her, mingling with a sense of responsibility to diffuse the situation and guide him towards a path of healing.

"I'm here for you, Chance. I support you. I love you."

As she uttered these words to Seth, Cassandra remained acutely aware of the delicate balance they walked. Each step required caution and compassion, seeking a resolution that would ensure the safety of all involved. She hoped to navigate this fragile moment, offering Seth the possibility of healing and redemption.

Seth, further consumed by the illusion, seamlessly adopted more of Chance's persona, with his voice taking on a softer tone as he leaned nonchalantly against the shotgun. His focus fixated on Cassandra; he seemed oblivious to the chaos and turmoil of nature surrounding them. In his distorted reality, he yearned for her touch, a desperate plea for the connection he believed they shared. "Please, hold me," he entreated, vulnerability and longing seeping through his words.

Suppressing her inner turmoil and hatred for the man, Cassandra summoned all her strength to sustain the facade, her mind racing to conjure loving gestures that would maintain the illusion. Though bitter, her words danced upon her tongue. "Oh, my poor dear," she responded, her voice laced with a feigned tenderness.

Cassandra embraced Seth, the weight of their shared history heavy upon her. Memories flooded back, reminding her of the perilous truth that safety remained elusive as long as he remained alive. As her hand gently patted his back, she stole a fleeting glance over his shoulder, catching sight of Chance approaching from behind. In that brief moment, her heart filled with relief and apprehension.

Seth's body tensed instinctively, his grip on the shotgun tightening. Sensing his reaction, Cassandra mustered every ounce of composure, desperate to keep Seth ensnared in the illusion they had created. "No, my love, just hold me," she pleaded, her voice tinged with compassion and concern.

A sigh escaped Seth's lips as he yielded to the comfort of Cassandra's embrace. The affection she offered enveloped him, a sanctuary from the storm within his mind. In this moment, he felt a renewed sense of purpose and belonging. The thought of his daughter's loving embrace and the success of his thriving business in Boston infused his twisted thoughts, fueling his determination to make his twisted dreams a permanent reality.

In the eerie silence that hung heavy around them, Seth's heightened senses detected a creaking floorboard from behind.

Sensing an intrusion, he released himself from Cassandra's embrace, turning to see his brother who now stood before him. Raising the gun, his voice trembled with confusion and aggression. "Seth, what are you doing here?"

His brother played along, maintaining the charade. "Chance, don't shoot. I need your help."

Seth stared at Cassandra. "Can you believe this lying monster?"

He aimed the shotgun at Chance's chest, ready to pull the trigger. Cassandra's panic overwhelmed her, causing her to abandon the ruse.

"Seth, don't do it!" she cried out desperately.

Seth's eyes darted uncontrollably as he struggled to grasp the truth. "I'm Chance," he muttered, tightening his grip on the shotgun.

As Seth stood amidst the chaos of the storm, his mind was a tempest of conflicting emotions and fragmented memories. Haunted by delusions that blurred the line between reality and hallucination, he struggled to discern truth from fiction. The weight of his past bore down upon him, each haunting memory of abuse and solitude a dagger to his fractured psyche. In the midst of the raging storm, he found solace in the sanctuary of his delusions, where he was both victim and perpetrator, hero and villain. The shotgun in his hands became a talisman of power, a symbol of control in a world spinning out of his grasp. Yet, beneath the veneer of aggression lay a profound sense of loss and longing, a yearning for connection and redemption that eluded him. As he confronted the specter of his twin brother, he was torn between the desire to reclaim his fractured identity and the fear of confronting the demons that lurked within.

Undeterred in his twisted mission, Seth advanced toward Cassandra, the gun steady and ready. He turned to face his brother, a sinister determination in his eyes. "He's still breathing. But not for long."

Chance's hands trembled as he pleaded, desperation filling his voice. "Please, Seth, I'm your brother."

"I have no brothers," Seth declared, taking aim. "I have a thriving business in Boston. I have a daughter named Angel."

Cassandra interjected, attempting to diffuse the situation. "We can fix this!"

Seth laughed bitterly. "Don't worry, Seth, your suffering will soon come to an end. Say hello to Grandpa!"

* * *

Seth steadied his aim, the cold barrel of the shotgun trained at Chance's chest. In that frozen moment, he relished the fear that flickered within his brother's eyes, seeing it reflected through the metallic gaze of the weapon. The allure of eradicating all his troubles, of vanquishing the haunting ghosts, danced before him.

As Seth's finger tightened on the trigger, the world erupted in nature's wrath. A blinding flash of lightning cleaved the sky, its brilliance illuminating the entire lake. The thunderous roar reverberated in Seth's chest, drowning out even the sound of his own heartbeat. In the split second of illumination, raindrops became shards of glass, slashing through the air with a ferocity that matched the storm's fury.

Simultaneously, a deafening crack shattered the air, splitting the darkness with the force of a thousand cannons. The explosion of the ancient tree sent tremors through the earth, the ground quivering beneath Seth's feet as if protesting the violence of the moment.

Seth peered over the barrel of the gun, his eyes widening in astonishment in a frozen moment of impending doom. The acrid scent of ozone mingled with the musty odor of damp earth, assaulting his senses as he struggled to maintain his grip on reality amidst the chaos. Cassandra darted out of the doorway and onto the shore, narrowly evading the devastation, her movements a blur of desperation and determination.

The impact of the broken tree propelled both brothers into the waters, their bodies tossed amidst swirling debris and remnants of the destroyed structure. Rain poured from the heavens in sheets, each drop a tiny hammer against their skin. The waves grew fierce, rising like angry giants, threatening to swallow them whole and drag them into the abyss.

In the midst of the wreckage, Cassandra's eyes strained through the curtain of rain, searching for any sign of her husband. She screamed out his name, her voice barely cutting through the chaos, lost in the cacophony of wind and water. Finally, she spotted an arm flailing in the air. "Hold on, Chance! I'm coming!"

She extended her arm past twisted nails and tattered roofing, clutching onto his arm while fighting to maintain her footing on a floating section of the boathouse wall. "Is that you, Chance?" she questioned, the words barely audible over the roar of the storm.

One arm desperately clung to him, while the other fought against the tangled debris that threatened to ensnare them further. The man's feet became entangled in the snarled mess of old wires, his hold slipping with each passing moment. Amidst the chaos, Cassandra's attention was abruptly drawn to another arm reaching out from the wreckage.

"Help me!" cried the second brother, his voice barely a whisper amidst the howling wind and crashing waves.

Both men sounded the same, looked identical, and even their clothing provided no clues in the darkness and downpour. Ignoring the confusion, Cassandra fought against the elements, striving to bring both brothers to safety. Thunder roared overhead, drowning out her shouted question to find the truth.

"Chance, where is Angel hiding?" she cried out, clinging to the hope of a clue that would guide her through the darkness.

"It's me," pleaded both brothers in a twisted duet of survival.

As they slipped further from her grasp, Cassandra's mind raced, frantically searching for a crucial detail to provide clarity. She tried to see or feel his wedding ring, but could not amid the darkness and mucky water. She strained to locate the Ace bandage on Chance's wrist that had unraveled in the waters, but it remained elusive in the chaos of the storm. And then, a realization struck her like another lightning bolt—Chance was left-handed!

A surge of confidence welled up within her as she released the man's right arm, leaving him grasping for any debris that evaded him in the tumultuous waters. Gasping for breath, he floated away, his final words filled with rage and bitterness.

"You bitch!"

Cassandra clung steadfastly to the surviving brother's arm, pulling him towards the shore with every ounce of strength left in her weary body. Exhausted, she took a moment to catch her breath, her gaze shifting to the now-vanished boathouse, swallowed by the churning waters. She pinned the man to the ground, her grip firm upon a piece of lumber to defend herself against any further threats.

"Where is your daughter hiding?" she demanded, her voice laced with urgency and determination.

"Angel and Brad," he gasped, his words barely audible over the howling wind, "are hiding in the gas tank."

"Chance!" Cassandra exclaimed, getting down on her knees to embrace him. With trembling hands, she reached out to touch his face, reassuring herself that he was indeed safe.

* * *

Later, Cassandra's gaze fell upon Chance, who stood at the water's edge, his demeanor weighed down by the magnitude of his loss. In that instant, she recognized the profound complexity of emotions that swirled within him, the turbulent sea of sorrow, anger, and conflicted feelings he wrestled with. With empathy and understanding, she approached him, her hand gently resting on his shoulder, offering a silent support.

Chance's struggle to contain his emotions became evident as tears streamed down his face. His gaze fixated upon the vast expanse of the lake, a reflection of his introspection and contemplation. Thoughts of Seth's tormented life lingered within his mind, mingling with the contemplation of the dangers his brother had subjected them to—the threats against Cassandra, Angel, and Brad. It was an unfathomable web of torment and despair, the complexities of Seth's troubled soul eluding complete comprehension.

The haunting echoes of Seth's words before the boathouse collapsed resonated within Chance's being, serving as a stark reminder of the darkness that had consumed his twin brother. The desperate look in Seth's eyes when he assumed Chance's identity lingered vividly, etched into the depths of his memory. In that moment, Chance grappled with the knowledge that Seth had endured immense pain throughout his life, a pain that had birthed the chaos and destruction they had just endured.

Together, standing by the lake, Cassandra and Chance shared an essential bond—a deep understanding that transcended words. They silently acknowledged the weight of their past, the complexities of the present, and the uncertain future that lay before them. As tears continued to cascade down Chance's face, Cassandra offered her support, telling him they would face the aftermath together, united in their journey of healing and moving forward.

231

"Cassandra," he whispered, his voice filled with anguish. "I failed him," he cried and fell into her waiting arms.

Soon, the rain subsided, leaving an eerie stillness in the woods. Cassandra peered out at the water, half-expecting Seth to swim back to shore, ready to resume his reign of terror. Her heart skipped a beat as a board floated towards the shore. Chance picked it up and hurled it into the water, watching as it joined the jumble of shattered debris.

"Let's go get the kids," he said determinedly.

* * *

Cassandra shifted her attention to the paramedic who approached her, his voice filled with concern. The moon cast an ethereal glow, bathing the scene in a surreal light that accentuated the flickering police and ambulance lights surrounding the property. Exhaustion settled upon her, a tangible weariness that seemed to seep into her very being. With a nod, her response conveyed the relief and fatigue that had accumulated throughout the unfolding events.

"Yes, I'm okay." Cassandra's gaze followed the paramedics as they wheeled Morgan and the injured officer toward the waiting ambulances. The chaos of the past had finally subsided, but its impact lingered, leaving her drained and emotionally spent. Turning her gaze back to the property, she contemplated the arduous journey that had led them to this moment. It was over—the darkness had been confronted and overcome—and now the process of healing could commence.

"Will he be all right?" she inquired, her concern evident.

Morgan raised his head, grinning. "Just a nasty bump, Sis."

"Stay still," the paramedic instructed him.

"I'm sorry for all of this," Cassandra said, gripping his hand.

"Never a dull moment," Morgan replied, casting a glance at Chance. "Any more surprises?" Chance shook his head, unable to find the words to express his remorse for what had transpired.

Cassandra scooped Angel into her arms. "You're riding with me and Daddy," she said, brushing dirt from her daughter's face and planting a kiss on her cheek.

"Brad too?" Angel asked.

"Yes," Cassandra reassured her.

Brad stood by Cassandra's side, feeling a hollow emptiness in his stomach. He reflected on the shared experiences with Chance—the tree fort they had built together, the joyous celebrations of holidays, and the invaluable lessons imparted on honesty, friendship, and family. The realization of how deeply entwined their lives had been left him grappling with the magnitude of the ordeal they had faced.

Amidst the lingering shadows, Brad's gaze shifted towards Chance, observing his tender interaction with Angel. The love and gratitude that emanated from Chance's touch and embrace melted away some of the heaviness that hung in the air. In that simple act of caressing Angel's hair, Brad caught a ray of light amidst the darkness that had threatened to consume them.

For Chance, the fear of losing his precious daughter had remained a constant undercurrent throughout the arduous events. The initial belief that his family would be spared from harm had been clouded by the overwhelming uncertainty that Seth's delusions had brought upon them. However, in this moment of safety and relief, those worries seemed to recede into the distance like storm clouds fading away.

As Angel embraced her father tightly, their connection radiated with a profound sense of love and resilience. The horror of the recent events lingered, but in the presence of his daughter's love, he felt a renewed sense of hope and strength, knowing that they had overcome the darkest of trials together.

"I knew you would find us, Daddy."

Moments later, they drove away from their summer cottage, leaving it behind forever. Several police cars stayed back, their officers awaiting assistance to search for Seth's body.

Part VI

"Come on, Angel. We have a long drive," Chance called out to his daughter, weeks after their harrowing ordeal. Cassandra stood by the car, making the final preparations for their much-needed family vacation. Angel rushed out the door, clutching her beloved panda bear.

"I almost forgot Truffles," she said, then noticed her friend standing nearby. "Hi, Brad." She blushed.

Brad playfully tickled her stomach. "Hey, Angel Eyes."

Cassandra beamed with gratitude. "I think we're all set. Brad, thank you for everything. We'll bring back lots of pictures to share when we return."

Angel eagerly climbed into the front seat. "We should go now!"

Cassandra double-checked her belongings. "Do you have everything, sweetheart?"

Angel nodded enthusiastically. "Yes, Mommy! I'm not that little anymore."

Cassandra planted a gentle kiss on Brad's cheek. "Thanks for taking care of the house."

"See you soon, buddy," Chance said from the driver's seat. He started the car, waving goodbye as they pulled out of the driveway.

As Angel waved back to Brad, she couldn't contain her curiosity. "Daddy, how far is Florida?"

"It's a long way. I hope you won't ask if we're almost there every ten minutes," Chance teased.

"Is that where Disney World is? Hurry!" Angel's excitement filled the air.

"Angel, remember what I told you about being patient?" Cassandra interjected, placing her hand over her stomach. "Chance, I felt the baby kick."

Sitting between her parents, Angel's eyes widened with awe. "Can I feel it too?"

Cassandra gently guided her daughter's hand to her stomach. "Just wait a moment, it will happen again."

Angel's face lit up as she felt the tiny movements. "Tell me again who's inside?"

"Your little brother or sister," Cassandra replied, her voice filled with tenderness.

Angel turned to her dad, her eyes shining with amazement. "Did you hear that? I'm getting a new brother or sister!"

Chance chuckled. "Are you expecting twins, dear?"

Angel playfully scrunched up her face. "I certainly hope not!"

As they settled back into their seats, a mischievous smile played on Angel's face. "Daddy?"

"Yes, sweetie?" Chance responded.

She burst into laughter. "Are we almost there yet?"

Cassandra joined in the laughter. "Yeah, and I need to use the bathroom!"

As Chance watched Angel bobbing her head and singing out of tune, his heart swelled with warmth and happiness. He glanced at Cassandra, struck by the realization that his wife possessed the same spirited and joyful nature as their daughter. Their mutual exuberance for life served as a beautiful reminder of the deep connection they shared as a family.

Amidst their playful banter and the sound of Angel's laughter, Chance felt an overwhelming sense of gratitude for the incredible women by his side. Cassandra's joy mirrored that of their daughter, a testament to the love they had nurtured within their family.

Epilogue

"And... cut! Okay, everyone, that's a wrap. Good work." Richard Massey, the stage director, emerged from behind the camera, extending his congratulations to Elizabeth and Brad. "I'm sure we'll have you back for the sequel."

Elizabeth agreed. "Brad, how about some coffee?"

"Thanks."

As they strolled through the sound stage, Brad felt awestruck by the advanced technology surrounding him. Witnessing the behind-the-scenes intricacies of television production firsthand was a dream realized.

Upon reaching the control room, his eyes widened at the sight of rows of state-of-the-art computers and servers. Richard explained some technical details that sparked new ideas for Brad's sequel.

"Over the past several years, media stations have transformed, harnessing cutting-edge technology for immersive entertainment," Richard began.

At FusionVision Network, advanced technology redefined the television experience. Skilled technicians in the broadcasting hub coordinated a seamless integration of 3D cameras, personalized satellite links, and advanced control panels. FusionVision's 3D cameras, suspended from sleek robotic swivels, created dynamic angles and lifelike visuals, rendering scenes with a realism that transcended traditional screens.

Brad and Elizabeth weaved through bustling technicians. He couldn't help but notice Elizabeth's striking figure, secretly hoping her movements were exaggerated for his enjoyment.

Navigating the hallway to Elizabeth's dressing room, she turned to Brad. "I hope the show helps boost book sales."

"It certainly can't hurt," Brad replied.

In her dressing room, Brad admired Elizabeth's organization. Bins labeled for research notebooks and meticulously arranged discs lined the room. Her dedication was evident in the well-lit mirrors adorned with makeup and personal recording equipment.

As Elizabeth prepared coffee, she slyly remarked, "Aren't we sneaky?"

A knock came at the door. "Come in."

Stan, Elizabeth's assistant, entered. "Sorry to interrupt."

"No problem, Stan. What's up?"

Stan handed Elizabeth a message. "It's addressed to someone named Angel. Seems like a joke. The show hasn't even aired yet."

Elizabeth shared a meaningful glance with Brad, who flashed a sly grin. Seizing the page, she scanned the opening words, a blush spreading across her cheeks. Stan, dumbfounded, asked, "Wait. Are you telling me that you're Angel?"

"Yes, that's me," she replied, defiance masking her panic.

"The same Angel from the story? Cassandra's daughter?"

"Stan, if you tell anyone, you'll regret it. Consider yourself warned."

"But how is this possible?"

Elizabeth turned to the mirror, wiping off her makeup. "Stan, this must remain a secret. Do you understand?"

Stan nodded. "I won't breathe a word to anyone."

"Thank you. This means a lot to me," she said, opening the door for him to leave.

"Have a nice day, *Angel*," Stan whispered in the hallway.

"That was close," Brad remarked.

"This goes way beyond close! Now I'm in deep trouble," Elizabeth said, glaring at the page in her hand. "I need to tell my mom to stop calling me Angel."

"But why? I love your nickname," Brad interjected, trying to lighten the mood.

"Brad, my job is at stake here."

"What does the note say?"

"Good luck with the show. We'll be thinking of you. Give our regards to Brad. Love, Mom and Dad." She fed the page into a shredder. "Couldn't they have just called?"

"What time does the show air tonight?"

"Eight." She nervously bit her nails. "Damn it."

"Relax. Everything will be fine," Brad reassured her. "At least Stan didn't realize we're married."

"Great consolation. Just one more nail in my soon-to-be coffin." Brightening, she added, "Ross and Sally are coming. He's graduating from the academy in six weeks. I'm so proud of him

"Come on. Let's go grab some lunch."

"Okay, but you need to leave first. I'll meet you across the street at the Friendly Deli."

As Brad left, he whispered, "See you soon, my Angel," brushing past her and planting a kiss on her cheek.

* * *

"Come in, Ross. The show starts in five minutes," Angel greeted her brother and his girlfriend, Sally, that evening.

Ross stepped in, followed by Sally. "Thanks for the invite."

"Nice to see you, Sally. Make yourself at home," Angel welcomed with a warm hug.

Admiring the upscale Boston condominium, Sally's eyes fell upon a Chagall print she recognized. "The Lovers… It's one of my favorites," she remarked, captivated by its romantic and dreamlike style that mirrored Angel's personality.

Changing the subject to something that piqued her curiosity, Sally turned to Brad with a curious grin. "So, I understand you used to be Angel's babysitter."

Ross stared at Sally, politely saying, "Honey, I asked you not to bring that up."

Intrigued, Sally said, "I'm just interested in how it all started."

"It's okay. I love telling this story," Angel smiled, causing Brad to sigh and step toward the TV, idly checking the settings. "Brad lived in Europe for eight years, immersing himself in his craft. When he returned, his mom threw a welcome-home party, and I met him there. I was seventeen. I could tell Brad was attracted to me, but he seemed shy and awkward. I asked him out to dinner, and we started casually dating. It took him forever to kiss me, so I kissed him first. Two years later, I practically proposed."

"Here it comes," Brad noted, eager to change the subject back to the show.

As everyone took a seat with excitement permeating, Angel's attention fixed on the opening credits. "Shh… it's starting!" A slight smile played on her lips as she anticipated the beginning of the show.

As the announcer's voice echoed through the spacious living room, dramatic theme music captured the mood. Simultaneously, vibrant graphics began to unfold on the large screen, marking the auspicious moment with a visual spectacle.

In their luxurious condominium, bathed in the warm glow of the setting sun, a hushed silence filled the air. Angel glanced out of the veranda window, hoping that the entire world had tuned in to watch.

* * *

"Seraph! Come!"

A peregrine falcon responded to its master's call from within a secret underground facility in Havana. The man put away a textbook on advanced human biology and adjusted the settings to record his niece's show. "Topics Above The Line" had begun, and it was time for the sixty-three-year-old twin to delve into the past.

Author's Note:

The first edition of "Twin Crossing" (previously titled "Double Jeopardy" and published in 2015) portrayed a slightly different story from the one you've just read. At that time, I believed the story had concluded with Seth Macklin's death.

Or so I thought...

In 2021, I penned a sequel titled "Second Chance," which delved into additional factual events surrounding Seth Macklin. Months after its release, Cassandra stumbled upon Seth's revenge journal, illuminating new facets of his life during his incarceration and the abuse he endured from his grandfather. After thorough examination of the material, I made the decision to rewrite "Double Jeopardy," change its title, and integrate Seth's account, along with Angel's interviews from her show "Topics Above The Line."

– Brad Genova, Boston, Massachusetts, March 6, 2023

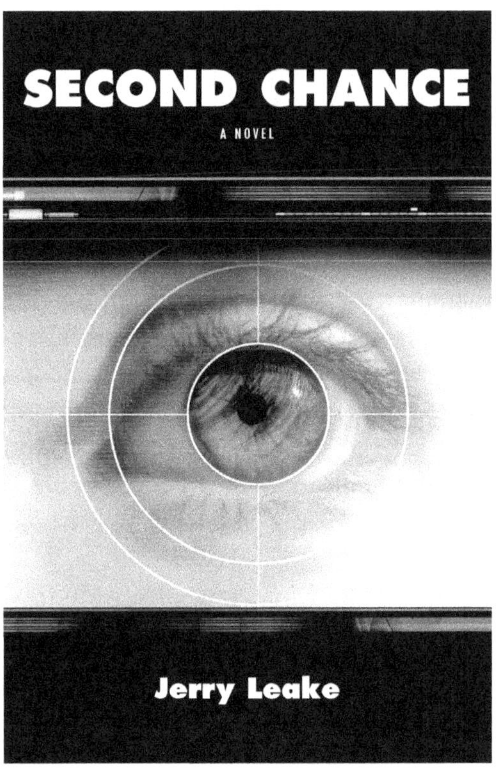

In 2031, Seth Macklin confronts his harrowing past as abuse survivor and ex-convict, now a reclusive benefactor funding humanitarian missions through groundbreaking microbiology. Brad Genova's bestseller resurfaces Seth's vendetta against his estranged twin, Chance. Amid Havana's turmoil, a high-stakes game unfolds within a futuristic Virtual Reality Internet, as Chance and Brad navigate to save loved ones from a perilous scheme that defies imagination.

— Novels by Jerry Leake —

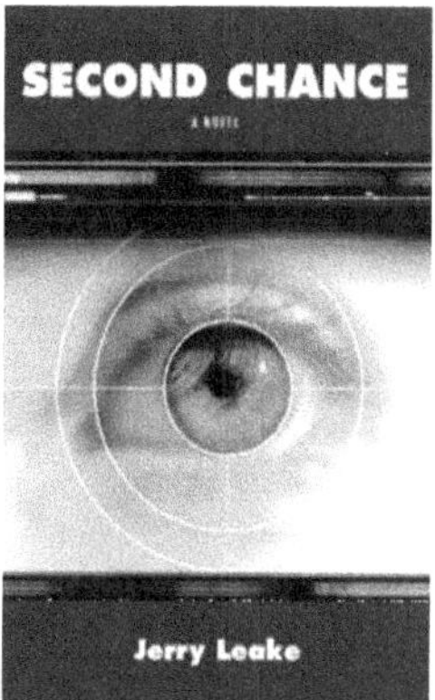

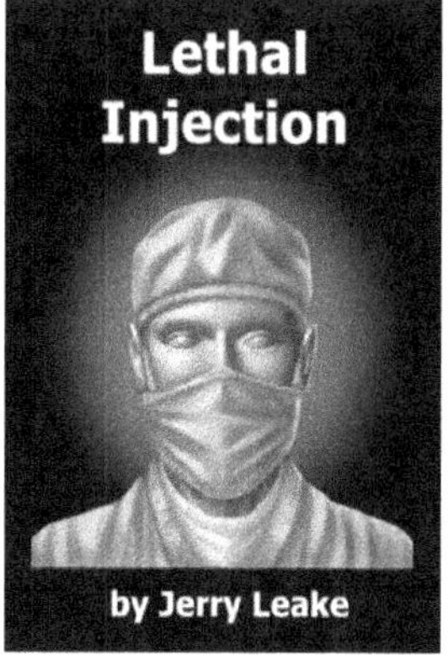